CROSSING PROMISES

KIMBERLY KINCAID

CROSSING PROMISES

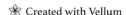 Created with Vellum

DEDICATION

*This book is dedicated
to you.*

*Without readers clamoring
for more, I wouldn't have
the best job in the world.*

1

Owen Cross sat back against the driver's seat of his Ford F-250 and prayed for either a time machine or a body double. Sure, he'd already knocked back the sixty tasks that had headlined the Friday edition of his To Do list—after all, he'd been up and at 'em for two hours before the sun had even thought about climbing over the horizon. But there were sixty more things that needed doing before quitting time, and, now that the clock on his dashboard had made three P.M. official, he really needed to get his ass in gear.

Cross Creek Farm wasn't going to operate itself. And thank God for *that* favor, because sore muscles and over-taxed body aside, there was nothing Owen would rather do with his life than fulfill the family legacy of running the place with his father, his brother, and his own two hands.

Speaking of which...

Owen reached for the two-way radio clipped to the belt loop of his faded Wranglers, thumbing the button on the side of the receiver and waiting out the hiss of static that went with the action before saying, "Hey, Hunt. I'm out at the hay barn. Gonna start loading up some bales to get them down to Nathan. You comin'?"

More static paved the way for his brother's answer. "Copy that. I'm helping Dad finish up in the north field. Be there in a minute or two."

Although it had been on the tip of his tongue to tell his brother to make it sooner rather than later, Owen stuck to a succinct, "Copy. Out."

Their old man was tough as nails and just as sharp, to be sure. But between the nasty bout of heat exhaustion he'd suffered early last summer and the forty-plus years of operating the farm that had come before it, there was no denying he moved a little slower than he used to. Owen and Hunter had an unspoken agreement by which they both picked up the slack without comment or complaint. That included not putting the screws to each other when one of them was working with their father.

Still, time was time, and, here lately, the stuff was at a massive premium. Getting out of his work-tested pickup, Owen adjusted his equally work-tested baseball hat against the warmth and shine of the afternoon sun. A mild March meant good things for crops and cattle, both of which they had in abundance on their 750-acre farm. Still, the balmier-than-usual temperatures made them busier than they'd normally be at this time of year, and the huge increase in business they'd seen at the end of the harvest last season had barely let up, even over the winter.

CSA shares, local businesses wanting fresh produce, distributors looking for corn feed, companies eager to buy farm-raised cattle, the project to build a fixed-structure farm stand/storefront on their property...the boom in business was great in theory. Hell, it was great in reality, too.

Except for the fact that in addition to the heftier workload, they'd been down a man ever since his youngest brother, Eli, had left Millhaven six months ago to become the journalist half of a hotshot photojournalist team with his girlfriend. Owen would never begrudge his brother the happiness—they might have butt heads a little in the past (okay, a lot. It wasn't *his* fault Eli could be a righteous pain in the ass on occasion), but he would have to be legally blind not to see how perfectly the career change suited his brother. Eli deserved to be doing what he truly loved, just like the rest of them.

Even if the last day Owen could remember taking off *was* Christmas, and he'd still ended up doing a page-by-page review of the blueprints for the soon-to-be-built storefront as he'd downed his egg nog and cookies. He might be happier than a pig in a puddle that Cross Creek's business had exploded over the last six months, but damn, having half an inch of breathing room wouldn't suck. He could throw back a few beers with his buddy, Lane. Go fishing down at Thompkins Lake. Or, hell, maybe even meet a pretty woman so he didn't wake up solo seven days a week.

Unease sent a pang right between Owen's ribs, causing his chin to jerk a few inches higher into the sunlight. He'd gotten far too good at that last part here lately, much to the dismay of his libido—which was not only as alive and kicking as any other thirty-three year old's, but also starting to get moderately indignant at being shown the back burner.

Shaking his head, he kicked his boots into motion over the dirt and gravel path leading into the two-story hay barn. He'd never shied away from hard work, and—unlaid or not —he had no room to bitch about being busy. The slow business and strange growing season they'd had a year ago had been a stark reminder that the alternative to a full workload was ten times worse. Anyway, Owen couldn't deny loving every second of running the farm, even when those seconds stretched into unending hours and backbreaking labor.

Family and farm, Owen. Never forget how important they both are. Never forget...

His mother's voice, long gone but never forgotten, echoed in his ears, making his heart beat faster. Carrying on the tradition of family and farm might be his birthright as the oldest Cross brother, but he didn't do it out of obligation. He'd made a promise to his mother before she'd died, and the farm was where he belonged, plain and simple.

No time like the present to work the land that bore his family's name.

Owen unlatched the barn door, sliding the thing open with a heavy clack-clack-clack. Both the hardware and the tracks that held the rolling, double-wide door had seen better days, and he paused for a visual inventory, making a mental note to fix up what he could and replace what he couldn't ASAP.

Stepping fully into the coolness of the barn's interior, he gave up a pair of slow blinks to let his eyes get used to the shadows. The musty-sweet scent of hay filled his nose, and one corner of his mouth tugged into a rare half-smile at the slivers of sunlight cutting white-gold paths between the boards making up the far walls. His smile grew as he slowly took in the open, two-story space, then threatened to become an actual grin when he climbed the rough-hewn ladder leading up to the hayloft that spanned much of the barn's second level.

Right up until his size eleven and a half went through the floorboards.

"*Shit!*" The abrupt shift in balance threatened to send him yard-saling across the hayloft, and Owen threw his arms wide out of sheer instinct. Thankfully, he connected with one of the support beams angling down from the roof, gripping it with enough purchase to steady himself on the foot that was still above level and yank back the one that had broken through the wooden planks beneath him.

"Owen? You good?" Hunter's voice, tinged with concern, filtered up from the ground.

"I'm fine," he answered, although his slamming pulse sure as hell wanted to disagree. "Looks like one of the floor-boards up here had a rotten spot."

Hunter appeared at the top of the ladder, his brows lifting toward the brim of his baseball hat at the sight of the boot-shaped indent a few feet from where Owen now stood. "Oh, yeah. I noticed that the last time I was up here."

"Thanks for mentioning it," Owen muttered, capping his reply with a frown.

But if Hunter was put off by the gruff response, he didn't show it. "The spot wasn't *that* bad when I saw it, jackass." His easygoing grin filed the edge off Owen's irritation in that way only Hunter could manage. "Otherwise, I would have. Plus, after all that rain we had over the winter, it's not really a news flash that some of these older boards might not hold up another season."

Sobering, he darted a glance at Owen's work boot, which —aside from bearing a few new scratches in the already scuffed leather—was no worse for wear. "Seriously, though. Are you okay?"

Ah, hell. Hunter wasn't wrong about the floorboards likely needing some TLC, and, once again, Owen had sent his words out with more steel than he'd intended.

"Yeah." He brushed his palms over the front of his dark gray T-shirt, turning away from the trouble spot. "We're going to have to check all of these boards from below to be sure it's safe up here, though."

Not that they really had the time for that, since their cattle manager, Nathan, was surely waiting on the hay bales they still had yet to move. But the last thing any of them needed was to go tango uniform and fall twelve feet to the hard-packed ground below.

Hunter nodded in agreement. "Yeah. I've almost taken a header out of this thing once, myself. I'm not too keen on a repeat."

"Let's get to it, then."

Ten minutes and one careful inspection later, Owen was relieved to confirm that all the other boards were intact. He could deal with the busted-up section later, albeit in time he'd have to manufacture from thin air. For now, they had more pressing issues; namely, cows that would go hungry if they didn't get fed and distributors who wanted anything other than bony cows.

He backed the trailer hitched to his truck past the barn doors, re-hauling himself up the ladder and studiously avoiding the rotten board as he set his sights on the hay bales in the loft. His muscles squeezed at the motions his body knew by heart, his now-gloved fingers hooking beneath the baling twine to lift the closest bale from the stack beside him. They'd have to put the hammer down to make up for the lost time, so Owen quickly found a rhythm, tossing each bale briskly over the side of the loft for Hunter to load into the trailer, then calling down to make sure his brother was ready for the next one. The exertion he'd welcomed in his muscles only minutes before became a burn far too easily, but he pushed past the discomfort to work up a quick sweat.

"So, I'm going to do a thing," Hunter said, his voice

reaching Owen with ease even though the two of them were separated by over a dozen feet of vertical space.

He hefted another hay bale over the side of the loft, waiting for the thump that marked its arrival on the ground, before answering. "Please tell me this thing involves catching up on invoices and payroll."

"You haven't done that yet?" Hunter asked, and Owen's corresponding laugh was sadly humor-free.

"In what time, exactly, would I have managed to lock myself in the office to tackle the bookkeeping?" There was a mountain and a half of it from this week alone, for Chrissake.

His brother nodded without breaking stride with the job in front of him. "Fair. Now that things are booming and we're going to break ground on the storefront soon, we really do need to hire someone to take care of the books."

It was a topic that had come up more than once over the last six weeks, with all three of them in agreement that a new hire was not just in order, but overdue. Busy or not, Owen could handle the labor of running Cross Creek with one arm tied behind his back. But the books? God, he'd never had the patience—or the know-how, to be honest—to manage them with anything other than a metric ton of effort.

"So, what's this thing you're going to do, then, if it's not number crunching?" he asked, reaching for yet another bale of hay.

"Actually, I was thinking I'd ask Emerson to marry me."

Owen's heart went on a line drive toward his sternum. "What?" he asked, the hay bale in his grasp falling clumsily back to the floor of the loft. He knew Hunter and his girl-friend, Emerson, were serious—hell, a person would have to have one foot and both eyes in the grave not to see that they were crazy about each other. But *married*?

"Yeah." Hunter looked up at him from the ground, his gargantuan smile telling Owen his brother had done a hell of a lot more than "think" about proposing. "I mean, at the risk of sounding like a Hallmark card, I've loved her since the minute I saw her. She's always been the one, you know? We spent a lot of years apart, but now that we've fixed that, it seems dumb to waste any more time not being married to her. So, yeah. I went into Camden Valley and I bought Em a ring and I'm going to propose."

"Wow." Owen's mind spun as he moved toward the ladder, their task momentarily tabled. "Does anyone else know?"

Hunter waited until Owen's boots had hit the hay-strewn ground before answering. "I talked to her parents last night," he said. "They gave me their blessing, so I told Dad this morning, and now you know. Eli and Scarlett are in Rome, but I left them a message to call me, and I haven't had a chance to tell Marley just yet."

Whoa. Owen took a step back, his brows kicking up. "You're going to tell Marley?"

"Of course. Whether she likes it or not, she's still family," Hunter tried, but Owen met his middle-brother's peace-keeping ways with a whole lot of oldest-brother candor.

"She's made it pretty clear she doesn't like it."

The half-sister they'd only recently learned of might've been living in the main house since coming to town last fall after her mother passed away, but she was an ace at keeping her distance despite all of their efforts to bring her into the fold.

Hunter—being Hunter—tried again. "She's licking some

serious wounds, O. Until six months ago, she didn't know any of us existed, either, including Dad. Plus, she lost her mother." The pause that followed reminded Owen that they both knew what that felt like. Not that he needed the memo. "She got that job in Lockridge and she's getting back on her feet. Maybe we should just cut her some slack in the meantime."

Owen adjusted his baseball hat and blew out a heavy breath. "Ah, I guess you're right." If they wanted Marley to act like family, they'd have to treat her as such. No matter how surly she was in return.

"I know," Hunter joked, delivering a healthy jab to Owen's shoulder. "But it's right nice to hear *you* say so, you old hardhead."

"Screw you," Owen said, but the words lost any heat he could've possibly pinned to them as he gave in to his laugh. "Seriously, though. Congrats. Emerson's great, and I know you two will be really happy together."

A weird feeling he couldn't quite label crowded his chest. It was gone by the time Hunter's palm hit the one Owen had extended, their shoulders coming together for a half-hug that was as close to the real deal as the two of them were going to get.

"Thanks, man. That means a lot to me."

After a second, they parted, and Hunter sent his gaze up to the damaged boards overhead. "Anyway. We should probably get back to work. Once we're done loading these up, I can get up there and replace that rotten board, easy."

He turned back toward the trailer, but Owen stopped him with a quick, "No." He didn't wait for Hunter to argue before adding on, "You're gonna do this proposal thing tonight, right?"

His brother paused. "Well, I kind of have a shitty poker

face, especially when it comes to Emerson. So, yeah, that's what I was planning on."

"Then go. Get out of here. Do...whatever it is you're going to do to make it romantic."

"Are you sure?" Hunter asked. His voice carried his doubt loud and clear, and, Christ, Owen wanted to tell the truth. But since that would involve the word "no" and he was damn certain his brother was only going to propose once in his lifetime, he couldn't make himself shove the word past his lips.

"Of course, I'm sure." Owen lasered a stare at the open barn doors to punctuate the sentiment, and Hunter's grin won out.

"I s'pose I probably could stand to get a few last-minute things in place," he said. "But only if you're—"

"Sure," Owen said. "Don't make me tell you twice."

"Okay. Thanks," Hunter said, shucking his work gloves and amping up his smile. Owen forced his nod and smile combo to last until Hunter had made his way through the barn doors and into his pickup, but as soon as his brother was out of sight, his shoulders slumped.

The only way he'd be able to balance all the work around here was with a miracle.

Cate McAllister had baked nine dozen cookies before sunrise. Which wouldn't necessarily be a bad thing, except this was her third baking binge in as many days, and she'd blown her paltry grocery budget on flour, butter, and sugar, rather than anything that would pass as an actual meal.

Lucky for her, she'd rather bake than eat.

She sighed and pulled into one of the handful of parking spots lining Town Street's main drag, which consisted of about three blocks and just under a dozen storefronts and businesses, including the farming co-op, the Hair Lair, and Clementine's Diner, which was this morning's destination. Tucking the box full of cookies (today's offering was oatmeal raisin) under one arm, Cate got out of her Toyota Corolla and slammed the door as gently as she could. The car was more fossil than mode of transport, and with the suspicious noise the driver's side door had been making upon use lately, and the fourth-time's-a-charm magic she'd needed to get it to start this morning, not babying it wasn't an option. Despite having two part-time jobs, she'd had to play some serious roulette with her bills for the past three months, each one of which had been tighter than its predecessor.

Cate had known a lot of things about her husband before he'd died three years ago in that car accident. How much debt he'd gotten them into?

Hadn't exactly been on the list.

"Good morning, Cate!" Clementine's voice was as warm and smooth as butterscotch, and the smile she gave up from behind the counter of her diner was a perfect match. "How you doin' today?"

"Great, Clem." God, she felt terrible lying to her boss, who had to be the nicest woman in the entire Shenandoah Valley, although—to be fair—Cate had been equal opportunity with that lie for years now. "Sorry I'm running a little late. My car was acting up a bit."

"Don't you worry about a thing, darlin'."

Clementine's tone and eyes both softened enough to take a jab at Cate's belly, and she busied herself with putting her purse behind the counter and her apron around her waist as she waited for the nasty pairing of frustration and guilt to pass. Folks were just trying to be kind, she knew. But after three years of being 'poor Cate McAllister', she really just wanted everyone to move on from the wreck that had killed both Brian and their daughter, Lily.

After all, she had. She'd had no choice. As much as she'd thought it might not in the beginning, the sun still came up every day. The roosters still crowed and bread dough still rose and bills still came. Brian's modest life insurance policy had kept her above water—albeit barely—for a while, but the reality was, the slew of temporary, part-time gigs Cate had picked up here and there were no longer cutting it.

She was going to have to bite the bullet and find a full-time job. Yes, the thought of something so permanent gave her hives the size of silver dollars, but it beat the thought of living in a cardboard box.

Even if only by a thread.

Smoothing a hand over her cheery orange half-apron, Cate turned back to Clementine, the box of baked goods in-hand. "I couldn't sleep last night, so I made a few cookies to share."

"A few." Clem's brows traveled up toward the green and white scarf keeping her long, sleek braids at bay.

"Okay," Cate admitted, sending her gaze over the bustling diner so she wouldn't have to look her boss in the eye. "A few more than a few. I guess I just got into a groove."

A bitter taste flooded her mouth in the wake of the second lie she'd told in as many minutes, but in this instance, pretzeling the truth was better than telling it. Coming out with the real reason she'd spent the wee hours in her kitchen instead of asleep in her bedroom would only up the poor-Cate ante.

Not that it made her feel like any less of a shit when it worked. "That is one heck of a groove, sugar," Clementine said, popping the lid off the box with an appreciative smile. "When are you going to get smart and start charging people for this magic?"

Cate's heart stuttered, her sneakers squeaking on the checkerboard floor tiles as she turned to stare. "What?"

"You heard me," Clementine said without heat. "You bake some of the best cookies in Millhaven. Why not turn it into something lucrative?"

"Because—" Annnnnd crap. Wasn't she just lining up lies like dominoes today? But she *really* couldn't back up her answer out loud, especially not in front of God and everybody having Sunday breakfast in the diner, so she said, "I only bake for fun."

Whether Clementine believed her or decided to let her off the hook, Cate couldn't be certain, but after a pause, the woman murmured, "Hmm. Well, if you're going to bring me the results, I'm certainly not going to complain."

"I made more than a hundred cookies." Cate let a sassy smile take over the edges of her mouth. "If I kept them to myself, I'd need a cardiologist *and* a personal trainer." Neither of which they had in Millhaven. Not that she was going to split hairs if it meant she'd score a full-frontal subject change. "Anyway, I've got the front of the house."

"Okay, doll. You get swamped up here, just holler," Clementine said before heading into the kitchen, probably to do some baking of her own. Cate swept a gaze over the dining room, scanning the shiny Formica tabletops and the cozy, high-backed banquettes, along with checking to see who sat at each one. Harley Martin and his daughter, Michelle, were tucked in at Table Four with what looked like their usual breakfast orders. Amber Cassidy sat across from Mollie Mae Van Buren at Table Nine, both of them guzzling coffee and—if Cate had to guess—copious amounts of weekly gossip.

But it was the two men sitting at Table Twelve who really caught her notice. Silly, honestly, that her stare would stop and linger on Owen Cross and Lane Atlee. She'd known them since they'd all been in kindergarten together, and, anyway, Owen in particular was pretty tight-lipped. Gruff. Borderline broody, even. She had to admit, though, from a strictly visual standpoint, her stare had impeccable taste. From his dark, tousled hair to the jawline that might as well belong to a statue of some Roman god to the leanly sculpted and totally bitable biceps peeking out from the sleeves of his T-shirt, Owen Cross was pure eye candy.

And Cate definitely had a sweet tooth.

One that had been *really* hungry as of late.

"Don't be an idiot," she whispered to herself as she set her shoulders and grabbed the nearest coffee carafe. Sure, Owen was gorgeous. He always had been. But he'd never shown her any interest, and, besides, she wasn't looking for anything that would last more than a night or two. Having a fling in a town the size of a thimble wasn't an option. She was already whispered about enough, thanks.

"...and I heard her ring is an en-tire carat and a quarter, princess-cut diamond with those, oh, what do you call those little teeny diamonds on the band? Right! Pavé stones the whole way around. It must have cost a fortune!"

Cate bit back a chuckle at Amber's exaggerated pronunciation of pavé that came out pah-VAAAAAY, lifting the coffee carafe with a smile she hoped reached her eyes. "More coffee, ladies?"

"Oh!" Amber fluttered a hand over her sequin-studded top, her dark purple fingernails flashing with their matching glitter tips, and Cate's stomach tightened as the woman's expression tripped immediately into poor-Cate mode. "I'm so sorry, Cate. I didn't see you there, otherwise I wouldn't have...well, you know."

Ugh, really? People couldn't even talk about impending weddings around her now? "It's fine," Cate said, although her smile now felt tighter than a pair of skinny jeans after Thanksgiving dinner. "Who's the lucky couple?"

Mollie Mae bit her brightly shellacked lip. "Hunter Cross and Emerson Montgomery. He proposed on Friday night."

"Oh, good for them," Cate replied, and meant it. Emerson had been back in town for almost a year now, and she and Hunter seemed really happy together. "Can I get you anything for breakfast?"

"No, thanks. We're watchin' our figures. Just coffee'll do," Amber said, her smile still loaded with syrup-sweet sympathy.

Cate scooped in a deep breath and topped off both of their cups. "Okay. Just let me know if you change your minds."

Before she could scream—or, worse yet, say what was really on her mind—she aimed her Keds toward the corner booth where Owen and Lane sat with their menus in front of them.

"Morning, you two. Coffee?"

The words slipped out with more of a scrape than she'd intended, and, *crap*, Owen's eyes crinkled in concern.

"Morning." He tipped his baseball hat at her with a quick lift of his fingers, and even though she knew the gesture was likely as subconscious as breathing and eating (thank you, Southern manners), her guilt still doubled up when he asked, "Is everything okay?"

"Mmm hmm!" she answered far too gleefully before finally finding a balance between bitchy and overly bright. "Everything is great. What can I get you for breakfast?"

After a brief pause for her to fill their coffee cups, Lane said, "I'd love one of Clementine's breakfast specials, eggs over-easy, with an extra side of home fries. Oh, and an order of toast. And could I get some extra bacon, too?"

Cate was powerless to stop her wry smile. "You do know

how much food is already in the special, right?" Of course, she knew he did, because A) Clementine's breakfast special had been the same three pancakes, three eggs, three strips of bacon, and one serving of her legendary home fries since the dawn of ages, and B) as long as Cate had been part-timing it at the diner, Lane had ordered said breakfast special every single time he'd crossed the threshold before noon, no exceptions.

He looked at her as if she'd just asked whether he was aware that one and one did, in fact, equal two. "Yes, ma'am."

She shrugged. Lane was built like a retaining wall, with not one ounce of fat on his six foot four frame. If anyone could do right by that breakfast, it was him. "They're your arteries, Sheriff. How about you, Owen?"

"I'll take a special, too. Scrambled on the eggs, please."

"Sure thing," Cate said, doing her level best not to look at the play of his muscles against the thin, white cotton of his T-shirt as he handed his menu over. But before she could get herself and her mutinous eyes safely behind the counter, Clementine appeared beside her with a cookie-laden plate balanced between both hands.

"You boys want to try some cookies? Oatmeal raisin."

Cate's heart did an aerial backflip into her breastbone. "I don't think—"

Clementine, traitor that she was, cut Cate off with an ear-to-ear smile as both Owen and Lane descended on the plate like locusts.

"Is this a new recipe?" Owen asked after a bite, and Lane slid another pair of cookies from the plate to follow the one that had just gone into his mouth. "These are even better than usual."

"Not a new recipe. A new baker," Clementine corrected. "Cate made them."

"Oh. *Oh.*" Owen's shoulders bumped against the red vinyl of the banquette. "I apologize. I mean...not that I wasn't being honest about the cookies." He darted a stare between her and Clem, clearly scrabbling for something to say that would keep from offending them both. "Your recipe is, you know, great, Miss Clementine. But Cate, these are—"

"Ridiculous?" Lane asked around a mouthful of oatmeal raisin.

Cate's cheeks burned so warmly, there was a zero percent chance she didn't have a blush on full display. "Right. I'm glad you like them. I'll just go"—*run and hide under the counter 'til I'm a hundred and five*—"put your breakfast orders in."

Dodging their stares, she cut a fast path to the kitchen, where she handed Owen and Lane's breakfast order over to Clementine's husband and cook/co-owner, Mason. Clementine came back a few minutes later, her plate decidedly less heavy and her expression soft.

"Your cookies were a hit. The Martins' agreed they're wonderful. Mollie Mae and Amber even broke that infernal diet of theirs to split one."

"Oh. Good." Cate grabbed a towel, swiping away at the already-clean stretch of countertop in front of her.

"I didn't mean to put you on the spot." Clem's voice was low, not quite at poor-Cate status, but close enough to put a twang in her chest.

Wanting very much to do anything other than have this conversation and also not hurt the woman's feelings, Cate said, "You didn't. I'm glad the cookies went over well. I noticed we're running low on napkins in some of the dispensers, so I'm just going to go grab some from the store room. Be right back."

She measured her footsteps along with her breaths,

keeping both even until she got to the cool quiet of the dry storage room in the back of the diner. Pressing her back to the far wall, away from the din of the kitchen, she closed her eyes and let out an exhale that was shakier than she wanted to admit. The sensation didn't last long, though, before the chime of her cell phone captured her attention from the pocket of her apron.

"What the hell?" She had the bare-bones, pay-as-you-go model, which meant no email or Facebook notifications, only good, old-fashioned phone calls. More importantly, the only person who would be calling was running her diner about twenty feet away. So this was either a wrong number, or...

Peterson Savings and Loan.

Shit. "Hello?" Cate asked tentatively, praying to every deity she could think of that this was a cold call offering her a great, low rate on a new credit card.

No such luck. "Hello, I'm trying to reach Cate McAllister," came the crisp, businesslike voice on the other end.

"This is she."

"Mrs. McAllister, I'm calling from Peterson Savings and Loan regarding your mortgage and the home equity line of credit taken out against it four years ago..."

She juggled the conversation as well and as quickly as she could, trying to digest phrases like *ineligible for refinance, file for bankruptcy*, and—oh, God—*foreclosure*. She had to promise to send an exorbitant-to-her payment in order to buy time, but thankfully, it did the trick. Cate lowered her cell phone, her heart lodged firmly in her windpipe and dread filling her belly to the brim.

Start her own business and sell cookies for a living. Ha. What a pipe dream. She couldn't even pay her electric bill, let alone her mortgage.

She needed a miracle. Fast.

But since there weren't any of those in the dry storage room, and she wasn't one to cry over her heartaches, Cate did what she always did. Squaring her shoulders, she grabbed the napkins she'd come in here for and headed back to the front of the diner. There had to be a way out of this. All she needed to do was buckle down and find it.

"Orders up!" Mason called, placing a handful of plates in the hot window. Cate ditched the napkins she hadn't really needed in favor of doing her job, loading up a tray with Owen and Lane's order and making her way back to their table.

"Oatmeal raisin cookies without walnuts are an abomination," she overheard Lane say, but Owen, whose back was to her, simply snorted.

"You're cracked. Simple is better. Plus, they're not called oatmeal raisin *walnut* cookies. Still—" A soft thunk sounded off from beneath the table, followed by a less-than-polite hiss from Owen. "Ow, dude! What the...oh, *hell*." He snapped to attention, his coffee mug meeting the Formica with enough force to slosh some of its contents over the rim. "Cate. Hi."

She thought of the walnuts that had been in every single one of the cookies she'd baked at oh-dark-thirty this morning and arched a brow. "Still hungry, I take it?"

"Sure. I mean"—he closed his eyes. Exhaled. Damn, eyelashes like that were honestly unjust on a man. Also, really freaking hot—"the cookies were great, and I've got room for breakfast, too."

"Glad to hear it. Two breakfast specials, one with scrambled eggs, one with eggs over-easy, extra home fries, and extra bacon." She delivered their respective plates. "Can I get you anything else?"

"Just the check, if you have a minute," Owen said, and shit. She might be a little light in the filter department (okay, fine, so she didn't really have one. Potato, po*tah*to), but the last thing she wanted was to piss off one of Clementine's customers. Not to mention lose her tip.

"You don't have to rush," Cate started, and, jeez, those eyelashes were even more lethal when they framed his wide, gray stare.

"Unfortunately, I do. Got a date with the invoices and books at the farm, and it's gonna take me all day if I'm lucky."

Confusion kicked in, good and hard. "But it's Sunday."

"Yes, ma'am," he agreed.

A prickle worked its way through her, half irritation at the politeness that bordered on poor-Cate sympathy, half something else that headed decidedly south.

She tried again. "You're working all day?"

Most everybody around here held Sundays pretty sacred out of self-preservation. Working the land seven days a week was brutal, even for the most well-practiced farmers. And from the look of Owen's biceps, he was *extremely* well-practiced.

He dropped his chin but not his stare. "Don't really have a choice. Cross Creek's books aren't going to balance themselves."

"You don't have a bookkeeper?" She shifted back on the linoleum, her confusion turning to outright shock.

"If we did, I don't reckon I'd be working the books on a Sunday."

Huh. Looked like she wasn't the only one who was a little light in the filter department. "Okay, fair," she said. "But Cross Creek is the largest farm in Millhaven. I just figured you'd have someone who handles that for you full-time."

"Believe me, I wish we did," Owen said, and her mouth opened of its own volition.

"Do you."

Cate heard the non-question before she even knew she'd spring it past her lips, but oh, how she wished to have it back. This was a bad idea. No, check that. This was an epically shitastic idea, with don't-you-even-think-it sprinkles on top. A full-time job was more commitment than she'd had in three years. The thought of something so regular, so *permanent*, gave her the shakes.

But then Owen was looking at her with a not-small amount of curiosity, and backpedaling was as impossible as catching smoke in her bare hands. "As a matter of fact, yeah," he said, straightening against the booth. "I'd love to hire a full-time bookkeeper. Why? Do you know someone who's interested?"

No. Nope. Sorry, buddy, I sure don't. These were all things her brain instructed her mouth to say, but her mouth—which liked to eat—betrayed her by going with, "Actually, I am."

The stunned silence that followed told her she'd better start making her case before he dismissed the idea as downright nutters. "I mean, I don't have a degree or any formal training, but I'm really good with numbers, and I'm not afraid of hard work. I can start as soon as you like, tomorrow, even, and—"

"Done."

"—I don't need...wait, what?" Cate asked as his answer caught up with her verbal landslide.

"You said you're good with numbers and you can start

tomorrow, right?" Owen's piercing gray stare was as tough to decipher as the rest of his expression.

She managed to nod. "Yes." She was only on evenings and weekends at the diner and The Bar. Time would be tight, but she could swing it. She *had* to. "I can."

"Great. Then you've got yourself a job."

3

Owen was late and filthy, although not really in that order. But he'd had no way of knowing the irrigation system in the south field would decide to spaz out just after sunup, or that it would take both him and his old man precious hours and all his clean clothing to get the thing back on track. He was supposed to meet Cate at the main house at—oh, *hell*—eight o'clock, and judging by the definite later-than-that slant of the sun over the tree line to the east, he was going to have a lot of explaining to do once he hauled himself up the drive.

Provided she was still there, that was.

"Great," Owen muttered, using one hand to steer his truck over the path leading to the house and the other to yank his dirty shirt over his head. Of course, he'd flung the stupid thing into the hinterlands of the backseat before realizing that's exactly where the clean one he kept as a spare was, and Jesus, Mary, and Joseph, this couldn't be any more of a Monday.

Please let her still be here...

Owen had to admit, Cate offering to be the bookkeeper they so desperately needed at Cross Creek had surprised the hell out of him, especially since he'd been borderline rude to her over the cookies. He wasn't charming like Eli, or even easygoing and friendly like Hunter. He hadn't *intended* to jam his boot in his mouth, and he sure hadn't meant to put a frown on her pretty face over what Lane—the jackass—was still referring to as walnutgate.

Of course, he'd done just that anyway, and damn it. Damn it! If he were her, he wouldn't kick around waiting for his tardy, ineloquent ass, either.

Pulling up in front of the main house, he put his truck in *Park* and heaved a sigh of relief at the sight of Cate standing a dozen feet away on the porch. "Hi," he said, jumping out of the F-250 and slamming the door. "I apologize for being late. It's been a really crazy morning."

"Let me guess. You've been chasing down shirt gremlins," she said. One mahogany-colored brow lifted over the rim of her sunglasses, her gaze raking over him palpably, even though he could barely see her shaded eyes.

Everything about Owen froze, except for his pulse. "Oh," he uttered lamely, because of *course* he'd forgotten to grab that clean shirt in his haste to get out and apologize. "Yeah. I mean, no. We had a problem with the irrigation system and I..." He forced himself to stop talking and just make a quick grab of the non-filthy T-shirt in the backseat of his truck. "I'm sorry."

"Oh, don't be."

Cate's reply barely reached his ears, more of an under-the-breath murmur than anything else, and he looked up in confusion with his arms halfway through their respective holes in the cotton.

"Beg pardon?"

Her spine went straight as an axe beneath her light blue sweater dress. "You don't have to apologize. It's really not a problem. The late thing, I mean."

"Okay," Owen said, following his answer up with a beat of awkward silence that stretched into two. He'd managed to make himself decent and they'd already agreed on the basics, like her salary, at Clementine's, so... "I guess we should go ahead and get started, then. Feel free to come in every day on your own when you get here. The regular work day for full-timers is technically eight to five, although we unlock the house as soon as we head to the fields at six or so. No one other than me, Hunter, our father, and Emerson has access without permission. And, well, now you, I suppose."

His boots thumped over the porch steps, Cate's shiny black heels clicking lightly in unison. "Eight to five. Eeeeevery day. You got it," she confirmed.

"We've got some paperwork to do to make things official. A W-4 for taxes, an application stating your past work history and qualifications, a few forms for your personnel file. Things like that."

She blanched a little, following him over the threshold and into the main house, which also held the office that was their operational hub. "Right. My personnel file."

"You did that for Miss Clementine, too, didn't you?" he asked, a little confused. The forms were standard-issue for their employees at Cross Creek—contact information, who to notify in case of emergency, and so on. He'd thought they were pretty much boilerplate for any full-timer, but the look on her face suggested otherwise.

Funny, the expression was gone as quickly as it had appeared, to the point that Owen questioned whether he'd been seeing things. "Yep," Cate said with a smart nod. "Of course."

"Great. Then we can go ahead and dive in."

After twenty minutes of check here, sign there, Owen slid the papers she'd filled out into a file folder and gestured to the cluttered space around them. "So, this is the office."

"Clearly," she replied, and, wait, was that a smirk playing at the corners of her mouth?

Owen straightened. He took this job more seriously than a heart attack with a triple bypass chaser. He might be desperate for a bookkeeper, but he expected her to do the same. "This will be your work space," he tried again. "Hunter and my father and I have split the bookkeeping up until this point, and Emerson comes in part-time to do some marketing stuff. Eli handles a decent amount of the marketing, too, but he obviously does that remotely now."

"Okay." Cate's smirk had disappeared, but he couldn't say he was in love with the frown that had moved in as a replacement. "Can you walk me through the system the three of you use for basic office management?"

"The system," Owen repeated, looking warily at the cardboard boxes jammed with folders, the expandable files full of purchase orders and receipts that littered nearly every flat surface in sight, and the desktop computer that was as old as it was overworked. "We all sort of have our own version of that, actually."

Her whiskey-brown eyes went round and wide, and he scrambled to answer her question more effectively. "Here are the files for all the vendors we currently have contracts with, and the payment and delivery schedules."

He pointed to the pair of cardboard boxes on the floor beside the roll-top desk. Owen knew the details of many of the contracts by heart, of course—hell, a few of those agreements were decades old and had been forged on little more than a good, strong handshake in the beginning. Still, demand for cattle, corn, hay, and—his personal favorite— seasonal and specialty produce had damn near doubled from last season. Keeping *all* the details in his melon just wasn't feasible.

"Here are the personnel and payroll files, including how many employees we have and all of their time sheets for the past six months," he continued, although now that he got a good eyeball on the tower of boxes in the corner of the room, he realized the month-count was probably more like nine or ten. They usually put the hard copies of anything from more than half a year out in storage once the information had been put into the system, but...yeah. "Payday is every other Friday. Nearly everybody has direct deposit, but we still have to log all the hours. Profit and expenditure reports are here"—Owen tapped the top of the nearby file cabinet—"and these are all the plans, contracts, budgets, and bills for the storefront we're breaking ground on in a couple of weeks."

Cate dragged a hand through her hair, her gaze moving over the boxes in disbelief. "Let me see if I've got this right. You don't do any of your bookkeeping online. At all?"

"We do. Just not a lot of it," he amended. The Cross men lived to work the land, not the ledgers. Sure, their current system was a little time consuming, but it wasn't totally ineffective. Cross Creek had been running on it for decades. "We have software right here on the computer." He paused to pull up the program they used for much of their bookkeeping before adding, "It's just that none of us are great at using it."

"So I see," Cate said after a quick perusal over his shoulder.

Irritation splashed through Owen's chest. "Our books aren't *that* bad."

The parting of her lips said she was primed and ready to take him to the mat on that count, and damn it, he really didn't have time to argue with her. "Look, I know it's going to take some work to get things running smoothly in here."

"It's going to take a lot more than that," she murmured with a shake of her head, and just like that, Owen's patience redlined.

"Can you do it, or should I find someone else?"

Once again, his words came out gruffer than planned. But before he could even think of cooking up an apology, Cate's arms had snapped across the front of her sweater dress to form a don't-mess-with-me knot that was far, *far* more of a turn-on than it had a right to be.

"That's what you hired me for, isn't it? To manage your books effectively?"

"Yes," Owen answered carefully, still caught between the desire to be annoyed, the desire to apologize, and, well, just plain desire.

"Well, then. Since I have my work cut out for me with a chainsaw, I suppose I should get to it," Cate said.

After a quick internal debate, Owen nodded. Brash or not, he needed her. More than he cared to admit. "Okay, then."

She answered by way of pushing up her sleeves and sliding an elastic from her wrist to secure her hair in a knot at the crown of her head. Even with the more casual edge, the powder-blue dress still hugged her curves, her calves flexing and releasing as she moved from one stack of boxes to the next in her heels, and he cleared his throat.

"Just so you know, we're pretty casual around here. You don't have to look nice."

Cate's cheeks flushed a shade of pink that, while highly pretty, didn't bode well for him in the mending-fences department. "Good to know," she said, and holy hell, why did his mouth refuse to cooperate with his brain around this woman?

"Not that you don't look, uh. Fine like that. All I meant was, you don't have to get dressed up. Jeans are okay."

She stared down at the toes of her shiny black shoes, but only for a split second before meeting his stare with her own. "Got it, Casanova. Is that all?"

For just a heartbeat, Owen was tempted to say no, to dig deep into his Neanderthal brain for the right words to tell her she actually looked fucking beautiful. To surrender to the hot demands coming from both his chest and his cock, and cross the room to impulsively kiss her sexy, sassy mouth.

But this was Cate McAllister. His buddy Brian's widow. He shouldn't think she was pretty. He shouldn't wonder if the skin on her shoulders bore the same provocative dusting of freckles as the neck she'd just put on display. And he *damn* sure shouldn't be turned on like floodlights at the fire in her eyes that he'd never quite seen before, but seemed to somehow fit her perfectly.

So, he simply said, "Yes. That's all," and walked out of the room.

CATE WAS GOING to need a pitchfork and the patience of Job to get through these books. She'd been camped out in Cross Creek's office for nearly three hours, and she still didn't even know where to start. Payroll, invoices, bank statements—every time she thought she had a snag untangled, five knottier things took root and did their damnedest to confuse her.

She hadn't even made it to lunch and she was in over her head.

Can you do it, or should I find someone else?

Owen's ultra-serious face appeared in her mind's eye, complete with that moody, broody scowl that did funny things low in her belly. Okay, so maybe she'd been more blunt with him than was necessary, but the whole showing-up-late thing had knocked her for a loop before he'd even arrived. Cate had been certain—and terrified—that he'd come to his senses and changed his mind about hiring her.

And the whole showing-up-shirtless thing? Sweet Jesus in the manger, *that* had nearly sent her over the edge. She'd had no way of knowing that not only did Owen possess supernaturally defined abs and a happy trail that had made her lady bits squeal with rapture, but that she'd get an eyeful of both right off the bat. The unexpected, visceral shot of heat in her blood had booted Cate's already-jumpy nerves into overdrive. Most women stammered or got shy when they were flustered. But not her, oh no. When her nerves hit, she had to go and let her sarcasm flag fly, loud and proud.

It was a wonder Owen—and his fantastically chiseled midsection—hadn't fired her on the spot. Even if she hadn't been wrong about his farm's books being a ten-car pileup.

"Okay," Cate said, shaking her head to bring her mind back to the present. Having ditched her heels less than thirty minutes in (for pity's sake, she hadn't even gotten the dress code for a full-time job right), she examined the boxes labeled "payroll", figuring it was a good place to start now that she'd sorted everything into piles. Of course, the three cups of coffee she'd slung back this morning chose that moment to let out an oh-hi-there, and, right. She'd need a quick bathroom break before tackling anything else.

Poking her head out of the office, Cate took in the empty hallway. She'd been too nervous to think of asking where the powder room was when she'd arrived, and the office was at the back of the house. There didn't seem to be anything else back this way, so she tiptoed down the hall until she reached the sun-filled kitchen.

"*Oh.*" Although Owen had led her through both the living room and the kitchen on their way back to the office this morning, the three-second trip had been little more than a blur in her mind.

Until now. God, the kitchen was the stuff of dreams, all full of space and light. Cate's heartbeat sped up as her gaze lingered on the white bead-board cabinets and the long expanse of the L-shaped countertop. A no-frills coffeepot sat nestled on the far end of the counter by the sink, the rich, enticing smell of its contents making her mouth water, and —okay, wow—there was even enough room to house a six-person table by the windows.

This kitchen put anything Cate had ever known to shame. Her fingers itched to roll out dough on the butcher block island in the center of the airy room, to fill both ovens with as many cookie sheets as they could handle, to see how many pies she could fit on the sill above the double-bowled stainless steel sink to cool.

A dream like that isn't for you. Best to wake up and remember that.

"Huh." An unfamiliar female voice sounded off from Cate's right, and even though it was neither loud nor threatening, she jumped clean out of her skin anyway.

"Hello." Cate's greeting came out far more question than anything else, and she scrambled to figure out why a willowy, sleepy-eyed woman wearing a tank top, pajama pants, and a henna tattoo that covered the majority of one forearm would appear in the Cross's kitchen.

"Hey," the brunette said, padding over the kitchen tiles on a straight path to the coffeepot. "Who are you?"

"I'm Cate. The bookkeeper," she added, although the clarification did nothing to send any recognition over the young woman's borderline-sullen face. "Owen just hired me."

A sound drifted past her lips, caught somewhere between a sigh and a snort. "Oh. Well, that figures. He never tells me the important stuff."

The dots lined up, connecting with a snap a second later. "I take it you're Marley."

Even Cate, who studiously avoided anything resembling gossip, had heard about Tobias Cross's long lost twenty four year-old daughter. Not that anyone in town had ever seen her.

"That's the rumor." Marley lifted a too-thin shoulder halfway before letting it drop. Her eyes stayed on Cate's for a heartbeat longer, and then she took a long draw from her coffee cup. "You don't have to worry about me being in your hair, or whatever, while you work. I might live here for now, but I won't for much longer. Anyway, I keep to myself."

"Unless you want coffee," Cate pointed out, causing Marley's lips to part.

Shit. Shit, crap, shit! Her nerves *seriously* knew no bounds today. Cate raced to come up with something— pretty much anything would do at this point—to soften the sarcasm that had launched from her mouth without permission.

But then one corner of Marley's mouth tilted into an

approximation of a smile, and, whoa, for just an instant, she looked exactly like Owen.

"I guess. Anyway, see you around. Maybe."

As Cate watched Marley walk back down the hallway with her cup, she couldn't help but wonder what the hell she'd gotten herself into with this job.

4

Three days later, Cate qualified as a walking, talking zombie. But when the manager at The Bar had called and asked if she'd wanted the Wednesday shift in addition to her already-scheduled Tuesday night slot, she couldn't say no. Picking up the additional hours had meant back-to-back eight A.M. to eleven P.M. workdays, but it had also meant extra money.

Not that she'd have nearly enough by bright and early Monday morning, which was when she'd promised the bank manager she'd have that mortgage payment ready to go.

"One train wreck at a time," Cate whispered to herself. Rolling over in her bed, she sucked it up and finally let herself squint at the clock on her bedside table.

5:42 A.M.

A tiny part of her was tempted to yank the blankets over her head and try like mad to go back to sleep. But since that trick had never once worked despite all of her truest efforts, she decided to forfeit her nice, warm bed in favor of the only part of her house that would soothe her under-rested body and her over-active mind.

Destination: kitchen.

Pausing only for a quick trip to the bathroom and a tango with her toothbrush, Cate pulled her hair into a low-slung ponytail and sock-footed herself to her kitchen. The room was the size of a Lego, but still. It was hers. At least, for now.

She opened the cupboard above the coffeepot. Flour, sugar, salt...everything she needed was there. Cate took out each ingredient and placed it on the counter. She slid a deep breath into her lungs, ordering the process in her mind and letting it calm her. Okay, yeah. She had just enough to make a double batch of lemon bars before she had to get out the door to Cross Creek.

Her stomach tightened at the reminder of her full-time job. Yes, she'd found a little bit of a rhythm over the last three days, even though there was conservatively ten times more work to be done than she'd imagined. But the thought of working at Cross Creek all day, every day, still made her nauseous. For the last three years, Cate had studiously swerved around anything that hinted at commitment, and for damn good reasons. She might need this job, but that didn't mean she had to like it. *Or* the serious, scowly man who had hired her.

Now her stomach did something entirely different, and the sensation crept lower, settling warmly between her thighs. Although she'd checked in with Owen twice daily since that first awkward morning in the office, their conversations had been as sparse as possible, mostly containing phrases like, "Do you know where the purchase orders for last June might be?" and "I updated this week's payroll." Which was a-okay by her, really. The less chance she had to inadvertently reveal that she was flying by nothing more than intuition and the seat of her Levis, the better.

Even if Owen's abs did make regular appearances in her mind's eye when she was drifting off to sleep at night. And in the morning while she drove to the farm. And when things got really slow at The Bar. And...

"Good Lord, girl. Simmer down." Cate reached for the fridge handle, tugging the thing open with enough force to make the condiments lining the shelf on the door rattle. Yes, Owen's abs were spectacular. But she had no business daydreaming about them, or any other part of him for that matter. If she wanted to take the edge off her libido, she could use that dating app to find a nice, yet nondescript, guy two towns over in Lockridge like she had last year. Granted, both times she'd done so, the sex had been pretty meh. But at least finding someone for a safe, no-strings-attached night in bed would be better than fantasizing about what that happy trail of Owen's led to, and exactly how happy he might make a girl with it.

Butter. Eggs. Flour. Lemon juice.

Right. Now.

Inhaling a much-needed breath of cool air from the fridge, Cate slid two sticks of butter from the top shelf and shut the door. Her kitchen was small, little more than a six by eight galley, lined on both sides by slim stretches of scuffed countertops and appliances that had been manufactured the same year she'd graduated high school. She set the butter on the counter to soften, taking out the square ceramic baking dish she'd picked up last year at the Salvation Army's annual yard sale. With motions as familiar and vital as breathing, Cate pulled a stainless steel bowl and her ancient hand mixer from the over-stuffed cupboard next to the sink. She opened the drawer above it to liberate one of the three kitchen towels she kept on a steady rotation, but a flash of bright blue and purple made her fumble to a stop, mid-reach.

The sight of the ceramic trivet shouldn't be a shock; after all, it had been nestled in the same drawer for three years now. For one sharp, impulsive second, Cate was tempted to take it out, to trace the indent of the kindergartener-sized handprint with her own, much bigger fingers, to read the uneven print of the letters that made up Lily's name, squeezed in tightly at the end of the inscription because she'd misjudged the print to space ratio like most five-year-olds did.

TO MOMMY, LOVE, LILY.

Cate shut the drawer with a wood-on-wood clap. The trivet was the only item in her kitchen that never got used. That hadn't always been the case, but now the trivet was exactly where it belonged and exactly where it would stay.

Because it had to.

Turning toward the oven, she reached for the button that had once been labeled "bake" but had long since lost its lettering. Cate tapped the up arrow until the display read 375 degrees, busying herself with greasing the baking dish. The familiar whir of the mixer smoothed the sandpaper-edges of her nerves as she creamed the butter and sugar, then added enough flour and salt to form the dough for the crust. Her shoulder muscles, which had been holding her neck hostage since she'd pulled herself out of bed, relaxed further as she pressed the dough evenly into the baking dish. Things might not be turning out the way she'd hoped or wanted, or even planned. But if Cate knew anything, it was how to be pragmatic and land on her feet. She had a solution. She could save her bank account by working at Cross Creek, and she could save her sanity by baking.

"Wait a second..." Cate frowned, peering into her oven. The light had popped on just like always as soon as she'd opened the door. But the way the interior temperature felt no different than the air in the kitchen around her, and the ominously dark heating coils that usually glowed orange-red when the oven was good to go?

Those were definitely new developments. And *not* good ones.

"Okay, okay. Think." Placing the baking dish on the counter beside the oven, she fiddled with the settings, going from bake to broil and back, and trying a handful of different temperature settings with the oven door open, then closed, before the dread in her belly spread out to her bones.

Nothing was working. Her oven was broken.

She pressed the button to turn the thing off—for all the damned good it would do—and dropped her chin over the neckline of her night shirt. The emotion of her week rushed up in her chest, threatening to break free and spill over. The debt, the commitment of a full-time job, and now this? Her oven? Her fucking *sanctuary*?

No. No, no, no, no, no.

Cate closed her eyes before the tears that wanted to fall could fully form. Swallowing the scream in her throat, she flattened her hands on the cool surface of the countertop, metering her breath against the rattling of her heart until both were controlled.

Standing here on the verge of a breakdown wasn't helping anything. She needed to *do* something. She couldn't sleep, she couldn't bake, and she couldn't stay here, where the options that weren't options would taunt her at every turn. A glance at the digital clock on the microwave told her it was a few minutes after six, which—damn it!—took every place in Millhaven off the table.

Except one.

Owen had said they started with the roosters, which meant no one's head was still on the pillow at Cross Creek. The office in the back of the main house wasn't her first choice of destinations, or really, even her tenth, but it was better than staring down her broken oven and unbaked lemon bars. If only by a freaking thread.

Cate carefully packed up the unbaked dough and put it in the fridge before heading back to her bedroom, then the itty-bitty bathroom attached to it. Her get-ready-and-get-out routine didn't take terribly long, especially since she'd heeded Owen's advice and ditched her dressier clothes in favor of jeans and—in today's case—a light, berry-colored sweater. After filling a travel mug to the brim with the strongest coffee she could afford to brew and still have enough to last the rest of the week, Cate grabbed a can of soup from the cupboard that stunt-doubled as her pantry and made her way out the door.

A chill hung in the still morning air, sending a shiver up her spine on the quick hustle to the carport attached to her house. Her Toyota cooperated for once, the engine turning over on the second try and not sputtering or stalling out on the entire ten-minute drive to Cross Creek. The first floor of the main house was quiet, but unlocked and empty as usual, so Cate headed inside and slipped into the office. Her morning routine kept her mind occupied, and, three hours later, she'd managed to take a small dent out of the latest stack of invoices and temporarily forget both her bills and her broken oven.

But all the stress came winging back into her chest at the unexpected sight of Owen standing in the office doorway.

"Oh, jeez!" She clapped a hand over the front of her sweater, half out of reflex and half because she was certain her heart would slam its way across the floor. "Make some noise next time, would you?"

"Sorry." He rocked back on the heels of his work boots and stuffed his hands in his pockets, his expression impossible to decipher. "I didn't want to interrupt you."

"It's a little late for that, huh?" Cate asked.

If the hard set of Owen's mouth was anything to go by, her attempt at humor had fallen way short of the mark. "I just wanted to know if you filled out the form for your benefits yet."

Shit. Speaking of stress. "No, I—"

Cate clamped down on her lower lip, hard. She could not, under any circumstances, admit that she'd never had a full-time job in her life and had no idea how any of this worked. Not to mention that even if she *had* been able to squeeze in enough time to figure out the fifty two-page benefits booklet Owen had given her to "take a look at", she probably couldn't afford any of the options for health care, anyway. "No. I didn't fill it out."

His eyes widened in all their long-lashed glory. "Oh. I didn't mean to pry. You know, if you've got...things in place from before Brian...um..."

"Died?" Cate asked after the silence that followed grew to roughly the size of a tour bus. Her nerves jangled, making her rib cage tighten. She didn't want to put Owen on the spot—really, she didn't. But between her crushing debt, her busted oven, and her overwhelming unease at the commitment of a full-time job, her heart was pounding triple-time.

Please, God. Please don't let him do the poor-Cate thing. Not here. Not today.

"Yes." Owen stared at the edge of the area rug. "I'm sorry.

You know what, I shouldn't have brought it up."

Her composure teetered, right on the brink. "You don't have to tiptoe around me, you know."

"I'm not," he said, but damn it, even his argument came out on cat's feet, all soft and loaded with pity, and in a white-hot instant, Cate's calm completely unraveled.

"You might not think so, but you are," she insisted. If he needed a primer on how to give his argument some backbone, she was more than willing to offer up an example. "It's been three years since the accident. I might not want to discuss every detail, but it's not necessary to avoid the truth like some sort of virus."

"I know." Again, Owen's words sounded like charity.

And again, she'd reached her limit. "But you don't. I'm so tired of everyone in this town feeling sorry for me." Cate lifted a hand to stop the argument he was clearly putting together, unable to keep her frustration corked. "I get that you think you're being nice, but you know what would *really* be nice? If you could treat me like a regular person. Not like poor, sad, widowed Cate who deserves to be pitied. God, for once, I'd really just like to be *me*."

Four rapid-fire heartbeats passed, then a fifth before Owen cleared his throat, his gray eyes blazing as he said, "Fine, then. The forms will need to be turned in tomorrow if you want your health insurance to start by the first of the month next week."

Cate took a long, large breath, mostly so she wouldn't scream, or—worse yet—cry. "I'll have them done before I leave today."

"Great."

But as he turned to walk out of the office, she couldn't help but feel about as far from great as she could possibly get.

5

Owen had a very bad feeling about the next hour of his life. On the surface, everything looked normal—the pot of spaghetti sauce bubbling away on the stove, the waning sunlight that said the workday was finally in the past tense, the sight of his old man sitting at the kitchen table, reading the *Camden Valley Chronicle* with their family mutt, Lucy, at his feet. But Hunter had requested a family dinner on a Thursday of all nights, then specifically came down to the greenhouse to ask him face-to-face if he'd be willing to make a pot of his signature spaghetti sauce for the occasion. Not that Owen minded the cooking. Between the homegrown tomatoes and onions and herbs, the sauce pretty much hit all of his happy places. Still, while his brother might be a lot of things, a dumbass had never been on the list. A family dinner, and a special one at that, on a weeknight?

Something was up, and whatever it was, it wasn't giving him the warm freaking fuzzies.

Taking a deep breath, Owen reached for the wooden spoon he'd propped over the lip of the stock pot and swirled it through the sauce. Between the billion things on his To Do list and getting all the last-minute details in order for next week's groundbreaking for the storefront, he'd admittedly been on edge today. Of course, the dressing down he'd received from Cate this morning hadn't exactly helped matters.

You know what would really be nice? If you could treat me like a regular person.

Owen frowned, a shot of irritation blooming in his veins. He might not be great, or—okay, fine—even passably decent at the whole expressing-himself thing, but he wouldn't dish up pity for pity's sake. All right, so maybe he'd treated Cate with kid gloves today, the same way everyone in town had since Brian had died. So sue him for trying to be nice.

Except...

Everyone in Millhaven really *did* tiptoe around her. No one ever mentioned Brian or Lily's name if Cate was within a forty-foot radius, and, even now, three years later, a hush tended to ripple over a lot of conversations when Cate was near. Most folks were trying to be kind—what she'd been through couldn't possibly have been anything less than devastating. But now that Owen thought on it, if that boot was on the other foot, three years of whispered pity would almost certainly drive him bat shit crazy, too, and damn it. For all her prickly delivery and fiery attitude, Cate might have kind of had a little bit of a point when she'd given him what-for.

"Ooooooh, that smells great."

The words—and the genuine smile from his soon-to-be-sister-in-law, Emerson—knocked Owen back to the moment.

"Thanks. How are you feeling?" he asked. Emerson had MS, and while she was fiercely independent about running her own physical therapy practice in town, she'd also come to let Hunter, and by extension, the rest of them, help her out on her not-so-good days.

Family and farm. Always remember...

"A little tired, but overall, I had a pretty good day today," Emerson said as Owen rubbed a hand over the weird ache that had just spread out behind his sternum. "Can I help with anything?"

He nodded, wondering if all the stress he'd been juggling lately was giving him heartburn. "I could use a taste tester."

Emerson laughed, the tiny lines around her eyes that marked her fatigue easing. "I thought you'd never ask."

"He let you off easy," Hunter said from the spot where he stood at the island, slicing one of the cucumbers Owen had liberated from the greenhouse less than two hours ago. "I'm on full salad duty."

Heartburn or not, he wasn't about to pass up a chance to give his brother a good-natured ration of shit. "That's because Emerson is prettier than you. And she complains less."

Reaching for the loaf of Italian bread beside the cooktop, he broke off a bite-sized piece and dipped it into the sauce, passing it over to Emerson. Her blissful moan was likely an exaggeration to tease Hunter, too, but it made Owen smile all the same. Right up until he caught the look on his brother's face as he watched his fiancée wrapped up in pure happiness, and ah hell, Owen was seriously going to need to leave a stash of antacids around here if this heartburn was going to keep up.

"I couldn't agree more," Hunter said, his grin multiplying exponentially as Emerson headed over to the island to give him a mostly chaste kiss.

"Sweet talker."

"Hey, I'm just telling it like it is, Miss Montgomery."

"Ugh." The disapproving grunt sounded off from the entryway to the kitchen, where Marley stood in a pair of ripped jeans, a black T-shirt with the word *NOPE* printed across the front in big block letters, and the mother of all scowls. "I get that you're all engaged and stuff, but is the PDA a moral imperative?"

Owen's shoulders went instantly rigid, but Hunter didn't skip so much as a beat. "Yep. 'Fraid so."

"Awesome," Marley said, her tone painting the word with the same brush someone would use on a phrase like *please drag me over a bed of tangled barbed wire*. She took a few steps into the kitchen, but stopped at the edge of the counter, her stare studiously avoiding the spot where their father sat at the table even though he'd clearly looked up with interest when she'd entered the room.

Owen frowned. "Marley. I didn't think you'd be joining us for dinner."

She worked a lot of evenings at some clothing store in Lockridge, and she hadn't graced them with her presence at a family dinner since January. Maybe before.

"Hunter told me I had to." She gave up half a shrug, like she couldn't even be bothered to go for the full shot of apathy. "Plus, there's food."

"I didn't say you had to," Hunter said gently, and Christ, his brother really ought to be sainted for his unending patience. "I said it's important."

"Same difference."

"Well, it's right nice to see you, Marley," their father said. A pulse of silence followed, thick enough to spread over corn bread, before Marley crossed her arms over her chest and made it clear she wasn't going to reply.

Oh, *hell* no. Owen opened his mouth to launch his irritation. His sister might still be angry about their father's promise to Marley's mother not to contact them for all these years, but he hadn't just blown her, or her mother, off. He'd made sure Marley was provided for. So she hated that he'd kept her mother's secret and stayed away. That didn't mean she had to be so hurtful. Hell, they were all thrown by the change in their family dynamic, and their old man was genuinely trying to connect with her now.

As if he sensed where Owen was headed, his father locked eyes with him, giving up the smallest shake of his head. "Dinner smells great. Those the plum tomatoes you canned at the end of the summer, Owen?"

"Mmm hmm." Clamping down on his bottom lip even though he really didn't want to, he turned his attention back to the stock pot, and yeah, it wasn't tough to let the produce adjust his attitude a little. "We should have a really nice crop of heirlooms this season, too."

"You sure planted enough," Hunter joked. "You can't swing a cat by its tail in the greenhouse without hitting at least three different kinds."

Owen scowled. "The demand for specialty produce spiked by over three hundred percent last season, you know." Of course, much of that demand had been driven by making the more unique varieties readily available in the first place—something Owen had been busting his ass on for a year now.

"Well, *I'm* happy to hear that," Emerson said, giving Hunter a healthy dose of side eye even though there was little heat in the gesture. "Those Cherokee purples you grew last year were my favorite."

"You have better taste in produce than you do men," Owen said, managing to crack a smile as he dodged the balled up paper towel Hunter tossed in his direction. "And I'm glad you liked 'em, because I added Cherokee chocolates to this year's rotation."

Emerson's blue eyes went as wide as her grin. "Stop."

Owen held up one hand in a nonverbal oath before draining the spaghetti that had been boiling away next to the pot of sauce. "So far, they're coming in great. They're known for their high yield anyway, but I'm thinking they might be our top seller for heirlooms once the farmer's market gets going next weekend."

"I like the sound of that," his father said. For a few minutes, they all got lost in the din of getting the table set and the pasta, salad, and garlic bread into serving bowls. The five of them settled in around the farmhouse table, with his father at the head of the table (as usual) and Marley as far away from him as possible, two seats down and to the left (as usual). The seat at the other end, opposite their father, always remained unoccupied. For Owen, and for Hunter, too, he suspected, leaving it that way was largely habit. They just always had. But for their old man, Owen had a feeling it was more bittersweet nostalgia than anything else.

Family and farm.

"So," Hunter started slowly, and Owen's warning flags went on instant red alert. His brother spent so much time being legitimately laid back that when his nerves actually made a rare showing, you could see the signs from the next county over. "Now that we're all together, Emerson and I wanted to talk to you all about the wedding."

"Alright." Their father, who could read Hunter as well as Owen, put down the bowl of salad without serving himself.

Hunter took a visible breath, scooping up Emerson's hand. "We've been thinking about it a lot, and the thing is, we don't want to wait to get married. Neither of us is really a big-ceremony kind of person, and we'd rather go small, surrounded by the people who are most important to us."

"That makes sense," Owen said, the weird jumble of nerves in his gut easing a little. They didn't have a whole ton of family; really, it was just the five of them. Why have a big to-do?

"We're really glad you think so." The tension fell away from Hunter's expression, and wait... "Because we'd like to have the wedding here on the farm. In five weeks."

Holy. Shit. "I'm sorry. Did you say five *weeks*?" His brother had to have lost every last one of his faculties. It was the growing season, for Chrissake!

"I get that it sounds a little crazy and the timing could be better," Hunter said quickly. "But we've already done the legwork."

Emerson took the conversational baton and ran. "Daisy and my mother agreed to coordinate all the details so none of you would have to do a thing, and, of course, we'll go around the farm's schedule. We'd like to have both the ceremony and the reception right here behind the main house, so the setup would be out of the way of operations, and we'd do it on a Saturday anyway, which would provide plenty of time for cleanup. It might be a bit crazy in the main house for a day or two." She cast an apologetic glance toward the head of the table, then at Marley, who—surprise, surprise— had a frown etched deeply over her face. "But, truly, this farm means everything to Hunter, and it's come to mean so much to me, too. We can't imagine a better place to start the rest of our lives together."

Hunter's face grew serious, and he looked from Owen to their old man, whose expression was damn near impossible to read. "I know you need me here now more than ever, and

I intend to honor all the work that needs done," Hunter said. "Emerson and I would postpone our honeymoon until after the last harvest in October, and even then, Eli said he and Scarlett will be stateside for a while at the end of the year. He promised to come help out while I'm gone."

"So, Eli knows about this?" Surprise and unease tag-teamed to form a heavy lump in Owen's stomach. "And Daisy and Emerson's parents, too?" Not that he didn't like Emerson's best friend, but she wasn't even technically family. How could he be so out of the loop?

"Well, yeah," Hunter said apologetically. "Eli's schedule is pretty unpredictable, so we wanted to be sure he could be here for both the wedding and after the harvest before we even thought about moving forward. And, obviously, we don't want anything about this wedding to interfere with Cross Creek's operations. So we had to be sure we could make that happen before we came to you three with the idea."

At that, the fork Marley had been gripping lowered to her plate with a clatter. "You mean those two." She gestured down the table at Owen and their father, who sat right next to him. "I don't have a say in this."

Hunter shook his head, adamant. "You're family. Of course, you do."

"I'm just living here for now," she insisted, her blue stare turning steely and cold. "No, I don't."

The lump in Owen's stomach doubled, then tripled at the flicker of emotion that whisked through their father's eyes at the words. "Is this really the best time to argue semantics?"

"No." The single word from his father made the rest of Owen's argument fade in his throat. "I don't reckon it's the best time to do anything other than plan a wedding."

"Really?" Emerson asked, her gaze lit with hope, and the old man sealed the deal with a nod of his graying head.

"Of course. If you two want to get married here at the farm in five weeks, I wouldn't dream of standin' in your way. In fact, I'd be honored."

Hunter's grin sent a sharp feeling through Owen that he didn't recognize and definitely didn't like.

"I know it'll take some juggling to keep everything running smoothly when we get close to the day of the wedding," Hunter said. "But this really means a lot to me, Pop." He looked at Emerson, their entwined fingers squeezing tighter. "To us."

"It means a lot to me, too, son."

Emerson hopped up to hug both Owen and his father, then smiled cautiously at Marley, who at least returned the favor by not frowning. Both Emerson and Hunter chatted happily about some of the wedding logistics as the meal resumed, and Owen did his Sunday best to follow along with the enthusiasm he knew they deserved. Yeah, having a wedding here at the farm during the growing season was going to make life a little crazy, and, yeah again, they were already pretty crazy with the farm stand project set to break ground next week and the upswing in business. But when it came to family and farm, family was first for a reason. This was his brother's wedding they were talking about here. His put-the-ring-on-her-finger, promise-to-love-and-cherish, say-I-do-forever-and-ever moment. Crazy or not, Owen should be happy as hell for him. No, check that. He *was* happy for Hunter.

Even if that feeling in his stomach only got worse as dinner went on.

∼

EIGHTEEN HOURS LATER, Owen was convinced he was either developing an ulcer or becoming a full-fledged hypochondriac. Between the definite ache in his chest and the even stranger heaviness in his gut, his money was sadly behind door number one.

"Ah, shit." He looked up at the sky, measuring the position of the sun against the backdrop of the fields and the hay barn in the distance. At least right now, he could blame his physical woes on the fact that noon had come and gone without the courtesy of allowing him a lunch break. But since Owen had zero interest in folding over from low blood sugar, he dusted his hands off and headed for his truck. He had a trillion tasks ahead of him, so he'd have to dine and dash. God, just this once, he'd love to start the weekend ahead of the curve instead of so far away, he couldn't even *see* the curve.

Ordering his afternoon by both urgency and importance, he made his way to the main house. If he could make decent time in the south field and get all of his work done in the greenhouse—which would take some balls-out effort since he'd recently added six different varieties of tomatoes, plus more asparagus, Chinese eggplants, artichokes, and kale—he might, just maybe, be able to leave work on time tonight.

Right. So you can spend time with whom, exactly?

The question prompted a fresh set of corkscrews to crank through Owen's chest. He might not be any closer to finding a pretty woman to spend a bit of time with, but come on. He was thirty-three, not a hundred and three. Anyway, there was work to do. He had to focus on the "farm" part of family and farm right now.

Putting his F-250 in *Park*, he got out of his truck and stabbed his boots into the gravel path. Cate's aging Toyota was parked beside the main house next to Marley's equally aging car, just as it had been at seven o'clock this morning when he'd driven by on his way to the greenhouse. Like yesterday, Owen had been shocked to see her there so early. But not as shocked as he'd been when he'd looked at her time sheet after she'd left yesterday evening and discovered she'd only clocked in from eight to five, and, now that he thought about it, he should probably remind her to record things accurately. If the work warranted extra hours, they'd pay her as such.

Owen bypassed the kitchen even though his stomach was giving him what-for and why-not. Moving toward the office, he tugged his baseball hat off to run a hand through the crow's nest that lay beneath it, replacing the thing just in time to walk over the threshold into the office...

And into Armageddon.

"What the hell happened in here?"

Okay, so he'd bypassed his manners just a little more than was proper. But from baseboard to baseboard, the office floor was plastered with invoices and work orders, with no apparent organization or system to keep them in order. Owen's pulse went from a steady push to an outright oh-shit slam as he registered the now-empty box labeled *Storefront Project* sitting in the center of the mess, with Cate perched next to it like nothing-doing.

"Hello to you, too," she said wryly, plucking a pencil from the dark brown twist of curls at her nape and scratching out God-knew-what onto the legal pad between the fingers of her free hand.

Frustration rising, Owen tried again. "What are you doing?"

"Playing Tiddly Winks with manhole covers." Cate looked up just enough for him to catch the arch of her brow that piggybacked her answer. "What does it look like I'm doing?"

"It looks like you're making an unholy mess," Owen said, the words pumping out unchecked.

Cate looked up from her legal pad, but funny, she continued to be unfazed. "You mean I'm bailing you out of *your* unholy mess."

"That's not what it looks like from here." For Chrissake, she had every single piece of paper on the giant make-or-break project they were about to start scattered to the four goddamn winds of the place.

Her spine unfolded, her shoulders forming a rigid line beneath her body-hugging black top. "I'm creating a system. One you need pretty badly," she added.

Whether it was the stress of the project itself looming so closely on the horizon, the toppling nature of his list of things to get done before said project began, or the ache still lodged firmly behind his sternum even as he stood here in the doorway of the office, Owen couldn't be certain. But all of it balled together, and the next thing he knew, he heard himself say, "Dumping everything into a giant pile is hardly creating a system. We're breaking ground on this project in less than a week, Cate. How am I supposed to find anything in this tornado you've created?"

"I told you, I've got everything under control. I guarantee that by the time the first shovel hits the dirt for your storefront, you'll be able to find anything you need far faster and easier than ever before."

"But—"

"No. No buts." Cate stood, leaving both her pencil and the legal pad at her feet so she could knot her arms over her chest. Her brown eyes blazed with both confidence and heat, and for a split second, Owen couldn't tell if he was more angry or aroused. "You hired me to get a handle on your books, and that's what I'm doing. Either you trust me to do the job or you don't, Owen. What's it going to be?"

The sassy, no-holds-barred ultimatum was one he hadn't expected, and it stunned him into silence. Drawing a slow, deep breath, Owen shifted back on the only non-papered section of the floorboards and made his very best effort to scrape up some patience. Not that it was easy; or, hell, anything less than an earth-moving effort. He needed this level of stress like he needed a punch in the face right now.

Unfortunately, he didn't have time to undo the mess she'd created, which meant he needed Cate more. No matter how much of a cluster fuck she was currently making out of his books.

"Fine. But I'm going to hold you to your word."

Rather than backing down, or even batting so much as a pretty, chocolate-brown eyelash, Cate simply slid her hands from her ribcage to her hips.

"Well, that works out perfectly, because I intend to live up to it. Now was there anything else you needed? Because, like you said last week at Clementine's, these books of yours aren't going to balance themselves."

6

Cate was ninety percent full of shit and the other ten was pure moxie. At least she'd managed—although barely—to wait until Owen had about-faced his way out of the office before letting her exhale escape in a whoosh of relief.

He hadn't called her bluff. She was still employed.

Also, about as on-edge as an industrial-sized roll of razor wire.

Framing the bridge of her nose with her thumb and forefinger, she pressed at the headache starting to form behind her eyes. She'd been up to her two front teeth in Cross Creek's books for nearly a week, and God, she'd barely made a dent in getting things organized. But despite feeling overwhelmed (read: terrified) by the sheer volume of work, Cate hadn't been blatantly lying to Owen. She *was* creating a system, and that system was allowing for progress, slow and steady.

The problem was, slow clearly wasn't going to keep her employed, and damn it, damn it, damn it! She couldn't think with all this pressure banding around her rib cage, threatening to squeeze her senseless. She needed space. She needed to be able to breathe, to shake some of the horrible stress in her chest and get her thoughts organized.

She needed to bake something.

"Wishful freaking thinking," Cate muttered under her breath. She'd had to make the rock/hard place decision not to pay her gas bill on time and to forego more than twenty dollars in her grocery budget for the week in order to scratch together enough money to cover her mortgage. No way could she afford to have anyone come out to do something as extravagant as fix her oven.

Her eyes surprised her by forming tears, hot and unbidden, and she clamped them shut to ensure that the tears wouldn't fall. Sure, things were bleak right now, but she'd been through worse, most of it without breaking down for a boo-hoo. She just needed to grit her teeth and muscle through like always.

Not that she'd ever done that without her oven. But she'd figure out a way.

Probably.

After a few rounds of deep breathing, Cate opened her eyes. While the unease that had parked itself inside her rib cage like a Buick hadn't budged, at least her stupid tears had taken a hike. Now, all she needed to do was grab a lightning-fast lunch and get on the rest of this paperwork.

She grabbed her bargain-brand canned soup du jour—vegetable, today—and headed into the Cross's kitchen. Pretty, golden sunlight streamed in through the windows on the far wall, illuminating everything around her in a happy glow. It should've lifted her mood, Cate knew. Instead, the view just reminded her of everything she couldn't have right now, and God, what was with her and the tears today?

How am I supposed to find anything in this tornado you've created?

No. *No.* She would not think of Owen and his storm-colored stare that seemed to cut a direct path right to where she felt most vulnerable.

Because on top of everything else, feeling vulnerable around her beautiful, brooding boss just might break her right now.

The sound of the back door squeaking on its hinges captured Cate's notice, and by the time Hunter had taken the half-dozen steps into her line of sight, she'd tacked a business as usual expression over her face.

"Oh, hi, Cate," he said, his blue eyes crinkling as he gave up a friendly smile. "I just came to grab some extra bottled water. Hope I'm not bothering you."

"It's your house." Her cheeks burned at the unintended gracelessness in her words, and she scrambled to add, "You're not bothering me at all."

Hunter glanced down at the can she'd popped open and poured into the chipped ceramic bowl she'd brought from home. "Canned soup, huh? You must really like that stuff."

Cate bit her tongue—not lightly—to keep from pointing out that nobody liked bargain-basement canned soup enough to eat it for lunch for a week straight. "It's not so bad," she said, because it was better that than a lie.

Hunter's expression said he thought otherwise, although he was too kind to say so out loud. Instead, he surprised her by going with, "You know, we've got more salad greens and tomatoes in the fridge than we can probably eat, and there are a bunch of strawberries in here, too."

More shock made her lips part. "You have fresh strawberries? How is that even possible?" They weren't in season for another two months. Even the ones The Corner Market had in those little plastic containers were pretty much impossible to get this time of year unless you were willing to settle for fruit that was either anemic-looking or way past its prime because it had been shipped from so far away.

"You'd be surprised what a good greenhouse will yield off-season. Plus, Owen tends to all the produce in there like a mother hen."

Hunter paused, just for a blink, but his wince in hindsight at the maternal reference didn't slip by her. Owen wasn't her favorite topic of conversation, but she'd take him over a poor-Cate pity party—even a subtle and well-meaning one—any day.

"Your brother does seem pretty serious." She stirred a can of water into her soup, which didn't add to the appeal of the blah-brown broth or the mushy vegetables, but hey, beggars and choosers and all.

"He does," Hunter agreed, reaching into the refrigerator for two oversized bottles of water. "But don't take it too personally. The legacy of being oldest might make him kind of a drill sergeant about the farm sometimes, but deep down, he's really just a big ol' softie."

Cate couldn't help herself. Despite the unease still bundled in her chest, a smile slipped out. "Does he know you're spilling his secret?"

"No, ma'am." Hunter smiled back. "I was kind of hopin' you'd keep that under wraps for me."

"My lips are sealed."

"Well. I've got a whole bunch of things to get done before the day is through," he said, and Cate's breath re-cemented itself to her lungs in response.

"I know the feeling," she muttered, her nervous system springing right on back to DEFCON 1 at the thought of getting the storefront project paperwork organized and entered into the database in a manner that made sense.

Hunter tipped his baseball hat at her and turned toward the door. "I won't keep you, then. Enjoy your lunch, and feel free to help yourself to anything in the kitchen, too, okay?"

"Thank you."

Cate dropped her stare to her soup, sliding it into the microwave and pressing the *start* button, even though her appetite was lukewarm at best. She had a minute to kill, so she let her stare coast over the big, beautiful double oven beside her, the long stretches of counter space just begging to be used, the white ceramic canisters labeled "flour", "sugar", and "salt" that stood close enough to make her fingers twitch.

Feel free to help yourself to anything in the kitchen...

Salad greens and fruit were one thing, and a generous offer at that. But what if Cate wanted more?

What if she wanted the kitchen itself?

Her chin whipped up, common sense quickly stamping out the suggestion from her clearly delirious brain. Was she crazy? She couldn't hijack the Cross's kitchen just to get her baking fix. It would be improper on so many levels. She'd not only have to invade their space, but she'd have no choice but to use ingredients from their pantry. She couldn't possibly justify either, not even in the name of calming her French-fried nerves.

Except.

While she'd have to raid the Cross's cupboards for ingredients, she *could* leave whatever she baked here for them to enjoy, and—of course—she'd clean up after herself. So the only thing she'd technically be taking would be the space, and she was already in their house for nine hours a day, anyway. She wasn't some stranger walking up the lane and into their kitchen without permission.

Cate's heart beat faster at the burst of excitement flooding her veins. It was nearly one o'clock. All three Cross men had come and gone for lunch. She usually didn't see any of them again until three or four o'clock, and, even then, those sightings were hit or miss.

She could totally borrow their kitchen without getting in anybody's way, and no one would know until after the fact.

Soup forgotten, Cate opened the fridge with a gentle tug. Not one, but two pints of strawberries greeted her, and oh, God, they were gorgeous. Not humungous or oddly shaped like some of those imported berries that had likely been sprayed with nine kinds of chemicals to "enhance" growth, these were bright red and bite-sized. She slid the closest container from the shelf, placing it on the counter next to a bowl of oranges and lemons, and she smiled instantly.

Strawberry lemon quick bread.

The idea echoed through her brain first, then quickly migrated to her heart. It was the perfect recipe to whip together on the fly. The summer-sweet bread didn't require any ingredients that weren't common pantry staples. She wouldn't need a mixer to make it, and she'd know the recipe even if she were in a coma—plus, the bread lived up to its name. She could put the double-batch recipe together, start to finish, in the time she'd normally take for her lunch break. No harm, no foul, no time missed from work.

Cate's fingers wiggled impatiently, her breath catching in her throat at the thought of soothing away the worries of her week with the simplicity of the ingredients and the motions she knew by heart. The motions that would offer her more sustenance than food or drink or sleep.

The motions that would calm her enough to let her get the books organized and keep her job.

She moved before her brain even registered the command it had sent to her legs to get in gear. Within minutes, she had all the ingredients assembled in front of her. Finding two loaf pans took a little doing, but didn't prove impossible. Now, if she could only dig up a mixing bowl big enough to—ah! Cate struck gold (or, in this case, stainless steel) in one of the cupboards beneath the island, and she didn't waste any time putting her newfound tools to work.

Flour, baking soda, salt, butter, sugar...she measured and stirred and mixed, letting each step chip away at the tension in her shoulders. This, *this* was the only thing that could calm her. Baking made her feel not only awake, but alive. The routine flooded her with relief, like that first gasp of air after diving to the bottom of a deep, dark pool, like some sort of vital puzzle piece that fit only her and didn't make sense to anyone else.

I like cookies as much as the next person, Cate, but we have a baby now. Anyway, no one ever makes money off a hobby...

She sucked in a sharp breath, her hands freezing mid-motion before she locked down on the memory and parceled it back to the basement of her brain. Nope. No way. She wasn't going to wreck the one shot she had at kicking her shitastic week to the curb by dwelling on a past she hadn't been able to change then, and damn sure couldn't change now.

Cate willed her muscles to unwind, stirring the batter with even turns of the spatula until it became a smooth, satiny mixture. Placing the bowl on the counter, she rinsed the strawberries and carefully patted them dry, the paring knife from the block on the counter sounding off in a rhythmic tat-tat-tat as she treated them to a quick slice. The jewel-toned berries popped against the pale yellow batter, to the point that she almost regretted folding them in. But she'd saved a handful of the prettiest ones for the top of each loaf—people ate with their eyes first, after all. And, wow, the strawberries really were some of the prettiest Cate had ever seen.

On impulse, she tossed one into her mouth. She hadn't really thought anything of the move; hell, she'd probably eaten truckloads of strawberries in her thirty-two years. But she realized, too late, that this was no ordinary strawberry. The flavors exploded on her tongue, juicy and ripe, and she let out a blissful moan before tasting another one, then another. The berries carried a flawless balance of sweetness to acidity, not too tart, not too cloying. Just perfect.

Kind of like this moment she'd craved more than food or water or air.

Getting the batter evenly distributed in the waiting loaf pans, Cate put both into the oven she'd preheated, quickly backtracking to tidy the kitchen and erase any signs that she'd been there. Even doing the dishes wasn't a chore, and as the last of her unease slipped down the drain along with the soap bubbles, she allowed herself to think that maybe— just maybe—she could tackle this job and pay her bills, and things would be okay.

ONE MEASLY HOUR LATER, Cate realized things were definitely not okay. She'd been so desperate to get into the Cross's kitchen for a little innocent baking that she'd forgotten the quick bread would make the entire first floor of the house smell like a strawberry-lemon paradise.

Which wouldn't be so terrible, except for the fact that someone had just unexpectedly opened the back door not even ten minutes after she'd turned out the quick bread to cool on the windowsill, and the increasingly louder echo of boot-steps in the hallway said that someone was headed directly for her. God, what had she been *thinking*, using the Cross's kitchen like that, even if it had been on her lunch break?

Cate whipped a panicked glance around the office. Of course, the place didn't look any better than it had when Owen had raised his eyebrows at it—and her—ninety minutes ago, even though she'd actually made more progress than she'd hoped. The lack of stress had cleared her mind enough to let her really dig in to the multiple options the software offered. Not that *that* little tidbit was going to help her right now.

Owen crossed the threshold of the office, and Cate's gut bottomed out on the floorboards. She couldn't have been busted by Hunter or Mr. Cross, could she? It just had to be grouchy, gorgeous Owen, standing there with a tea towel-wrapped loaf of quick bread balanced between his big, rugged hands and a stupidly sexy crease bisecting his brows.

"What is this?"

In a lot of cases—most of them, even—the question would be totally innocuous. But this wasn't going to be one of those cases, so despite her hammering heartbeat, Cate stood up and said, "It's a strawberry lemon quick bread."

The only change in Owen's expression was the slight lift of his stubbled chin. "You baked a loaf of quick bread in our kitchen?"

She bit back the no-filter urge to point out that she'd actually baked a pair of them.

"I did it on my lunch break, and I know it was really

brash to just raid your pantry like that. But I wouldn't dream of taking it home with me. It's, you know. For you to enjoy," she said, the words tumbling out in a rush. Better to just rip off the Band-Aid in one painful tug. "I apologize for overstepping my bounds. Hunter said I should help myself to anything in the kitchen, but I'm sure he didn't mean this. I just...the oven at my place is broken, and I can't afford to fix it right now, but I wanted...I needed..."

Cate trailed off, unable to finish the sentence without sounding like a bigger wingnut than she already did. How on earth could she expect Owen to understand why she'd needed to be in the kitchen so desperately? That when she had her hands on the ingredients and her mind on the recipes, it was the only time she ever felt *right*?

She cleared her throat. "Anyway. You're my employer, and this is where I work. It was wrong of me to take such a big liberty with the house. I won't do it again."

"Cate—"

Oh, God, his eyes were brimming over with equal parts question and pity, and really, she just *couldn't*. "Look, I have a lot of work to do if I'm going to get these books organized before the construction on your storefront project begins next week, so can we just forget about this? Please? I really won't ever do it again."

For the longest minute of Cate's life, Owen said nothing, simply looked at her with that steely gray stare that she was certain could see every single thing she wanted to hide. Her throat knotted, her palms going clammy with the certainty that he was going to call her out or fire her, or maybe even both.

So she was shocked right down to her toes when he said, "Okay, then. I guess we should both get back to work."

7

Owen huddled down low in his thermal-lined jacket, warding off the early morning chill with a cup of coffee strong enough to strip the paint off his truck. He loved Cross Creek in all lights and seasons, but there was something a little exceptional about the place right after dawn, just as the sun warmed the tree line over the east fields. The way the sky morphed so seamlessly from dark blue to purple to pink, the sun ushering the shadows into the past tense and turning the fields all green and gold...Christ, it was enough to take a man's breath away.

Even if he *had* been working those fields so much lately he could feel it in his fingernails.

"Well. I s'pose that face is one way to go."

Owen shifted against the fence line and gifted his brother with a single-fingered salute, although the corners of his mouth edged up in enough of a smile to take most of the heat out of the gesture. "Yeah, yeah. It's six thirty on a Wednesday morning and we're about to get our asses kicked by a twelve-hour workday. Sue me if I'm not all rainbows and unicorns right now."

Hunter laughed, leaning against the planks of the split rail fence so they were shoulder to shoulder. "You should be all unicorns and rainbows right now, seeing as how we're breaking ground on the storefront in a couple of hours *and* you weaseled the last piece of that quick bread for your breakfast. You sneaky bastard."

So many things to unpack there. Owen decided to go with the easiest. "I can't help it you stayed in bed an extra ten minutes and missed out on breakfast. You snooze, you lose, brother."

Hunter's laugh became a snort, lickety split. "Pretty sure I win, considering I spent those ten minutes enjoying something even better than quick bread."

Ah, shit. He'd waltzed right into that one, hadn't he? "Right. Well, good for you, then."

His brother's reply was—blessedly—cut off by the buzz of his cell phone, which he slid from the back pocket of his jeans. "Oh, hey! It's Eli on FaceTime."

Hunter swung the phone around, and a few taps had Eli's face on the screen, his cocky, up-to-no-good grin firmly in place.

"Hey! Morning, slackers," he said, the words arriving on enough of a delay to remind Owen that his youngest brother was easily a half-dozen time zones away.

"Slackers? Are you kidding me?" Hunter replied with mock indignation, and Eli laughed.

"I'm in Athens. It's already afternoon here, and there y'all are, just getting started."

Owen shook his head. Six months later, it was still so hard to picture Eli, who hadn't set foot outside of King County for twenty-eight years, jet-setting all over the globe. He worked hard, though, and even though his career one-eighty had caused a whole lot of changes on the farm, Owen couldn't be mad that his brother was following his true passion with a woman he loved.

"It's been a while since I caught both of you together," Eli said. "So, tell me, what's new out there?"

Owen opened his mouth to give Eli a full farm report, but Hunter beat him to the punch with a wry grin. "Nothing much. I was just ribbing Owen for his complete lack of a sex life."

"Dude." Owen gave up a look of pure *what the fuck*. Not that it fazed either of his brothers.

"What?" Hunter arched a brow high enough for the thing to disappear beneath the brim of his baseball hat. "It's not like I'm wrong."

Owen frowned. "And it's not like we're not busy around here."

"I work as much as you do, and I'm still having sex," Hunter pointed out, and Eli—the little turncoat—nodded sagely.

"I've been in three different time zones this week alone and I still got lucky last night, man. Sorry-not-sorry."

Great. This conversation was officially hell. "So, what? You two have formed some elite club now?" Owen asked. He resisted tacking on "you assholes," but only just.

"Sure have," Eli said, not skipping so much as a beat or a breath. "It's called the Get Laid On a Regular Basis Club. You should try it. It's spectacular."

That weird feeling Owen had been battling for over a week now came twisting back through his chest in full force. "You're a dick."

"No, dude. I'm not, and neither is Hunt. That's precisely why we're giving you a hard time. Look"—Eli's voice canted lower, his face growing unusually serious, and Owen noticed the loaded stare his brothers had exchanged too late

—"I get that you love the farm, and that Cross Creek is your legacy. I really do. But work isn't everything, no matter how much you love it. Even legacies that are meant for you get lonely after a while, you know?"

Family and farm.

"I guess," Owen said slowly, because as much as it pained him to admit it, Eli wasn't entirely wrong. "But Millhaven's not exactly busting at the seams with available women."

As usual, Eli pushed his luck *and* Owen's buttons. "We found some."

"You fell for a woman who was only visiting for a series of online articles, and Hunter's marrying his high school sweetheart." Owen split a frown between both of his brothers. "It's hardly the same as me trying to find someone to date in a town where I've lived my whole life that's not even big enough for its own dot on the map."

"Okay, okay. You might have a point," Hunter admitted.

"Point or not, you're still not getting laid," Eli said, the last of his words turning into an *ooof* as a flash of light blond hair and a deceptively sweet pixie-like face appeared on the screen.

"Don't let him harass you, Owen. You'll find someone in your own time."

Owen's mouth twitched with a smile, mostly at the fact that Eli had fallen in love with a woman who put his ass in its place just as often as she got out of bed in the morning. "Hey, Scarlett. Thanks."

"Oh, don't thank me yet, honey," she said, her New York accent toughening up her words. "You might find a woman in your own time, but it'll almost certainly be the *wrong* time."

"Yeah," Hunter said, and Eli nodded in an agreement trifecta.

Jesus. This just kept getting better and better. "Great. Now that you're all in agreement on my extra-curriculars—"

"Or lack thereof!" Eli interrupted with glee.

Owen rolled his eyes, even though his brother's statement was painfully accurate. "I'm going to get moving. Today's going to take forever, and I need to get my chores done early so I can supervise the groundbreaking on the farm stand." As it was, he'd barely have enough time to review the paperwork before the contractors arrived at nine, and that was *if* he could find what he needed in the wreckage of the office. Considering the state of the place the last time Owen had seen it, he'd put his chances of success somewhere between slim and none.

Eli surprised him by letting him off the insult-to-injury hook, then again by replacing his usual cocky grin with something a whole lot more genuine. "Okay. Give Clarabelle an extra apple for me, would ya? I miss that old girl."

"Will do," Owen said, shaking his head at the irony of a former cattle farmer having a nine-hundred pound Jersey brown as a pet. Lucky for Eli, that cow of his was as sweet as could be.

"Thanks. And, hey, O?"

"Yeah?" He turned around, and funny, Eli's expression had grown even more serious.

"I know you're gonna work too hard even if Hunter and I tell you to take it easy, so do me a favor and just don't forget what I said about bein' lonely, okay? When the wrong woman shows up at the wrong time, at least give her a chance."

For a white-hot instant, his mind's eye was flooded with a spill of rich brown curls, a sharp and sexy mouth he'd alternately cursed and been dying to taste for over a week now, and a set of curves that rivaled every back road Millhaven had to offer. Owen's pulse kicked, the lowest part of his belly stirring in oh-hell-yes agreement.

Which was totally fucking crazy. The wrong woman at the wrong time was one thing. Beautiful, brash Cate McAllister was entirely another.

Even if he *could* still describe every nuance of the look on her face when she'd confessed to commandeering their kitchen in the name of some quick bread.

Realizing a few beats had passed and that both of his brothers were certainly waiting for him to speak, or at the very least, move, Owen worked up a sound resembling a soft laugh.

"You got it," he told Eli, waiting just a second more before being unable to resist adding, "Slacker."

"Ahhhh, there's the brother I know."

Owen said one last goodbye to Eli and Scarlett and lifted his chin at Hunter in parting. Setting his sights on the greenhouse in the distance, he began to order his tasks for the morning although his nerves did their best to submarine his calm. Today was a bigger day than he'd wanted to admit out loud, one he hadn't been sure would ever come. Of course, Hunter and their old man—and even Eli, in his own way—loved Cross Creek. They all wanted the place to prosper. But Owen had always had visions for the farm that seemed a little different than everyone else's. Bigger. More modern. Even cutting edge.

The storefront was the first leap in getting them there. If it brought in revenue as projected, the options could be— no, *would* be—limitless. His brothers might give him shit, and his dick might be increasingly disgruntled at the idea of all work and no play, but he needed to focus on the farm part of his legacy now more than ever.

There couldn't be a worse time for a woman to walk into his life.

OWEN TOOK a deep breath and stared down the door to the main house. He was T-minus fifty-seven minutes from the contractors coming to literally dig in to the biggest construction project Cross Creek had seen in more years than he could count on one hand. Even then, that had been when they'd built his cottage on one side of the property and Hunter's on the other. That work had been a big deal, sure, but it hadn't impacted operations like the expansion they'd begin today. From the business plan to the floor plan, this on-site storefront had taken no less than thousands of hours of brain power and determination. Owen had dreamed about it. He'd worked himself senseless to coax it from concept to reality, and now, *finally*, after years of effort and research and planning, they were breaking ground.

Well, they would be as soon as he got his mitts on all the paperwork, anyway. And after the sinkhole Cate had made of the office last Friday, that was really going to be one hell of an endeavor. Yeah, she'd promised to right the ship by today, but come on. She might be fierce (and smart. And damn, so sexy), but unless she dealt in miracles, there was no way in hell she'd been able to get that promise out of the wishful-thinking stage.

Brushing the dust off his Wranglers, Owen palmed the doorknob and made his way into the house. Cate's car was parked outside in all its Wednesday-morning glory, and he straightened his shoulders as he headed for the back of the house, fully preparing himself to have to sift through a huge mess of papers for the handful of ones he needed to review.

But the office was spotless.

"What...what happened in here?" he stammered, his face—and a few other, less-than-proper parts of his anatomy—heating at the sight of the brassy, sassy smile on Cate's heart-shaped mouth.

"First, you don't like the mess, then you miss it when it's gone?" She sat back in her desk chair, her warm brown stare pinning him into place at the edge of the area rug.

He shook his head, partly in response and partly to clear his mind from the very unexpected, very wicked thoughts that had just run through it. "I don't miss the clutter," Owen managed, a new round of surprise blooming in his rib cage as he caught sight of the wide-open space by the window that had, up until a few days ago, held a six-foot stack of boxes. "You didn't, ah, throw it all out, did you?"

"Funny." Cate backed up the claim with a laugh that replaced the surprise in Owen's chest. "Of *course* I didn't throw it all out, although I have to admit, I was tempted a couple of times."

"Okay," he said, his tone marking the word as more question than anything else. "So, what *did* you do with all the boxes that were in here?"

"The boxes are in storage. Hunter showed me where to put them. But the information"—she gestured to the computer sitting on the now-tidy desk in front of her—"is all in a new software program."

"A new software program," Owen repeated. He was pretty sure his expression was as dumbfounded as the rest of him.

But Cate simply nodded and said, "Mmm hmm. The whole thing is pretty streamlined. Well, it is now," she self-corrected. "After I ran updates on your computer and backed up your existing records—which you really should do more often, by the way—I saw that the latest version of the software you'd been using has some really great new options for payroll, invoices, tax information, you name it. I was able to organize everything by category, season, and year, scan and enter the data into the new system, and merge it with the already-existing records, so now all of your bookkeeping is right here online. I still have a few more boxes of the older records and past invoices to go"—she pointed to the neatly stacked trio of boxes tucked beside the desk—"but I should have it all scanned in by the beginning of next week."

Owen blinked, and nnnnnope. His shock hadn't budged. "So, what about all the plans and contracts for the storefront?"

"They're all right here, too. I did those first since I knew you'd need them this week." Cate navigated confidently through a few screens that pretty much looked like they'd been written in Sanskrit for all he knew. "Once you click on the projects tab right here, you can use the menu to find whatever you need. Plans, work orders, materials, budget proposals...I divided everything up into categories, and we can add new ones or merge others if we need to down the line."

"And the software just does that automatically?" he asked, skeptical. They'd had the same bookkeeping program for years, and more than one or two. Granted, Cate hadn't been wrong about them needing to update it, but could the answer to getting everything organized *really* have been right there in front of him the whole damned time?

"Yep," she confirmed. "It's pretty easy to use once you get the hang of it."

"I'm not so sure that's accurate."

Cate's face fell, her spine snapping into a rigid line against the back of the desk chair. "I thought this would be a better way to manage all the bookkeeping. I know it's not what you're used to, but frankly, you guys were stuck in the dark ages with all those hard copies, and—"

"No, no." Ah, shit. Owen closed his eyes, wishing like hell that just once, he could work up some charm like one of his brothers, or even enough of his father's bottomless patience to muddle through his chronic case of foot-in-mouth disease. "I didn't mean it like that. This is, ah, helpful."

"It's what you hired me for," she said quickly, and his heart beat faster at the spark in her eyes, like bourbon going over ice.

"Yes, but—"

"You didn't think I could do it, did you?" Cate cut him off without a breath of notice, and dammit, he answered in the exact same manner.

"After Friday? To be honest, no. I didn't."

"I see." She pressed her lips together, and the deep breath that lifted the front of her sheer white blouse did nothing to help Owen regain his composure *or* put the right words in his mouth. "Well, then. I'm not sure if I should say 'I'm sorry' or 'I told you so'."

"I don't think either is necessary," he said, but, of course, the damage was done.

"Great," Cate replied tightly. "Now that we got that out of the way, was there something you needed?"

"I was just going to go over the plans for the storefront one last time before the contractors get here," he said. Maybe he could still smooth this over.

Or not. "I printed them out for you. Since I knew you

were breaking ground today." She nodded crisply and handed over a sheaf of papers, tucked neatly into a file folder. "Everything is already in the system, of course. But I know you like hard copies."

"Right. Okay, then."

Some voice deep inside of him screamed that he should thank her six ways to Sunday for the incredible job she'd done, to humbly apologize for not believing her when she'd promised to get things straight in time for the groundbreaking, to let her know she'd singlehandedly done something in five days that would've taken him five freaking months to figure out. But, as always, his brain couldn't form the right words, so Owen relied on what he did best.

He walked out of the office with his sights set on the farm, even though for the first time in his life, he was torn between work and something else.

Because it turned out, the answer *had* been right there in front of him the whole time, and right words or not, he needed to do something other than nothing.

Otherwise he was going to lose it.

8

Cate stared down at the screen on her laptop, reviewing the numbers and columns and ratios one last time, even though she'd memorized them after the fourth pass. Tomorrow was her first payday as a Cross Creek employee, and as much as the full-time commitment part of things still made her consider throwing up, the deposit that was set to arrive in her bank account at midnight definitely didn't suck.

Scrolling down to the window she'd hidden at the bottom of the screen, she hovered over the bright red *submit payment* button, her common sense forcing her to click the damned thing before her heart could intervene. Of course, Cate knew her gas bill—tardy as it was—outranked getting her oven fixed. But she also couldn't deny that between last Friday's ill-advised kitchen takeover at Cross Creek and the less clandestine, yet not as much fun, griddle duty Clementine had put her on for half of the following Sunday's shift, she'd found enough of a groove to whip the books at the farm into tip-top shape.

Much to her insanely handsome, insanely tight-lipped employer's surprise.

Cate exhaled, forcing herself to ignore the warmth that had been making a *very* inconvenient habit of forming between her thighs every time she thought of Owen Cross. For God's sake, he was blunt enough to border on being churlish. She had no reason to find his gruff demeanor so freaking attractive.

Except, damn it, she *did* find it attractive. The truth was, while most people probably found Owen's personality overly curt, Cate kind of found his honesty refreshing. Maybe not yesterday, when he'd told her he hadn't believed she could do the job he'd hired her for. That one had kind of pinched. But she hadn't entirely believed she'd balance those books in the beginning, either, and she *had* told him to treat her like a regular person.

He'd been the only person to actually do that in over three years.

A knock sounded off on her front door, rattling her pulse. She didn't live too far from the main road, but everything was pretty much off the beaten path out here in Millhaven. She certainly wasn't expecting anybody at five-forty on a Thursday night.

Creeping to the door, she asked, "Who is it?"

"Hey, Cate," came a slightly familiar voice. "It's Mike Porter. I heard you need your oven looked at."

Cate unlatched the front door, even though nothing Mike had said—other than his name, anyway—had made a lick of sense. "Hey, Moonpie." She paused to bite her lip at letting the guy's elementary school nickname slip, but he waved off her obvious chagrin with a smile. "I'm sorry, I don't think I heard you correctly."

"I heard you need your oven looked at," he repeated,

holding up the tool box Cate just noticed he had in his grasp. Mike worked for a contracting company that specialized in appliance repair, mostly on the bigger, newer houses in Camden Valley and Lockridge, but he did his fair share of fix-it jobs in Millhaven, too. Only, how the hell he'd gotten the news flash about her oven being broken, she had no clue.

"You did," Cate replied slowly.

"Yep. Owen Cross mentioned it."

At her continued stare, Mike added, "Yesterday evening, when I saw him making a delivery at The Corner Market. He told me your oven wasn't working and asked if I'd come fix it for you."

Cate's cheeks prickled, but at this point, she had to choose disclosure over dignity. "I'm sorry. I can't let you do that. I can't pay you."

"You don't have to." Mike shook his head. "Owen took care of it."

Shock merged with something a whole lot less identifiable, both of them settling low in her belly. "He...what?"

"The job's paid for. Labor and parts," Mike said, holding up an invoice that was—sure enough—emblazoned with the words PAID IN FULL across the bottom.

So much for Owen treating her like a regular person. "I'm not letting Owen Cross pay you to fix my oven."

Funny, Mike didn't look surprised by her answer. "He said you might say that. So he wanted me to tell you"—Mike shifted his tool box to his left hand, removing his cell phone from the back pocket of his jeans with his right—"And I quote, 'There's a difference between sympathy and kindness. Consider this a bonus for the great job you did on the books. Now, let Mike fix your damned oven. Please'."

A minute slid off the clock, then another, before Cate

could process what had just happened. Her sledgehammer-serious boss, who hadn't strung together more than sixteen syllables in her presence since she'd shown him the new bookkeeping software yesterday, had gone out of his way to help her get her oven fixed, and he hadn't done it out of pity. He'd done it out of gratitude. In his own brusque way, Owen was treating her like a regular person.

And oh, God, it felt so good, she could cry.

Mike looked at her, and she belatedly noticed the sheer panic blooming over his face. "I'm sorry. I thought you'd know what Owen meant by that, since you're out there, workin' for the Crosses and all now. But I sure didn't mean to offend—"

"No. No, no, no," Cate said, shaking her head adamantly to make sure she got the message across. "It's fine, Mike. I know exactly what Owen meant."

"So, did you want me to get started, then?" The poor guy looked at her in the same manner one might reserve for rattlesnakes and raving lunatics.

But, for once, the tiptoeing didn't bother Cate one whit. "That would be great. Why don't you come on in?"

OWEN HAD NO SOONER PULLED AWAY from the main house on Saturday afternoon when his cell phone made a bid for attention from the back pocket of his jeans.

Hey, you fucking workaholic! Everyone's headed to The Bar tonight to celebrate the engagement. Stop making that face. You're going.

Blanking his frown, Owen stuffed his phone back in his pocket without answering Hunter's text. In his defense, he'd probably clocked a seventy-hour work-week, with a solid two-thirds of it being manual labor and the other third over-seeing the biggest project they'd started in a decade. Anyone who wasn't bulletproof or subhuman would've pulled a face at the prospect of heading out on the town after that.

Jesus. What was wrong with him? This was his brother's engagement they were celebrating. He should be diving headfirst into the festivities along with everyone else.

Fuck, he felt so alone.

Owen's chin hiked upward, his pulse kicking at the unexpected thought. Not that he could deny it, exactly—after all, he *was* alone. At thirty-three, he wasn't totally on the shelf, but he wasn't drowning in prospects, either. At some point, he'd have to focus on the family part of the family and farm legacy.

"Come here, sweet boy. Hop right on up here with me." His mother leaned forward from the pillows stacked behind her and patted the blue and white quilt tucked around her frail body. Her eyes were startlingly clear, even though the aggressive chemo and radiation had taken whatever vitality the breast cancer had left behind. Her dark blond hair had long since fallen out, replaced by floral scarves brought by Clementine and Harley Martin's wife, Louise, but even then, Owen had never thought her any less than beautiful.

"Hi, Momma." Owen climbed up to the center of the four-poster bed. He wouldn't admit that it was still a little hard for him to get up there without a step-stool. He wasn't little like Hunter, and he definitely wasn't a baby, like Eli. Plus, he knew his momma couldn't lift him anymore, even though she looked like she wanted to, so he wouldn't complain.

"I want to have a talk, just me and you," she said. She looked so sad that he let her smooth his hair with one hand, even though that might normally make him feel like he wasn't the oldest.

"Okay," he replied. He was six now. He could have a grown-

up talk with her if that's what she wanted. And Owen could tell that she did, because her eyes got very serious, like they had when Hunter had fallen off the rocking chair last year and needed four stitches on the back of his head. "Is this about my chores? I did 'em just the way Pop asked, but"—he bit his lip before ultimately deciding to tell the truth—"I couldn't lift all the watermelons to put them in the crates. And I dropped one outside the barn door. It made a big mess."

To his surprise, his mother laughed. "Well, I reckon the bees will be right thankful to you for that." She slid her fingers through his. "I know you're working hard on your chores, Owen. I wanted to talk to you because your daddy's going to need a lot of help around here soon, and not just with what needs done around the farm."

His momma stopped for a second, like she was already tired. Just when he thought maybe he should say something, though, she kept going. "He's probably going to be sad, and you might be sad, too. So I'm going to need you to look out for him and your brothers a little extra for me when that happens. Do you think you can do that?"

Owen nodded, even though he was a little confused. "I'll be strong, Momma. Don't you worry."

And he would. He always drank his milk and ate his greens. Even the peas, which baby Eli hated. But Owen could hide them in the mashed potatoes, just like their momma did. He'd seen her do it. Even though he thought it was pretty gross, he could do it for Eli, too, if that's what she needed.

"Thank you, sweet boy." His mother wrapped her arms around him, her pretty white nightgown soft on his cheek as he snuggled against her shoulder. "There's one other thing I want you to remember. Your brothers aren't quite old enough to understand it yet, so this one will just belong to you and me, okay? But it's very important, so listen carefully."

"Okay," Owen said, returning her squeeze as her fingers tightened over his hand.

"As you get bigger, there are going to be a lot of things that mean something to you. But two of those things are always going to matter most. Family and farm, Owen. Never forget how important they both are. Never forget..."

Owen pulled up in front of his cottage with his heart in his windpipe. The memory came back from time to time, and, with it, the reminder of what was important. Channeling all of his energy into the farm part of things had been easy. He loved working the land, the planting, the cultivating, the vitality—all of it. But he'd let the family part fall by the wayside. True, the friction that had existed between him and Eli had mostly eased, but things with Marley were still a hot mess, and while his brothers had both found happiness with women who were perfect for them, he was still alone.

"Screw it."

Owen got out of his truck and headed for his cottage, his shoulders set and his mind made up. He wasn't going to miraculously stumble over true love at The Bar, that was for damn sure. But for tonight, he could do the next best thing.

And that was drink.

After a hot shower and quick change of clothes, Owen shot off a text to Lane and grabbed the keys to his truck. Being Millhaven's sheriff, Lane wasn't much of a drinker even when he was off-duty, and, although it didn't happen often, the guy had carted Owen's drunk ass home on more than a few occasions over the last ten years. Better to make the get-home plan now, rather than after he couldn't drive. He liked The Bar as much as the next person, but sleeping in one of the booths—or, worse yet, on the beer-stained floorboards—definitely wasn't on his bucket list.

Owen cracked the window of his truck, catching a full

handful of stubble as he scrubbed a palm over his face and pulled out onto the main road. In his haste to get out the door and get to sipping, he'd made the executive decision to skip shaving, just as he'd made the same judgment call last week on the haircut he needed but didn't have time for. Guess it was a good thing he wasn't lookin' to fix his loneliness problem tonight, because other than the clean T-shirt and jeans he'd managed to rustle out of his dresser drawers, he wasn't going to win any awards for impeccable grooming.

The trip to The Bar was a fast one, and Owen parked under a street lamp, surveying the gravel lot through the growing twilight on his trip toward the door. Hunter's truck stood a few spots away, sandwiched between Billy Masterson's pickup and Amber Cassidy's cherry-red convertible. His jaw tightened involuntarily as he caught sight of Greyson Whittaker's dented and dinged Silverado on the far side of the parking lot. God, he fucking hated that guy, and not just because he was the only son of the man who ran the farm that gave Cross Creek the most competition for business.

Healthy rivalry, he could handle. Arrogant, entitled douche bags with chips on their shoulder the size of the Grand Canyon? Not so much.

Owen shook his head, forcing the thought to go with it. He was here to blow off steam a different way, which meant he was already late for his date with a nice, cold pitcher of beer and a shot or three of Jack Daniels. Pivoting on his boot heels, he turned toward The Bar, where he could already hear the steady thump of music pulsing from behind the brightly lit windows and wide double doors. But then a slightly rusty, very familiar Toyota caught his attention, and damn it, he must be thicker than a brick not to have realized Cate might be working tonight.

He'd had his balls to the wall ever since they'd broken ground on the storefront three days ago, which meant he'd barely seen anyone in his family since then, let alone had time to go up to the main house to touch base with Cate. Owen did, however, know her oven was now in perfect working order, but it wasn't the invoice Mike Porter had emailed him yesterday for the new heating coil he'd installed that had tipped him off. No, that little heads up had come courtesy of the box of cookies that had been left on the desk in the office with his name on it.

Oatmeal raisin. Not a walnut in sight.

Owen exhaled and finished crossing the parking lot, the soles of his boots crunching steadily over the gravel. He was here to loosen up, maybe have one drink too many. To forget everything that had been jammed on his plate, even if it was only for one night.

And that's just what he intended to do.

Palming the handle on the sturdy wooden door leading in to The Bar, he made his way over the threshold. The country music that had been a muted thump in the parking lot became a full-bodied blast of bass and twang, backed up by the ambient buzz of at least a dozen nearby conversations. The place was more full than not, with a handful of couples already on the wood-planked dance floor and nearly every seat at the bar occupied. Rather than zeroing in on the section of bar tables where he and his family and friends usually threw a few back, though, Owen found his stare traveling to the far side of the room—specifically, to the spot where Cate stood behind the bar.

Her head was tilted to the side, her long, dark hair piled on top of her head in a knot that would probably look messy on anyone else. But not on her. Nope. On Cate, it looked unvarnished and naturally pretty, putting the long line of her neck on display and showing off just enough of her collarbones to make his pulse sit up and take note. A few defiant wisps had broken free from where she'd pinned the rest at the crown of her head, framing her face in a way that, for a stupid split-second, made Owen's fingers jealous, and a sinking feeling took root in his gut.

This was going to be a long-ass night.

"Hey, you showed!"

Owen slapped together a smile before turning toward his brother's voice. "With an invitation like yours, how could I say no?"

"Okay, okay. Maybe I could've been a little more cordial," Hunter said, clapping his brother on the shoulder in greeting. "But then you wouldn't have come, and I'd have had to drag you off the farm kickin' and hollerin', and everyone would talk for weeks about how your younger, better-looking brother outmuscled you. Figured this way, at least I'd save you a little face."

Ah, hell. The guy looked so happy, it was impossible not to take one for the team. "Well, that's damn nice of you, man."

"What can I say?" Hunter grinned and opened his arms wide. "I'm a giver."

"You are somethin'," Owen agreed, and Hunter let out a laugh.

"Well, I'm glad you came out, because actually, there's something I wanted to ask you, and I thought it'd be best done face-to-face."

Concern sparked in Owen's chest. "Everything okay?"

"Everything's fine," his brother said, tucking his hands in the pockets of his jeans and giving up a sheepish smile. "Except I'm getting married in four weeks, and I don't have a best man, so I was kinda hoping maybe you'd help me out and do the honors."

Jaw, meet kneecaps. "You want *me* to be your best man?"

"You look surprised."

"I am. I mean"—Owen cranked his eyes shut, and God, would he *ever* say the right thing at the right time?—"Don't get me wrong. I'm flattered, but I assumed you'd ask Eli. You two have always been closer."

Hunter nodded, stepping a little closer to keep their conversation personal despite the din and bustle of the crowded bar around them. "Eli and I *are* close. But I don't know anybody who holds family more important than you, O. I'd be honored to have you stand beside me at my wedding."

Damn. Owen swallowed past the rare shot of emotion tightening his throat. "I don't know what to say."

"How about that you'll do it?" Hunter asked with a laugh that loosened the mood perfectly. "Because you're leaving me hanging a little bit here, and..."

"Jesus, Hunt." Owen rolled his eyes, although he couldn't help but let his laugh creep in and have its way with him. "Of course, I'll do it."

"Thanks, man. Now, what do you say we grab a couple of beers and get to celebrating?"

"I say that sounds like one hell of a plan."

9

Cate really needed to stop watching Owen from across the damn bar. The place had been packed, as usual, for a Saturday night, and even though she had help from the manager, Brett, and the crowd was beginning to thin out, she had to be on her toes. She didn't have time to be sneaking covert glances at Owen, his biceps, or the overly sexy stubble he'd let grow over the last few days.

Which was kind of ironic, seeing as how she'd unlocked expert-level Owen-scoping skills over the past three hours.

Her sneakers squeaked over the thick black mats behind the bar as she turned to grab a box of straws she couldn't justify needing. Okay, fine. So Owen was attractive, and he'd done an unexpected thing that had made the last two days of her life exponentially easier. This was still Millhaven, and he was still her boss, whose birthright was an entire farm. A *family*-run farm. No matter how much a dark and dirty part of her wanted to throw caution out the window and discover all the dark and dirty parts of *him*, Cate needed to keep herself in check.

A man like Owen Cross wasn't for her. Even if he was right there in front of her with an empty glass and she was the only person behind the bar while Brett closed down the kitchen.

Tucking a strand of wayward hair behind her ear, she pulled together a smile and covered the few steps to the spot where Owen stood next to Lane, one of them looking a whole lot happier than the other.

And here Cate had thought Owen's scowl was sexy. "What can I get you, boys?" she asked, trying to think of something—God, *anything*—that would erase the heat on her face at the very unusual sight of his smile.

"Owen needs a glass of water and a slap upside the head," Lane groused, which turned Owen's smile into a laugh and Cate's panties into a hot zone.

"I'll have another beer, actually. And Lane needs a shot of courage. Or tequila."

"They're not the same thing?" Cate asked, pouring both a glass of water and a beer for Owen and another Coke for Lane, since that's what he'd been drinking all night.

"No." Lane nodded in thanks as she passed his drink over the bar. "And I have plenty of courage, thank you very much."

Owen snorted. "He's trying to work up the nerve to ask Daisy Halstead to dance," he said.

Lane's hand connected with Owen's bicep in a solid thump that wasn't at all shocking since Lane was built like a Sherman tank and Owen's reflexes were probably a little rusty from the four shots of Jack Daniels she'd watched him chase with just as many beers over the last few hours. Smack to the arm notwithstanding, no wonder Owen was full of smiles.

"I already told you," Lane bit out. "I don't need any courage to ask Daisy to dance."

Before she could think better of it, Cate said, "Actually, I'm going to side with you on this one. You probably don't."

Both men blinked at her in a nonverbal equivalent of "huh?", and she tucked her smile between her lips before continuing. "Look, you're a nice guy, Lane, so I'm going to give it to you straight. Daisy's been sneaking looks at you all night. If you don't ask her to dance, then Billy Masterson's going to, because he's been sneaking looks at *her* all night. Daisy will probably say yes, since she knows Billy and he's a decent enough guy and all. But then she might actually have fun with him. In fact, she might even let him walk her to her car and kiss her goodnight."

Cate paused to let the words sink in, but only for a beat of the song filtering down from the overhead sound system. "And since that's really what *you* want to be doing and what I'd also guess *she* wants you to be doing, since she just looked over at you again—don't *look*, Owen," she warned, stopping him mid-swivel before capping the whole thing off with, "maybe you should just cut to the chase and ask her to dance before Billy does. Courage optional, of course."

After a pause, during which Cate was certain she'd over-stepped her bounds in pretty much every direction, Lane pushed back from the bar with a nod. "Fine. But now I'm not just going to ask her to dance."

"Okay," Owen said, his brows lifting up to his tousled hairline. "What else did you have in mind?"

"Now, I'm going to ask her to dance *and* go out to dinner with me next week."

For a guy who rarely smiled, Owen was doing a bang-up job making up for lost time. Thank you, Jack Daniels. "Are you sure? Because you've only been talking about her for like, six weeks straight, and—"

"Owen?" Cate interrupted, making certain her smile was as sweet as possible before she added, "Shut up and let Lane have his moment."

"Thanks, Cate. I couldn't have said it better myself," Lane replied, tipping his chin at her and turning toward the jukebox, where Daisy stood next to Emerson and Hunter. He blew out a breath. "Here goes nothing."

Owen waited until Lane was out of earshot before appraising her with a warm gray stare. "Okay. I've been harassing that big baby to ask Daisy out forever. How did you just manage to get him to do it in less than two minutes?"

"I don't know." She shrugged. "Billy Masterson's harmless, but he's kind of a tool. I'd way rather see Daisy end up with Lane, especially since she really has been making eyes at him all night—and by all night, I really mean for the past six months. So, I guess all I did was tell Lane the truth."

Owen huffed out a soft laugh and took a sip of his beer. "You're good at that. Being honest," he clarified.

"Turns out, honesty can get you into as much trouble as the alternative sometimes," Cate said, her heart smacking against her sternum for letting the omission slip out loud.

Of course, even with his beer buzz, Owen caught it. And, of course, because he had said beer buzz, he got bold enough to ask, "Yeah? How do you figure?"

It was on the tip of her tongue to dodge the question with some smart remark. But the truth was, beer buzz or not, Owen's kindness deserved more than a baked-goods thank you. No matter how vulnerable the words would make her feel.

"You did a really nice thing for me the other day," she said, and he coughed into his pint glass.

"Shit. You really do dive right in, don't you?"

His candid reaction scattered the tension that had been building in her shoulders, and she forked over the truth. "Yep. Why did you send Mike to fix my oven?"

"Because."

Owen waited out the minute it took Cate to replace a pair of beers for Greyson Whittaker and Billy Masterson, and pour a round of Chardonnays for Michelle Martin and her usual crew for girls' night out.

"Because?" Cate prompted upon her return, but Owen just lifted one leanly muscled shoulder in reply. Anyone else would've taken the cue to let it go, she knew. But she *so* wasn't anyone else, and, what's more, she really wanted to know. "Come on, Owen. We got this far in the conversation. You're not really going to go tight-lipped on me now, are you?"

The edges of his mouth curved just enough to form the hint of a smile, and ha! Gotcha. "You fixed my books. It only seemed fair."

"You're paying me to fix your books," she pointed out, handing over a couple of checks to people waiting to settle up and head home for the night.

"Okay, fine," Owen said when she was done, this time without prodding. "How about this? I sent Mike to fix your oven because you needed it. And I...get that."

"You do."

Cate's breath hitched behind her navy blue top. No one knew how much baking meant to her—she'd certainly never told anyone how she felt when she was in the kitchen, how she craved the ease and calm that baking provided. She *couldn't.* But something about the glint in Owen's eyes told her that not only did he see how much she'd needed her kitchen, but he wasn't bluffing or bullshitting about understanding that need, and when he nodded, she said the only thing she could think of.

"Thank you."

"You're welcome." He lowered his stare to the half-empty beer in front of him. "I wanted you to know I appreciate your hard work, but I'm not always so great at knowing what to say. In fact, I kind of suck at it." A self-deprecating laugh punctuated the admission, and God, did Cate know the feeling.

"Then you could just say that. Look, I'm not great at expressing myself, either," she said, and Owen arched a brow.

"What? You? I never would've guessed."

Cate's laughter snuck up on her, but, oh, it tasted dangerously good. "Ha-ha. Did you want to be the pot or the kettle, there, Casanova?"

Funny, his corresponding laugh sounded even better than hers felt. "Fair enough."

"Why don't we call it a draw and agree to stick with honesty from now on?" she asked. "Deal?"

"Yeah. Deal."

A pause opened up between them, but before either one of them could fill it, Lane reappeared at the bar, an oddly concerned look on his face as he looked at Owen.

"Hey, so, ah, here's the thing." Lane shifted his weight from one foot to the other, running a palm over the back of his tightly cropped crew cut. "Daisy caught a ride here with Hunter and Emerson, and they're ready to call it a night. She and I are kind of having a good time, though. So I told her if she wanted to stay and hang out for a little while longer, I could give her a ride home instead, but...uh..."

"Oh. *Oh.*" Owen straightened in realization. The look on his face said the second-last thing he wanted to do was cock block his buddy after the guy had finally made a move that —from the sound of things—was working. But it also said the *very* last thing he could do was safely drive himself home, and, oh, screw it.

"Go," Cate said. "Take Daisy home. I've got Owen."

Both men turned toward her with surprise that would've been amusing if she wasn't also feeling it with equal measure.

"You do?" Owen asked, and Cate served up a no-nonsense stare.

"I do. Unless you've got a better idea."

He shook his head, dropping his voice as he leaned toward her. "I was out of those two beers ago."

"Then I guess it's settled." It wasn't as if she didn't know where he lived, or Cross Creek was more than five minutes out of her way. She could give Owen a ride home, no harm, no foul.

Lane's goofy smile was pretty at odds with his tough demeanor and his linebacker-esque physique, but Cate had to admit, it still looked good on him. "Thanks, Cate. I really owe you one."

She laughed, shooing him from the bar. "I'm going to make Owen help me clean up before I drop him off. Believe me, we're square."

"Greeeeat." Owen tried—unsuccessfully—to hide the smile that canceled out his sarcasm in his pint glass, then focused his attention back on her. "So, what should we talk about now that you're stuck with me and we've got this honesty policy in place?"

"Work?" Boring, maybe, but at least it was something they had in common.

Or not. "Nope." Owen shook his head. "I came out tonight to forget work." At her doubt-filled frown, he amended, "At least 'til tomorrow. Try again."

"The weather?" Cate asked, and, ugh, she had no small-talk game whatsoever. She was totally and completely game-fucking-free.

Thank God Owen seemed to have enough of a beer buzz not to notice. Of course, he didn't do her any favors, either. "No on that, too. I'm a farmer, which makes the topic of the weather awfully close to work."

"You have a point." Cate paused for a quick scan of the bar, picking up a handful of empty glasses from the notice-ably less-populated stretch of mahogany on either side of them. "Got any non-work-related ideas, then?"

"What's your middle name?"

If he'd asked her to jump up on the bar and dance a jig, it might've surprised her less. "*That's* what you want to talk about?"

"Seems as good a thing as any," he said, relaxing against the ladder back of his bar stool, and for the love of God, couldn't the man own a single T-shirt that didn't make his biceps look like pure arm porn? "Here, if it makes you feel any better, I'll go first. My middle name is Nicholas."

Cate snuffed out the heat between her legs before it made her say something stupid. Or, worse yet, vault over the glossy wood and glassware separating them so she could get a firsthand feel of those corded, sexy, arm muscles. "Owen Nicholas," she managed. "That suits you."

After she didn't fill the ensuing pause with anything other than a smile, he said, "Come on, I told you mine. Are you really going to leave me hanging?"

There were no less than ten reasons—good, solid, *sound* reasons—why flirting with Owen was a bad idea. But, funny, not a single damned one of them could keep her from doing it.

"I'm thinking about it, yeah." Before he could loosen the protest that he was clearly working up, Cate gave in. Sort of. "Okay, okay! Guess."

"Are you going to give me any hints?"

"It's not Nicholas," she offered. Although he arched a brow at her in reply, that tiny half-smile still played on his lips, and, she had to admit, this bolder version of him was even more attractive than the broody side that she already didn't hate.

"Okay. Let's see." Owen tapped his index finger against his bottom lip. "Cate is short for Catelyn, so…"

Shock worked its way through her veins. "You remember that?"

Nobody ever called her by her full name, largely because she'd never answered to it. Catelyn had always felt so frilly to her, especially with how her parents had decided to spell it. Cate was far more to the point.

"We were in the same class every year from kindergarten to graduation. Of course, I remember it," Owen said, and small town: 1. Cate: goose egg.

Assessing her with an up and down look that sent a shiver up her spine despite the warmth of the bar around them, he continued, "How about Ann?"

She laughed. "Nice try, going generic. But no."

"I suppose that means Mary and Elizabeth are out, too, then."

"Not even close."

He held up his hands. "You can't blame a guy for trying. I should've figured this wouldn't be easy."

Cate took a turn with the brow-raise they'd been trading all night. "Careful, Casanova, or I'll think you just called me a pain in the ass."

"A challenge," he countered, his forehead creasing in thought. "It's not anything totally off the wall, like Esmerelda, is it?"

More than anything, she wanted to hang on to her stick-straight stare and make him panic. But the peal of laughter in her chest refused to let her. "No. It's not Esmerelda. And, yes, it's something I'm sure you've heard before."

"Grace."

"No."

"Melissa."

"Nope."

"Ah!" He snapped his fingers in triumph. "Abigail."

"Still no," she said with a laugh.

"You're killing me here, you know."

The words were simple. But Owen's eyes flashed, storm-gray and intense as he delivered them, and, suddenly, inexplicably, those seven little syllables went right into Cate's center.

"It's Sophia."

Owen's blink lasted for less than a second before his smile took over. "Sophia," he repeated, testing it out on his tongue. "I don't think I would have guessed that."

"Mmm." Her heart beat faster, whooshing against her eardrums in a rapid *thump-thump-thump* as she pressed her hands over the bar and leaned forward. "There are probably a lot of things about me that you'd never guess. But I don't go sharing my middle name with just anybody, so you'd better take that one to the grave, Owen Nicholas."

He leaned in, too, close enough for Cate to be able to smell the crisp, clean scent of his soap, see the sweep of his coal-colored lashes even though his stare never budged. "Your secret's safe with me, Catelyn Sophia."

And wasn't that just what she was afraid of?

10

"All right, everybody, that's it! You don't have to go home, but you can't stay here."

Cate eyeballed the half-dozen patrons still dotting the dance floor even though Garth Brooks had crooned his last note of the night. Millhaven was a small enough town that last call clocked in at midnight, which might be considered early for the bigger bars and chain restaurants in Camden Valley, but was definitely later than anything else within a twenty-mile radius of The Bar, or any other place in town, for that matter.

Echoing a couple of "goodnight"s, Cate ushered everyone toward the door. "Have you got a ride, Amber?" she asked as the woman teetered on her four-inch boot heels.

"Yes, ma'am!" Amber giggled. "Billy's gonna drive both me and Mollie Mae home. Isn't that sweet?"

"As pie," Cate replied, exhaling in relief. At least the guy had only had two beers all night. As opposed to Amber's four mango-ritas, which had been three parts 'rita to one part fruity mixer. "Be safe getting home."

She closed the door after the trio, leaving the bar eerily quiet, save the muffled clink of the glassware Brett was loading into the industrial dishwasher in the kitchen. She had already tidied up and restocked everything behind the bar, as well as run inventory and lined up clean pint glasses and plastic pitchers for whoever was working tomorrow's shift. Brett had taken mercy and sprung her from the drudgery of putting up the bar stools and mopping the floors, so that left her with only one thing on her agenda.

It was time to take Owen home.

Cate turned toward the spot where he sat at the bar, looking just as infernally sexy as he had when he'd flirted with her an hour ago. "You doing okay over there?" she asked.

A swath of dark hair tumbled over his forehead as he measured her with a glance. "Well, that depends."

"On?"

"You don't have a long-lost twin I don't know about, do you?"

She lost the battle with her smile. "I'm afraid not."

"Then I'm good," Owen said, recanting a little with, "also, a little drunk."

Cate nodded. He was a big enough guy, and even though he'd downed most of the ice water she'd poured after he'd finished his last beer, he'd still had his fair share of liquor tonight. He didn't seem sloppy enough to be full-on wasted, but the flush on his cheeks said all the alcohol had finally soaked in to tag him right in the happy place. "Let's get you home, then."

After a quick trip behind the wood to grab her jacket and purse, and another one into the kitchen to say good-night to Brett and let him know she was leaving, Cate fished out her keys and made her way back around the front of the bar. "Ready?"

"Mmm hmm. Yyyyyep."

Owen found his feet, clearly taking a second to recalibrate his balance, and Cate stopped halfway across the floor.

"You sure about that?"

"What? Oh, yeah," he said. But the hand he waved through the air was wobbly enough to prove otherwise.

"Okay." Cate's legs were in motion before her brain had fully registered the command to go. Ducking under his shoulder, she threaded her arm around the back of his rib cage, leaning into him until he had no choice but to sling his arm around her for support. "Come on."

"You really don't...o-kay, and we're moving."

Thankfully, Owen abandoned his protest in favor of falling into step beside her. He leaned in just enough to make her hyper-aware of all the places their bodies touched —the fit of his upper arm over her shoulder blade, the warmth of his rib cage where he pressed against her side, their skin separated by only the too-thin layers of their shirts because her jacket had fallen open when she'd moved to help him. As if the contact wasn't enough, each tandem step created just enough friction to make Cate's heart pound. Step, Owen's thigh on her hip. Step, her jeans brushing his jeans in reply. Step, his palm curving over the top of her bicep, and, oh, God, she should've just risked letting him stumble his way to her car.

"Here we go!" she said far too cheerily as they reached her Toyota. She sent up a fervent prayer that it would cooperate, releasing a relieved breath when the engine kicked over on the first attempt. Owen managed to get his seat belt on, and they made the trip to Cross Creek in ten minutes that were both quiet and quick.

"So, I'm not sure where to go from here," Cate said after pulling off Millhaven's one central road and onto Cross Creek's property. She knew Owen and Hunter both lived on different parts of the farm, but she'd never had occasion to go anywhere other than the main house, which stood in the shadowy distance.

"My place is on the west side of the property. So head left at the fork instead of going right, toward the main house."

It took Cate a second to realize he hadn't opened his eyes. "Don't you need to look?" For all he knew, she could've passed the fork already. Not that she had, but...

"Nope," Owen said. "I was born and raised on this farm. Running the place is my legacy. I'd know where I was with my eyes closed." He seemed to get his own joke after the fact, letting out a laugh before adding, "Turn right up here, after you pass the greenhouse. My house is up a ways, around the curve and on the left."

Damn, he really wasn't kidding about that internal compass of his. Cate paused to make the turn by the greenhouse, slowly navigating the pitch-dark path. A pair of tiny lights twinkled up ahead, dimly at first, then growing brighter and warmer as she made her way around a gentle curve in the gravel road. The lights illuminated the porch of a cozy two-story cottage just enough for Cate to see the stone pavers leading up to the porch steps and the beautiful, natural wood exterior that made the place seem more like a cabin than a traditional farm house. A sturdy, oversized rocking chair stood sentry a few feet from the front door, and between that, the wide, wood-and-copper planter boxes gracing the length of the porch railing, and the pretty, lantern-like fixtures casting a golden glow over it all, the house might as well have leapt off the pages of a home and garden magazine.

"Wow," she whispered, and again, Owen laughed.

"See you found the place." His eyes fluttered open, and he indulged in a batch of slow blinks before shaking his head. "Just let me figure out what I did with my keys. Ah!"

His victory was short lived as he held up his key ring in one second, then dropped it to the floor of her Toyota in the next. "Damn it," he muttered. He leaned forward to search for them in the dark, promptly bumping his head against the dashboard and letting out a darker, harsher curse.

"Oh, jeez! Are you okay?" Cate asked, but Owen just sat up and rubbed his forehead.

"Sorry. That wasn't a very polite thing to say."

She bit back her surprise, then her smile. Looked like the Owen she knew from the farm wasn't too far beneath the surface. But that was okay. She pretty much lived above the surface. "Lucky for you, I don't put a whole lot of stock in sugar-coating things—including the F-bomb. Come on. Let's get you inside."

Owen located his keys easily enough once Cate opened her door and the dome light clicked on, and she slid her arm under his to guide him up the walkway. He fumbled with the whole key/lock thing, but only for a second before getting both where they belonged and freeing the front door with a turn of his wrist. They got over the threshold without fanfare thanks to the light filtering in from the porch, and, come on, come on, there had to be a—yes! Cate's hand connected with a light switch on the wall in the foyer a second later.

"Huh. That's much better. It's so...light," Owen said, prompting a laugh to slip past her lips.

"Okay, Casanova. Why don't I help you with the stairs,

here?" The full flight in front of them looked sturdy enough, but was also pure hardwood—pine, if she had to guess—and definitely not something she'd want to climb unattended if she were a little sloshed. Owen seemed to feel the same way, because he let her make the trip beside him, although he managed most of it on his own with deliberate movements and a whole lot of assistance from the railing. That water he'd chugged must be starting to work its magic.

"Which way is your bedroom?" Cate asked, her cheeks prickling hotly when Owen stopped in the center of the hallway to stare at her through the shadows.

"Cate McAllister. Are you flirting with me?"

She opened her mouth. Considered all the words she could send out of the traitorous thing.

Oh, she didn't want to use it to talk.

Owen tensed visibly, his expression sobering and slipping into panic. "Shit, I'm sorry. That just flew out. I shouldn't have been so—"

"No."

"No?"

"No." She stepped toward him until only half an arm's length remained, her pulse knocking faster against her throat. "We're not doing that, remember? You and I have an honesty policy. So, yes."

"Yes," he said slowly. "Now I'm confused."

Cate laughed. "Yes, I'm flirting with you. But it's not my fault you're an adorable drunk."

"I'm not *that* drunk," Owen argued.

"You're a little drunk," she argued back, but the step he took toward her was startlingly sure.

"And you are very pretty."

The sound that left her mouth was more of a sigh than she intended. "Okay. I'm pretty sure that's the Jack Daniels talking."

"I mean it, Cate." Reaching down, Owen grabbed her wrist. Although the move had been far from rough or intimidating, her breath hitched in her chest all the same. How long had it been since a man had touched her? Told her she was pretty and made her feel breathtakingly good, way down deep where it mattered?

How long had it been since any man had looked at her with the sort of hunger that was in Owen Cross's eyes right now?

"You are beautiful," he whispered. "And the crazy thing is, you don't even know it."

The words slid right through her, under her skin and into her veins, and she knew, she *knew* she needed to say goodnight and get herself back to her car as fast as humanly possible. A man like Owen Cross was serious. Solid. Steady. He wasn't for her.

She kissed him anyway.

For a fraction of a second, Owen went completely still, his breath coming out in a quick, sharp burst. But Cate reached up to knot her arms around his shoulders—holy *God*, they were as hard and lean and sexy as they looked— and his shock gave way. Grabbing her hips, he hauled her close, joining their bodies in an abrupt thump and parting her mouth with a single firm press of his own that she didn't even consider resisting. His tongue darted out to swipe over her bottom lip, the relentless back-and-forth motion making her sensitive skin tingle even as she craved more, and Cate arched into him in an effort to find it. She kissed Owen back with urgency, her tongue tangling with his.

More. She needed more.

The words must've slipped from her lust-clouded brain

to her mouth, because he responded by tightening his grip on the denim at her hips.

A sound grated up from his chest, proprietary and hot. "You're not making it easy for me to pace myself, here," Owen said against her mouth.

She felt the proof in the firm press of his cock on her belly. Wetness gathered between her legs, desperate and greedy and daring her to let him fill the tight space there. "Who said anything about pacing yourself?"

"Cate—"

She interrupted him with a hard slide of her lips. "Owen, please," she whispered, letting him kiss her deeply, then kissing him back with equal need before he broke from her mouth to look at her.

"Please, what?"

Please, ease this ache inside me. Please, make me feel good, just for tonight.

"Please, take me to bed," Cate said.

Without another word, Owen turned toward his bedroom.

11

There was a marching band in Owen's skull. Check that. There were two marching bands in his skull, and they were duking it out for the top honors of Loudest Band Standing. Rolling over, he covered his head with his pillow, while pieces of his memory came back in fits and starts.

Doing that last, ill-advised shot of whiskey with his brother (never again. *Damn*, his head felt like it was going to cave in). Lane finally balling up the courage to ask Daisy out. Cate's sassy, sexy smile as she leaned over the bar and told him her middle name, the feel of her body, soft yet strong, as she guided him into the house and up the stairs...

Owen, please. Take me to bed.

His heart thwacked against his rib cage, going from zero to holy-fucking-shit in about four nanoseconds. Bolting upright in his bed, he flung a panicked gaze around his room, forcing himself to take in the rumpled sheets, the side of the mattress opposite him that was—shit!—totally empty, and the sun relentlessly streaming in through the slats in the blinds. His head spun, and, after a second, his stomach went along for the ride. But he couldn't afford to be foggy, here. He had to figure out where Cate was.

And, more importantly, exactly what had happened between them last night.

"Okay. Okay, okay. Think." Owen commanded himself to take a slow, deep inhale even though it took herculean effort. The jeans and T-shirt he'd been wearing last night were strewn messily on the floorboards beside his bed, along with his socks and boots. His boxer shorts were in place on his hips, which would have been a good sign if he could remember with total certainty whether they'd been there the whole time or he'd done the now-you-see-them, now-you-don't routine with them at some point after he and Cate had crossed the threshold of his bedroom.

But he couldn't have. He might not remember the finer details of his night—fucking Jack Daniels!—but come on. The kisses he and Cate had shared had been damn near incendiary. She was freaking gorgeous, and as impulsive as it had been, he'd wanted her like water and air combined. If he'd slept with her, it would be tattooed in his memory. Damn it, why couldn't he *remember* anything after they'd gone into his bedroom?

And what was that smell wafting up from his kitchen?

Shoving the blankets off his legs, Owen stumbled out of bed and tiptoed to the door. The warm, enticing scent grew stronger as he peered out into the hallway, earthy coffee mingled in with some baked good he couldn't quite identify. Although he was tempted to take a straight path down the stairs to investigate, his current state wouldn't win him any favors, so he skinned into a pair of sweats and a fresh T-shirt, stopping to scrub his teeth and throw back some much-needed ibuprofen before heading quietly to the kitchen.

"Oh, hey. You're awake," Cate said, looking up at him from behind the rectangular island. She wore the same clothes she'd had on last night, although her low, neat ponytail and fresh face suggested she'd washed up since waking. A plate of golden, slightly misshapen baked goods sat by her elbow, next to a nearly empty cup of coffee and a copy of *The Camden Valley Chronicle* that was open to the business section, and, okay, he'd officially gone around the bend.

"Are those homemade biscuits?" Of all the questions flying through Owen's mind, that one seemed the most innocuous. Albeit definitely weird.

Funny, Cate didn't so much as blink. "Yep. For a single guy, your pantry is freakishly well-stocked. Although I had to cut them out by hand, so they're not very pretty. I hope you don't mind." She hesitated, biting her lip even though her stare never wavered. "I know I'm making a habit of invading your kitchen space, but I thought you might want something hearty to feed your hangover. And I like to bake. Obviously. So..."

"No, I don't mind," Owen said. All the less-innocuous questions that had been filling his brain fought for his attention, and he cleared his throat. "So, ah, you...stayed."

"I did." Now, her stare did drop, just a fraction, but it was enough to make his breath go tight. "Which was really presumptuous of me, too, I know. But I figured we should probably talk about last night privately. And sooner rather than later."

Translation: before I see you at work tomorrow, and Owen's mouth worked independently of both his brain and his better judgement.

"Oh, hell. I didn't...we didn't...did we..."

Cate's brows traveled up, but she followed his fumbled question easily enough. "Don't look so mortified, Casanova."

"I'm not mortified," he said automatically. "I mean, I am, but I'm also not. I think." Jesus, could he ruin this any more thoroughly? "What I mean is—"

"Owen. Stop." The quiet words were at odds with the firm tone she'd used to deliver them, and both made him do what she'd asked. "Nothing happened."

Relief moved through Owen's gut, followed by a swift shot of disappointment that was gone before he could even kick himself for it. "Nothing," he said.

She must have heard the question in his voice, because she amended her claim with a quick hint of a smile. "Well, not *nothing*-nothing. I mean, I am here. But as far as the rest, you walked me down the hall to your bedroom last night. We kissed a little. And...you fell asleep."

Owen took it back. Mortified wasn't even in the same *hemisphere* as this. "Cate," he started, but she shook her head.

"And this is why I slept on your couch instead of going home. We have an honesty policy, and it doesn't just apply when you've had a few and you're flirting with me."

Cate took a biscuit from the larger plate in front of her and placed it on a dish, sliding it toward him on the island before continuing. "You got a little drunk. You said some things you might not otherwise say, which led to some things you might not have otherwise done. It's not a big deal, unless—"

Owen pulled back to look at her carefully. "Unless, what?"

She brushed a few crumbs off the granite with a paper

towel, saying nothing, and he watched his hand leap out to touch her forearm over the small expanse of the island.

"If we're going to go with this honestly policy, it can't be a one-way street. Help me out and talk to me, here," he said. Cate exhaled slowly, but to Owen's relief, she didn't dodge the question.

"It's not a big deal unless you regret what happened."

"I don't." His answer flew out as quickly as his hand had, and he realized that not only was he still touching her, but he didn't want to break the connection. "I think we've already established that I kind of suck at this, so I'm just going to say it straight. Being a little drunk might have motivated me to say and do what I did, but that doesn't make me sorry that we kissed, and it damn sure doesn't make my words untrue." Although his pulse kicked at his next thought, he knew he still had to give it voice. "But I don't want you to feel uncomfortable about what happened last night, either."

Cate's chin lifted. "Why would *I* feel uncomfortable?"

"Because I kissed you," Owen said. He might not be sorry they'd kissed; hell, for over a week, he'd wanted to do way more unspeakable things than put his mouth on hers. That still didn't change the fact that he'd acted less than respectably by turning his impulse into action, then topped the whole thing off by being an idiot and falling asleep on her.

None of which seemed to be bothering Cate in the least.

"Actually, if you want to split hairs, I kissed you first." Picking up her coffee cup with a matter-of-fact shrug, she took one last sip before turning toward the pot on the counter. "Coffee?"

Surprise sent his brows on a one-way trip toward his bedhead, and his manners made a showing about nine hours too late. Tardy little bastards. "Yes, please. And you might have technically kissed me first, but I still kissed you back"—*impulsively. Deeply. So fucking hungrily*—"a lot. That wasn't very honorable of me."

"We're two consenting adults. What's not honorable about that?" Cate asked. She took a mug down from the open shelf above the coffeepot, filling both it and her empty one before returning to the island, and were they seriously having this conversation as easily as they'd chat about the weather?

"The fact that you're Brian's widow, for one," Owen said quietly.

Everything about Cate stilled except for her eyes, which lifted to meet his. "Do you think I haven't had sex since Brian died?" she asked, and, oookay, it looked like they sure as shit were.

"I don't...I'm sure that's none of my business," Owen managed to cough out. But Cate gave up that glittering no-holds-barred stare that read *well?* for a breath, then two, before he had no choice but to actually answer her question. "I don't know. Have you?"

A wistful laugh puffed past her lips. "It's been more than three years, Owen. Of course, I've had sex. I mean, not a lot, and not...very meaningfully." She broke off a piece of a biscuit, although she didn't take a bite. "But don't feel guilty about what you said to me last night because I'm Brian's widow. For three years, all I've heard from people is 'I'm sorry' and 'how sad for you' and 'poor Cate'. It actually felt kind of nice—normal, I guess—that you got a little drunk and flirted with me."

His pulse picked up the pace, and he opened his mouth to argue. Not tiptoeing around her when it came to health insurance benefits was a hell of a lot different than kissing her senseless in his hallway. But she'd said she wanted to be treated like a regular person, and her actions *had* backed up her claim, one hundred percent.

Which meant he had no reason to hold back.

"The beer had nothing to do with what I said to you," Owen told her, and now her laugh came out louder and less restrained.

"Yeah, right."

But oh, no. If she could go for broke in the honesty department, then so could he. "Maybe I had a few more drinks last night than was smart. But the only thing the alcohol did was give me the courage to say what I think every time I see you when I'm sober. You really are very pretty."

Cate's cheeks flushed as if to punctuate the statement. "And you really should get courageous more often."

"I'm just being honest," he said. Speaking of which, if he was going to go all in... "I wasn't trying to frustrate you by bringing up Brian. I'm sure being a young widow isn't easy, especially in a town as small as Millhaven."

"I know you weren't trying to frustrate me. It's just that I feel like I've got a giant spotlight on me sometimes," she said, her voice softening along with her expression. "I mean, for three years, I've been Poor, Widowed Cate. Lily's mom. Brian's wife. No one looks at me without seeing them. Some days, it's enough to make me want to scream." She gave up that no-nonsense stare that said she was measuring her words with care. "To be honest, Brian and I weren't exactly the perfect couple everyone thinks we were."

Owen froze, his coffee cup halfway to his lips and his chest chock-full of shock. "You weren't?" She and Brian had gotten married right out of high school, for God's sake. They were always the couple voted most likely to...well, couple.

"We weren't unhappy," she amended. "But our daughter was born less than a year after graduation." She paused to clear her throat. "Specifically, nine months after."

"Oh. *Oh.*" Holy shit. She'd gotten pregnant by accident? "I'm sorry, I didn't realize."

Cate nodded. "Obviously, it's not something we advertised. Brian and I fibbed a bit about our due date and said Lily surprised us by arriving six weeks early, so nobody realized the pregnancy wasn't planned. Or if they did, they never had the balls to say so. And then we had Lily, and she was a sweet baby. Slept like an angel, right from the start. I even took her to Doc Sanders because I thought something was wrong with her. She was always so happy."

Her expression grew suddenly tender, the brief, unexpected emotion in her eyes arrowing directly to Owen's gut. But it lasted for less than a breath, quickly covered by her careful, practical smile, and he ditched caution without thinking twice.

"But?"

"But the past is in the past," she said after a pause. "What I'd really like now is to move forward. Not as Brian's widow or Lily's mom. Not as Poor Cate. Just as me."

Owen thought, but only for a second before nodding. "Okay."

"Really?"

The shock dominating her features was so genuine, he laughed, which made her laugh in turn, and, God, she really was beautiful.

"Yes, really," he said. "What, you thought I was going to argue with you?"

The arch of her brows told him that's exactly what she'd thought. "I don't know. Maybe a little. I mean, no offense, but you're not exactly a go with the flow kind of guy."

He'd take exception, save the fact that she wasn't wrong. In truth, it was kind of nice not to have to wade through any bullshit with her. "No, but I am an honesty guy, remember? I'm not big on pretenses. From here on in, you're just you, and I'm just me. We're starting fresh." He stuck out his hand to prove it. "Hi. Owen Cross."

Smiling, she wrapped her fingers around his firmly. "Cate McAllister."

Even though he knew he probably should, Owen didn't let go. "It's nice to meet you, Cate McAllister. Since you were so kind as to make breakfast this morning, I was wondering if you might like to stick around and enjoy it with me."

"Well, I'm not normally a breakfast person, but since we're starting fresh, I suppose I could make an exception."

He moved around the island, pulling out one of the bar stools tucked beneath it for Cate to sit on before taking the other one around the opposite side to face her. "Don't you eat the things you bake?"

"Sometimes I take a small bite, just to be sure nothing went horribly wrong, but no. I don't usually eat what I bake," she said, settling in with her coffee.

Owen's curiosity kicked in good and hard, but he couldn't resist the smirk tugging at one corner of his mouth. "Horribly wrong. That sounds reassuring."

"Very funny. Anyway, you don't have to worry. I've made these biscuits a thousand times, and this batch seems okay."

"All right, then. I'm going in."

Breaking off a piece of the biscuit in front of him, he reached for the butter Cate had taken out of the refrigerator, applying enough to melt into the flaky layers of dough. He popped the bite into his mouth and reached out to ready another, but the flavors bursting over his taste buds stopped him mid-move.

"Holy..." Manners lost, Owen took a second, bigger bite, torn between wanting to eat as much as possible and slowly enjoying every light and fluffy crumb. The biscuit was both savory and sweet, with the slightest tang from the buttermilk playing perfectly with the heady flavor of the melted butter, and God *damn*, his pie hole had just beat out Disney World as the happiest place on earth.

"I think you need to examine your definition of 'okay'," he managed a few seconds later. "Did you seriously just throw these biscuits together out of regular old ingredients while I slept?"

Cate laughed. "I told you they weren't bad. Although for the record, good biscuits aren't really that hard to make."

The sound he let slip was *this* close to a snort. "Uh, yeah they are," he said, reaching for another two from the stack on the plate between them.

"How do you know?" Her tone was loaded with curiosity, but lucky for him, the question was a total no-brainer.

"Because I've tried."

Her lips parted into a pretty, peach-colored *O* that outlined her shock. "You bake?"

"I cook," Owen corrected. "I run a farm, so food is kind of my thing, especially the specialty produce like heirloom tomatoes and harder-to-find varieties of some vegetables and herbs. I'm a decent cook, but I don't really have the hang of baking. My biscuits always turn out like stones."

"Hmm." Cate took a long draw from her coffee cup, clearly thinking. "You're probably overworking the dough, although you might also be going heavy-handed on your flour. You're not just dunking the measuring cup in the container, are you?"

Shit. "Is there another way to do it?" he asked.

She was off her stool in a flash of dark brown curls and

total determination. "Oh, my God, come here. I can't let another minute go by without you knowing the answer to that question."

A quick grab of the flour from his pantry and the measuring cup sitting in the drying rack beside his sink told Owen she was dead serious about a tutorial, and, yeah, with a look like the one that was on her face right now? He wasn't about to say no.

"Baking isn't like cooking, where there's more room for error and you can make recipes to taste. If you want to get things right, you've got to follow the rules pretty strictly," Cate said.

"I do use those measuring cups, you know," he replied drily. "I'm not a total heathen."

Her expression remained serious, although if he wasn't mistaken, a flush crept high over her cheeks, and, note to self: sarcasm + Cate = oh, *hell* yes.

Squaring her shoulders, she pointed to the half-empty bag of flour she'd placed on the counter. "I'll reserve judgment until after I see *how* you use them."

She handed over the measuring cup expectantly. Owen took it by the handle, reaching into the bag to scoop up enough flour to fill the cup to brimming, but Cate stopped him before he could get the thing all the way over the counter.

"Argh, stop! That's what I was afraid of. Look"—she gestured to the measuring cup in a wordless *may I?* and he passed it over with a nod—"see how there's a mound of flour on top, over the measuring line?" She shook the excess back into the bag, and, whoa, how had he never noticed how much extra that could add?

"Yeah," Owen said. But rather than give him crap, even

good-naturedly, Cate turned so he could see exactly what she was doing.

"Flour is easily mis-measured. Scooping from the bag not only gives you that extra crown on top, but it can also cram more flour into the cup than belongs there. Since all-purpose flour also packs a decent amount of gluten, using too much can totally throw your biscuits out of whack."

Huh. He had to admit, that made sense. "Okay. So how do I measure accurately if using the cup alone won't do it?"

"Where do you keep your teaspoons?" she asked, and talk about the last thing he expected her to say. It must've showed on his face, because she added, "Trust me."

"You're the boss." Owen tucked his fingers beneath the oiled bronze handle on his utensil drawer and gave up a tug. He passed over a spoon, which Cate used to fill the measuring cup with light, heaping scoops of flour. Her movements were wholly natural, as perfectly made for her as her fingerprints, and his heart tripped beneath his T-shirt. Instinct and impulse combined to draw him in closer as she flipped the spoon around, sweeping the handle over the edge of the plastic cup to even out the flour inside.

"See?" She handed over the measuring cup, which was noticeably lighter than when he'd filled it. "Spooning the flour in and leveling it off gives you a more accurate measurement."

"And that's your secret, huh?" Owen asked with a grin. The edges of her mouth twitched in a borderline smirk, and damn, he should've known her sassy side had been dying to make an appearance.

"That's how you measure flour. But it's going to take a hell of a lot more than a sexy smile to get me to give up my secrets."

In that moment, he realized she hadn't shifted back

when he'd leaned in to watch her work. Only a few scant inches of daylight separated their bodies. Hips. Chests. Shoulders.

Mouths.

His pulse flared. "You think I'm sexy?"

"I do," Cate murmured, her stare glinting like double-barrel bourbon over ice. "And you know what else I think?"

"What?"

"I think we could try that kiss again. If you want."

Holy shit, she was full of surprises. "Are you sure that's what *you* want?"

She lifted her chin, so close that Owen could feel the heat of her exhale. "Come here, Casanova. I'm not going to bite you. Not even if you ask me nicely."

He closed the slice of space between them in one forward press. For a second, their mouths rested together as if getting acquainted, warm and whisper-soft. But then a sound came out of her, low in the back of her throat, and Owen's belly tightened in demand. He slid his tongue across the seam of her lips, tasting his way past them and into her mouth. Cate met him halfway, her tongue darting out to tease his, to flirt with his teeth, then the curve of his bottom lip.

Christ, her mouth was perfect. Warm. Lush. Brazen, just like the rest of her.

He wanted that mouth everywhere.

Reaching up, Owen cupped the back of her neck with both palms, his fingers hooking up into the thick fall of her curls while his thumbs cradled her face to hold her close. He tasted and took, his cock going hard against the press of their bodies as she did the same right back, and, finally, with one last sweep of her tongue, Cate pulled back.

"You are an adorable drunk, but you're an even better

kisser when you're sober," she said with a smile that did nothing to ease his arousal. "I'm glad we cleared the air about last night. Enjoy the rest of your breakfast. I'll see you tomorrow."

Owen felt her on his mouth for the rest of the day.

12

Cate sat back in her desk chair with a smile on her lips and her chest full of triumph. It had taken all of her morning and most of her energy, but she'd tamed the mountain of work on her desk into a molehill. Okay, so it was a moderately large, sort of messy molehill, but she had to admit it. After two weeks of working at Cross Creek, she was feeling pretty damned good about herself.

Right. And being thoroughly kissed by your boss, not once, but twice, has nothing to do with that.

Her chin sprang up, a prickle of heat washing over the back of her neck and up into her hairline. She'd known Owen would wake up thoroughly hung over and just as distressed once he realized he'd fallen asleep on her. Staying to reassure him once he woke up had seemed practical, and a hell of a lot less awkward than having the conversation here at Cross Creek. Of course, she hadn't counted on their conversation turning to her past, or actually telling him she'd gotten pregnant unintentionally at eighteen.

One reckless night under the stars. One roll of the dice as a teenager, and her life had changed forever.

And now she wasn't the only person on the planet who knew it.

Cate straightened in her chair, reaching out to gather the purchase orders in front of her with a brisk snap. Okay, so she'd gone a little more personal with Owen than she'd intended, but her past was still just that. Her past. Obviously, otherwise she wouldn't have kissed him.

Damn, she'd felt that kiss in her toes. And way down deep in her belly.

And a couple of other places that had been *far* too neglected lately.

She pushed back from her desk and pushed the thought from her mind. Owen was sexy as hell, and, no, she didn't regret having kissed him (fine. Twice). But he hardly struck her as a one-night stand kind of guy, and since she was a no strings attached kind of girl, it was probably for the best if that kiss of theirs remained a one and done.

Making him a pound cake really quick might not hurt, though, just to be sure he knew there were no hard feelings. She'd seen both Hunter and Mr. Cross this morning, and they'd encouraged her to make use of the oven any time she wanted. She could replace the ingredients with ones from her own kitchen tomorrow—even when she left the fruits of her labor behind for them to enjoy, it still didn't feel right to raid their pantry. Plus, she had her whole lunch break in front of her, and that ho-hum package of instant noodles she'd brought from home would take less than five minutes of it.

Thank God.

Mind made up, Cate turned toward the door, her sights set on the Cross's kitchen. Her heart tapped out a giddy little rhythm at the idea of losing herself in baking. Pound cake could be finicky sometimes, but she prided herself on adding the ingredients in just the right fashion to make the end result both moist and dense.

After heading to the sink for a date with the soap and water, she slid two sticks of butter from the refrigerator with a smile. She preheated the oven, which was a beautiful, sturdy model twice the size and a third of the age of the one in her tiny little kitchen. Cate started by gathering the necessary utensils—hello, hand mixer—and placing them on the counter before rummaging for the rest of her ingredients. Eggs and milk joined the flour, sugar, and vanilla extract she'd been lucky enough to score from the cupboard that held all the spices, although she preferred almond extract in a pound cake for that extra level of flavor.

"Ah, next time," she said, her heart climbing rapidly into her throat at the sound of a sardonic laugh over her shoulder.

"Next time, what?"

"Oh!" Cate whipped around, the measuring cup that had been in her grasp falling to the ceramic floor tiles with a clatter. The sight of Marley, this time in a black muscle T-shirt and a pair of leggings dotted with brightly colored sugar skulls, registered a second later. "You scared the shit out of me," Cate said.

The words flew out like an accusation, burning her cheeks upon their exit, but Marley's lips just quirked slightly.

"I was just trying to get to the coffeepot." Her piercing, almost navy blue eyes traveled to the appliance in question, which stood a few feet from where Cate had set up shop. "I wasn't being sneaky or anything. You seemed kind of lost in your own world."

"A little bit," Cate admitted, because why the hell not? It was true. "I get kind of focused once I get a task in front of me."

Marley tilted her head at the ingredients Cate had lined up neatly on the counter, eyeing the mixing bowl and Bundt pan as she moved to grab and fill a coffee mug. "You made that cake thingy we had in the house last week, right? With the strawberries in it?"

"Guilty as charged." Cate reached to pick up the measuring cup, bringing it to the sink for a quick wash. She didn't want to be rude, but the clock was ticking on her lunch break, and she couldn't risk rushing through this pound cake and having it come out wonky.

Not that Marley seemed to notice, let alone mind. "It was good." She capped the words with a quick shrug. "I mean, at least that's what I heard. Owen and Hunter and Tobias kind of hogged it."

God, the *don't touch* was strong with this one. Not many people called their own father by his first name. No one Cate had ever met, anyway. "I'm sure if you'd said you wanted some, they'd have saved you a few slices," Cate said. She filled the ensuing silence by popping the butter into the microwave for a few seconds to get it soft, testing out both sticks with a press of her thumb before returning to the counter to unwrap them and place them in the bowl.

"Whatever." One slender shoulder rose and fell. "I don't really eat here if I can help it."

"Well, that's too bad, because I'm about to make something even better than that quick bread."

Cate wasn't trying to wheedle the woman into talking; if anyone respected the whole close-to-the-vest thing, it was definitely her. But with a tight-knit family like the Crosses, she'd bet even money Marley's indifference wasn't winning her any fans or favors, just like she'd bet all that bravado was little more than a cover.

"Yeah. I'm just here for the coffee, thanks," Marley said, lifting her mug. Her tone had lost its sharper edge, though, and she didn't make a move to leave, and, oh, screw it. Cate had never been one for social graces, anyway.

"I heard your mother passed away recently," she said, fitting the beaters into the hand mixer with a soft *snick*. "I'm sorry for your loss."

Marley's shoulders snapped to attention around her neck, her lips flattening into a thin, pale line. "What do you know about loss?"

Cate paused. But the truth wasn't anything the woman couldn't find out from her brothers or anyone else in town— hell, the story followed Cate like a thick, dark storm cloud, always looming—so she said, "A lot, actually. My husband and daughter were killed in a car accident three years ago."

"Oh." Marley's eyes went saucer-wide. Cate used the opportunity to cream the butter and sugar together, the whir of the hand mixer smoothing over what was sure to be an otherwise awkward silence.

"That sucks," Marley said quietly when Cate finished with the mixer a few minutes later. "I mean"—she dipped her chin in a soft nod—"it's really sad."

Cate took a long inhale, gripping the edge of the mixing bowl with one hand and the mixer with the other.

"It is sad," she agreed, because it was also the truth. Fact. Irrefutable. "But sometimes, it's how you feel. Mad, too. I felt a lot of both, especially in that first year."

"And people didn't, you know, give you crap for being mad a lot of the time?"

Now it was Cate's turn to shrug. "I kept a lot of it to myself. I didn't really have many people to talk to."

"Not even your own mom?" Marley asked, and hell. Cate had been honest up until now. Changing course seemed kind of stupid at this point.

"I've never been really close with my parents. They retired and moved to Florida when my daughter was two. They came back to Millhaven for a while after the accident." Those days full of forced conversations and heavy, awkward silence had been some of Cate's worst. "But to answer your question, no. I didn't have anyone to talk to who really understood what I was feeling."

A sound left Marley's lips, too joyless to be called a laugh, although that was probably its intent. "Yeah. I get that."

More quiet stretched through the sun-filled kitchen. Cate waited Marley out, cracking eggs into the bowl and mixing them in one at a time, then measuring the flour and salt into one bowl and just the right amount of milk into another. "Anyway, I know it's not exactly the same kind of loss, but if you ever feel like you want to talk, I'm a pretty good listener."

"I don't," Marley said, swift and certain. "So, what are you making?"

A subject change Cate would take any day of the week and twice on Sundays, especially since baking was pretty much her version of going to church. "Oh, this? It's pound cake. Or, I guess, it will be."

"It smells pretty decent." Marley's stare flicked down to the pale yellow batter in the mixing bowl, and Cate had to laugh.

"Anything with this much butter and sugar usually does."

For one bright instant, she burned to ask Marley if she wanted to help. But she'd already been prickly about Cate's offer to talk, and anyway, the younger woman wasn't actively trying to run off like the last time she'd seen her. No sense in giving her a reason to ghost.

"This recipe is one of my favorites, actually," Cate said instead.

"Because of the butter and sugar?"

"That, too. But the truth is, I like it because it's kind of a pain."

From the look on her face, Marley's laugh surprised them both. "You like it *because* it's a pain."

She peered at Cate from beneath the dark swoop of her bangs, but Cate only nodded. "Mmm hmm."

"I don't get it."

Her pulse accelerated. The calm she always got from baking was spiked on occasion by a shot of proud satisfaction, like the first time she'd gotten the flaky layers and filling of those pain in the ass éclairs just right, or when she'd baked the perfect chocolate lava cake even better than the Pinterest photos. Like all the hard work paid off in the end.

Like she'd been made to get there from the beginning.

"I guess I just feel like the tough stuff gives you more of a sense of accomplishment when you beat the odds and nail it," Cate said.

All at once, Marley's arms whipped over her chest, her expression turning stony and shuttered. "That's a little rah-rah for a bunch of butter and sugar, don't you think?"

Whoa. "Maybe a little, but—"

Marley's coffee cup met the counter with a hard clunk. "Yeah, well, I can read between the lines. I'm not some charity case who needs a pep talk to get over my mom. I'm just fine the way I am."

But as she turned on her heels and stalked out of the kitchen, Cate couldn't help but think that was far from true.

∼

FOUR AND A HALF hours and one pound cake later, the mole-hill on Cate's desk had become a speed bump. She still had no less than a dozen major tasks on her To Do list, especially where the storefront project was concerned, but at least now the books were manageable. She had a schedule. Order. A plan.

And, more importantly, her bills were getting paid.

The back door off the kitchen opened with a now-familiar squeak, and the equally familiar sound of boot-steps sounded off on the floorboards in the hallway. Cate's heart tripped in her chest, and, oh, for the love of Christmas, it had only been a couple of *kisses*.

Hard, hot kisses that reminded you exactly how long your vagina has been a ghost town...

"Hey," Owen said, the sight of his tousled, slightly-too-long-but-still-wildly-sexy hair doing nothing to squash the heat growing low in her belly. "Do you have a second?"

Taking a deep breath in an effort to get her girly bits to stand down, Cate said, "Sure. What's up?"

"The contractors are making really good progress on the storefront. I'd like to be sure the next phase is really solid on the books since it seems we'll be getting to it on or maybe even a little ahead of schedule."

"Okay," she said. She'd put everything he'd given her so far into the system, but it made sense for them to cover the details of the next steps of the project to be sure they were both on the same page.

Cate reached for a pen and a legal pad. But instead of grabbing the spare chair that sat on the other side of the desk so they could get to business, Owen stood firm just two steps inside the doorway. He glanced down at his boots, running a palm over the back of his neck before sliding his gaze back in her direction.

"Actually, I was thinking, if you're free for dinner, we could go over the plans tonight." Quickly, he added, "I'd pay you for your time, of course, since it would be work-related, but I've got some garlic chicken marinating at home. There's plenty for both of us. We could kill two birds with one stone."

Surprise parted her lips, but only for a second before they found the smile that had started in her chest and worked its way up. "The first bird, I get. We'd be talking about the project. But what's the second one?"

"Oh. Well, the second one is that I'd really like to spend time with you."

The unabashed honesty of his words made a shiver move through her. "Okay, then. My answer is yes, but on one condition."

"And that is?"

Cate was certain she shouldn't flirt with him. Folks were going to start lifting eyebrows and wagging tongues, and she didn't want the attention. Dodging their whispers was already hard enough, and nothing would ever come of her spending time with a man like Owen Cross.

Yet, still, she heard herself say, "You let me make dessert. A girl can't go to dinner—even a working one—empty-handed."

"Deal," he said, finally breaking into a smile. "I'm going

to head over to my place and get cleaned up. How does meeting there in half an hour sound?"

Feeling this good was risky. Dangerous, even. Cate knew that all too well. But right now, in this moment, she didn't care.

"Great. I'll be there."

13

Cate stood on Owen's magazine-worthy porch with a grocery bag in each hand and her chest full of butterflies. She'd been perfectly calm until now, using twenty-eight of the thirty minutes before they'd agreed to meet on a quick trip to The Corner Market and a pit-stop at her house to pack up what she needed and quickly change her clothes. She'd had a plan, with objectives, none of which had included thinking of Owen in the shower. But now she had two whole minutes to kill. One hundred and twenty seconds to let her mind wander to whether his long, black eyelashes would spike together with drops of water clinging to them, or how his hands might look roaming over the ridged muscles of his chest and abs as he lathered and rinsed.

"God! Down, girl," she whispered, shuffling the bags to jab the button for the doorbell with one finger. Yes, Owen was sexy as hell, and, yes, they'd traded a pair of very hot kisses. But at the end of the day, a man like that, so serious and family-driven, wasn't meant for her. Plus, he was her boss. They might work well together, but she still had to see him every day. As much as she wanted to, she couldn't just sleep with him, and she damn sure couldn't do something insane like *date* him. She had to dial it back and keep this dinner platonic, no matter how good it had felt to flirt with him a little while ago.

The door swung open, and sweet baby Jesus, why did this man have to make her work so hard for her composure?

"Hey. You made it," Owen said. He'd traded his work clothes for a pair of fresh but faded jeans and a navy blue button-down shirt that Cate would swear was made specifically to complement the steel-gray of his eyes. He'd rolled up his sleeves just high enough to showcase his corded forearms, completing the casual look with a blue and white checked dish towel slung over the broad line of one shoulder. His dark brown hair curled over his ears and his forehead, damp from the shower and perfectly imperfect, and she had to swallow twice before rummaging up a smile and a suitable reply.

"It's easier to navigate during daylight hours," she said. The truth grounded her, turning her smile more genuine. It was only dinner, for cripes' sake. No reason not to enjoy it. "Plus, I figured if I really got turned around, I could just call."

Owen stepped back to usher her over the threshold. "Ah, good luck getting cell service if you're not at the main house. Here, let me take those."

"Oh, no, it's okay. I promised I'd make dessert. That includes the hard labor."

She lifted the bags and did a no-frills twirl to show him how light they really were—just an eight-by-eight baking pan and a few plastic containers full of dry ingredients, plus one holding some canola oil.

But he didn't step back to start walking her down the hall to the kitchen. In fact, he moved closer.

"Cate," he said, slowly, as if measuring his words with precision. "I don't want to take your bags because I think they're particularly heavy."

"They're not," she assured him. She'd thought the twirl would kind of hammer that home, but then again, she forgot most people weren't really fluent in her brand of sarcasm.

"I know, and I also know you're perfectly capable of carrying your own things."

"Okay." She extended the word into a question, and Owen blew out a breath in nonverbal defeat.

"I'd like to carry your things for you because it's nice. So, could you please do my manners a solid here, and let me?"

"Oh. *Oh.*" God, her social graces needed a good dusting off. "Well, in that case, ah, go for it."

Cate passed the bags over, making sure not to let his fingers brush hers in the exchange, even slightly. He led the way through the foyer and living room, turning to aim his next words over one shoulder as he went.

"I was just getting the chicken ready to go into the oven. If you don't mind sharing the kitchen space a little, you're welcome to bake while I get dinner ready."

Yes, yes, yes. She needed to get her hands on the ingredients and her sanity, ASAP. "That sounds great. I hope you like brownies."

"Are there people who don't?" He gestured to the kitchen island, placing the bags on the pretty, light gray granite after she nodded.

"I suppose in theory. But I'm not sure I'd trust one."

Cate moved to the sink to wash her hands, stealing a long look around Owen's kitchen as she went. Of course, she'd had plenty of time to catalogue the place yesterday morning while she'd waited for him to wake up, but now, with the evening light streaming in through the bank of windows along the far wall, the room was even more gorgeous.

"Your kitchen is really nice," she said, walking back to the island to unpack her grocery bags. With its stainless steel appliances, sleek countertops, and spacious antique-white maple cabinets, it was a hell of an understatement. But since Cate was fairly sure that "your kitchen gives me a giant lady boner" would make Owen send her straight home, pink slip in hand, it would have to suffice.

"Thanks." Owen turned toward the L-shaped counter, choosing the small space at the end for prep so he was still half-facing her as he spoke. "I can't take a ton of the credit, though. The architect and designer pretty much did all of it. I just made a couple requests."

Huh. "Like?"

"Well, I like to cook, so I definitely wanted function to go with the form. And I don't plan to really ever move out of the place, so I figured it wouldn't hurt to have things I'd want down the line even if I don't use them too much now, like a big pantry and a double oven."

Cate rubbed a hand over the ache that passed beneath her breastbone and reached for the baking dish, hitting it with a liberal dose of cooking spray. "Lucky for us that you did, since we're about to put that double oven to use. Do you mind if I preheat the lower oven for the brownies?"

"Not at all," Owen said, breaking into the half-smile Cate was starting to find even more attractive than its full-wattage counterpart. Somehow, it just seemed to fit him better. "In fact, I can't think of anything I'd rather have in there for its maiden voyage."

"You've *never* used it?" Cate asked, thoroughly shocked. "Are you crazy?"

Owen's laugh made her realize—too late—how blunt the question had been. "Not last I checked. Just busy. Anyway, we do all of our family meals up at the main house, and it's just me here for now, so, nope. I've never used both ovens at the same time."

"I'm so glad we're fixing that, because really, for an oven this nice, it's a crying shame."

She preheated the oven with a few quick taps of the buttons, then returned to her spot at the island. After asking for a mixing bowl and a pair of eggs, both of which she'd known he had after yesterday and neither of which would have traveled easily from her house, Cate reached for the container with the dry ingredients. Owen worked at his end of the counter, putting the chicken into a large baking dish, then the dish into the oven, before trimming the ends off some of the prettiest asparagus Cate had ever seen. The silence that rolled out in the sunlit space between them wasn't uncomfortable, and the fact that she didn't feel some awkward urge to fill it took her ease up another level. She stirred and mixed and breathed deeply, adding in the ingredients for the brownies one by one until the batter was satiny smooth and ready to go.

"Damn, even the batter smells good," Owen said, lifting a brow over his steel-gray stare as she slid the pan onto the shiny oven rack and closed the door. "Is there anything you don't bake well?"

Ah, the question was loaded like a two-dollar pistol. "I find some things more challenging than others," she offered, but Owen read right between the lines.

"That's a no."

After a second, Cate admitted, "Okay, yeah. I mean, I've

had some master disasters to go with my masterpieces, but I've also loved baking forever. The tougher the recipe, the more I tend to like it. So, I suppose I do bake pretty much everything well. Even if that does sound immodest as hell."

"I don't think that sounds immodest at all," Owen said, setting the asparagus—which was now wearing a liberal dose of olive oil and some earthy-smelling fresh herbs Cate couldn't name but definitely wanted to eat—aside in favor of a saucepan and a box of rice. "You work hard, and you're great at what you do. No shame in being honest about your accomplishments."

Cate paused with her fingers over the timer app on her cell phone, her pulse quickening at her throat. The steady *thump-thump-thump* went for broke when he added, "Miss Clementine is right, you know. You should go into business and sell some of this stuff."

"I wanted to."

She heard the words only after they'd made a jailbreak, and she pressed her lips together even though it was too late to snare them back.

Funny, though, Owen didn't seem too stunned. "How come you never did?"

Well, shit. Her choices now were to either fess up or tuck tail and run, and she couldn't exactly run without him noticing. It was just the two of them, standing there, shooting the breeze in his kitchen. What would a little selective sharing of the facts hurt?

"It was ages ago," Cate said, qualifying the claim with, "before Lily was born, so buying in on an actual space to start a bakery was out of the question. The initial investment, plus the overhead costs, made even renting way out of my reach, and I was too young to know anything about business plans or profit margins. No bank in their right mind gives a loan that big to an eighteen-year-old with no credit, no collateral, and a kid on the way."

She didn't add that she knew because she'd tried. Cate had never even made that admission out loud—not to Brian, not to her friends at the time, all of whom she'd grown apart from after she and Brian had gotten married, anyway. Letting it loose now, when it didn't even matter and nothing could be done to change things? No, thanks.

Owen nodded slowly, shifting back from the saucepan full of broth and rice, which was now burbling happily over one of the burners on the stove. "Yeah, that makes sense. Cross Creek has established credit and sources of income, and securing the loan to make the storefront happen still took a bunch of hoop jumping. Which I guess you know since you're managing the books," he added with a self-deprecating smile. "Anyway, I hear you. Business loans can be tough to secure. Still, that was a long time ago. Why don't you apply for one now?"

The question blew right past selective sharing, sticking into the soft, vulnerable part of her that warned her she shouldn't have opened her mouth to begin with. Damn it, she needed to build some sort of immunity to Owen's straightforward appeal.

"Because I'm scared I'll die of boredom filling out the paperwork," she volleyed, hoping like hell that her smile didn't look as ill-fitting as it felt. Admitting that she'd once wanted to bake for a living was one thing. Forking over why she couldn't possibly do it now was quite another, and not one that would ever change. "Anyway, I already have a job or three. Unless you're trying to get rid of me already."

"No." The response flew out of him, and he paused to put the lid on the saucepan before turning all the way toward her. "I'm really not. The way you've organized our books is nothing short of amazing, to be honest. I don't know how we survived as long as we did without the change."

Cate shrugged. At least this was easier territory. "You had a system you were used to. Most people have to be dragged out of their comfort zones, kicking and screaming. All I did was grab you guys by the boot heels and tug a little."

"You did much more than that," Owen said. His voice was quiet, but oh, it slid through her deeply all the same. "We're really grateful for your hard work, Cate. *I'm* grateful."

Pride warmed her face, feeling both unusual and tantalizingly good. "Thank you," she whispered, clearing her throat a second later. "So, we've got a lot of ground to cover. Did you want to get to work while the ovens do their thing?"

"Sure."

Armed with a pair of legal pads and Owen's laptop, they relocated to the kitchen table, taking over two of the four sturdy ladder-backed chairs there. Early evening sunlight streamed in through the windows to provide an abundance of light, and between the cozy setting and Owen's clear enthusiasm for the project, not getting excited—even about work—was pretty much a no-go.

"Okay. I was thinking we could start with a review of the overall plan, then talk about the budget and timeline for the next phase to be sure we're still on track for both. Sound good?"

Cate nodded. While she'd managed a decent grasp of the farm's finances over the past couple of weeks, she had to admit the specifics for this project were still a bit outside of her wheelhouse. A plan overview wouldn't hurt. "You got it."

"The goal of the project is to build a place where a wide variety of our produce will be available to folks on a daily basis," Owen said, his gray-blue eyes crinkling around the edges as he clicked to open Cross Creek's website. A banner appeared at the top, with a slide show of gorgeous, vibrant photos—that had no doubt been taken by Scarlett—showing off everything from the produce to the landscape. God, she'd even captured a great picture of the henhouse. "Not just tomatoes and corn and melons, although those are things we'll certainly have in abundance, like always. But we want to use this storefront to really showcase the specialty items people can only get here. Heirloom tomatoes, a wide assortment of greens and herbs, varieties of fruits and vegetables that are a little more upscale than their everyday counterparts. Things like watercress, pattypan squash, Chinese eggplants, purple cauliflower. "

He ticked each item off on his fingers, his face growing more animated as he went, and Cate's stomach dipped down low beneath her jeans. "So, you're essentially combining the best of both worlds by offering both the staples everyone is used to and broadening your customers' horizons with new and unique produce. Kind of like running your own personal farmers' market every day."

"Exactly," Owen said. "We had a lot of success with our late-season marketing bringing people out here for Pick-Your-Own crops like apples and pumpkins in the fall, and to our tent at the farmers' market in Camden Valley every Saturday, too. But this storefront will let us expand on that even more."

Cate nodded, her brain turning her thoughts over one by one. "You have a lot of momentum from the marketing Emerson is doing and the visibility you gained when Scarlett was here, doing that series for her friend's online magazine. Building on that makes sense."

She knew the budget for the actual construction cost

was complete—familiarizing herself with what needed to be paid and when had been one of her first orders of business. Still... "What about the cost output once the storefront is complete?"

"Good question." Leaning forward in his chair, Owen pulled up the schematics on his laptop, scrolling to a sketch of the floor plan before turning the laptop toward her. "Part of the storefront will be completely enclosed." He outlined a section of the structure with one finger. "Running water, electricity, heat and air conditioning, the works. But we wanted to create that farm stand vibe while keeping the overhead costs manageable, so more than half the space is actually outdoors."

Surprise popped through her, and, she had to admit, the strategy was pretty frigging brilliant. "But it's covered, so you've still got protection from the elements."

"For both the people and the product," Owen pointed out. "We'll keep hardier produce out here, like corn and watermelons and pumpkins in the fall. The storage bins fit easily on pallets, so we can bring them inside after closing each day. Then the more perishable produce will go in these temperature controlled cases inside the enclosed part of the store."

Cate reached for her legal pad, scribbling off a handful of notes. "What sort of staffing are you looking at?"

"We won't be ready to open until the middle of the summer, so there's really no time for a soft opening. With the efforts Eli and Emerson are both sinking in on the marketing side, I'm hoping we'll be busy from the start."

She skimmed the page of the business plan he'd just pulled up, and, wow, he wasn't kidding. "So, you'll need two dedicated sales staffers a day, six days a week through the harvest, plus someone to re-stock and run inventory throughout each shift."

"To start," Owen agreed. "The proposed budget allows for five new seasonal hires, plus at least one person to manage the staff and the inventory."

"You don't have a manager yet?" Cate asked, surprised.

He hesitated. "Well, sort of. Right now, it's me."

Unable to help it, she laughed. "Of course, it is."

"What's that supposed to mean?"

Despite the directness of the question, Owen's tone said he was genuinely asking—well, mostly, anyway. God, he was probably gruff in his sleep.

Cate shook her head, although whether it was to reassure him or to tamp down the odd pang of attraction rippling through her belly, she couldn't be sure. "Nothing negative, Casanova. In fact, quite the opposite. This project obviously means a lot to you, and your work ethic is pretty much bulletproof. All I meant was that you being in charge of things from stem to stern doesn't surprise me."

"Yeah." For a second, something wistful flickered through his eyes, and the rare show of emotion startled her. But then it was gone just as fast as it had appeared, and even though she was certain she'd seen it, something warned her not to push. "Anyway," he said. "Now that we've talked about the basic overview, let's go through the numbers for the rest of the construction phase to make sure we haven't missed anything."

"You got it."

They worked together easily enough, which—considering their shared lack of tolerance for bullshit—didn't shock Cate in the least. Despite the dated way he'd kept his books, she had to admit Owen was both meticulous and innovative with regard to the project details, and by the time they'd finished their work a half an hour later, she'd caught a fair amount of his enthusiasm.

"This storefront really is pretty cutting edge," she said, tucking the three and a half pages of notes she'd taken into her purse before amending, "Well, for Millhaven, anyway."

"Thanks, I think." Owen's lips twitched just slightly, betraying the barest hint of a smile, and damn, who knew he had a playful side beneath that rugged, rough exterior?

"You're welcome. You know, I was thinking." Cate paused, too late. God, her mouth had a mind of its own! Owen had all of these smart, strategic plans, and here she was, two millimeters away from giving up what was likely to be a lame idea. "I mean, I don't have any business experience or anything, so this might be off the wall."

Serious Owen was back in a flash, arching a nearly black brow and leaning back to pin her with a stare that said he wasn't letting her off the hook. "You have enough business experience to manage Cross Creek's books. I'd say that's plenty. So, what's this thought of yours?"

Cate gathered up a large breath, and, oh, fuck it. "Well, you want to focus on the specialty produce that makes Cross Creek unique, right? Things like the best strawberries in the county and more varieties of heirloom tomatoes and greens than anyone else, right?"

"That's the idea, yes."

"But the startup costs and overhead for a project like this are high. The sooner you recoup them, the sooner your profit margins rise, the better for business all around," she continued.

Owen nodded. "Of course. But we're already using every inch of land and greenhouse space that we've got. I can't sell more than what I have."

"Actually, I think you can."

His expression suggested he was seriously reconsidering that whole off-the-wall thing, and Cate scrambled to tack on, "What I mean is, for an added stream of revenue, you could consider renting a little bit of the space in the store-front to other vendors."

"Okay, but the point is to be better than the competition. Not give them another way to reach customers," Owen said.

The timer on Cate's phone chimed softly, and from the chocolatey-sweet smell wafting through Owen's kitchen, it was spot-on. "I'm not talking about renting space to your competition. That *would* be dumb," she agreed, pushing up from her spot at the table to grab the brownies from the oven. "But think of people like Daisy Halstead. She does great business at craft fairs with all of those bath and body products she makes."

"She does?" He moved past the island to hand over two perfectly matched blue pot holders.

"She does," Cate said. At least, that's what she'd over-heard Daisy tell Emerson last month at Clementine's, but she had no reason not to believe her. Plus, Daisy had given her some samples of her honeysuckle hand lotion, and the stuff smelled divine. "Daisy's products have a good crossover audience with yours, and you're both selling local goods. I don't have to tell you that goes a long way around here."

"As it should," Owen grumbled, his chin lifting sheep-ishly a second later. "Sorry. I'm not a fast food, chain store kind of guy."

Cate gave up a utilitarian shrug. "Not something you should apologize for, then." She paused to open the oven, and, ahhhh, *yes*. The brownies were just starting to pull away from the edges of the pan. "Anyway, renting a little bit of space in your storefront to a vendor like Daisy seems smart. She gets added exposure for her products, and you widen your market without cannibalizing your sales. It's a win-win."

"Smart? It's more like brilliant. And not something I would have thought of on my own."

"It's just one idea," Cate said by way of argument. "I'm sure you'll come up with a ton of them to make the store-front successful."

For a heartbeat, Owen seemed primed to argue. But then his eyes dropped to the baking dish between her hands, and, God, that sexy little half-smile of his was going to either end her or make her hurl herself at him, right here in his beautiful gourmet kitchen. "Those smell unbelievable."

"Thanks," she said, grabbing a toothpick from her grocery bag to test the center, just in case. "I've tried bunches of different recipes over the years—peanut butter brownies, cheesecake brownies, you name it. I always come back to this one, though."

"You can't go wrong with a classic."

They filled the next ten minutes or so getting the last-minute parts of the meal prepared and on the table. The chicken Owen pulled from the oven smelled hearty and mouth-wateringly good—far better than anything Cate would have ever had the wherewithal to pull together at home. He added some touches to the rice while she set the table, and by the time they settled in to eat, her stomach was growling with uncharacteristic intensity.

"This looks really great. Thank you," she said, serving herself and passing dishes back and forth with Owen until their plates were full. They ate for a few minutes in silence, although the quiet was far from uncomfortable. The meal tasted even better than it had smelled, which seemed nearly impossible to her. But the simple ingredients mixed together perfectly, the hearty chicken and the freshness of the asparagus combining with the simplicity of the herbs and rice to create a comfort food feel that was satisfying without being overbearing or heavy, and the more she ate, the lighter she felt.

"So, I have to ask," Cate said between bites, giving in to a question that had been dancing through her mind for the last two days. "What made you go out and get all liquored up on Saturday night?" At his semi-panicked expression, she quickly added, "I mean, don't get me wrong. It was amusing as hell. But not really your speed, is all. You're usually kind of serious."

Owen's fork hovered over his asparagus for a full five seconds before he said, "I got drunk because Hunter asked me to be his best man."

Hello, bombshell. "You say that like it's a bad thing," Cate finally answered, once her shock let her.

"No." Owen shook his head and resumed eating, although a bit more slowly than before. "I mean, I'm really happy for him, and he's really happy with Emerson."

"They really are a great couple," she agreed.

"I know. I guess it's just...stupid." He let go of a soft laugh and shook his head. "Never mind."

"Oh, come on," she urged. "We have an honesty policy, remember? Consider this your cone of silence." She spun her finger to draw an invisible circle between them two of them. "Spill it."

"You're a pit bull, you know that? Fine"—he held up a hand before she could launch another argument—"it's just that Hunter and Emerson are getting married. Eli's got Scarlett. Even Lane has managed to find someone to date. So, I suppose I'm a little jealous."

Of all the things he could have said, Cate had expected

that the least. "You want a serious girlfriend?" Her stomach dropped, roller coaster-style, her appetite suddenly gone.

"I don't know. Maybe. I mean, I don't want to be with someone just for the sake of it," he qualified. "But my brothers are both really happy. I'm thirty-three, and I don't want to be alone forever. So, yeah. I guess in a way, part of me does want to find a serious girlfriend. Which probably sounds crazy, I know," he added sheepishly after a few seconds.

"No." Cate managed—barely—to get the word past her lips. Of course, he wanted a girlfriend, someone to eventually marry and have a bunch of kids with. His family was one of the tightest in Millhaven, maybe even all of King County, for Chrissake, and the farm was his legacy. His *family-run* legacy.

And she was an idiot.

"It doesn't sound crazy at all," she said, forcing herself to smile. "In fact, it sounds perfect for you."

Cate looked around his sunlit kitchen, with its fancy bells and whistles and more than enough space to accommodate the family he almost certainly wanted sooner rather than later. She thought of her own space, with its shadows and dinginess and the trivet she couldn't even bring herself to look at, much less use ever again, and, God, how had she let her impulses make her so naive?

A man like Owen Cross wasn't for her. Not casually. Not seriously. Not ever. She needed to keep him at arm's length, for his sake and for hers.

Starting right now.

14

Owen had fucked up monumentally. Not that he knew how or why or precisely when—but at some point between the dinner at his house and the nearly two days that had followed, Cate had gone the all-business route on him. Despite their great start the other night, she hadn't even stayed for dessert, claiming to be stuffed after having picked through most of her meal. She'd been polite enough, thanking him for dinner and ducking out with a lukewarm smile and a wave. While Owen had tried not to overshoot in the expectations department, he had to admit, he'd been hoping for a repeat of Sunday morning's slow and sexy goodbye kiss. But not only had Cate all but dashed out of his place as soon as they'd finished eating (fine. He'd eaten. She'd pushed her food around her plate), but she'd mastered the art of holding up her end of all their conversations since then with as few cordial yet boring words as possible, including the quick "have a nice night" and corresponding "you, too" they'd exchanged ten minutes ago.

Bracing his hands over the kitchen counter in the main

house, he dropped his chin to his chest. Cate might have been distant, but he knew her far better than to think she'd keep it to herself if he'd pissed her off outright. As much as Owen hated it, that probably meant one thing, and one thing only.

For whatever reason, she wasn't interested.

"Wow. And here I thought you couldn't get any more serious."

Owen's head whipped up at the sound of Marley's voice coming in from the entryway to the kitchen. "I'm not that serious," he said by default. But the argument rang hollow in his ears, and Marley's expression was proof she wasn't buying it, either.

"Okay." Her tone slathered the word with a double-coat of sarcasm as she moved toward the fridge and pulled out a bottle of water. Instead of hightailing her way back upstairs like she usually did, though, she lingered, her stare flickering over the last piece of pound cake sitting wrapped up beside the coffee pot.

"Is that pound cake?" Marley asked, and Owen nodded.

"Yeah. Why?"

Her chin hiked in a stubborn lift. "Cate said if I wanted some, I should tell you guys to save me a piece, so I thought...it would be okay to try some."

"You've talked to Cate?" Owen asked, utterly stunned.

Marley snorted, although more softly than usual. "Uh, yeah. She's in the house pretty much every day."

"Oh. Right." He shook his head, although more at himself than anything else. Of course, it figured they'd have crossed paths a few times. "She just didn't mention having met you."

"Huh." Marley's lips parted in surprise, but only for a

second before her mouth pressed right back into its permafrown. "So, what'd you do to make her mad?"

"I beg your pardon?" Owen asked, his heart clapping against his rib cage.

Marley made a sound that was half snort, half laughter. "God, you're so polite. I was just asking what you did to Cate. I mean"—she moved around him to pick up the pound cake, unwrapping it for a tiny bite—"Hunter's too nice to piss anyone off, and you work with her way more than anyone else, so I figured it was you."

"I didn't do anything to piss her off," Owen said, his brain scrambling to process exactly how observant Marley had been. "Why, did she, ah, say something to you about it?"

Marley took a bigger bite of pound cake and shook her head. "She didn't have to," she said after a few seconds of chew and swallow. "But she only bakes the really hard stuff when she's got her panties in a twist, and those macarons she brought in yesterday? Let's just say they're one of the top ten hardest desserts to make."

Owen plucked the first question from the pile of them growing in his head and sent it down the chain of command to his mouth. "How do you know that?"

"Duh. I Googled it."

"No," he said, quietly so he wouldn't scream in frustration. "I meant, how do you know she only bakes the really hard stuff when she's..." *Do not talk about Cate's panties. Seriously, dude. Don't do it.* "Upset?"

Marley paused, only for a heartbeat or two, but it was enough. "Lucky guess."

The silence drew out between them, growing heavier by the second. Owen sucked at this sort of thing—truly, Hunter, or even their father, who Marley avoided like every strain of the plague, would know what to say here. But this was the longest conversation he and his sister had ever shared, and, frankly, Owen was pretty fucking desperate for advice.

So he said, "Cate's not shy about letting people know when she's mad, so I don't think I pissed her off." He looked at the counter, where the giant plastic container full of brightly colored macarons sat, and, yeah, Marley didn't seem to be wrong about Cate's baking jags. "But she does seem a little, ah, distant lately, and I'm not sure why."

"Have you asked her?"

"What?"

Marley sent her gaze skyward and shook her head. "It's not advanced algebra, Owen. If you think there's something bothering her, just ask her what it is."

Owen turned to lean against the counter beside him, parceling through the thought. "Okay, but what if she doesn't tell me?"

"Then she doesn't want to tell you. But you're not going to know unless you ask."

He opened his mouth to argue, but quickly found he couldn't. He and Cate had agreed to be honest with one another. As tight-lipped as she'd been for the last two days, she hadn't broken that agreement.

And as much as it was going to crush his comfort zone, if he wanted to know what was going on with her, he was going to have to find the words to ask.

Owen realized Marley was still looking at him with that shrewd, sharp-edged stare of hers, and he straightened as tall as his six-foot-one frame would allow.

"Are you going to eat that for dinner?" he asked, gesturing to the now half-gone piece of pound cake in her hand.

Marley's frown deepened. "I'm twenty-four. I don't need parenting, thanks."

Shit. *Shit.* Why didn't he hear his words before they came out? "I didn't mean—"

"And in case you didn't notice," Marley interrupted, breaking off a huge chunk of the pound cake to pop it into her mouth. "This cake is really good, so, yes. I am totally having it for dinner. In my room."

"Awesome," Owen said under his breath as she turned on her heel and marched out of the kitchen, the admittedly awkward invitation to go grab a burger at Clementine's Diner disappearing from his lips. A burst of odd emotion pressed up from his chest, and he turned to grab his keys from the spot where they sat on the counter. He was done fumbling his way through conversations. He might not be able to fix his mess of a relationship with his sister—God knew *that* wasn't going to happen in a night. But there was something he could go fix.

And he was going to do it right now, come hell or high tide.

OWEN KNOCKED on Cate's door hard enough to make his knuckles sing. He knew turning up on her threshold unannounced, wearing dirt-streaked jeans, a T-shirt that had seen months' worth of better days, and a look of sheer determination was just shy of crazy. But he also knew Marley was right—he wasn't going to get any answers unless he had the balls to ask for them.

If Cate shut him down, so be it.

She opened the door, her dark brown curls loose around her face and her bare feet peeking out from beneath the cuffs of her faded, body-hugging jeans, and for the love of Christmas, how did she manage to look prettier *every* fucking time he saw her?

"Um, hi?" Cate's whiskey-brown eyes went wide, but not even her obvious shock was enough to deter him.

"Hi. I want to know what's bugging you."

She made a small noise of heightened surprise, but nope. Owen had come all this way. She might slam the door in his face when he was done, but he wasn't going to stop until he'd aired out everything he'd come to say.

"Look, we agreed we were going to be honest with each other, so that's what I'm going to do. I know you work at Cross Creek, and the last thing I want is for you to feel uncomfortable there. With me. Because we kissed. And then I asked you to dinner."

He paused long enough for her to—thank God—shake her head. "Good. Okay. So, what happened between us over the weekend wasn't very conventional, or planned, or anything, but I thought we had a good time together, and I really enjoyed our dinner. Clearly, I did something to mess with that, and I'm not sure what, and we have this honesty policy, like you said, so I came out here to find out what's bothering you."

Owen's words kept pouring out in an artless rush, and, what the hell, he was already in for a penny. Might as well go for the whole goddamned pound. "Look, if you're not interested, that's okay. It won't stand in the way of us working together. But spending that time with you at my place, and those talks we had...I liked that. I like *you*. And now you're barely speaking to me unless you have to, so if I did something to upset you, I just want to know."

The quiet that followed was punctuated by the persistent *whump-whump-whump* of his pulse against his eardrums. The longer it drew out, the faster the rhythm became, until finally, Cate stepped back to swing the door open wide.

"Come in."

"Thank you," Owen said. About two steps over the threshold, he realized that, while he'd known where she lived for over a decade—hello, benefits of small-town living —he'd never actually been inside the place. Between the limited square footage and the sparse furnishings, taking in the foyer/living room was a two-second job. Although meticulously clean, everything from the carpet to the curtains easily dated back to the year he'd gotten his driver's license. Cate led him deeper into the house, not surprisingly stopping in her galley kitchen, where an aging laptop and a Styrofoam cup of instant noodles sat on the slim stretch of chipped Formica that served as a breakfast bar.

"Oh." A pang of guilt stabbed at Owen. Of course, he'd probably interrupted her dinner. It was six o'clock, for God's sake. "I apologize."

Cate followed his gaze to the cup a few feet away, and she waved off his worry with one hand. "Oh, please don't. That stuff isn't all too great, and, anyway, I was pretty much done." She clicked her laptop closed, clearing the remnants of the soup to the single-bowl sink before gesturing to the dining area off the back of the kitchen. "We should probably sit."

"Okay." Owen waited for Cate to pull out a chair at the four-person table that took up ninety-percent of the space before origami-ing himself into the seat across from her. As much as he'd run off at the mouth after she'd opened the door, something cautioned him to give her some breathing room right now, so even though it damn near killed him, he waited out the handful of seconds before she finally spoke.

"I didn't want to come work at Cross Creek, at first."

Okay, *so* not what he'd been expecting. "But you offered," he said, and Cate nodded in agreement.

"I know, and please don't misunderstand. I'm really grateful for the job."

The flash of genuine emotion in her stare backed up the claim one hundred percent, so Owen waited for her to continue without protest.

"I told you, not everything about my marriage was what it looked like," Cate said. "We had—*have*—a lot of debt I didn't really know about until after the accident. Brian didn't want me working outside of our house. It was really important to him that I be here for Lily all the time. So much so that he maxed out a home equity line of credit he opened without my knowledge, along with all of our credit cards."

Oh, hell. "I'm so sorry," Owen said, because it was the only thing he could come up with that was both true and appropriate. Her former marriage was none of his business, but damn. No wonder she was so insistent on honesty now.

Cate's smile was bittersweet. "I'm sorry, too. I went from high school to marriage to motherhood so quickly. I loved my daughter." Her voice caught, the sound jabbing into a part of Owen he couldn't quite name, and it took every ounce of his willpower not to reach out and grab her hand. "But I don't exactly have a lot of career skills, so when I first scraped up the courage to ask you for a job, I was really nervous. In fact, I was pretty sure you'd fire me before the week was out."

"You're wrong," Owen said, and, yeah, so much for his gruffness going on any sort of sabbatical. "You have plenty of career skills."

She laughed in a soft, humorless huff. "And not a lot of social skills, as it turns out. I like spending time with you, too. You're the only person who treats me like *me* no matter what the topic of conversation is, and I shouldn't have pushed you away without at least telling you why."

"Is it work?" he asked, unable to keep the concern tamped down. "Because if it is, we can—"

"No." Cate reached over the small section of the table that separated them, her fingers wrapping around his forearm in enough of a squeeze to tell him she really meant it. "Owen, we kissed on our own time, and it would've happened regardless of whether I work at Cross Creek or not." Looking down, she withdrew her hand, but rested it on the table instead of back at her side. "It's just that long-term commitments are...a big leap for me."

He paused. Retraced his steps through the conversation they'd had at his place the other night.

And promptly wanted to bitch-slap himself.

"God, I'm kind of an idiot," he said, shaking his head in disbelief. Cate might have clearly grieved the loss of her husband and be ready to move on, but that didn't mean she wanted to jump into another relationship with both feet first. Of *course,* all that talk about weddings and serious girl-friends had probably rattled her. Hell, in its own weird way, the idea still rattled him, too.

Cate's laugh surprised him, but it also took the steely edges off the unease that had opened up in his rib cage. "You're not an idiot, Owen. There's nothing wrong with you wanting a serious relationship. But it was hard enough for me to take a full-time job with you. A commitment like a relationship..."

She trailed off, leaving Owen to fill in the blanks. The topic was loaded with conversational potholes, each of which had the potential to torpedo him and his ingrained gruffness in less than a second. He hadn't come this far to scale back now, though, so he took a deep breath and a giant fucking leap.

"Look, to be honest, I'm not entirely sure I'm up for that, either. Don't get me wrong—I meant what I said the other night. I don't want to be alone," he clarified. "But the idea of going from zero to married with someone, especially for the sake of settling down, isn't really appealing, either. I guess I just want to find someone who I like hanging out with and see how it goes."

One slender brow arched, quickly accompanied by a smirk that had enough brass for a marching band. "Unless you want to end up hitched to Lane, you might want to narrow that game plan down."

Yeah, serious topic or not, if she was going to flirt with him, there was a zero percent chance Owen wasn't flirting back. He leaned forward in his chair, just slightly, until his hand was two inches away from hers. "Mmm. Lane's a cool guy and all, but he's sort of taken now that he and Daisy are seeing each other. Plus, he's not really my type."

"Ah." Cate shifted, and now only an inch separated their fingers. "And what is your type, exactly?"

"Female, for starters. Smart. Likes to bake. Dark hair. Very pretty eyes." He let his stare linger on hers for just a beat before his half-smile took over. "Unbelievably brash mouth. You know anyone who fits the bill?"

The blush that stained her cheeks made Owen want to taste every part of her just to keep it there. "This is going to get complicated," Cate said softly. But she didn't pull away—in fact, she angled even closer—and, *God*, he didn't even think twice. With one finger, he traced a line over the back of her hand from her knuckle to her wrist, and even though his darker, baser instincts screamed for more contact, more heat, more everything, he lifted his hand from hers, letting it hover over her skin after only the one slight touch.

"No, it's not," he said. "And here's why. If we do this, we're going to be honest with each other. Straight up. No bullshit. Everything on the table. When we're at Cross Creek, we work."

"Of course, work should stay separate." She paused, her pupils dilating and her voice taking on a breathy quality that traveled directly to his cock. "But what about when we're not there?"

With careful control, Owen leaned in just a fraction closer. "That ball is in your court, Cate. I promised not to tiptoe around you, so I'm going to give it to you straight. I think you're sexy as hell, and I'd love to spend more time with you. If that's not what you want, I'll understand, no harm done. But if you do want it"—Owen smiled, and even though it took every ounce of willpower he owned, he forced himself to get up from the table—"you're going to have to come and get it. In the meantime, I'll see you tomorrow."

15

Cate stared at the financial projections she was entering into Cross Creek's system even though she didn't see a thing. Actually, scratch that. She *did* see something. But since she was certain Owen's sexy, steel-gray stare wasn't going to get these notes on the next phase of the storefront project put into the system, she should probably blink a few times and move the hell on.

The only problem was, she'd tried that trick sixty times in the last six hours to no avail, and the longer she sat there all hot and bothered, the more obvious the truth became.

She wanted Owen so badly she could taste it, feel it in every heartbeat like a living, breathing, carnally wild thing.

And as dangerous as Cate knew that was for both of them, it was getting harder and harder to deny.

Maybe...

Something on the paper in front of her snagged her attention, yanking her from the impulsive thought. She read the passage, then read it again before going for a three-peat. But even though the words that marched across the page in Owen's tidy, precise handwriting made sense, as far as the whole subject-verb-object thing went, they might as well have been written in Cantonese for how much *actual* sense they made.

Unless—

Before she could think twice, Cate had scooped up the two-way radio sitting in the charging station in the corner of the office. Owen, Hunter, and Mr. Cross used the walkie-talkie-like devices to communicate on the farm since cell service wasn't always reliable, and they always left one on in the office during working hours. Owen had shown her how to operate the controls on her first day, just in case. She'd figured she'd only ever use the thing in case of an emergency, and while no one was breaking in or bleeding out up here at the main house, the paperwork in front of her was enough to make her press the "talk" button without so much as a heartbeat's worth of a pause.

"Owen, this is Cate, over," she said, having overheard enough conversations from the unit that stayed in the office to know the correct protocol. "Do you copy?"

"Yes, ma'am," came the serious and seriously unreadable reply. "Everything okay at the main house, over?"

Well, shit. Hunter and Mr. Cross were some of the nicest folks in Millhaven, and both of them were probably listening to this exchange. If she answered in the negative, there was no way in hell all three Cross men wouldn't drop whatever they were doing like a red-hot poker to come barreling up to the house.

"Everything's fine," Cate borderline lied. "I've got some, um, information in front of me on the storefront project that doesn't quite add up and I was hoping we could talk about it, over."

"Copy that. I'll be at the house in five. Out."

Despite her very best efforts, her hands shook as she

replaced the two-way in the base. She had to be calm about this. Rational. Smart. She paced over the area rug to offset the adrenaline riding through her veins, elongating her breaths to a slow, controlled in and out and slowing her pulse to a nice, steady rhythm.

A steadiness that vanished the instant Owen opened the back door to the house and made his way into the office.

"Have you lost your mind?" Cate asked briskly, her heart making the involuntary climb toward her throat.

The noise that came out of him was part shock, part barked-out laughter. "Not that I'm aware, although something tells me you've got a different opinion on the matter."

Nope. Not even that sexy little half-smile was going to save his equally sexy ass now. "What is this?"

He looked at the sheaf of papers she'd just snapped up off her desk. "That is the list of local business owners we'd like to partner with once we get to the next phase of the storefront project."

"And why is my name on this list?"

"Actually, it's at the top of the list," Owen said, pointing to the page in her hand, and Christ on a cupcake, he *was* insane.

"Yes, I can see that," Cate said, sending each syllable through her teeth. "What I'd like to know is why."

Owen took a few steps farther into the office, but he didn't break eye contact with her. "Because we'd like to offer your baked goods to our customers once the storefront is open for business."

"No." The word vaulted out of her mouth despite the whisper of a *yes* that had stirred in her chest.

A muscle in Owen's jaw tightened. "Why not?"

"Because," she said, slowly, to buy time. "It's crazy."

"It was your suggestion to add vendors with unique

products to entice new customers," he pointed out. His reply was low and perfectly controlled, yet definitely still an argument, and damn it, she should have known better than to think he'd let her off the hook with a simple protest.

Too bad for him, she could stand her ground like a champ. "Okay, but I didn't mean *me*. I'm not a vendor."

"But you could be."

"No, I really can't."

Where Owen's logic had grown stronger with each assertion, Cate's had faltered, and her heart kicked so fast, surely he was able to see it from the spot where he stood in front of her.

"Yes, you really can. Look"—his hands went to his hips, each of his words chipping away at her resolve—"I'm not asking for something outrageous, like a kidney, here. All I'm suggesting is that we give this a try."

An image of the trivet hidden away among the dish towels in her kitchen sailed into her, stealing her air. "It's not a good idea," she managed.

Something shifted in his stare, turning it one degree softer and surprising the hell out of her. "Actually, it's a great idea," Owen said quietly. "And I can prove it before the next phase of the project even starts."

Cate stepped back in shock. "How?"

"With a test run at the farmers' market this weekend."

"Owen—"

"Jesus, Cate. Would you at least hear me out before you say no?"

Although the words were technically a question, they came out with enough of a demand to pin her into place. Something deep in her belly made her acquiesce in spite of her defenses, and a flash of surprise added more gray than blue to Owen's eyes as he registered her lack of protest.

"I'll make a deal with you," he said. "I'll advance you the money to make and package as many baked goods as you're able between now and Saturday morning. It's an advance, not charity," he reiterated, turning her brewing argument to stone. "You can pay it back with your profits. You'll also have Cross Creek's produce at your disposal for baking. Right now, there's a decent crop of strawberries in the greenhouse and a ton of fresh herbs if you want to make savory bread. I've also got more eggs in our henhouse than I know what to do with."

Ah, hell. Using Cross Creek's produce would not only ensure top-notch quality in the baked goods, but it was a stroke of marketing genius on Owen's part. Still... "That's a lot of baking in the next two days."

He shrugged, undeterred. "Something tells me you're good for it. Plus, you're welcome to use my kitchen if the double oven will help, and if you need to take a shift off at The Bar, I'll compensate you for lost wages."

"What about the space?" Cate asked, crossing her arms over the front of her pale yellow top.

"What about it?"

This was a full-on negotiation now, so hell if she was going to pull any punches. "Cross Creek has one of the biggest tents at the farmers' market. I'm sure King County charges you a fortune for it, and I doubt I can afford a portion of the rent."

"Consider the space part of the trial run. We're already renting it anyway so it's not an added expense, and your baked goods are an added draw, which is a win for the farm. We can shuffle things and rotate stock to make room for both Cross Creek's inventory and yours. If you feel that strongly about it, you can work the market with me and my father to offset the day's rental costs."

Oh, well played. Of course, he just had to appeal to her Kevlar-reinforced sensible side. "So, hypothetically, I bake a bunch of stuff and work the farmers' market with you. Then what?"

"Then you sell out of said stuff and realize how much money there is to be made by partnering up with Cross Creek on a more permanent basis once the storefront opens." Owen pointed to the notes she still held between her fingers in a nonverbal *may I?* and Cate unwrapped her arms from her chest to reluctantly hand them over.

"This is the buy-in for rental space in the storefront," he said, flipping to the third page in the pile and tapping a section with one finger. "Along with projected sales and profit margins. Obviously, none of it is a guarantee. But..."

Cate scanned the figures on the page, her jaw unhinging as they fell into order in her head. "Holy *shit*. If this works, you could make a killer profit."

"*When* this works, *we* are going to make a killer profit."

Lowering his notes to the desk, Owen took a pair of steps toward her, until only a few feet remained between them, and Cate's breath tightened in her lungs.

"Look, I'm really good at what I do, but I can't make this idea work without vendors," he said, lowering his chin to lock their gazes together. "Great ones. And you're at the top of that list for a reason—my father and Hunter and I agreed you're a perfect fit. All I'm asking is that you give this an honest shot. If it doesn't work, we can drop it. But if it does, you'll be able to pay your debts off a hell of a lot faster than working at Clementine's and The Bar, plus, you'll be doing something you love."

Oh, my God, he had to stop hitting her in her soft spot. "Since when are you so pragmatic?"

"Since I learned from the best."

"Oh, now you're just flirting with me," she grumbled, and he reduced the space between them to only a few scant inches.

"No, I'm not. When we're at work, we work, remember?"

Cate's chin snapped up. "I didn't mean I think you're flirting with me to get me to say yes." Stupid, stupid sarcasm!

Owen laughed, and the sound sent a bolt of heat through her that felt far more like hope than it should. "I know. What I meant was, I'm not bullshitting you. You're really, really good at what you do, Cate." He tilted his head to look at her. "Look, you said most people have to be dragged out of their comfort zones, kicking and screaming, right? All I'm doing is grabbing you by the boot heels and tugging a little. So, what do you say? Will you at least give it a try?"

Time passed for the span of a breath, then two, then a third before she finally let go of a long exhale. "Low blow, using my own logic against me like that."

"Yeah, I know." God, he even made looking genuinely sheepish sexy. "Did it work?"

Don't do this. You cannot do this. Don't...

"Yes, Casanova. It worked. But be careful what you wish for." Cate waited just a beat before fixing him with a smile as sweet and thick as buttercream frosting.

"If you think I turned your office into a tornado a couple of weeks ago, that's nothing compared to what I'm about to do to your kitchen.

EXCITEMENT PUMPED through Owen's veins despite the subhuman hour. Even though he'd been able to sleep in (somewhat—he was, after all, a farmer) on Saturdays for the last four and a half months while the farmers' market in Camden Valley was on hiatus, opening weekend always filled him with the sort of electric buzz usually reserved for kids on Christmas morning. This year held a little extra kick because of the deal he'd struck with Cate.

Owen's pulse flared, and he placed a hand on the cool granite countertop in front of him to ground himself. Cate hadn't been kidding about unleashing hell in his kitchen. Over the past day and a half, he'd helped her scrub flour, sugar, and, in one unfortunate instance, molasses, from places in his house he hadn't even known he had. To be fair, she had also taken her end of their agreement as serious as grand jury testimony. She'd baked dozens of loaves of quick breads, scones, biscuits, and cookies, packaging everything up in cellophane with red and white ribbons that matched the colors in Cross Creek's logo. She'd even gone so far as to print specially designed labels on red and white stickers for each item, along with a complete list of ingredients in case anyone had food allergies. By the time they'd loaded everything up in crates and put it all in his truck at ten thirty last night, she'd grudgingly admitted there was a tiny chance this might not be a total failure.

Please, God, don't let it be a total failure.

Owen poured half a pot of black coffee into the Thermos on the counter and dismissed the possibility. He'd meant what he said the other day in the office—she *was* an unbelievable baker, even if she was far too stubborn to admit it.

In fact, Cate was a lot of things he'd never realized. Over the past two nights, Owen had discovered her weakness for Hawaiian pizza ("Come on! Ham and pineapple on a pizza. It's like a full-time luau for your mouth!"), her freakish ability to name a song after only hearing the first five seconds ("Seriously. How can you not tell that's Thomas Rhett?"), and her secret love for Wonder Woman ("Between the lasso, the killer boots, and that invisible jet, who *wouldn't* want to be that chick?"). Aside from some veiled flirting, they'd stuck to business—she took the whole work-when-we're-at-work thing as seriously as he did, much to his dick's chagrin. But Cate was the first woman he'd enjoyed spending time with in conservatively a dog's age. He might've suffered through a couple of very cold showers after she'd gone home both nights, but he'd also given her the reins.

Which meant he'd let her set the pace, no matter how badly he wanted to strip her naked and put his mouth on every place that would make her sigh and shake and scream.

A crisp knock on his front door ripped Owen out of his dirty thoughts not a second too soon. Adjusting his jeans to make sure his appearance was one hundred percent socially acceptable, he forced himself to think of cow manure and tractor sludge, which—thank fuck—did the trick by the time he reached his destination.

"Good morning," Cate said, looking way cuter than anyone in a hoodie, jeans, and cross-trainers ever should. She'd corralled her curls into two loose braids that framed her pretty face, and Christ, he was never going to lose this hard-on now. "It's six. Are you ready to go?"

"Absolutely." He cleared his throat, then did it again just for kicks and grins. "Just let me grab my coffee and my keys and we can head out."

He put his words into action, and, a few minutes later, they were side by side in his F-250. They sat together in quiet for a few minutes as he drove, which was neither unusual nor uncomfortable. Except for the fact that it allowed Owen to focus on the smell of Cate's shampoo, which she must have used very recently, because the herbal scent, deep and woodsy, yet with a hint of sweetness like rosemary, filled his truck, then his nose, and, okay, he needed to find something to talk about before he pulled over and laid ruin to the whole work-while-we're-at-work thing.

"You really didn't have to get up this early," Owen said, because it was the first thing he could think of that was both appropriate and true. "Meeting us when the market opens at eight would've been just fine."

Cate shook her head, which did nothing to lessen the unnervingly sexy scent in the cab of his truck. "Nope. I said I'd work the market with you and your father, and that means all of it."

"Suit yourself," he said, trying to offset his unintentional gruffness by explaining, "The setup is mostly manual labor. Putting the tents together and unloading the crates and managing inventory. Stuff like that." He and Hunter and their father had loaded nearly everything, save the few really perishable items like the heirloom tomatoes and asparagus and the more fragile greens, into their box truck yesterday evening before he'd left to go help Cate in his kitchen.

She dipped her chin in a nod. "That's okay. I don't mind."

"You might want to reserve judgment until after we start setting up," Owen said as playfully as his personality would allow—which, admittedly, wasn't much. But, of course, Cate didn't budge.

"Owen, I tackled your books on little more than a wing and a please-Jesus. When have you known me to shy away from hard work?"

She buried her smile in her travel mug, and, okay, she kind of had him there. "Fair enough."

Cate looked out the passenger side window even though the sun had barely started pinking the horizon and there wasn't much of anything to see. "Anyway, it'll keep my mind off what I'm going to do with all these baked goods if nobody buys them."

"Why do you do that?" Owen asked, loosening the question before he didn't. At least she was too smart to go the "do what?" route, letting out a slow exhale instead.

"I know it probably doesn't make much sense to you, but this"—she gestured to the crates and bins stacked along the bench seat of his truck, all of which held some form of home-baked goodness—"is hard for me."

His heart tripped behind his breastbone. "Do you want to help me understand why?"

"Not really," she said, and damn, Owen should've known she'd go for no holds barred honesty. "But that has a lot more to do with me than you."

"Okay."

The soft sound of her surprise echoed through the shadows between them. "Okay?"

He had no choice but to laugh. "Yeah, okay. What, did you think I was going to put the screws to you until you caved in and told me?"

"No." She laughed, too, and it broke the last of the tension in her voice. "Not exactly. It's just that I needle you about being straight-up with me all the time. I guess I just thought you might pull the turnabout card."

Owen knew he could've done exactly that, that he could do it still. There was no denying he wanted to get past her tough exterior, to get to know the parts of her that lay beneath. But instead, he said, "Just because we have an honesty policy doesn't mean we're always going to want to use it. If you change your mind, you'll let me know."

"Thanks," Cate said. She reached out to brush her fingers over the knuckles of his right hand, which sat on the console between them. The touch was slight, but Christ, at the same time, it felt like everything.

He tilted his hand to return the gesture, and damn, he felt the touch of her impossibly soft fingers everywhere.

"You're welcome."

16

The excitement of opening day lasted for exactly twenty seconds before the prospect of ball-busting labor kicked Owen in the ass, good and hard. He'd pulled into the pavilion and parked next to his old man, who had driven the box truck into Camden Valley from the farm. They'd gotten smart at the end of last season and hired extra hands to help unload and set up, but things were still hectic with all that needed to be done in such a limited amount of time.

Ah, he still loved every fucking second of it. "Hey, Pop," Owen said, adjusting his Cross Creek baseball hat against the early morning chill as he approached their usual setup spot. "I see you're not wasting any time this morning." A pang of guilt expanded in his belly as he realized his father had already unloaded their bright red canvas tent and all the hardware that accompanied the thing.

"Don't see much sense in that," his father said. His gaze traveled over Owen's shoulder, his eyes crinkling around the edges. "And I see *you* brought help."

The back of Owen's neck prickled with unusual heat,

making his mouth default to his standard-issue gruffness. "She insisted."

"Owen," his father quietly warned, but Cate surprised them both with a laugh.

"Oh, it's okay, Mr. Cross. I'm used to Owen's charming personality. Anyway, he's not wrong. I did insist."

"I see." His father's tone suggested that he saw all too well, and Owen jammed his hands into the pockets of his canvas jacket, wishing for the conversation to endure a quick death.

"Well, in that case, we're right glad to have you, Cate." His father tipped the brim of his caramel-colored Stetson at her, showing off the source of Eli's charm and Hunter's even keel. If Cate still felt any unease at the prospect of the day ahead she didn't show it, giving up a smile and bending down to scratch the family mutt, Lucy, between the ears.

"It's the least I can do. I really appreciate you and Owen giving me a chance to come out and sell some of my baked goods at your tent today."

"Ah, something tells me it'll be a walk in the park for you, darlin'. That pound cake you made the other day was delicious. As good as Rosemary's, if I do say so."

Family and farm.

The casual mention of his mother, and the unexpected whisper of his memory, sent a whipcord of pain between Owen's ribs, the old wound aching as if it was freshly made.

They were about to officially kick off the season, potentially the best one they'd ever had. He should be focused. Working. Not standing around feeling things he couldn't control.

"We've got a lot to get done before the gates open at eight," he said, turning toward the box truck in an abrupt pivot. "I'm going to get started on the tent before we lose too much time."

"Oh." Cate blinked, and damn it, he was such an ass. "Right. I don't want to get in the way, so I'll just unload the crates from your truck and keep them over here until you've got the tent ready to go. Then I can set up while you unload the produce, if that works?"

"Sounds good."

With a clipped nod and a deep breath, Owen took advantage of the litany of tasks in front of him, keeping both his brain and his body busy as he ticked items off his mental list, one by one. He felt his father's eyes on him a little more sharply than usual, but thankfully, his old man didn't give the sideways glances voice. They spent the next hour getting everything ready to go from tent to tables, and, finally, the unease that had knotted both his muscles and his mind dissipated enough to allow a twinge of excitement back in.

"Hey," Cate said as he approached the area where she'd set up a rectangular folding table covered in a cheery gingham tablecloth and arranged all of her baked goods in a pretty yet straightforward display. "I think I'm all set up here. I've got a complete list of my inventory so I can keep track of sales as they're made. This is everything I could fit on the table, with all the extras in the bins underneath." She gestured to a sturdy plastic plate in front of her, filled with bite-sized versions of chocolate chip, sugar, and—ah, his weakness—oatmeal raisin cookies. "I made some smaller treats for people to sample. It seemed to work pretty well when Clementine did it at the diner, so..."

Owen nodded. God, she'd thought of everything. "That's a great idea. We do it sometimes, too, when things that are easy to eat out of hand are in season." Cracking open one watermelon to sell fifteen? So worth it.

"Oh. Good."

She tucked her hands into the pockets of her jeans, scraping the toe of one cross-trainer over the asphalt and biting her bottom lip just slightly as a weighty silence settled between them, and Owen's chin lifted a degree in surprise.

Holy shit. Headstrong Cate, with all her mettle and moxie and fire that lit him up like fireworks on the Fourth of July, was *nervous*.

He opened his mouth—to say what, he had no fucking clue—but his stomach sounded off in a low, rumbling growl that made body betrayal a very real thing.

A soft pop of laughter crossed Cate's lips. "Did you eat breakfast?"

Thoroughly busted, Owen admitted, "No. Truth be told, I get pretty excited for opening day. I must have forgotten."

"Hmmm." Reaching down low for one of the crates beneath the table, she unearthed a plastic storage container full of scones. "Savory or sweet?"

"Let's try savory," he said, his mouth involuntarily watering at the sight of the hearty golden triangle of dough she plucked out of the container and passed in his direction. His taste buds went for a full-on riot a second later as he took a bite.

"Damn." Another bite followed the first, his brain trying to process the perfectly balanced flavors and textures amid all the primal noises that wanted to shamelessly vault out of his mouth. "Did you put crack in these?"

"Close. Bacon," Cate said with a wry grin. "It went great with the chives from the greenhouse, so I couldn't resist. I made a batch of cheddar and rosemary, too."

Owen's mind spun, when his taste buds finally let go of it. "We should get these scones front and center by the herbs, in case folks want to grab some to eat for breakfast."

Cate's brows lifted. "Do you really think that'll happen?"

He polished off the rest of his scone in two bites flat. Holy hell, they were a flawless trifecta of dense, buttery, robust flavor. "I really think people would be crazy not to."

He grabbed two packages of scones while Cate did the same, and they walked the handful of paces beneath the tent to strategically place them near the wide, side-lying baskets overflowing with chives, rosemary, basil, and other assorted herbs he'd cut from the supply in the greenhouse yesterday afternoon. Across the triple-wide canopy tent, his father was deep in conversation with Lucas Clifton, who they'd hired as an extra hand for the season, but as far as setup went, they actually looked pretty good to go with about ten minutes to spare.

Cate looked at the baskets of herbs and crates of greens Hunter had spent a good part of yesterday afternoon cutting, weighing, and bagging. "So, tell me about some of this specialty produce."

"You want a tutorial on kale and collards?" Owen asked, and she lifted a slender brow in reply.

"I'm working the farmers' market with you, aren't I? Someone might have questions, so, yeah, Casanova. I want a tutorial on kale and collards and whatever else you've got here."

Damn, her moxie was bottomless. Also, incredibly hot.

Owen cleared his throat and turned toward the tables they'd set up along the perimeter of the canopy tent, with a few smaller ones in the center of the space to maximize their allotted square footage while still allowing for a good flow of foot traffic. "Most of our produce is pretty straightforward. Strawberries, asparagus, rhubarb, sweet onions, mixed greens."

His heart tapped faster, a familiar, intoxicating buzz

spreading out in his chest at the sight of the jewel-toned berries in their cardboard baskets and the thousand shades of green from the leeks to the baby spinach. "We're a little limited with what's available right now since it's still early in the season, but we're also lucky that the yield from our greenhouse has been high."

"Somehow, I doubt that's just luck," Cate said, but Owen lifted his shoulders in a shrug.

"A lot of variables go into it, and any one of them could make or break a crop. Soil composition, amount and type of fertilizers—"

Cate interrupted him with a laugh that, while brassy, carried no heat. "Come on, Owen. It's not all circumstance. Anyone with functional vision and half a brain can see how seriously you take the farm."

"I do," he said, the admission sliding out with ease. "Farming doesn't just feel like a job to me, though, you know? Not that it's not ball-busting work. But even on the hardest days, even when things go sideways and the weather turns and we lose crops or cattle, I still love it."

The excitement he'd been dancing with all morning spread out and strengthened, allowing the words to pour right out. "There's something...I don't know, vital about working the land with your hands. Watching each plant grow from this tiny little seed into something sustainable, something that comes directly from the earth the way nature intended it to. Like it shouldn't be possible, and yet, under the right circumstances, it happens without any effort at all. Just humble and real and right."

Owen looked up from the produce in front of them, Cate's wide, whiskey-colored stare tugging him out of his thoughts and making him realize how insane he probably sounded.

A hard shot of embarrassment sent heat over his face. *Jesus.* "Which, I'm sure, is probably the craziest thing you've heard in a while. But—"

"No. It's not."

The pared-down honesty on Cate's face sent a different feeling through Owen, one he couldn't quite pin with a name, but God, it felt frighteningly good. *I get it*, the look said. *I see you. I understand.*

She didn't actually speak the words, and hell if that didn't make the feeling in his gut—whatever the hell it was—that much stronger.

"So, how about these?" Cate asked, pointing to the small baskets of heirloom tomatoes, and, just like that, his comfort zone snapped right back into place.

"These are Cherokee purples. We've also got some Brandywines, and these here"—he paused just long enough to cradle one of the pretty, bright yellow tomatoes he'd plucked from the vine yesterday morning—"are Kellogg's Breakfast. They're all heirloom tomatoes."

"They look pretty wild." She ran her fingers over the fat, rippled curves of the tomato in his palm. "Are they all so different?"

Owen nodded. "Yep. I mean, I can almost always tell what variety a tomato is just by looking; and by taste, I'm even more accurate. But each one of these babies is as unique as a signature. You never know how they'll turn out."

"Sounds like baking." A wry smile played at the edges of her mouth, making her so much more beautiful than even a full-wattage, pose-for-the-camera variety would. "I could put together the same recipe a thousand times and the yield is always a little different. I don't think anyone can tell but me, but...I can."

"You know your stuff," he said, his pulse speeding up as Cate's smile bloomed into a laugh.

"And clearly, you know yours."

A flash of movement grabbed his attention from over her shoulder, making him grin down at her as he said, "Well, that's a good thing, because it looks like the gates just opened up. So what do you say we go knock opening day out of the park?"

CATE SHOULD'VE BEEN NERVOUS. No. That wasn't quite right. She should've been curled up in a ball on the asphalt, rocking back and forth and channeling all of her will into not throwing up.

But she wasn't. Not that her calm had much to do with her at all. From the minute Owen had opened up about farming, to the sexy stunner of a grin he'd given her when the gates opened, to now, two hours and a steady stream of customers later, Cate had been able to breathe for one reason, and one reason only.

And he was standing ten feet away, looking as intense and as gorgeous as ever.

"Cate? Is that you?" came a kind, familiar voice from across the table, and she dialed up a smile to—*please, God, let it work*—cover up the dark and naughty thoughts that had been having a field day with her brain.

"Hi, Mrs. Ellersby. Would you like to try a cookie this morning?" Cate offered the plate of samples to the elderly woman, who politely took a bite-sized sugar cookie.

"I'd heard you were working down at Cross Creek, helping them out with their books and such. Such nice boys, those Crosses."

Cate followed the woman's gaze over to Owen, who was re-stocking leeks and spring onions with all the seriousness of brain surgery. "Yes, ma'am," she murmured, although *nice* didn't even make the top ten of words she'd use to describe Owen. Not that she'd expect any of those to make Mrs. Ellersby's list, either.

"Balancing the books for such a big farm can't be easy," Mrs. Ellersby said, peering over the rims of her glasses. "I always knew you had a good head on those shoulders."

Shock pinged through Cate's chest at the words, and the same sentiment showed on Mrs. Ellersby's face a second later as she tasted her cookie.

"Well, my land! Cate McAllister, did you make these?"

Cate nodded hesitantly. "Yes, ma'am."

Mrs. Ellersby fluttered a hand over the front of her blouse, taking another bite. "I didn't know you could bake like this. These cookies are soft as a pillow!"

"Thank you," Cate said, the back of her neck heating even though she was under the full protection of the canopy tent. "I had a lot of help from the Crosses. All the herbs, fruit, and eggs that I baked with came right from their farm."

"Sounds like a match made in heaven," Mrs. Ellersby clucked, picking up a package of sugar cookies. "I've just got to take some of these home with me. They'll be perfect with my afternoon tea."

"Enjoy them," Cate said, marking the sale on her inventory sheet as Mrs. Ellersby smiled and continued on to the rest of the tables beneath the tent. Cate had kept a careful tally of the money she'd spent on ingredients and materials, along with the inventory she'd used from Cross Creek's greenhouse and henhouse, and the hours she'd spent in the kitchen. Paying Owen back every dime of that advance was priority number one, and from the look of the list right now, she'd already turned enough profit to do so with ease. If things kept up, those earnings would amount to not only the ability to make a healthy mortgage payment, but also a litany of "I told you so"s from Owen.

Which would also present her with one hell of a quandary, she realized with dread. If she was actually successful selling her baked goods, she wouldn't have any logical reason not to keep doing so on a regular basis.

Not that the reason she hadn't taken the plunge before now had ever been sensible to begin with. But it was the only thing she felt more deeply than her ingrained sense of practicality. The only thing that followed her like a shadow, just waiting for the darkness to settle in so it could become stronger, growing teeth and claws that sliced to the bone.

Jesus, Cate! You're putting your hobby in front of our kid?

Oh, God, what was she doing? This dream wasn't for her. It couldn't be. Not now. Not ever.

The ache she'd felt for far too long thudded hollowly through her veins, and, for a slice of a second, she nearly gave in to the deep temptation to run. Owen's voice stopped her in her tracks, though, filtering in from the spot where he now stood a few paces away. His back was fully to her, and she edged closer on legs that weren't quite under her command.

"Ah, that fennel is a good choice. It's coming in even better than last year," he said to Jenny Porter, whose back was also mostly to her as well. "We've got some great-looking rosemary, too."

"Oooh, rosemary," Jenny gushed. "My favorite. I'd put it in everything if Mike wouldn't make fun of me for it."

"Bet you'd love Cate's rosemary and cheddar scones, then." Owen pointed to the package sitting on top of the wooden crate full of assorted herbs in front of them, and Cate's heart pounded against her rib cage so hard, she was sure the sound of it would give her away.

"Scones, huh?" Jenny's voice lilted higher in interest. "They look great."

Owen's dark hair brushed over the back of his neck as he nodded. "They are great. I had one of the bacon and chive ones for breakfast, myself."

"Quite the seal of approval. I'm sold," Jenny said, scooping up the package with one hand and a bunch of fresh rosemary with the other. Cate slipped back to the periphery of the tent just in time as Owen walked Jenny to the opposite side of the space so his father could ring her up, and she watched him covertly, replaying the conversation in her mind. For all of his sharp corners and rough edges, Owen was unapologetically himself. He worked honestly and hard, doing what he loved, and a spike of jealousy stuck between Cate's ribs.

She'd wanted that once, so badly she'd been able to taste her ambition, spicy and deep like a hit of cinnamon.

It's not for you.

But that's stupid, came a whisper from somewhere in the back of her brain, in a voice that wasn't hers, and her breath caught on the realization that it wasn't wrong. Owen took his business seriously. He wouldn't have hired her, and he *definitely* wouldn't have said those things about her baking if he didn't believe in her ability.

And as she watched him from across the tent, with his serious smile and unabashed dedication to the legacy that fit him like a fingerprint, Cate couldn't help but wonder if she shouldn't take a risk and start believing in it, too.

17

Owen made it exactly four minutes through the drive back to Millhaven before he couldn't hold back any longer.

"Admit it," he said, glancing sidelong at Cate from the driver's seat of his truck. "You kicked ass today."

She pressed her lips together, although it did damn little to kill her smile, and hah! He had her.

"It killed you to wait this long to say that, didn't it?" she asked. "Like, I'm betting it caused you actual physical pain."

"*Brutal* physical pain," Owen corrected, even though he knew damned well he wasn't so much pushing his luck as shoving it off a cliff. "Which is why I'm going to need to hear you say it out loud."

Okay, so it wasn't usually in his nature to gloat unless his brothers and some serious bragging rights were involved. But between the adrenaline-laced buzz of the start of the season, the upward trending success Cross Creek had seen over the past six months, and how thoroughly Cate's sales had to have surpassed the profit threshold they'd calculated last night, he just couldn't manage to rein himself in.

Which she must have sensed, because she laughed and said, "Fine. I sold a lot more than I expected to."

Christ almighty, she was tough on herself. "We're going to have to work on your confidence between now and when the storefront opens."

"What about Cross Creek?" she asked after a beat, looking out the window. "You seemed to move a lot of produce today."

A bit of an abrupt subject change, but not one Owen hated. "We did, actually. We'll have to run the numbers and the inventory on Monday for exact counts, but at first blush, it looks like our best opening day in the last few years."

"Sounds like I'm not the only one who should be singing her own praises," Cate said, and despite only being able to spare her a quick glance because he was driving, he still caught her wry smile right in the solar plexus.

"Okay, okay, okay!" He lifted one hand off the steering wheel in concession, laughing along with her. "We *both* kicked ass today."

"So." She gestured to the mid-afternoon scenery flying past the windows, all bathed in muted sunlight. "Are we officially off the clock, then?"

Owen nodded. She was probably dying for a break, with how hard she'd worked over the past three days. "Yes, ma'am. It seems we are."

"Excellent. How do you feel about sex?"

His heart boomeranged through his chest. "I'm...sorry?" he sputtered. Certainly, he was hearing things. Because no way in hell had Cate just asked—

"How do you feel about sex? Specifically, having sex with me."

Holy *shit*, she had. "I, ah. Should probably buy you dinner first."

Cate met his weak attempt at humor with a shake of her head. "You could, but it's really not necessary. Look, you said the ball was in my court, right?"

"I did," Owen said slowly, still trying to get his brain around the conversation.

Cate, however? Seemed to have no problem whatsoever in that department as she continued, "And we're two consenting adults who are attracted to each other."

Fuck, yeah we are! Stop overthinking this and take off your pants! his libido screamed, but he managed to go with a slightly more subdued, "Yes."

"Okay, then. I'm free tonight, if that works for you."

Owen laughed, because the alternative was to pull over and take her up on her proposition right there on the side of the goddamn road. "You really do get right to it, don't you?"

"I don't see any reason not to," Cate said, her voice hitching by the slightest degree when she added, "Unless you're not interested."

"Oh, believe me. I'm interested." The words came out low and covered in gravel, and Owen swallowed to regain his steadiness. "But, see, I've got these pesky manners, so I'm going to have to insist on that dinner."

She made a sound that was some cross between an exhale and a chuff of laughter. "That's sweet of you, but I really don't need that."

"Maybe not, but I do."

Owen caught the look of shock that crossed her face a heartbeat later, and it prompted a smile over his lips. "What? You thought this was going to be all about what you need? I mean, I'm happy to oblige." Okay, so *happy* didn't even begin to cover it, but now wasn't the time to fuss over semantics. "But if you want to have sex with me, you're going to have to meet me halfway."

"Alright," Cate said, her seat belt shushing softly over her T-shirt as she turned toward him more fully from the passenger seat. "Name your stipulations."

Well, at least the first one would be easy. "One, we're not talking about sex like it's a business transaction. I get that you like everything on the table, but I'm making requests, not rules."

"Okay. I guess I got carried away with 'stipulations'." She bit her lip, and Owen forced himself to focus on the road.

"Request number two, you let me feed you dinner. And, no," he said in a pre-emptive strike, "driving through at a fast food place or throwing back three bites of something doesn't count."

Cate's laugh came out edged in guilt. "That's fair. We haven't really had a proper meal today. Anything else?"

Owen paused. This would be the kicker, he knew, but it didn't stop him from saying, "Just one more thing. If we do this, I want you to stay the night."

"Owen—"

"Hear me out," he said gently, even though his pulse was rattling through him like a freight train. He might be gruff with her over a lot of things, and he might tease her about some others, but this had to be straight-up. "I know what you're asking me for, here, and, more importantly, what you're not asking me for. We're on the same page. But this one's a deal-breaker for me, Cate. We don't have to put any strings on the sex, but if we spend tonight in bed together, that's where I want us to wake up. After that, what you do is up to you."

A minute passed with nothing but the white noise of the road whooshing by around them. Just when Owen started to think he'd pushed too hard, Cate gave up an almost imperceptible nod.

"That's not unreasonable."

"Okay," he said, his heart beating faster for a whole new reason. "So, dinner tonight at my place. How does six thirty sound?"

He looked over just in time to catch her cat-in-cream grin, and damn, the next couple of hours couldn't go fast enough.

"Six thirty sounds great. I'll be sure to bring dessert."

TRUE TO OWEN'S SUSPICIONS, the time that had passed from their ride back to Millhaven and the minute the clock on his microwave struck six thirty had moved at a glacial pace. Not that he hadn't had plenty of things to keep him busy— taking a shower had been a definite must, as had putting clean sheets on his bed, making triple-sure he had plenty of condoms, and assembling everything he needed to make his signature spaghetti and meatballs for dinner. Even with his trip into town to grab a bottle of pinot noir from The Corner Market, he'd still ended up counting nearly every one of the last thirty minutes.

Christ. With all this anticipation, he wanted Cate so badly she just might get the fast path to sex that she'd asked for.

No, Owen thought at the same time a knock sounded off from the front of his house. They might have agreed not to attach any commitments to tonight, but he could still do this properly. Go slow. Take all the steps to ensure she'd enjoy herself.

But then Owen opened the door, and screw proper.

He wanted to do things to this woman that would make

her forget her name, then remind her who she was just so he could do them all over again.

"Hi," Cate said, her red-lipsticked mouth curving into a smile that made his cock stir against the fly of his jeans. She'd ditched her braids—a fact Owen would mourn if she hadn't replaced them with a loose, sultry twist that rested just behind her right ear. Her plain white button-down blouse was anything but plain on her body, with its short, fitted sleeves and fabric-covered buttons undone just low enough to give up a glimpse of her cleavage, surrounded by—good *Christ*—just a hint of a lacy, powder-blue bra. She wasn't wearing her slim black pants so much as surrendering her curves to the material that hugged her hips and legs before stopping mid-calf, and from her head to the poppy-red toes peeking out from her high-heeled sandals, Cate McAllister took his damned breath away.

"Hi," Owen made himself say, because the lift of her brows told him he'd already waited a beat too long to reply. "Ah, come on in."

"Thanks. Here's dessert, as promised." She tipped her chin at the foil-wrapped plate that he just now noticed she had balanced between her palms, her heels tapping a delicate riot on the hardwoods as she crossed the threshold.

He should have known better than to think she'd meant it metaphorically when she said she'd bring dessert. "You really didn't have to bake anything," he said, taking the plate from her and leading the way to the kitchen.

Her laughter spilled past her lips, so open and honest that it eased Owen's adrenaline-fueled nerves.

"I'm sorry, have we met?" she asked, coming to a stop at the island. "I had almost three hours to kill and all I could think about was sex. Of *course,* I needed to bake something.

Anyway, since you're so intent on feeding me, I'm really just returning the favor."

Owen laughed, too, his curiosity getting the better of his mouth. "What did you make?"

"Chocolate lava cake. You?"

Nice. "Spaghetti and meatballs."

Cate closed her eyes and inhaled, her breasts swelling perilously close to the deep *V* of her neckline, and, fuck, she was stunning.

"Tell me you made the sauce from scratch," she said, her lashes fluttering as she opened her eyes.

He let one side of his mouth kick up into a half-smile. "There's no other way to make sauce."

"You know, I'm starting to not regret this dinner-first thing."

Her words snared his attention, re-setting his determination to take the evening slow. "I did nearly all of the prep ahead of time. The sauce and the meatballs are done, but they can simmer for hours, so just say the word when you're hungry, and I'll put the water on for the pasta. In the meantime, do you want a glass of wine?"

"I'd like a gallon of it." Cate capped her reply with a tart laugh, and even though he didn't stop smiling, he also shook his head.

"You're determined to rush this, aren't you?" he asked, taking the bottle of pinot noir from the fridge.

Her brows furrowed. "I agreed to dinner," she pointed out.

"You did." Owen paused to grab two wine glasses from the cabinet where he kept them, then the corkscrew from a drawer in the island. Cate might balk at his next question, but still, something made him ask, "Are you going to enjoy it, though?"

"It smells fantastic," she said slowly, her guard inching up. "I'm sure I will."

Yep. It was time to start speaking her language. "You don't eat."

She barked out a laugh, but there—*there* it was, the wall he'd bet she didn't even know she'd put up. "Of course, I eat."

"No, you don't." Calmly, methodically, Owen removed the foil from the top of the wine bottle, sliding the corkscrew into place. "Not the way you should."

"Okay, fine," she said, taking the glass he offered her a minute later. "So, I maybe have a thing for junky cereal on occasion, and I can't say I've never turned wine and Doritos into a meal. But it's only a couple times a year. Nothing to get judgy over."

Owen lifted his glass of wine, clinking it against hers. "I'm not talking about *what* you eat, although I might judge you a little for the wine and Doritos, because, ugh."

"Okay, then what *are* you talking about?"

"I'm talking about the way you eat. Or, more specifically, the way you don't."

Cate took a large sip from her glass, arching a brow at him. "You're not making any sense, you know."

"And you're not slowing down to enjoy what's on your plate."

Ah, that got her. "I am, too."

"Okay," Owen said, putting just enough mustard on the words to turn them into a dare. "Prove it."

Without waiting for her to reply, he moved back to the refrigerator, tugging the door open for a quick search. Come on, come on, there had to be—*yes*. Perfect. He pulled the cardboard container full of the strawberries he'd washed and hulled earlier off the shelf and placed it on the island in front of Cate.

"You want me to eat some strawberries?" she asked with a laugh. "That's not exactly a hardship."

She plucked one from the top of the pile and went to pop it into her mouth. But Owen reached across the island to capture her wrist, stilling her movements and speeding up his heartbeat.

"Uh-uh," he said, rubbing one finger over the soft skin on her inner wrist, right where her pulse jumped. "Eyes first."

"I'm sorry?"

The question rode out on a velvety exhale, and Owen had to tamp down the hard, hot urge to say screw everything else and kiss her.

Focus. "The other night, when you were baking, you said people eat with their eyes first, right?"

She nodded, a tendril of hair falling loose to frame her face. "Yes."

"So, do it."

Keeping his fingers circled around her wrist, he reached for the strawberry with his other hand. She gave it over freely, watching as he held the sun-ripened fruit between his thumb and forefinger. He kept it steady just long enough to create anticipation, letting her gaze move from the strawberry back to his eyes before continuing.

"You can taste it, right? In your mind." Owen lowered her wrist, keeping his eyes steady on hers as he rounded the island to stand directly in front of her. "The way the flavors will burst over your tongue, sweet and citrusy, with just enough bite to make it perfect."

"Mmm hmm." Cate's murmur came out as thick and decadent as honey. His breath tightened in his lungs, daring him again to forget the food, to forget everything that didn't involve stripping Cate naked right here in his kitchen and fucking her until she came undone, but he refused to give in. She needed this more than sex.

And he needed to give it to her.

18

C ate stood perfectly still even though her body was vibrating with enough want to steal her breath. Less than an arm's length separated her from Owen, yet she was keenly aware of the distance, of the fact that he wasn't touching her, just standing inches away with that strawberry in his hand like a dare she was dying to take. The way his callused fingers gripped the delicate fruit with both intention and care sent a shiver over her, and oh, God, how would a touch like that feel on her nipples, which were now tight peaks behind the lace of her bra? What would it do to the sensitive skin on her thighs, or deep in the spot where they came together, where she ached to have him most?

"Go on," Owen said, his voice low and rough. "Taste."

She opened her mouth at the same time he lifted the strawberry to her lips. The berry was perfectly sized, and she closed her lips over it and started to chew. Flavors rushed over her tongue, first sweet, then heady and slightly tart, and the more she chewed, the more she wanted.

Please. Please, make me feel good.

Cate gulped down the bite, greedy for another. But Owen didn't move, just made a noise that was part protest, part something else she couldn't name yet still found unbelievably hot.

"No." He grabbed another strawberry, running the soft curve of the fruit over the edge of her lower lip. "Don't eat it. *Taste* it."

"What's the difference?"

God, she should feel self-conscious at how she sounded, so full of breath and need. But then Owen's pupils flared, filling his gray stare with a darkness that sent a jolt from her belly to her clit, and she held on to his stare even though she knew what he'd see when he looked at her.

"Tasting it is an experience," he said, holding the strawberry over her lips. "You focus on the flavors. The feel of the food on your tongue, the vitality of it. When you taste something—*really* taste it—you're surrendering to the flavors. You're letting yourself enjoy it. That's the difference."

Cate bit into the second strawberry without thinking twice. A moan caught in the back of her throat, and oh, God, how could such a simple experience make her feel so much?

"Oh," she whispered. Looking up, she realized how carefully Owen had been watching her. He stood close enough for her to feel the heat of his body, to see the tension humming in the hard, roughhewn muscles beneath his T-shirt and jeans, and, impulsively, she reached up to touch his face.

"What about you? Aren't you hungry, too?" she asked, her heart pounding faster as his heated exhale filled the scant space between his chest and the rise of her breasts.

"Oh, I'm plenty hungry, sweetheart. But the only thing I plan on tasting tonight is you."

Cate pressed forward to kiss him, but he was already

there, pulling her close and slanting his mouth over hers. Their lips crashed together, parting in a tangle of tongues so deliciously hot, she nearly cried out. Searching desperately, she latched on to Owen's upper lip, holding it between her own for one decadent second before gliding her tongue along his smooth, soft skin. But as quickly as she'd taken the lead, he took it right back, hooking his fingers in her hair to hold her steady as he turned her back to the island and pushed deeper into her mouth. He kissed her hard, but without urgency, as if he had an endless well of intensity and the only thing he wanted was to focus it on her. Their tongues slid together, lips tugging and taking and tasting in an erotic back and forth that sent a tremble through Cate's belly that quickly became a demand.

"Owen." His name spilled from her mouth as he parted from her lips, trailing a firm, hot path of kisses over her jaw to her neck. Cate reached for the hem of his T-shirt, surprise sparking through her chest when not only did he not protest, but he lifted his arms over his head to help her pull the thing off in one quick yank.

Whoa. She'd already known his body was gorgeous, thanks to the T-shirt mishap/miracle on her first day of work. But this close up, with his tanned skin and work-sculpted muscles and the dusting of dark hair leading from his chest to all points south, Owen was a work of freaking art.

Cate reached out to touch him, but she realized—too late—that he'd maneuvered his hands over her hips, angling closer to bring their bodies completely flush. Even in her heels, he still had a good four inches on her, which gave him the perfect leverage to splay his fingers over her ass and lift her to the countertop with ease.

"Oh!" she exclaimed at the same time he murmured,

"That's better." The change in vantage point brought his mouth in line with her collarbone, and he transferred his grip to her hips, hauling her close as he settled between her thighs.

"These freckles are incredibly sexy," Owen said, tracing a finger from the hollow at the base of her throat into the deep *V* of her blouse.

Her nipples tightened at the nearness of his touch and how badly she wanted him there, but still, she managed to laugh. "Are you serious? They're *freckles.*" In truth, she'd always hated them.

The edges of Owen's mouth moved just enough to hint at a smile, taking the tightness of her nipples to a needy tingle. "I'm always serious, remember?"

Leaning in, he pressed his lips to her neck, sliding the edge of his tongue from one spot to the next, tasting her just as he'd promised.

"Oh." *Goddddd.* Cate's head fell back. "Okay, maybe they're sexy after all."

"They're definitely sexy," he said, his lips parting over her skin in a wicked smile she both saw and felt. "I've been dying to find them all for weeks now."

Her heartbeat shifted from the steady pound of arousal to a pang of pure surprise. "You have?"

Owen pulled back to pin her with a stormy gray stare, his eyes glinting in the soft, pink-gold sunlight around them. "You really don't know how stunning you are, do you?"

Cate drew in a sharp breath. In all her life, no one had ever used that word to describe her. Yet standing here, all hot and bothered in the middle of his kitchen, when Owen looked at her, that's what he saw.

Hooking a finger under her chin, he tilted her face up

until their gazes met. Held. "That's okay," he said, brushing a kiss over her lips. "I'm going to show you."

And *oh*, he did. One by one, Owen freed the buttons on her blouse, each rustle of the fabric sending heightened want through her body. Finally, thankfully, he reached the last one, sliding his hands between the two sections of fabric to part them over her body.

"Christ," he bit out. But the curse was reverent, more like a benediction than a swear, and he slid his thumbs over the satiny straps of her bra. "Your body is perfect."

The irony caught Cate right in the center of her chest, so hard she nearly balked. The reality was, her body was far from perfect. Silvery stretch marks she'd kept covered for years, the C-section scar she'd earned by default, all of it had always made her a lights-down-low kind of girl.

But when Owen said she was perfect, she believed him. Even if it was just for this moment, this night. Right now.

Cate let go of a shaky exhale, letting him look his fill. "Then take it," she said with a defiant lift of her chin.

His laugh moved through her like a living, breathing thing. "Are you sure that's what you want?"

"Do you think I'd ask for it if I wasn't?"

"No," Owen said. Still, he shifted back to put some space between them—not much, just enough for her to see the seriousness in his stare—and she hooked her legs around his hips to haul him right back in.

"I'm very, very sure," Cate murmured against his lips, "that if you don't keep undressing me, I'm going to lose my mind."

"Ah." He kissed her deeply, just once before his fingers found the lacy edges of her bra. "That's where you're wrong. Because I'm going to keep undressing you." He slid her shirt from her shoulders as proof. "And *then* you're going to lose your mind."

Owen dropped his mouth back to her neck, and, just like that, she was lost. His fingers—clever things—hooked beneath her bra straps, moving them just far enough out of the way for him to kiss an unimpeded path from her neck to her shoulder, then the flat expanse of her upper chest. Cate's mind spun, the voice that always told her she wasn't meant for things like this lurking in the periphery of her thoughts, and she closed her eyes to try and stay in the moment.

Owen froze into place, his lips just above the curve of one breast. "Cate. Open your eyes."

"What?" she asked, blinking down at him in confusion.

"Eyes first, remember?" He raked his gaze to the spot where his mouth hovered over the hardened outline of her nipple behind the powder-blue lace, waiting for her to follow suit before saying, "Leave them open and watch. See how beautiful you are."

The idea was so provocative, so deliciously dark and dirty, that it sent a thrill all the way through her. Her position on the counter offered a perfect view of Owen's dark head, his strong, firm mouth, his callused fingers on her achingly sensitive skin, and she nodded, keeping her eyes wide. Lowering her chin, Cate watched as he splayed one hand beneath her rib cage, reaching between her shoulder blades with the other to release her bra with an economical turn of his wrist. Owen swept the lace away from her body, moving the hand on her rib cage up at the same time his mouth moved down.

A noise came from the back of his throat, primal and low. Cupping her breast to hold her steady, he closed his lips over her nipple, and the warm, wet friction made her moan.

"*Ah.*" Cate's hands found his bare shoulders, her nails

curving into his skin. But despite the sensations sailing through her and the fact that they should make her feel vulnerable, she watched. Arousal grew, hot in her belly, as Owen gripped her tightly and began to suck. He alternated slow, open-mouthed kisses with hard, fast swirls of his tongue, repeating both until her body was pulsing with pleasure and want. Her clit throbbed, her pussy clenching with the building need to have his cock buried between her legs, yet she couldn't tear her eyes from what he was doing to her, from how it made her feel.

And Owen refused to rush. He worked her body with his mouth and hands, licking and tasting and taking and giving, until finally, he pulled back to look at her.

"See?" His fingers skimmed her breasts, then the top of her waist, his smile growing dark at the sight of her nipples, dark pink and glistening from the attention of his mouth. "Fucking beautiful."

"I want more," Cate said, her body humming like a live wire, full of energy in need of a place to go. "Please, Owen. Show me more."

As quickly as he'd lifted her to the countertop earlier, he unseated her, his arms around her until her feet found purchase on the hardwood floor. He moved with purpose, his muscles bunching and releasing as he reached for the button on her pants.

Her sex grew slick, even as her belly tightened at the renewed potential for vulnerability. But just as she'd been hypnotized by the sight of Owen's mouth on her breasts, her heart quickly pounded in excitement at the *prrrrrrp* of her zipper, the way his pupils dilated at the slide of the fabric moving lower, lower. Cate kicked out of her sandals, then her pants, leaving her in nothing but the pale blue panties that had been in the far reaches of her top drawer for half a decade. Her eyes registered the imperfections—the starker-than-normal jut of her hip bones, the stretch marks, the faded scar that lined up with the top of the lace. But what she *saw* was Owen's expression, and, in that moment, everything else fell away.

"Still sure?" he asked quietly.

She nodded before both words were all the way out. "Still sure."

His mouth quirked with seductive intention. "Good," he said.

And then he hit his knees.

"God, just look at you," Owen murmured. His gaze lit over her panties, which were level with his line of sight, his breath hot on her skin. A whimper worked at Cate's throat, ragged and needy, but she forced herself to swallow it, to feel everything about the moment she was in.

Owen didn't make it difficult. He dragged a finger over the seam of her pussy, the friction from the lace sending sparks across her vision, and her hips tilted, chasing his touch.

He did it again, then again, and oh, God, she was going to come before he got the damned things off her body.

"Owen," she said, part plea, part curse.

"Don't worry. I hear you." Slipping his fingers under the strings at her hips, he pulled the lace all the way off, leaving her completely bare. "Keep those eyes on me, beautiful. I'll show you everything."

Then his mouth was on her, and Cate lost the ability to breathe, let alone see.

"Mmm." Owen's voice rumbled, heightening the tension deep between her hips. Her lips parted on a soundless gasp, her body arching into his touch, and he held nothing back. Angling his shoulders between her thighs, he explored her

pussy with his lips and tongue. His fingers joined the movements a minute later, gently testing, stroking, lighting her
up. Cate's clit pulsed with the demand to be touched, even
as pleasure coursed through her from his other ministrations. Owen slid his tongue up, over her sex, and she rocked
her hips to get him where she needed him to be.

"*There*," Cate cried out, pleasure bursting through her
first at the contact, then again at the sight of his wicked
smile, buried between her legs. Owen didn't balk at being
given direction. Instead, he took full advantage, pressing his
tongue against her clit for a hard glide that tore a moan
from her throat.

And still, she watched.

Turning her chin against her chest, Cate fastened her
eyes on him as he pleasured her, stroke by stroke. His strong
hands bracketed her hips, one shoulder pushing up just
enough on her inner thigh to lift her foot from the floor,
and, oh. Oh, God, she'd never felt so good or needed so
fucking much. He tasted and licked, his tongue thrusting
inside once, then twice, before he returned to her clit. Uncut
sensation sang in her veins, her need coiling and doubling
and growing unbearably hot between her hips. Owen met it
with every movement, and she lowered a hand to the back
of his head, knotting her fingers in his hair. Release built,
powerful and bright in Cate's belly, yet still, she didn't close
her eyes.

She felt powerful. Sexy. Alive.

She felt *everything*.

Her orgasm ripped through her, bringing her breath to a
standstill and her back to a full arch against the counter.
Owen worked her through each wave, kissing and stroking
every last tremble from her before softening his touch and
eventually pulling back to look at her. For a minute that

could have been two, or even twenty, they stared at each other, chests moving up and down, eyes wide. Then Owen stood, grabbed her hand, and turned toward the hallway.

"What are you doing?" Cate blurted, her brain trying desperately to function.

He shot her a glance over his shoulder. His wicked smile was back in all its glory, his gray eyes glinting with intention that had the heat between her legs rebuilding in an instant.

"After that? I'm taking you upstairs to my bed, where I can fuck you good and proper. Now, are you coming, or do I have to pick you up and carry you?"

"Are you kidding?" She laughed. "I'll race you to the goddamned stairs."

They moved through his hallway—thank God for curtains and remote country living—stopping a few times along the way for some slow kisses that made Cate's heart race. They made it to his room in a tangle of arms and legs and mouths, and he led her to his bed, easing her over the dark blue quilt and settling between her thighs.

"Oh, no you don't." Palming his shoulders, Cate hooked a leg over his hip, switching their positions in a less than a breath.

Owen's eyes flared. "Cate—"

"Shh." She silenced him with a firm brush of her lips, shifting back until she straddled his thighs. "I want you, too, Owen. So shut up and let me have you."

He stared at her, but only for a second before his hands lifted in concession. Cate's pulse knocked at her throat, and, oh, she didn't want to wait. Reaching out, she ran her fingers over the top of his jeans, the soft cotton a complete contradiction to the hard muscles beneath it. Owen's stare followed her touch, and the intensity in his eyes made her even bolder. She undid the top button, undressing him in quick motions until they were both naked on his bed.

"*Oh.*" It was, of course, an understatement. Cate had thought the corded muscles shaping Owen's midsection were sexy, but clearly, she hadn't even known the definition of the word. His hips were lean, ridges and valleys of honey-colored skin suggesting latent power. A trail of dark hair arrowed from his navel downward, his cock jutting proudly over his lower belly, and, God, he was the hottest, most provocative thing she had ever seen.

She slid her fingers over his abs, her breath growing thicker in her lungs at the way his muscles jumped in reply. Arousal stirred, no longer a whisper in her core, and Cate moved lower, letting her hand find his cock.

Owen exhaled, his hands turning to fists at his sides. Still, his gaze didn't waver. He watched as she wrapped her fingers around him, testing different movements and measuring the best ones by the sound of his breathing. His hips lifted off the mattress to guide her, but after less than a minute, he grabbed her wrist with a soft curse.

"Cate," he said, shaking his head when she opened her mouth to protest. "We aren't going to be here much longer if you don't stop. And I'd really, really like to be here longer if that's okay with you."

The look on his face said he was actually asking, that if she argued in earnest, he'd give her what she wanted, exactly how she wanted it.

But she wanted more.

Cate let go and shifted forward to kiss him. "I want *you*, Owen. I don't want to wait."

He was out from beneath her in a heartbeat. Turning toward his bedside table, he grabbed a condom, putting it on with a quick, careful glide. She lay back on the quilt, letting Owen settle between her thighs. He ran a fingertip over her sex, lingering on her clit for just a stroke, then slipping inside her with ease. The sensation made her inner muscles squeeze, giving both the sense of fullness and the promise for more. The blunt head of his cock followed his finger, and Cate couldn't wait. She angled her hips to take him deeper, but he was already there, pushing inside with one swift thrust.

"Holy..." Owen sent the word through his teeth, his hands gripping the quilt by her shoulders.

"I know," she breathed. The pressure between her legs felt almost too much to bear, so intense and darkly good. She shifted, just a tiny movement back, and when he pressed forward to fill her again, Cate cut out a moan.

"Just don't stop."

He didn't. Drawing back, Owen balanced his weight between his hands and his knees, thrusting into her in slow, long movements. The back and forth became a rhythm, and Cate set her hands on his hips, rocking along with him to meet it. He leaned in, his chest providing just enough friction on her nipples to tempt her to scream.

"Cate," he said, placing his forehead on hers, his lips just over her lips. "Watch. Watch how pretty you are when you come."

Owen moved back, redistributing his weight to his knees. The change in angle let him find some hidden spot inside her pussy, his cock stroking it and daring her closer to release with every pump of his hips.

"*Look.*"

The word was rough-edged and covered in gravel, and Cate was powerless against it. Dipping her chin, she fixed her eyes on the spot where their bodies joined, and the primal intimacy of what she saw sent her over the edge. She came with a keening cry, bowing up to let Owen fill her over and over again. His movements grew more intense, his breath sawing past his lips.

"Ah, *fuck*," he grunted, his jaw like granite. With one last thrust, he filled her to the hilt, his body shuddering as he buried himself deep and came.

Cate's heartbeat was the first thing that registered, although how much later, she didn't know. The soft press of it against her eardrums served as the soundtrack for everything else as her body came back online—breath, muscles, hearing. Owen shifted off of her, then into the bathroom for a minute. Emotions lurked in the periphery of her mind like shadows, and she wasn't naïve enough to think she could keep them at bay.

A man like Owen Cross isn't for you. Keep your stupid heart to yourself, for both your sakes.

But then Owen lay down bedside her, his body warm and his mouth on hers in a soft, sweet press, and even though Cate knew this feeling couldn't last, she pushed the voice aside for just a little while longer.

19

Owen spent fifteen minutes trying to figure out what to say before he threw in the towel. He'd run through everything from "so, how about this weather we've been having?" to "that was the most mind-blowing sex I've ever had in my life", and while the latter was startlingly true, he didn't want to give Cate a reason to tack her guard back into place. Lying here with her, their bodies warm and spilled together in the evening shadows, felt as good as the sex they'd just shared, although in a different sort of way, and if he opened his gruff, graceless mouth, her willingness to let herself feel it might fade along with the daylight.

She shifted against him, her stomach letting out a healthy growl, and Owen gave up a soft, surprised laugh. "Are you hungry?"

"Maybe." Cate laughed quietly back. "We did kind of skip dinner."

It had been worth every second, but he stood by what he'd said earlier about her not tasting her food, and he damn sure still wanted to feed her. "I don't mean to brag, but

I have it on good authority that my spaghetti and meatballs are a bit of a religious experience."

"Is that so?"

"It is," he confirmed, making sure his smile hung in his voice. He might not know what to say or how to say it, but food? Now *that*, he could do.

But Cate didn't move from her spot on his bed. "I need to be sure this is still no strings attached, Owen. I'm not..." She exhaled against his shoulder. "I promised you I'd stay, so I will, but I can't give you anything other than this."

A pang centered in his chest. The last thing he wanted was for her to gather up her clothes and run, but she'd given him the courtesy of uncut honesty. The least he could do was be truthful in return.

"Look. We had sex—"

"*Great* sex," Cate corrected, and, despite the gravity of the topic, Owen had to smile.

"Definitely great sex," he agreed. "And I do really want you to stay. But I'm not going to pressure you into it, or anything else. We still have that honesty policy, right?"

She nodded, her hair shushing against the bed sheets. "We do."

"So, let's use it. I like being with you, Cate. It doesn't have to be anything serious. We can take each day as it dawns if that's what you need. I just want this."

After a heartbeat, then two, her body relaxed against his. "Well, then. With a promise like religious-experience spaghetti and meatballs, how can I refuse dinner?"

Since her clothes were still strewn all over his kitchen floor and a chill had crept into the nighttime air, Owen gave her a flannel shirt from his closet. The thing pretty much swallowed her, with the red and blue fabric covering her fingers and draping her body to mid-thigh, but she looked as comfortable in it as he felt in the jeans he'd just slid back over his hips. Deciding to forego a shirt—at least for now—he led the way back to the kitchen, flipping on enough lights to cast a warm, golden glow around what was probably his favorite room in the house.

"Can I do anything to help?" Cate asked after picking up her clothes, folding some and replacing others, most notably, the pale blue panties that he'd had to fight himself not to literally rip from her hips less than an hour ago.

Focus, jackass. "There's not much to do," he said, grabbing a stock pot from a cupboard beneath the island and beginning to fill it with water.

"I could set the table." She shifted toward the spot where he kept the plates, but something indefinable made Owen step directly in her path.

"Or you could relax with your glass of wine and let me do it."

A tiny shadow flickered over her whiskey-brown stare, but she tempered it with a bold enough smile that he almost didn't see it. "I'm perfectly capable of setting the table, Owen."

"You're perfectly capable of a lot more than that," he said. "But this is supposed to be about me feeding *you*, remember?"

"You really don't need to do that." Cate's reply was automatic, both her smile and her shoulders growing tight. "I promise, I do eat every day."

A burst of frustration sizzled in his chest, and he almost put it to words. But her guard was up in full force, and there was only one way he was going to get her to let it down.

"I was honest with you a few minutes ago when we were upstairs, right? And we agreed that's how we're going to do this?" he asked, turning off the kitchen faucet and turning to look at her with a no-nonsense stare.

She stared back. "Yes."

"Then talk to me, Cate." Owen's legs took a step toward her even though his brain had thoroughly cautioned not to, but he wasn't dumb enough to think his brain was actually in charge here. Not when his heart was slamming away like it was. "How come you don't let yourself enjoy things?"

"I do," she said. But her gaze slipped along with the argument, and Owen closed the rest of the space between them in two long strides of *fuck it*.

"You don't. You make all of these incredible desserts and you only taste little bites to make sure they're right. You won't open yourself up to the possibility of starting a career doing something you clearly love—not even when an incredible opportunity is right in front of you. You keep everyone at arm's length. I get that you don't want to be hurt again, I really do. But why don't you let yourself feel anything good?"

"I..."

Cate broke off, the fight in her protest falling hollow. Her eyes glittered, not so much with tears as pure emotion that tore at Owen's chest.

But it was nothing in the face of what she said next.

"Because I was supposed to be in the car the day Brian and Lily died."

CATE'S heart ricocheted around her rib cage, part from the shock of her admission and part from the truth itself. The words had flown out without her permission, as if they'd been some rabid, caged animal, mindless and desperate to be let loose.

"You...what?"

Her face flamed from the weight of her words. Of course, Owen was stunned. No one—not *one* living, breathing person—knew the truth. The confession left an odd, jagged hole in her rib cage, but now that it had surfaced from the spot where she'd kept it buried for so long, the rest of the truth just rushed right out of her.

"We were supposed to go to the movies in Camden Valley, all three of us. There was a new Disney movie out, and Lily wanted to go. I was surprised she asked," Cate continued, guilt stabbing through her at the memory, at the argument that had come after.

She's nine now, Cate. We're running out of time to have another baby. You already stay at home—I don't understand what the problem is...

She stuffed the echo of Brian's voice down, but still, her own words came, sharp in her mouth like shards of glass. "Lily had been outgrowing a lot of that little girl stuff. But she asked, and Brian never told her no." Another source of contention, another slice of guilt over all the times she'd played the role of the stern parent and Brian had spoiled Lily rotten.

"Cate."

Owen's voice, notched just above a whisper, told her she didn't have to say anything else, that if she wanted to yank her armor back into place and say "forget it", he'd let her. But he wouldn't forget—damn it, she felt so good when she was with him that *she* couldn't forget—and she shook her head and continued.

"The trouble was, it was a Saturday afternoon. That was the only day I really got to lose myself in the kitchen, and I'd started making croissants from scratch. They're a righteous pain in the ass, with all the folding and rising, and the timing is really tricky, so leaving the batch I'd been working on pretty much ensured they'd have been ruined."

Owen nodded. He stood in front of her, completely unmoving, giving her enough space to talk, but staying close enough for her to feel his quiet steadiness.

"I told Lily I didn't think the movie was such a great idea. I know it was selfish," Cate added quickly. "But we'd had a long week with her school science fair project and the PTA's fundraiser, and between that and all the household stuff like cooking and laundry and driving all the way to Camden Valley for both ballet lessons and Girl Scouts...well, I wanted some time in the kitchen."

"Taking the time to do something for yourself isn't selfish," Owen said, his eyes growing suddenly stormy despite the soft overhead light of his kitchen.

The irony of it forced a joyless laugh past Cate's lips. "I didn't think so, either, not in that moment. It was the first time I'd ever really chosen what I wanted to do over what Lily had asked for. Don't get me wrong," she added, "I'm not a martyr. I spent my Saturdays in the kitchen. At least, I did whenever we didn't have a practice or a birthday party or an activity to go to."

Which pretty much meant she got one Saturday a month to get right with the flour and butter and sugar, but she'd made it work. She'd *had* to. Her kitchen had been the only place where she wasn't Brian's wife or Lily's mom or anyone other than herself, pure and simple. It had been the only place where she'd known how to breathe and just *be*.

"But when I told Lily no, Brian got really angry," Cate said, her breath shaking the slightest bit. She knew what was coming, what her memory would cough up next. God, she knew it by heart.

Jesus, Cate. You're putting your hobby in front of our kid? It's just a batch of stupid bread. We'll buy some on the way home if it means that much to you...

"Angry," Owen repeated. She caught the steel in his voice a heartbeat later, and immediately shook her head. Brian might have been a lot of things, but he'd never been hurtful in the physical sense.

"I think mean is a better word. At least, when it came to me baking."

Owen frowned, his brows cinching together in obvious confusion. "I'm sorry. I don't follow."

Cate's pulse peppered her belly with dread. But she'd already poured half the story all over his kitchen floor. There wasn't any practical reason to hold back now.

"Just before graduation, I got a scholarship to the Culinary Arts Academy."

His lips parted, but nothing came out for a long second before he finally asked, "The one in Harrisonburg?"

"Yeah. I knew it wouldn't make me a celebrity chef." She nearly laughed at the thought. "I mean, the academy is a great school, but the Shenandoah Valley is hardly New York or Chicago. I didn't need all that, though. I just wanted my own bakery." Her chest suddenly felt like there was a steel band around it, gripping tighter and tighter, and damn it, this shouldn't be so hard to say after all this time. "But Brian wasn't as...enthusiastic. He blew it off as a pipe dream. Joked that cookies were for bake sales, not businesses. Stuff like that. He made it really clear he thought culinary school was a waste of time and money, and that my owning a bakery one day was about the craziest thing he'd ever heard, including stories of Bigfoot *and* aliens at Roswell."

"I don't mean to speak ill of the dead," Owen said, sawing off each word. "But I didn't realize Brian needed a lesson in proper manners."

Cate shrugged. She'd come to terms with this part of things long ago. "He was scared I'd leave Millhaven and never come back if I pursued baking, and, to be honest, the fear probably wasn't unfounded. I'm not close with my parents. Nothing was tying me here, and I'd have had better luck opening a bakery in a bigger city like Harrisonburg or Charlottesville or Staunton. I cared about him, but culinary school...God, it held so many possibilities. And I wanted them all so badly."

"So, you were going to go?" Owen asked.

"Yes." Cate nodded. "I hadn't told Brian for sure, but I think he suspected. I had half my things packed in boxes when I found out I was pregnant with Lily."

She took a second for her conscience to slide between her ribs and squeeze. The first thing she'd felt when she'd seen that test turn bright, undeniable blue, had been dread. *No. Not this, anything but this*, and she'd never be able to erase that. Not even with the love that eventually came after and would never, ever come again.

Cate cleared her throat. "So, obviously, I gave up my scholarship to get married to Brian instead. We made a good life together for our daughter, but he did everything he could to keep me from baking. Guilt trips, making fun and calling his meanness a 'joke'. Promising we'd look into renting a space for something small here in Millhaven, then going back on his word. But I never stopped baking"—God, it had been her lifeline, her oxygen on some of those days, when Brian's contempt was on full display—"and he never stopped hating it. On the day of the accident, we'd argued even before Lily asked about the movie. It was why I'd chosen such a difficult recipe to begin with, actually."

"What did you argue about?" Owen asked.

"Brian wanted another baby." *Wanted* probably wasn't the best word, she knew. What he'd really wanted was more leverage over her, more reasons to keep her busy and out of their kitchen. He'd made that clear in the argument, even though she'd have said no regardless. *A baby will keep you focused on what's really important around here*, he'd said, as if the sliver of stolen time she spent in the kitchen every month had been some sort of national threat. "He told me I was being self-centered because I didn't want to have any more kids, and that I had no right to put baking first. The thing with Lily only made it worse. He said he wasn't going to put up with my foolishness anymore, and he threatened to throw out the batch of dough I'd been working on."

Cate shivered. God, she could still hear the hiss of his words in her ear, the malicious bite of *it would serve you right for being so selfish* as fresh as if he'd just uttered it. "For the first time in my life, I snapped."

"That doesn't seem unfounded," Owen said quietly, and if anyone else had told her the same story, Cate probably would've agreed. Of course, this was *her* story. One she'd kicked into motion. One that drowned her in so much guilt that she couldn't even open the drawer in her kitchen that held the trivet Lily had made for her without wanting to break down and cry.

One she couldn't undo.

"I was just so angry," Cate whispered. "I told Brian I was going to stay in the kitchen and finish the recipe I'd started, and that he wasn't going to guilt me about it anymore. I said it was past time for him to make good on all those empty promises he'd made that I'd own a bakery one day, and that this time, I wouldn't let him blow it off. The fight was the worst one we'd ever had," she said, her heart beginning to thump faster behind the borrowed flannel of her shirt. *You're never going to have a bakery, Cate. A dream like that isn't for you. Best to wake up and remember that.* "It ended with him storming out to the movies with Lily. I stayed home, and, well, the rest is...the rest."

She let go of a shaky exhale, her heart climbing into her throat. Owen had asked her a question, and though she'd taken a roundabout path to get there, it still needed an answer. "I've played that day back in my head a million times. What if I'd given in and just said yes? Would Brian not have stormed out of the house so fast, into the path of that deer he'd had to swerve to try and avoid? What if I'd said no, we'll all go tomorrow instead? Then it wouldn't have been raining, and even if he'd had to swerve, the car wouldn't have flipped over or smashed into that tree. Or"— hot tears filled Cate's eyes, as they always did when she got to this what-if, the one she'd wondered in those early days if she'd truly deserved—"what if we'd all been in the car together, and I died instead of Brian or Lily? What if my daughter—"

"*Stop.*"

Owen's hands were on her shoulders, his stubbled jaw unyielding and his eyes full of a brand of fire she'd never, ever seen before. "Your fight with Brian was terrible, yes, and the accident, even more so. But don't do that to yourself."

In a white-hot instant, her guard came crashing down. "Why not? It's my *fault*, Owen! I said no. I fought with Brian. I told him I wouldn't leave the house. I yelled at him that if he wanted to take Lily to the movies so badly, they should just go. I'd never done anything like that before, ever. But I was so angry at him for pushing, for making me feel like a bad parent when I loved Lily so much, for continually belittling my dream—God, for *all* of it—that I just snapped."

She started to cry at the same time Owen's arms came around her, so honest and strong and right, and she selfishly soaked in the feel of him even though she knew she didn't deserve it.

"Don't you see?" she asked into his shoulder, the words ragged in her throat. "That's why I can't have my own bakery now, and it's why I don't let myself feel good. How could I possibly have anything happy when I'm here and they're not? When if I'd just done one thing differently—"

"Cate." Owen pulled back, cupping her face between his big, callused hands, holding her steady without force. "That accident wasn't your fault."

"But—"

"No." He shook his head. His voice carried no heat, but the truth in the single word sent goose bumps over Cate's skin. "You were mad—with good reason, I'll add—and you got into an argument. But you didn't put that deer in the road, and you didn't make Brian swerve to miss it. That accident wasn't your fault, and it's past time for you to stop believing it was. I know you loved Lily, and that you were left behind." Owen thumbed the tears, which were falling in earnest now, from her cheeks, his gaze never wavering, his words low and strong. "And that makes you feel guilty, but you are worthy of happiness. You're talented and beautiful and smart as hell. You deserve to live your life."

Cate opened her mouth, primed to argue. But, oh, God, Owen's hands felt so achingly good wiping away her tears, and when he said those words to her—the same words she'd adamantly denied for three long years—she realized the truth.

He meant what he was saying. And she might not believe it on her own, but when he stood there in front of her, telling her she was worthy of pursuing her dream and feeling good, she began to think at least maybe it was possible.

They stood there together, her crying and him silently dispatching every tear, for an amount of time Cate couldn't measure, until finally, she nodded, shifting forward against his chest. Owen kissed the top of her head before parting from her wordlessly, moving to the sink to transfer the stock pot full of water to a burner on the stove. He finished preparing dinner, and she set the table in between long sips of wine. Eventually, they started talking about easy topics like what sort of books they both liked and their favorite flavor of ice cream, and when they sat down to eat twenty minutes later, some laughter threaded through the conversation, too.

And Owen wasn't wrong. His spaghetti and meatballs were the best thing Cate had ever tasted.

She had two huge servings to prove it.

20

"**O**kay, jackass. You've been sitting over there, smiling like the cat that ate the canary for thirty minutes now. What gives?"

Owen looked across the table at Lane, glad as hell they'd snared the corner booth at Clementine's so no one could see the smile he was unable to keep from commandeering his mouth. He'd always been a terrible liar, mostly because he never saw the point, but since he'd also never been one to kiss and tell, he went with, "Nothing."

Hunter laughed, his cheeseburger halfway to his mouth. "Ah, here's where I call bullshit. I know what he's smiling about, and her name is Cate McAllister."

Owen's heart took a whack at his rib cage, piñata-style. "Really? And what makes you think that?"

"Uh, the fact that her car was at your house from dinnertime Saturday night until five-thirty this morning, and you were late to work for the first time in the history of mankind."

Lane coughed out a laugh that matched Hunter's cocky

I-dare-you-to-argue expression, and shit, Owen hated them both right now.

"You've dragged your ass on plenty of Mondays. Besides, I was only ten minutes late, you dick," he grumbled, but his smile had too much staying power to stick the words with the proper amount of grit.

"Uh-huh." Hunter lifted a brow, along with one corner of his mouth. "I told you a man can do a lot of things worthy of making him late in ten minutes."

Lane's laugh grew loud enough to make the handful of people having dinner at Clementine's look in their direction, and, yeah, this conversation needed a kill switch, stat.

"Oh, for the love of...fine. Yes." Owen dropped his voice to just above a whisper. "Cate spent the weekend at my house. Are you happy now?"

"Not as happy as you, I bet," Lane said, waggling his light blond brows before shoving a pair of fries into his mouth. But his buddy wasn't the only one who could ration up some good-natured shit.

"You're one to talk, Sheriff. I overheard Amber Cassidy telling Billy Masterson at the co-op this morning that you and Daisy are practically attached at the hip now."

"I doubt that's where they're attached," Hunter said, his smile losing some of its luster a heartbeat later at the warning look Lane shot in his direction.

"Careful, wedding boy." At Hunter's lifted hands, Lane continued. "Anyhow, I'm not trying to hide the fact that Daisy and I have been spending time together. I like her."

"I like Cate, too." Ah, hell, the words slipped out before Owen could stop them. Not that they weren't true, but still... "We're just kind of taking things slow and seeing where they lead."

It was one hell of an abridged version. After their talk in the kitchen, during which Owen had been alternately furious and heart sore, he and Cate had fallen into a rhythm that had surprised him with its ease. They'd talked and eaten, then talked some more, and when he'd taken her back up to his bedroom for a slower yet just-as-hot round of sex, then she'd stayed all day yesterday and until the tiny hours of this morning for more of the same, Owen had realized the truth. He *did* like Cate, maybe more than was good for him.

Which meant he had to tread very carefully for both their sakes, because she'd made it wildly clear she wanted no strings attached.

"Taking things easy to start out makes sense," Hunter said, bringing Owen back to the quiet din of Clementine's Diner, and, ah, the shot was too good to pass up.

"Says the man who's getting married in less than a month."

"Shut up." His brother's laugh took all the heat from the directive and sent a weird feeling through Owen's gut. Yeah, Hunter had always been a goner for Emerson, even in the twelfth grade. But the look on his face right now was nothing short of pure love, and not the sappy, roses-are-red kind, either. This love was real, the kind their old man had had for their mother. The kind that *lasted*, like family and farm.

The kind that Owen wanted, and Cate wasn't interested in.

"Speaking of which"—he took a long sip from the sweet tea in front of him in the hopes it would drown the sudden triple-knot in his throat. Talk about putting the cart before the horse. He and Cate hadn't even been on an official date yet, for Chrissake—"we should probably get to planning some of these wedding logistics."

Hunter nodded. It was, after all, the main reason they'd decided to meet up on a Monday evening for dinner. "I s'pose you're right. There's a lot to get in order."

"Great," Owen said, tamping down the last of the strange feeling in his chest. He had plenty of time to get from Point A to Point B, and Cate needed to go slow. Sure, he liked her. But he also couldn't push her, or she'd shut him out. So, he did what he always did.

He buckled down and got serious about what was in front of him.

"One Cross Creek country wedding, coming right up."

Owen shook off the early morning chill in the air, heading into the main house with an empty Thermos and a big ol' smile on his face. Yeah, he was running on a skimpy five hours of sleep, but after he'd come back from dinner with Hunter and Lane, he'd gotten a text from Cate. That had led to him shamelessly inviting her over, her quickly accepting, and them having incendiary sex on his living room couch because they hadn't even been able to make it up the stairs to his bedroom. They'd had sex there later, too—good measure, and all. But in between, they'd finished the chocolate cake she'd made over the weekend, laughing and talking about the details for Hunter's wedding, and, as tired as he felt, Owen couldn't think of one damn thing he'd rather trade sleep for than Cate McAllister.

He was so tangled up in the thought that he didn't realize the kitchen was occupied until he was a full three steps over the threshold.

"Marley?" He blinked, wondering if he was seeing things. But nope, his sister was definitely standing at the kitchen island with a mixing bowl clutched to the chest of her pajama top and a look of pure shock on her face. "What are you doing down here so early?"

"Nothing! Aren't you supposed to be *working*, or something?" Her mouth pursed in a scowl of frustration, and, a second later, Owen realized why.

"Are you baking brownies?"

Marley held the mixing bowl possessively, but didn't hesitate to look him dead in the eye. "No. Yes." She huffed out a sigh. "I mean, it's just some dumb recipe I found online, but...I don't know, I wanted chocolate and it didn't look so hard. So, I thought, you know. I'd try it."

"At six thirty in the morning?" he asked, and damn, her frown was at expert levels today.

"It's the only time I can get any privacy in the kitchen. You guys are always having some family meal or another in here, celebrating another Thursday, or whatever."

Owen dug deep for his patience and miraculously found some. "If you want to use the kitchen for something, all you have to do is ask." A beat passed, which Marley surprisingly didn't fill with a caustic comeback, so he impulsively added, "And if you want to join us for one of those meals, all you have to do is show up."

"I wouldn't want to intrude," Marley said. There was a hint of truth beneath the serrated edges of her answer, and it made Owen proceed with care.

He walked to the coffeepot like nothing-doing. "Well, that's a relief, because you wouldn't be. Like it or not, you *are* part of this family."

Okay, so he still had strides to make in the sense-of-humor department. Still, Marley didn't chuck the bowl at his head.

But she didn't look happy, either. "Only half," she

reminded him, putting the bowl on the butcher block and giving it a vigorous stir.

"Not to us, Marley."

"I know, but I am to me."

Irritation flashed in Owen's veins. He wanted to argue, to tell her blood was blood and she was being ridiculous—in fact, he had his mouth halfway open to do exactly that. Then he saw the glint of pain in her eyes, the one he'd bet his last dollar she'd rather die than admit existed, and he clamped his trap shut.

He knew that loss. He missed his mother, too. Only, he'd always had his brothers to remind him how important family really was.

Marley needed a brother, and he needed to give her that. Even if she wasn't ready to be his sister yet.

"So." Owen filled his Thermos to the top, the coffeepot softly clanking as he replaced it on the burner. "Does Cate know you're trying your hand at baking?"

"No! Don't—" Marley's chin whipped upward, her eyes bright blue and wide. "Could you please not tell her?" she asked quietly. "I'll probably suck at it."

He capped his Thermos with a nod. "I won't tell her if you don't want me to. That said, she won't care if you suck at baking."

"How do you know?"

It was an honest question with an easy answer. "Because I suck at conversational skills, and, miraculously, she still ends up talking to me. Somehow, I have a feeling she'd be fine with you muddling your way through a batch of brownies. She'd probably even think it was cool that you wanted to try it out."

Marley paused, long enough that Owen nearly gave up and made his way back out to the greenhouse. But then she asked, "Do you really think so?" and an involuntary smile tugged at the corners of his mouth.

"Yeah. I really think so."

A glimmer moved through his sister's expression, and Owen recognized it as mischief two seconds too late. "Oh, my God, you *like* her."

Shit. Shit! "Of course, I like her. She's"—*whip-smart. Totally fucking gorgeous. An insanely good kisser*—"uh, nice."

"You're going to want to work on that game face," Marley said with a snort.

Owen frowned. "That obvious, huh?"

"Oh, yeah." She reached for the bowl, stirring the contents one more time before reaching for one of the two eggs sitting on a dish in the center of the island. "But don't worry. I won't blab to Cate that you got all goofy at the mention of her name or anything."

He couldn't help it. He laughed. "Thanks. I appreciate that."

"Sure thing."

"Well, I guess I'd better let you get to the rest of your recipe," he said, waiting until he was most of the way across the kitchen floor before turning back around. "And, hey, if you ever change your mind, the invite to family dinner is always open."

"I know," Marley replied, just as she always did.

But for the first time since she'd shown up on their doorstep six months ago, she looked like she'd actually consider it.

Cate hummed a crooked tune under her breath as she entered the last of the payroll data into the system. She hadn't seen Owen yet today—well, okay, technically, she *had* seen his silhouette slipping out of bed at 4:45 this morning, and she'd felt the brush of his mouth on her forehead fifteen minutes later when he'd headed out of his bedroom. But she hadn't seen him face-to-face in the light of what was turning out to be a gorgeous spring day, which meant he was likely up to his elbows, perhaps literally, in work in the greenhouse. She'd slipped in to the main house at a few minutes before eight after a lightning-fast trip home for a shower and change of clothes, and even though she'd still technically been on time, snoozing until the last possible second in Owen's bed, all warm and soft and smelling of cedar and something that belonged only to Owen himself, had felt nothing short of indulgent.

Cate couldn't remember the last time her alarm had woken her. She'd thought it would be weird at first, sleeping in the same bed with someone else after so long. It had ended up being the opposite of weird, though, with Owen just gathering her up in that quiet way of his and the two of them simply slipping off to sleep. No fanfare, no big deal.

Mmm hmm. Unfettered bliss will do that to a girl.

Her chin hiked, and she spun a brisk gaze around the office as if she'd been caught doing something she shouldn't, then rolled her eyes at herself two seconds later. Cate wasn't naïve enough to think that what was happening between her and Owen was truly *just* sex—if that had been the case, she wouldn't have spent the last three nights drifting off to dreamland next to him in his bed. But it wasn't anything to get all panicky about, either. They weren't picking out china patterns or those cutesy coffee mugs labeled "Mr." and "Mrs.". Sure, they enjoyed spending time together, but he'd promised things were casual. Just for now.

She couldn't give him the life he ultimately wanted, the

family he deserved to have. So, yes. Things had to stay commitment-free in the long run, for *both* their sakes.

"Hey."

Cate's heart bolted against her sternum, bumping off no less than four of her ribs before settling back into place. Jeez! Had she really been so lost in thought that she hadn't heard Owen open the back door and head down the hallway? And, seriously, how could anyone who had just done five hours of manual labor look so freaking sexy?

"Hey," she said, her resolve locking into place as Owen crossed the room to drop a kiss over the top of her head. "Owen. We're at work."

Somewhere between thought and action, her protest grew weak. Cate couldn't blame herself, really. Just the outline of those biceps against his T-shirt sleeves was enough to make her want to swallow her tongue—or, at the very least, do very naughty things to said biceps with it.

He didn't help her cause by grinning. "Take a break," he said, the flash in his eyes all suggestion.

She knew all three Cross men respected the work she did for them, and, since she respected it, too, she said, "Nope. We agreed."

"I'm sorry. You're right." Owen straightened, taking a step back with a deferent nod. "When we're at work, we work. Speaking of which, I have a proposition for you."

"*That* doesn't sound like work." Cate let a smile play on her lips as she pushed back in her desk chair to arch a brow at him.

A bolt of heat moved through her when he arched a brow right back. "Get your mind out of the gutter, sweetheart. This proposition is all business."

God, that slow and sexy half-smile should be illegal. Or,

at the very least, come with a sternly worded warning label. "Okay. What's on your mind?"

"I sat down with Hunter and my old man yesterday, and after looking at the numbers, we'd like to offer you a weekly contract to sell your baked goods in our tent at the farmers' market until we can offer you a permanent placement in our storefront."

"You..." The words swirled through Cate's head on wings, each of them flying just out of her comprehension's reach. "You don't want to wait until the storefront opens at the end of the summer?"

"Nope. We don't."

At her continued silence and the look of pure *whaaa* that must be slathered all over her face, Owen added, "I know it's a bit of an unexpected ask, but it wouldn't be anything we haven't already done, to both of our success. All we'd do is write up a short-term contract to repeat everything from last weekend until the storefront opens. Cross Creek would take a percentage of your profits to cover the produce used and a portion of the rental fee for the space. We'd also ask that you work the farmers' market every other Saturday to help with setup and sales since that worked out so well last weekend, but otherwise, that's pretty much it."

Finally, a thought grew clear in her crowded brain. "I'd have to quit working at Clementine's and The Bar." She didn't mind the work, but not even she could be in two places at once.

"That's probably true, yes," Owen said. "We're happy to pay you competitively."

He gave up some numbers that made her knees weak, and she was already sitting down. "That's"—*crazy. Unbelievable. Enough to take a massive chunk out of my debt by the end of the summer*—"reasonable. What sort of timetable were you thinking?"

"Not to put too fine a point on it, but...well, now."

"*Now*? As in, today?"

He nodded, his handsome face perfectly calm. "If we're going to make this weekend's farmers' market, then yes, we'd ideally sign the contract today."

Cate's pulse whooshed in her ears. She'd spent so long thinking her dream was more of a fantasy, the big, out-of-reach kind like winning the lottery or living on your own island. The thought of getting paid to bake, to do what she truly, purely loved...

A dream like that isn't for you.

Owen looked at her, his expression all business. "I know this is more of a commitment than you're used to, and that you might be hesitant to bake on a regular basis. If you need some time to think about it—"

"I don't."

Her words startled her a little, but, oh, they felt so good in her mouth, the way she imagined a French truffle would, decadent and delicious.

"You don't." Owen's answer wasn't a question, but Cate nodded anyway. Yes, she was here when Brian and Lily weren't, and, no, that ache probably wouldn't ever ease all the way. But a dream like this *was* for her. It always had been. She owed it to her daughter's memory to be strong and go after the goals she'd pushed aside for far too long.

Starting right now.

"I don't need to think about it," she said with a smile. "I'd love to accept your offer."

21

"Okay. This is the last of them."

Cate pulled the cookie sheet loaded with snickerdoodles out of Owen's oven, placing it carefully over the wire rack on the island before letting out a sigh of relief. She'd planned her preparations carefully over the last three days, and having one farmers' market under her belt already, she'd at least had an idea of how long certain tasks would take. Still, there were no less than a thousand potential pitfalls in going from concept to reality. With T-minus fifteen hours to go, it was nice to at least have all the baking done.

"They smell unbelievable," Owen said hopefully, and she slid a cinnamon and sugar-crusted cookie off the baking sheet that had come out ten minutes before its brethren.

Ah, perfect. "One," she replied, trying—and failing—to give him a stern look as she broke the cookie in half and passed part over to Owen before popping the other part into her mouth.

The pleasured noise that came from the back of his throat made Cate's belly flood with heat of the non-kitchen variety. "Damn, and they're still warm?" He chewed, and the noise turned into a moan. "It doesn't get much better."

"Oh, it can always get better." She'd tweaked even her most reliable recipes for years.

Owen, however? Didn't seem to be buying it. "Haven't you ever heard the phrase 'don't mess with perfection'?"

"Right." Cate started to package up the cookies that had fully cooled into the cellophane bags sitting in wait on the counter, her smile as inevitable as the sunset in a couple of hours. The cookies had come out as soft and cinnamon-sweet as she'd hoped, but still... "Like you ever stop messing with soil compositions and planting schedules. Oh, and crop rotations—"

"Okay, okay! Point taken." His laugh ended quickly as he turned to look at the windows lining the back of the kitchen. "I just wish we hadn't lost so much time today because of the weather."

An unexpected stretch of storms had started blowing through at lunch time, making steady outdoor work all but impossible between the overly wet conditions from the bouts of heavy rain and the threat of lightning. The storms had been persistent and unpredictable enough that the Crosses had finally just called it a day a couple of hours ago, after three rounds of harried stop/start.

"I know the farm is important to you," Cate said, because, God, it was the pure truth. "But you really only lost a couple of hours, right?"

She pointed to the clock on the microwave, which read nearly five PM. She'd finished up all the bookkeeping early so she could focus on a few more batches of cookies for tomorrow's farmers' market. Between her and Owen, they'd found a system this afternoon that had been efficient *and* fun. Not that baking ever felt like work to her, but having an extra set of hands had made all the difference in getting things done both quickly and well.

"Yeah." Owen nodded, but that seriousness he always wore when it came to the farm didn't budge from his eyes. "Anyway, the rain seems to have finally tapered off now. I was going to head to the greenhouse to see if there are any last-minute heirloom tomatoes or greens we could pack up for the market tomorrow. They're so perishable, I'd hate to see any go to waste just because we missed 'em."

"Workaholic," Cate teased, and damn it, one day she'd learn to brace herself for that sexy half-smile of his *before* it took a potshot at her composure.

He stepped in front of her, taking the cellophane bag out of her fingers and placing it carefully on the island. "Takes one to know one."

After a slow kiss she felt in a lot more places than her mouth, Owen pulled back just far enough to murmur, "I really do need to head on down there for a quick trip, though."

"Mmm." Cate laughed. She couldn't really blame him for being ambitious. For loving what he did, right down to his boot heels? Even less. "Far be it for me to stand in your way, then."

But rather than stepping back as she expected him to, his arms remained solid around her rib cage. "It's not far. Truth be told, I was going to walk it. Now that you're done in here, you could come with me. I mean, it might be kind of boring for you, but..."

"Right. Because watching me mix the batter for half a dozen strawberry-lemon quick breads was riveting for you, I'm sure." Especially since it had been more like nine loaves, *and* three huge batches of cookies. "Am I okay to go like this?"

She gestured to her light green sundress, which had been perfect for the warm spring weather that had dominated the first half of the day. At least she'd had the wherewithal to throw on her Converse lowtops this morning instead of a pair of flimsy sandals, although now that she thought about it, her sandals were still upstairs in Owen's room, right where she'd left them two days ago.

A tiny warning bell jangled in the back of Cate's brain, but she snuffed it out. Yes, she'd kicked off her sandals at Owen's bedside and inadvertently left them there the next morning in favor of the ballet flats she'd packed in her overnight bag, but she was hardly moving in with him. In fact, she'd responded with a polite yet firm no thanks when he'd offered to let her keep a toothbrush and some toiletries in his medicine cabinet, preferring instead to haul them back and forth whenever she stayed. She'd just have to be sure to grab her sandals later tonight. No big deal.

"Sure," he said, bringing her back to the kitchen with a smile. "It's still plenty warm out despite the rain, and the path is all gravel, so we shouldn't run into any of the standing water or mud that we had to worry about in the fields."

"Great. Just let me finish bagging these cookies up and then we can head out."

A handful of minutes and a dozen or so packages of cookies later, they were headed over the threshold of Owen's front door. He hadn't been kidding about the temperature still being more than warm enough for shirtsleeves, and even though the sun was still well-hidden behind a bank of light gray clouds, Cate still twisted her hair into a knot to keep it off her neck in the humid, post-storm air. "Oh, hey," she said, pausing to run her fingers lightly over the herb garden exploding out of the planter box nearest to the porch railing where she stood. "Your lavender bloomed a ton this week. I'd love to know your secret. I always manage to kill mine."

Owen spread a hand over the front of his T-shirt in mock horror. "Please tell me you water it."

"Of course, I water it," she said, laughing and following him down the porch steps.

"Uh-huh. And where do you keep it?"

She bit her lip, knowing he wasn't going to like her answer. "In a pot in my kitchen, usually."

One nearly black brow lifted all the way up. "Your kitchen that gets as much natural sunlight as a dungeon, you mean?"

"Point taken." Cate held up her hands in concession, falling into step beside him on the gravel path leading toward the smaller of Cross Creek's two greenhouses. "Not everyone can be a natural when it comes to growing things. I think I'm more *all* thumbs than green thumb."

"First of all, Mediterranean herbs like lavender and oregano need a ton of sunlight to thrive, and it's a common mistake to keep them in a spot that's too shady. Secondly, most of what you need to know to grow things well isn't inherent. It's learned."

"Really?" Surprise worked a path through her chest. "You just seem to have such a knack for farming." Actually, he seemed to have been pretty much hand-crafted for it. If she recalled properly, he'd worked full-time through the harvest their senior year in high school without missing so much as one assignment.

But Owen simply laughed, one shoulder lifting and lowering in an easy shrug. "After doing it for fifteen years, I reckon I probably do. But I think that's because I love learning about it more than any sort of predisposition for knowing the land like some sort of plant whisperer."

Cate's curiosity perked, good and hard. "Did you always know you wanted to run the farm?"

"Yes, ma'am."

His answer was so immediate, so immoveable that she pounced. "*Always*? You never wanted to be an astronaut or a rock star or something wild like that?"

"When I could run the farm instead?" he asked, his tone wrapping the words in a healthy veneer of *are you crazy?* "No way."

"Wow." Her curiosity grew another layer. "That's some serious devotion."

They walked a little ways down the path, a breeze cooling the air and rustling through the bright-green stalks of corn that already stood a solid three feet from the wet earth where they were anchored. The silence between them wasn't awkward—Cate was coming to recognize the V-shaped crease between Owen's brows and that firm set of his mouth that anyone else would probably call a scowl as his default for deeper thinking. Far be it for her to poke at whatever had him lost in thought before he had the words to answer.

Finally, he said, "It's not hard being devoted to something you love. Running Cross Creek is the only thing I've ever wanted to do. I mean, don't get me wrong." He gestured to the landscape around them, which somehow managed to burst with vitality even beneath the gray, gloomy sky. "Some days are pretty hellish. Heat waves, crop infestations. Cattle falling to disease. Any one of those things could break an entire season."

"But?" Cate supplied, because she knew full well it was coming.

Owen didn't disappoint. "But even on the most difficult days, I wouldn't trade farming for anything. I feel like running Cross Creek is what I was born to do. Like working the land with my family just *fits* me, and I fit right back."

His cheeks reddened a breath later, and he gave up a self-deprecating laugh. "Annnnnd that sounded a lot less weird and new-agey in my head. Anyway, running this farm after my old man retires is my family legacy, and it's one I definitely intend to uphold. Not out of obligation, but because I can't imagine doing anything else and being truly happy."

"That's not weird at all," she said, an odd sensation laddering down her spine before disappearing with a shiver. She cleared her throat. "So, you inherited your love of the land from your father, then?"

"I did, but truth be told, I think the way I feel about the farm itself came more from my mother."

Cate nearly tripped over the gravel beneath her feet. "Really?"

"Crazy, right?" Owen asked, and she nodded, all truth.

"Yeah. I mean"—she heard her answer only after it had made a jailbreak, and, *God*, her lack of filter knew no limits —"your father is the one who inherited Cross Creek from his father, right?"

"Yep. But my mother loved it here just as much as he does."

He paused again, and Cate considered telling him they could change the subject. Lord knew she got how difficult it could be to talk about people you'd lost. But then Owen continued in that quiet, serious way of his, and she found herself not wanting him to stop talking at all.

"Hunter and Eli were really young when our mom died. I don't think they remember her very well. In fact, I know Eli doesn't." His expression grew wistful, as if he was caught more in memory than thought. "But there are some things I remember like they happened yesterday."

"I know that feeling," Cate said softly, because, oh, she did. A sudden chill sent a spray of goose bumps over her arms. Her heart threatened to climb into her throat, but then Owen's hand was there, wordlessly closing over hers with their fingers threading together, and she was able to breathe.

"My mother might not have been born into farming like my father was, but she still came by it so honestly," Owen said. "She and my father were both only children, so it was really just the two of them at first, running the place with all the farm hands. But she loved it like he does. She's the one who planted all the gardens around the main house."

Cate thought of the rows of blooms, spread out on either side of the main house in colorful starbursts and lush, green thickets, all flowing together so naturally that she'd wondered more than once if they hadn't simply appeared out of the earth one day rather than been planted or planned. "Your mom must have *really* loved it, then. They're beautiful."

"The farm was important to her," Owen said, his fingers tightening against Cate's just enough for her to squeeze back. "Family was even more important, though. She used to tell me all the time, 'Family and farm, Owen. Never forget'."

"Your family is pretty tight-knit," she said. Having never been that close with her parents, or had the sort of love with Brian that she suspected Mr. and Mrs. Cross might've shared, or that even Hunter and Emerson seemed to be in, the whole thing seemed so terribly foreign to her, like a lost dialect to a language she didn't even recognize, let alone know.

Owen huffed out a sound that was equal parts laughter and—oddly—irony. "I hope I'm doing right by her wishes. Anyway, my love of the land might come from my old man, but my love of the farm, of my family legacy and what this place really means? I think that comes from my mother."

Cate squeezed his hand, and God, despite the gravity of what he was saying and the reminder they couldn't get any more serious than *not* serious, it felt so good in hers. She slid a sidelong glance at him, opening her mouth to answer, but the words stopped short before they could reach her lips.

He was frowning. Not the lost-in-thought variety she was coming to know so well, but a full-blown, something's-not-right frown. "Cate," he said, at the same time a rumble of thunder echoed loudly through the air.

Her heart began to pound, and holy shit, when had the sky turned so angry and dark? "Owen?"

A streak of lightning split the sky, followed by a rip of thunder that sent her hair on-end. A gust of wind—no *wonder* she'd had goose bumps a minute ago—sent her dress into a tangle around her ankles and her hair into a much looser knot, and oh, hell, this storm looked downright freaking scary.

"Shit," Owen muttered, whipping a look over either end of the path. Lightning forked the sky again, this time even closer, with menacing thunder following quickly on its heels. "We need to get inside. If we run, we might be able to make the greenhouse before it starts to rain."

The words were no sooner out of his mouth than the sky opened up over their heads.

22

Owen kept a firm grip on Cate's hand and made a break for the greenhouse even though he knew it was fucking useless. The sky had torn open, the rain not so much falling as crashing into them like a tidal wave from above. In less than three strides, he was completely soaked. The proximity of that last lightning strike warned him not to slow down, though, and even though he knew it would do nothing to keep him dry, he ran the rest of the way to the greenhouse with Cate in tow.

"Oh, my God," she breathed from the doorway they'd just banged through, turning to look at the storm from the safety of the covered threshold. "That came out of nowhere."

Owen tugged a hand through his hair, but he knew a lost cause when he felt one. His chest rose and fell rapidly from both the sprint and the jolt of adrenaline from the storm, and he took a second to catch his breath before answering.

"The storms have been like this all day. I should've known better. Or, at the very least, been paying better attention."

Guilt pinpricked his gut. Of course, he and Cate were fine, but Mother Nature wasn't to be messed with. He'd gotten so caught up in the conversation, in the ease and shocking goodness with which his words had slid out, that he hadn't even noticed his surroundings.

He noticed them now. Specifically, the soaked and still-beautiful woman standing directly in front of him.

"Jesus. You're drenched," Owen said, running his palms over the tops of her arms to slick off some of the rain.

Cate's throaty laugh went directly to his cock. "I'm hardly going to melt," she pointed out, but not even her no-nonsense moxie could trump his manners.

"Come on. I keep some towels in here for cleaning up. Let's get you dry."

Grabbing hold of her fingers again, he closed the greenhouse door with his free hand, making sure to firmly secure the latch. The last thing he needed was for a gust of wind to blow the thing in and smash one of the panels, or worse. The rain—which seemed to be growing even stronger, although Owen had no clue how—rattled over the glass above them, sluicing down the walls and thoroughly blurring any view in or out.

The air in the greenhouse was still despite the noise, slightly humid and full of comfort. The smell of humus and earth filled his senses as he inhaled, and he moved easily through the rows of produce growing from various planter boxes, emerald-colored leaves sprouting so thickly in some places, seeing past them was nearly impossible. Owen would know where he was going in the dark, though—this greenhouse was his refuge, with its pathways of plants and its wooden work tables built in along the perimeter on three sides of the rectangular structure. He knew each variety of every plant, where their planter boxes stood and how they'd been cultivated, watered, and maintained. Not just because he and his brother and old man kept detailed records of that, because, of course, they did. But he knew because he'd tended to all of them personally, watching their growth and marveling at how something as natural as a seed becoming a fat, juicy tomato or a perfectly rounded bell pepper could be so simple, yet so full of complex, mysterious twists and turns that even a slight variation in the process could drastically change the outcome. Yet, still, these plants defied the odds and not only grew, but thrived. He made sure of it.

He felt the prickle of Cate's stare a half-second before he caught it out of the corner of his eye, heat covering the back of his neck despite the fact that his skin was covered in chilly rain. "What?"

"You look at home here."

Owen's boots clattered to a stop by the spot where the far wall joined the shorter side of the greenhouse in a corner workbench. He grabbed one of the towels stacked beside some empty wooden crates, turning toward her briskly.

"I work here every day," he pointed out, running the towel over her bare, rain-streaked arms.

She slipped his grasp, her fingers stilling his movements. "I know, but you're right. The farm, this greenhouse. It fits you."

Damn it. He should have known better than to open his yap and let any old thing fly right out. But he'd felt so at ease walking side by side with Cate on the path here that he'd done exactly that, complete with the confession that it was his mother who had really crystallized his love for Cross Creek. Yeah, it was true. But he'd still never told anyone that before. And now here they were, soaking wet in the greenhouse with Cate looking at him like she could see right *through* him, and shit, he should feel vulnerable as hell.

Yet, somehow, Owen didn't move. Instead, he stood perfectly still in front of her on the hard packed earth and let her look her fill. His heart slammed in his chest as the rain did its best to match the sensation on the slanted glass roof overhead. The clouds had darkened the space around them, yet even in the shadows, Owen felt the familiar comfort on all sides. Cate took the towel from his fingers, and his heartbeat shifted into a different sort of rhythm at the look in her eyes. Her hair had fallen loose from its twist, hanging around her shoulders and face in dark, wet waves. The rain had turned to a sheen on her face, beading softly on the curve of her cheekbone and in the indent above her upper lip, making her skin almost glow. The pale green fabric of her sundress was—ah, *fuck*—plastered to her body, clinging to every outline and curve as if they were lifelines. Her chest rose and fell against the row of tiny buttons down the front, her nipples pressing against the soaked material in shadowy peaks, and Owen's cock jerked beneath the wet denim around his hips.

She was, by far, the most beautiful thing he had ever seen.

"Cate." Christ, even her name felt right in his mouth, sexy and essential all at once. He reached for the towel—he'd promised to dry her off, after all—but she dodged him with a deft shift of her weight that brought their bodies even closer together.

"You don't have to take care of me all the time." She slid a finger over his mouth, leaving it to linger on his bottom lip long enough to quell his protest and make his pulse spark faster from the contact. "I know you want to, and, believe me, it feels good when you do. But I like it when you let me do things for you, too."

There was no mistaking the suggestion hanging in her

murmur, and Owen cut out an exhale, quick and hot. "We're in the middle of the greenhouse."

Cate nodded, pressing up to her toes until her mouth was just below his ear. "Is anyone going to come out here in this weather?"

As if to bolster her question, thunder rolled loudly from the other side of the panels, the wind and rain both competing to see which could make more noise.

Owen's pulse put them both to fucking shame. "No."

Between their location in the far corner and the height and density of the plants in here, nobody would see him and Cate even on the off-off chance they did wander out here in the middle of this monsoon. Not from the door, anyway.

"Mmm." Her lips curved against his skin, her smile making his dick impossibly hard even though he couldn't even see her face. "Are you okay with me seducing you in the middle of your greenhouse, then?"

"Hell, yes."

Cate pulled back, her eyes wide with surprise, and Owen faked enough nonchalance to raise a brow and slap together a half-smile. "I just wanted to be sure you knew what you were getting yourself into, is all."

She laughed, the full-bodied, unfettered sound echoing through the warm air around them. "I think we've already established that I'm not shy. Now, put your hands right here, on the work table."

Cate took a little sidestep, angling his back to the corner workbench and tilting her head at the wooden boards running the length of the room.

"Really?" he asked, his lips parting in surprise. "I don't even get to use my hands?"

She shook her head, staring at the workbench on either

side of his hips so pointedly that Owen had no choice but to put his hands on either side of him.

"My seduction. My rules." She took the towel in one hand, running the soft cotton over his forearms. She didn't get far before she realized his T-shirt was part of the problem, though, and, before he could blink, Cate's fingers were beneath the hem and on his skin.

"Do you know what I thought when I saw you standing outside the main house on my very first day at Cross Creek?"

The wet cotton cooperated with her touch shockingly well, moving up and over his head with only a few well-placed tugs.

"No," he said, his knuckles tightening as he replaced his hands on the workbench. Jesus, this was going to be an exercise in restraint.

"I wanted to touch your biceps. Actually, no"—Cate moved the towel over his shoulders, then his arms, trading it for her fingers a second later—"I wanted to bite them."

He barked out a laugh, unable to help it. "That's a little filthy."

"*You* were a little filthy," she reminded him, and the provocative smile on her mouth made his balls ache. Stepping in closer, she kissed his neck, her mouth warm and wet on his skin. "God, I wanted you."

"Cate." His fingers dug into the edges of the workbench, desperate with the need to touch her. She must have heard it in his voice, because she placed her hands over his, anchoring him into place as she trailed a line of kisses over his shoulder.

"I wanted to touch you." Her tongue slid hotly over the top of his arm, making his breath grow shallow, then catch in his chest. "I wanted to taste you." Her mouth traveled lower, her teeth scraping over his bicep in a move that was surprisingly sexy.

The laugh that came up from the back of her throat pushed the limits of Owen's already thin resolve. "So, now I'm going to make up for lost time and do both," she said. Kissing her way back up to his shoulder, Cate repeated her ministrations on the other side of his body. Every glide of her mouth made his skin prickle with awareness and want, and by the time she'd returned to his neck again, his desire to touch her had become a full-blown, screaming need.

But she didn't move her hands from his. Instead, she lowered her chin, kissing a path down the center of his chest.

Owen realized her intended destination a second later, and even though his cock jerked eagerly at the mere thought of her mouth heading closer, he had to make her stop.

"Owen. Please," she whispered, and only then did it register that she'd paused just above his navel. "Please, let me do this. Let me make you feel the way you make *me* feel."

She'd let go of his hands to gather her skirt between her fingers, lifting it around her knees as she'd kissed her way down his body. Her damp hair was wild around her face, her cheeks flushed with obvious desire. Her eyes were what wrecked him, though, pleading in that bold way that could only belong to her, and fuck, he wanted to give her everything she'd wanted on that first day, standing out in front of the main house.

He wanted to give her everything, period.

Afraid to trust his voice with anything other than a moan, Owen nodded. He helped Cate wrestle with his jeans and boxers—not nearly as accommodating as a flimsy T-shirt when wet, as it turned out—and they got things shoved down to his knees until they realized that was as good as it would get. She grabbed the towel from the workbench, dropping it to the ground and kneeling between his legs.

"*Oh.*"

All the air abandoned his lungs on a grunt as her exhale moved over his cock, her mouth tantalizingly close. She brushed her fingers up his length, and sweet Christ, he couldn't tell if he was in heaven from the pleasure or hell from the dark, greedy need pumping through his veins. But then Cate let her tongue dart out to trace a light, long line from root to tip, and that was when Owen knew the truth.

It didn't matter if he was in heaven or hell or any point in between, just as long as she didn't stop what she was doing.

Cate reached out, her touch soft as she explored his hips, the tops of his legs, the sensitive skin on the inside of his thighs. The friction from her fingertips sent sparks of pleasure through his blood, pulsing along with his heart-beat as she swept and stroked. She pressed her mouth over the midline of his cock, her lips parting just slightly in a wet up-and-down slide, and it took everything Owen had not to thrust blindly into her touch.

She had asked him to let her do this, and, by God, he *would* stand by his word and give her what she wanted.

Shifting forward on her knees, Cate wrapped her fingers around him, brushing a feather-light kiss over the crown of his cock before parting her lips to go farther. The heat of her mouth made his vision slip, but the sight of her nestled between his legs was too pretty, too provocative not to watch. Her hands gripping his hips and pumping the base of his shaft as she sucked, her tongue swirling harder on every upward glide—Owen shamelessly watched it all. He kept his eyes fixed on her, hypnotized as she tasted and gave and took.

She angled her head slightly to one side, and the change in sensation made his balls tighten with undiluted pleasure. A tingle of warning unraveled at the base of his spine, strong enough for him to unlatch a hand from the workbench and place it on Cate's shoulder.

"Come here," he said, his voice so guttural and rough, he barely recognized it as his own.

She lifted her head to pin him with a glittering stare. "I don't have to stop."

Just like that, his instincts overrode his control, snapping his composure in half and stomping it into dust. "You misunderstand. I don't want you to stop."

Reaching down to hook his hands under her arms, Owen hauled her to her feet. He yanked the hem of her dress up over her thighs, cupping his palms over the swell of her ass and pulling her off the ground in the same swift movement, turning to place her firmly on the workbench. Somehow, a scrap of decorum made it past all the carnal now-right-now controlling his thoughts, and he grabbed another clean towel from the nearby stack. He maneuvered it beneath Cate's body at the same time he pulled her panties from her hips.

"I want you to keep going, sweetheart," he said, tugging her shoes off and grabbing a condom from his wallet. "In fact, I want every single thing about you. I want you to sigh." He ran a finger over her slippery entrance, then did it again and again until a heavy exhale unspooled past her lips. *Yes.*

"I want you to scream." Owen's touch drifted up, finding the tight knot of her clit at the apex of her thighs. Cate arched into the contact, her thighs falling wide, and he made fast work of the condom. Notching himself firmly between her legs, he pressed the head of his cock just deep enough to feel the promise of full penetration, and she let out a sound that was half-cry, half-moan.

Good enough for now. "I want you to come so hard you can't stand or see or think. So, no, I don't want you to stop. But I do want all that to happen with my cock inside you. Please."

"Oh." For a stop-time second, nothing existed but the two of them, right on the edge of something Owen couldn't explain but really fucking wanted. Then Cate's hands found his shoulders, gripping tight as a seductive smile took shape on her lips.

"Well, if you insist. Take me, Owen. Any way you want."

With that, he was lost to all rational thought. He wrapped his hands over the back of her hips, tilting forward to fill her, inch by inch. Her inner muscles squeezed his cock so hard he nearly lost his breath, and he had to pull back a few times, easing his way inside so he didn't lose his goddamned mind, until, finally, he was snugly seated all the way inside of her.

"Oh, God, that's..."

Cate didn't finish her sentence. Instead, she moved, throwing her head back and thrusting her hips upward even though their bodies were already completely joined, and Owen didn't hesitate to do exactly as she'd asked. Keeping his grasp on her ass, he angled himself over her, withdrawing an inch, then reclaiming the spot deep inside her pussy.

"Good. So *good*."

Her words were so honeyed Owen could practically taste them. Cate's pleasure made his that much more demanding, and he buried his cock over and over in long, hard strokes. "Take it, sweetheart. Tell me how good you feel."

The pleasure/pain of her nails curving against his shoulders was her first reply. She knotted her legs around his waist, taking him even more deeply than before, the pressure of her inner muscles growing stronger and sweeter with every rock forward and back. Owen dropped a hand to the slight, hot space between their bodies and slipped his thumb over her clit. There, *there* it was, that bowstring tension in her body that he craved, the promise he wanted more than his own release. He circled his thumb above in time to the rhythm of his thrusts below, both becoming more purposeful, until Cate's mouth opened on a soundless gasp.

"Yes. Oh, God, please—"

She broke off with a ragged cry. Her whole body trembled in release, her pussy pulsing around his cock. But, oh, he was far from done. He worked her through every breath, then began softening his touch and expecting her movements to slow.

Only, they didn't.

"Owen," she said, quickly rebuilding the intense rhythm that had just sent her over the edge. She pushed her hips back up, reaching for his waist to set the pace, and there was no way in hell he could deny her.

"Ah, God, Cate." He thrust deep into her with ease, not losing any of the pleasure that had unfolded deep in his belly as he'd made her come.

"Don't stop." She looked up at him, her whiskey-warm stare seeming to see how close he was, how much he felt. Everything. "Please. I don't want to stop, either. Take me. Come for me."

Digging his fingers into her hips, Owen held her steady on the workbench, his thrusts quickening. Cate met each one with a push of her hips, locking her legs around him to hold him all the way inside her body. Release coiled in the lowest part of his belly, winding tighter and burning brighter. His orgasm slammed up his spine, pushing the breath from his lungs with a shout.

For some amount of time he couldn't measure, he stood there, his chest on Cate's chest, their bodies spilled together. Eventually, they began to unwind from each other, righting their clothing to the soundtrack of the rain now falling softly on the roof above them. She gave him the same sassy-sweet smile as always, brushing a kiss over his mouth like she'd done dozens of times before.

But as he took her hand and led her out of the greenhouse, Owen couldn't shake the feeling that nothing was like it had been before. Because Cate had seen him. *Really* seen him.

And he had let her.

23

Cate rocked back on the heels of her cross-trainers and surveyed the throng of people milling through Camden Valley's pavilion. The farmers' market was even more crowded than last weekend, thanks to upward trending temperatures and an over-abundance of the pretty, late spring sunshine that had chased yesterday's storms out of town. The increased foot traffic should have made her edgy; hell, just the thought of being here, putting her dreams on full display by selling the baked goods she'd made with her own time-tested recipes should have been enough to send her nerves into a complete tizzy. But she and Owen had simply gotten out of bed, falling into the same get-ready, get-out-the-door routine they'd cultivated over the course of the past week, then busying themselves with setting everything up for the market, and Cate had found she'd had neither the time nor the inclination for nerves. They simply hadn't made sense. She was here with Owen, doing something she enjoyed and making money, to boot. Plus, she had to admit, watching him in his element was enticing as hell. The way his eyes crinkled around the edges and lit from gray to blue when he told Mollie Mae Van Buren about the different varieties of summer squash they'd be sure to have later in the season, or the natural honesty of his smile when he helped Mrs. Ellersby choose just the right bunch of cut flowers to show off at her bridge club meeting —God, something about his ease just made her feel happy, too.

Careful not to get too *happy there, girl. You can't give that man the fairy-tale ending he deserves.*

"My, my. What have we here?" Clementine's voice tugged Cate back to reality with a jolt, and she slathered a smile over her face even though she knew it was a poor fit.

"Oh, hi, Clem!" She took a deep breath, forcing herself to dial it down. "Would you like to try a strawberry white-chocolate chip cookie? They're a brand-new offering this week."

"You know I would," Clem said, eagerly taking a sample from the plate Cate had placed front-and-center on the red and white tablecloth in front of her. "Delicious," she proclaimed a second later, turning toward the spot where Owen stood over by the baskets of radishes and kale. "I'm not sure what you did to get Miss Cate here out of her shell, but whatever it was, thank you."

Owen laughed, sauntering over as Cate flushed. "Much as I'd like to, I can't take any credit," he said. "All I did was ask her to give it a go."

"You must be mighty persuasive," Clementine said, her voice lilting up just enough to mark the words with suggestion, and, ahhhh, Cate should've known that between Amber seeing her and Owen flirting at The Bar and the fact that her car had been parked at his place every night for a week straight, the rumor mill would catch up with them sooner rather than later.

Owen's cheeks turned roughly the same shade as the strawberries in the pint-baskets behind him, and Cate camouflaged her laughter under the guise of a poorly constructed cough.

"I, uh. Yes, ma'am," he replied, adjusting his baseball hat.

Thankfully, Clem had the good grace to let him off the hook. "Well, I'm glad she listened to one of us. Truth be told, her talents were wasted in my diner."

"Yes, ma'am," Owen said again, his chin bouncing up a half a breath later, and once again, Cate suppressed a smile. "I mean, no offense. You know I love your diner, but—"

Clementine cut him off with a deep, melodic laugh. "None taken, child. I think you and I are of like mind when it comes to Miss Cate's abilities in the kitchen. I'm just glad you could nudge her out of the nest."

Cate crossed her arms over her chest, although she knew her deep-down smile made the gesture pretty much pointless. "I'm right here, you two. Totally close enough to hear you, and everything."

"Mmm hmm," Clementine murmured. "Now, do me a favor and *stay* here, would you? I won't lie and say I don't miss you on Sunday mornings, but baking cookies for Cross Creek looks good on you."

"Thank you, Clem," Cate said softly, her chest giving up a squeeze. She might not have been an open book when she'd worked for the woman—in fact, she'd probably been a smart-mouthed pain in the ass. But Clementine's genuine support was just one more sign that maybe she was ready to start her own business after all.

Clementine winked, scooping up two packages of cookies as she turned toward the checkout line across the tent. "My pleasure, honey. My pleasure."

Cate waited a beat, then one more for good measure before she looked at Owen. "You can wipe that smile off your face any time now."

He nudged her with one hip, his smile getting even bigger. "Not a chance. See, I kinda like this smile. Along with the person who put it there."

Damn it, now she was smiling, too. "Aren't you just living up to your nickname, Casanova?"

"Mmm hmm." Owen dropped his mouth to her ear, and, God, how could he make her feel so good with one little murmur? "Just wait 'til later and I'll prove it."

A snort caught Cate's attention from a few feet away, and she stepped back just in time to catch Greyson Whittaker's eye roll from the edge of the thoroughfare.

"Well, aren't y'all just sweet? I can practically feel myself getting cavities from here."

Owen stiffened beside her. "Greyson."

"Owen," he replied with an equal amount of under-enthusiasm, lifting his darkly stubbled chin in greeting. "See you've been busy."

Greyson's gaze lingered on Cate just long enough to turn Owen's hands into fists at his sides, and surprise lifted her brows. Greyson had never been particularly out of line with her, but, then again, pouring a man's Budweiser every Saturday night for the better part of a year could turn even the surliest son of a bitch into a lapdog. Cate didn't have any love lost for the guy, though. Especially not with the way he was sneering at Owen right now.

Unsurprisingly, Owen sneered right back. "If by 'busy' you mean 'working hard and enjoying strong crops this spring', then yep. We've been downright swamped."

"Sure," Greyson said, his laugh containing all the humor of a prize fight. "Let's go with that. Cate." He had the courtesy to tip his baseball hat at her, and, God, when he wasn't acting a fool (which, granted, was ninety-eight percent of the time), he was actually a good-looking guy. Not that the smirk that accompanied his greeting seemed to make Owen want to pummel him any less. "I see you've been *busy* this season, too."

Ooookay, that was enough. Owen might have a metric ton of composure, but she didn't want to find the boundaries of his asshole tolerance. Not in the middle of the farmers' market, anyway.

"Yep! I sure have. Cookie?" Cate asked, waiting until Greyson had taken one from the plate she held out before adding some teeth to her smile. "Looks like you could use a little sweetening."

Owen failed to stifle his laugh as Greyson's dark eyes widened in surprise.

"This is great," he said, chewing deliberately and sending a stare over the packages of cookies and biscuits and quick bread. "You sure you don't want to come on over to my side of the market and see how the better half farms? Whatever Cross Creek is doing for you, I'm sure Whittaker Hollow could do better."

She edged closer to Owen, turning her smile up to maximum wattage. "I'm all set on the better half, thanks. And after last year's Fall Fling, it might be just a little too soon for you to be getting so cocky."

At the mention of the bet he'd lost to Owen's brother, Eli, over which farm could earn more money before the harvest, Greyson's smirk flattened into a thin line. "Suit yourself, then. Y'all have a nice day."

"Mmm," Cate said, keeping her smile in place like she'd just won the Miss King County pageant. "You, too."

Owen let out a soft laugh in Greyson's wake. "Damn, I

wish I had a camera. The look on his face was freaking priceless."

"Guess that rivalry of yours is still alive and kicking," she said, pausing to offer up some samples to a few folks passing by.

"You could say that," he replied after all the potential customers were out of earshot. "But I'm not sure it's so much farm versus farm as it is Greyson just being a dick."

Surprise streaked a path through her veins. "So, whatever it is between you guys isn't some Capulets versus Montagues feud-type thing?"

"If I'm being entirely honest, I'm not sure exactly how the friction started all those years ago. But I do know this. I'd *love* to see someone knock that guy on his arrogant ass."

"Greyson's full of himself, I'll give you that," Cate said. All that cocky, tattooed bravado might be somebody's cuppa, but she'd stick with slightly broody and totally handsome, thanks. "I'm sure he'll get what's coming to him someday."

One shadowy brow lifted. "You don't strike me as the type of person to believe in karma."

"Oh, I don't." Lord knew she was far too practical to buy in to the universe and all its signs and signals. Give her reality any day. "But I do believe in payback, and I have a feeling Greyson's is going to be a bitch."

Cate stood next to Owen for a minute, quietly watching the milling crowd move over the thoroughfare. Finally, she gave voice to a question she'd been thinking about ever since he had asked her to work the farmers' market with him again. "So, do you work here every Saturday during the growing season?"

If he was taken aback by the change in subject, he didn't show it. "Pretty much, yeah. We used to swap farmers' market duty between me and Hunter and Eli. Sometimes my old man will get a wild hair and come like he did last week, too."

"Obviously," Cate teased, although she'd definitely noticed Mr. Cross's absence today.

The corners of Owen's mouth kicked upward in response. "For big-deal occasions like the Watermelon Festival, we all attend to represent the farm. But now Eli's gone, and after that scare my old man had last year with heat exhaustion, he's got to be more careful about putting in a lot of hours, too."

"He looks well," Cate said, and Owen surprised her by chuffing out a laugh.

"Oh, he's as tough as the day is long. Doc Sanders has him on a pretty decent regimen, although he drew the line at the high-fiber granola and kale chips she tried to work into his diet."

"Ugh." Cate wrinkled her nose. "Truth? Those are a hard no for me, too."

Owen's expression said that despite being a champion of the real deal, he wasn't a fan of turning kale into chips, either. "Hunter and I try to juggle the lion's share of the long hours and harder labor to make sure he doesn't get too worn out. But with Emerson's MS, it's more important for Hunter to stay close to home in case she needs help. He'd never say it in so many words; hell, he loves Cross Creek as much as I do. He loves Emerson, too, though. Family and farm. So I take most of the trips here on Saturdays now."

"Wow," Cate mused after Owen did a quick eyeball check-in with Lucas that consisted of one brows-up glance and a corresponding head shake from the guy that said he didn't need any help with the flow of customers wandering in and out of their tent. "Your family really *is* close-knit."

"Yeah." Owen's smile faltered slightly. "Well, except for Marley, but that's her choice, not ours."

Cate hadn't seen hide nor bedhead of Owen's sister since an early morning exchange at the coffeepot the other day that had consisted of a sum total of six syllables, five of them spoken by Cate. "I'm just guessing here, but I think Marley might be used to a bit of a different family dynamic."

"I don't know about that. She and her mother were close," Owen said, and Cate nodded, because even though Marley hadn't confided in her much since that day they'd talked about baking, she could still tell how strongly the girl had felt for her mother.

"Yes, but it was just the two of them, right?"

When Owen nodded, she continued. "Marley's not used to having siblings, or a father, and you guys are all *really* close. She might just need time to adjust to her new normal so she can figure out where she fits in to all of that."

A muscle ticked in Owen's jaw, his eyes going from blue to gray in a flash. "She's made it pretty clear she doesn't want us to be her new anything."

Ah, right. The old I'm-not-staying-for-long line. Cate laughed. "You don't actually believe that, do you?"

"I don't know," Owen said slowly, reaching out to fiddle with the edge of the cheery red and white tablecloth. "Not really. I mean, I don't know where else she'd go, but she's pretty convincing with that attitude of hers."

"I get that her don't-touch vibe is pretty strong, Owen." Cate's chest constricted, thinking of all the walls she'd put up right after Brian and Lily had died. "But she's hurting."

Owen, however, didn't budge. "That doesn't give her the right to say whatever she wants. Especially to my—" He caught himself, re-setting with a deep breath. "Our father."

"You're right. It doesn't," Cate agreed. "All I'm saying is

she's probably not being difficult for the sake of being difficult."

"Okay, but we're all trying," Owen said, his frustration on full display. "I even invited her to come to our weekly family dinner tonight. But she pretty much shut me down. That was on Tuesday, and I haven't talked to her since."

Cate thought about Marley, with all her prickly armor and the pain she thought she'd hidden in her eyes. "She barely spoke to me the first few times I saw her in the kitchen. It might take a couple of tries to get her to come to dinner."

"Maybe not if you're there."

Annnnd cue up the very last thing she'd expected Owen to say. "You want me to come to your family dinner? Tonight?" Cate asked, stepping back on the pavement.

This was exactly the sort of thing that should send her warning flags whipping in the wind. Family dinners, especially with families like the Crosses, were the sort of thing girlfriends attended. The sort of thing she needed to studiously avoid.

Funny, Owen looked as sure as Cate was surprised. "Why not? It's not as if we don't all know you, and, believe me, our family dinners are nothing fancy. Just the three of us and Emerson, kicking around the table on most Saturday evenings. But if you're there, maybe Marley might come, too. She seems to really like you."

"Like *me*? Why?" Cate blurted.

"Not to put too fine a point on it, but I'd guess it's because you're not one of us," Owen said with a shrug. "Maybe if she sees you there and realizes the dinner is no big deal, she'll feel more comfortable joining in. Or, at least, not running away."

Cate's defenses squalled despite the *yes* forming in her

chest. "I don't know," she said, reaching out to straighten the already-tidy rows of quick bread on the table in front of her. "I don't want to intrude on a family thing."

"That's just the point," Owen said, his voice both serious and soft. "It's not intruding, for you or for Marley. Come on, Cate. It's just dinner." He reached out to brush a hand over her wrist, and, God, how could one barely-there touch feel so comforting and *good*? "You work with all of us, and it's no secret we like you."

"I like all of you, too," she admitted. Even Marley, with all her barbed-wire edges. To be honest, the girl wasn't too unlike Owen, if Cate thought about it. And she definitely deserved to know her family, or, at the very least, give them a chance. If Cate could help with that, what would one little dinner hurt?

"Okay, then." Owen looked at her, his stare wide-open and his stance completely relaxed. "What do you say about joining us for dinner tonight?"

Her pulse tapped a rapid beat against her throat. The sudden rush wasn't fueled by the sort of unease she'd thoroughly expected, though. No, this felt different. Exciting, like standing on the edge of something brand-new and comfortable all at the same time.

It felt like hope.

"Okay," Cate said with a smile. "But you know the drill."

Owen threw his head back and laughed. "Let me guess. Only if I let you bring dessert."

24

Owen stirred the pot of spaghetti sauce on the stove top, unable to keep his ear-to-ear grin at bay. They'd had another incredible day at the farmers' market, bringing in such a steady stream of sales that there had barely been much to pack up and take home at the end. He and Cate had been on their toes from the minute she'd agreed to come to dinner until the powers that be had closed the gates leading into the pavilion, selling everything from radishes to rutabagas and a whole lot of cakes and cookies in between.

Business was booming. He was spending every night with a woman who was as smart and savvy as she was beautiful. Eli and Scarlett would be back in Millhaven in one measly week, putting his entire family back together for the first time in nearly five months.

Yeah. Owen couldn't deny it. Life was fucking fantastic.

"Ooooooh, spaghetti and meatballs," Emerson crooned, making her way from the back door to the middle of the kitchen with an armload of freshly cut wildflowers and the family dog, Lucy, at the hem of her skirt. "What's the occasion?"

Owen's pulse tripped, but still, his grin refused to budge. "I can't make spaghetti and meatballs for any old Saturday dinner?"

Hunter laughed, looking up from the spot where he'd been emptying the dishwasher. "Dude. Not only are you making spaghetti and meatballs for the second time this month, but you're smiling. A *lot*. So, in a word? No."

"I can frown if you want," Owen said, dropping his voice to keep his next words brother-to-brother before adding, "While I'm kicking your ass." He dodged Hunter's attempt at a laughter-filled potshot to his shoulder, adjusting back to normal volume. "And I only made it last time because *you* asked me to," he pointed out.

"Uh-huh. What about tonight?" Hunter asked with an arch of his brows, and damn it, now even their old man had looked up from his newspaper with interest.

"Tonight I just felt like making it. Plus, uh, Cate's joining us for dinner."

"Really?" Emerson drew the word out with interest, her blue eyes sparkling in a way that meant nothing good for Owen. "So, you two are a thing?"

Hunter shook his head, filling a glass with ice and water and passing it over to Emerson as he took the flowers from her and placed a kiss on her cheek. "They are. Just don't ask him about it," he said, giving up a wink and a nod that answered her question. "He gets snippy."

"I don't get snippy," Owen—*shit*—snipped. He stirred the pot of sauce, although it was mostly to smooth out his nerves. This whole conversation was stupid. It was just a meal. So what if he really liked her?

He cleared his throat. "Anyway, I asked Cate to dinner

because I thought it might make Marley more comfortable." It wasn't the only reason, of course. But for now, it'd do.

His father looked up in earnest now, the paper rustling to the pine tabletop. "Marley's coming to dinner?"

Ah, there was enough hope in the old man's eyes to make Owen's throat tighten. "She told me she'd think about it," he said.

Actually, his sister's words had been more along the lines of "I'll think about it, maybe, if I'm hungry, or whatever," but since she hadn't hit him with an unequivocal "hell, no" when he'd gone upstairs a couple hours ago to ask her if she wanted to join them, Owen had decided to go with the "maybe" part and call it a win.

"I see." His father nodded slowly, running his fingers over the brim of his Stetson. "Well, it'll be right nice to see Cate at the table."

As if on cue, the doorbell rang. Hunter's grin lasted only long enough for him to catch the warning look from his bride-to-be, and clearly Owen hadn't thought this through a lick before he'd opened his great, big mouth and invited Cate to join them.

"I'll get it," he said, grateful to be out from under the Cross family microscope. Setting the sauce-coated wooden spoon in the spoon-rest beside the stove, he turned toward the entryway to the kitchen, covertly checking his button-down shirt and jeans for any errant splatters as he made his way to the front door. Cate stood on the porch boards, looking pretty enough to steal his breath in a flowery sundress and her dark curls all soft around her face, and oh, hell.

He was in deep. Deep. Trouble.

"Hi," she said, her wide-open smile putting another nail in his I'm-stupid-for-you coffin. Jesus, he needed to get himself together before Hunter clapped eyes on him and gave him shit for this until he was ninety.

"You rang the bell," Owen blurted, and, right, so much for getting himself together.

Fortunately, Cate laughed. "Yeah. I know I usually walk right in for work, but it didn't quite feel proper for tonight. If you want, you can shut the door and I can barge in on a do-over, though. Your call."

The ease of her words and the sassy smile with which she delivered them turned Owen's nerves into dust. "Nah. It doesn't seem right to shut the door on a pretty girl. Especially one who comes bearing gifts."

He gestured to the plate balanced between her palms, which she lifted with a smile. "Apple pie," she said.

"Now I'm *definitely* not shutting the door on you," Owen said, gesturing her over the threshold with a flourish. He took the pie plate from Cate's hands, brushing a quick kiss over her mouth as he ushered her all the way into the house. They made their way to the kitchen, where Hunter was still grinning like an idiot, Emerson was trying her best to look like she hadn't just been eavesdropping, and Owen's old man was wearing a smile that flat-out busted them *both* for eavesdropping.

"Oh, hey, Cate!" Emerson said, subtly placing her elbow into Hunter's rib cage before crossing the kitchen to give Cate a friendly hug. "It's so nice that you could join us tonight."

Hunter nodded in agreement, and for all of his ribbing, Owen had to admit being grateful for his brother's genuinely easygoing nature right now. "Ooooh, pie. Why don't I take that off your hands for you, O?"

"Not a chance, little brother," Owen said, neatly side-stepping him and turning to put the pie in a safe place, a.k.a.

the sideboard, where Hunter wouldn't get his mitts on it because it would be in plain view.

"Thanks for having me over for dinner," Cate said. "It's really kind of you all."

Owen's gut squeezed at the sight of his father's genuine smile. God, it had been far too long since the old man had given one of those up. "It's our pleasure, darlin'. And the least we could do for our newest business partner. Owen tells us y'all had quite a day today at the farmers' market."

Cate nodded, her smile brightening. "We did. The specialty produce was flying out of the tent, and I even ran out of pound cake there at the end."

"Well, bein' a big fan of your pound cake, I can't say I'm too surprised about that."

"Thank you, Mr. Cross. That's high praise, for sure."

She slipped into the kitchen to wash her hands, continuing to chat with his father about the farmers' market and helping Hunter chop vegetables for the salad while Owen got the spaghetti on to boil. Emerson joined the back and forth about the farmers' market, asking questions about Cate's baking schedule and her signature recipes, and, damn, it felt better than Owen wanted to admit to have a house full of good food and happy conversation.

"So, Cate, I've been meaning to come by the office and talk to you," Emerson said, and, wait...what was that weird look she'd just exchanged with Hunter?

"Oh?" Cate asked, pausing with her hands chock-full of sliced cherry tomatoes. "I got your notes on the farm's ad placements for this month. All the accounts should be up to date in the system."

Emerson smiled. "Thank you, but that's not what I wanted to talk about."

"Okay." Cate's tone painted the word as way more question than statement, but Emerson—thankfully—got right to the point.

"Actually, Hunter and I were wondering if you would consider making our wedding cake."

Surprise filled Owen's chest at the same time Cate's brows shot upward. "You...I'm sorry, what?" she asked.

But Emerson's expression remained absolutely certain. "I know two weeks is really short notice. But the wedding is going to be small, only fifty people or so, and all the bakeries we've tried in Camden Valley and Lockridge are just okay."

"They're definitely nothing special," Hunter chimed in, and the implication that Cate's baking was *very* special put a pretty, pink tint on Cate's cheeks.

"That pound cake you made a couple of weeks ago was to die for, and Owen told us all about that decadent chocolate lava cake you made last weekend, and, well...Hunter and I thought we'd take a flyer and ask if you'd be willing to make a wedding cake for us."

"I don't know what to say," Cate replied slowly, the tomatoes now on the butcher block, clearly forgotten. "I've never made anything even close to a wedding cake before, although I guess I *have* worked with fondant a bunch."

The fact that she hadn't dismissed the request with an outright "no" made Owen's pulse hitch. Emerson must have noticed it, too, because she pressed onward, albeit with care.

"We really don't want anything terribly fancy," she said, and Hunter nodded in agreement.

"It's just us."

"It's your wedding cake," Cate said, doubt flickering through her stare. "Even if it's not fancy, it should still be perfect."

Owen opened his mouth before his brain fully got the command from his instincts to speak. "If anyone can make a perfect cake, it's you. Plus, you have a little time to try a few things out to be sure you get them exactly the way you want them."

"I'd happily volunteer to be your taste tester," Hunter said, and their old man tipped his head with a smile.

"It does seem like a right smart plan to have the best baker in the county whip up your wedding cake," he agreed.

The doubt in Cate's eyes turned into something else, something softer that sent a twist through Owen's rib cage. "I'd have to see photos of what you have in mind before I could commit."

Emerson didn't hesitate. "As it turns out, I have a bunch of ideas saved to a Pinterest board. I could show you right now, if you want."

"I'm sure Owen and I can manage to get dinner finished up while you two take a look," Hunter said, and Owen made a mental note to buy his brother an extra beer next weekend at The Bar.

That beer became the entire tab at the sight of Cate's smile. "Okay, then. Let's go through some cake ideas and see what we can put together."

After a quick rinse of her hands, Cate joined Emerson at the table. There wasn't much left to do for dinner, save grabbing the plates and cutlery from the cupboard and putting some finishing touches on the salad and the pasta, which he and Hunter easily handled. The conversation kept flowing after everyone had filled their plates, and Owen didn't even mind Hunter's poorly hidden snort when Cate commented how much she loved the signature dinner dish that—okay, fine—he only made on special occasions. They sat at the table, talking and laughing and having a raging debate about raspberry jam filling versus amaretto buttercream, and, God, this felt good.

With Cate right beside him and his family all around, this felt *right*.

"Hi." Marley's voice sounded off from the entryway to the kitchen, causing the conversation to thud to an abrupt and awkward halt and her face to flush at the ensuing silence. "Sorry. I didn't mean to interrupt."

Just like that, her expression snapped closed like a pair of old storm shutters. She pivoted on her thick black boot heels, but before she could bolt or Owen could open his graceless mouth to stop her, Cate stood up.

"You're not interrupting," she said. "We were just having dinner."

Marley chewed on her thumb nail, her gaze flicking over the table. "Yeah. I got that."

Owen's shoulders stiffened. Yes, he'd wanted Marley to join them, but he wasn't about to let her get chippy with Cate.

But then Cate's hand slid to his shoulder, stopping his protest in its tracks. "Emerson and Hunter asked me to make their wedding cake. We were talking about some of the options."

"Oh," Marley said, her voice lifting with just enough interest to make Owen hopeful that this whole thing wasn't a crash and burn just yet. "That's cool, I guess."

She looked from the stovetop to the table, and Owen finally made his mouth work properly. "There's plenty of spaghetti in the pot if you're hungry."

"I suppose I could eat," she said slowly.

Hunter was on his feet in less than a breath. "I'll go grab a chair from the dining room."

They shuffled their plates around the table to make room for Marley, who put a minimal amount of spaghetti and salad on her plate before sitting down next to Cate. She chose the spot farthest away from their father yet again, Owen noticed, but he guessed all the wins couldn't come in a day. The conversation picked up where it had left off, with Emerson and Cate trading ideas about cakes and him and Hunter chiming in here and there. Marley ate without contributing, and Owen's gut did a little free fall of disappointment as she cleared her plate and excused herself as soon as she finished.

"Let her go for now," Cate whispered, softly enough to keep the words private between them. His old man remained quiet, but the flash of emotion whisking through his stare was enough to give Owen hope.

"Okay," he whispered back, the hope in his chest tripling when Cate reached for his hand beneath the table and squeezed.

25

Cate surveyed the mess she'd made in the Cross family kitchen with a frown. She must have been insane to have agreed to make a wedding cake, of all things, right out of the gate, and with only a week and a half to go now, at that. Hunter and Emerson had been really easy to work with, though, clearly describing what they wanted and giving her enough leeway to be creative with some of the smaller aspects. Owen had been wildly encouraging, too, foregoing the rah-rah cheerleader route for the sort of quiet, truthful encouragement that felt far too good, yet right at the same time. Add to it the incredible sex they'd been having pretty much every night and the easy conversations they'd been having every day, and Cate couldn't deny it.

She was crushing on Owen Cross. Hard.

"Stop," she whispered, although her mutinous belly had already done a little backflip at the mere thought of him. Everything about Owen screamed "family man", and she couldn't give him what he'd ultimately want from her if they fell for each other. She *knew* this. Had known it from the beginning. Yet, somehow, she managed to still feel so good with him that that troublesome little fact got brushed to the back of her mind.

What if she didn't stop? What if, somehow, she and Owen could make things work, just the two of them?

"You look kind of lost in thought."

Marley's voice hit Cate with no small measure of surprise, and her head sprang up to meet the younger woman's stare.

"Oh!" She laughed, not wanting to scare Marley off since she hadn't seen her since she'd dined and dashed on Saturday night, but it still came out tinged with nervousness. "Yeah, I guess I was zoning out a little. I'm working on Hunter and Emerson's cake, and there's a lot to get done before the wedding next weekend."

Marley's shoulders tensed beneath her dark gray tank top. "So, I guess you're going to the wedding, then."

"Yes," Cate said. Cake aside, Owen had asked her to be his date the other night as they'd been drifting off to sleep. After the time she'd spent with both him and his family over the last four weeks, her *yes* had been as automatic as breathing. "I'll deliver the cake early on the morning of the wedding, but I'm also going to the ceremony and reception with Owen." A thought occurred to her, sending her brows creasing down. "Aren't you going, too?"

"No. I don't know." Marley knotted her arms around her rib cage, staring at the floor tiles. "Hunter and Emerson have asked me a bunch of times, but I just don't think it's a good idea."

"You don't." A shot of frustration moved through Cate's chest. It must have shown on her face, because Marley's scowl went from steely to ironclad.

"No. It's a small wedding for everyone who's really close to them, and I'm not part of their family."

"That's bullshit."

Cate heard the challenge only after she'd issued it, but still, she stood firm. Marley might be hurting, but she couldn't deny the truth. Not only was she biologically part of the family, but from her looks to her tough-edged spirit, she was a Cross through and through.

Of course, Cate should've known she'd argue anyway. "Excuse me?" Marley asked, frost crisping every syllable.

God, she was as serious as Owen. But Cate's pragmatism was equal opportunity, and it was past time for someone to stop tiptoeing around this girl and deliver some tough love, straight-up. "I said, that's bullshit. Also, here. Stir this."

She handed over a bowl full of buttercream frosting and a silicone spatula, which Marley was too shocked not to take.

"I probably shouldn't." Marley tried to push the over-sized stainless steel bowl back in Cate's direction. "I mean, it's for the wedding cake. I don't want to screw it up. And what do you mean, that's bullshit?"

Cate shook her head, picking up a bowl of her own. "It's just stirring. You can't screw it up. And I mean just what I said. You might not be okay with it yet, but you're part of this family. You're going to have to face that at some point."

Marley huffed out a breath, but put the spatula into the bowl and started to stir the frosting nonetheless. "Owen and Hunter and Emerson and Eli are part of this family. Not me."

Cate measured her words for a second, trying to temper them, but, oh, screw it. "Being Tobias's daughter won't make you any less of your mom's daughter, too, Marley."

"I don't want to talk about Tobias."

Marley delivered the words with enough brittle edges that Cate knew better than to push. Still... "Fine. Let's talk about your brothers, then."

Marley stirred the buttercream in her bowl, and, huh, she actually had some nice technique. "What about them?" she asked.

"Owen and Hunter love you, and even though Eli's not here all the time, I'm sure he does, too." Cate replied. "They're good men, and they want to be part of your life. It might not hurt to let them."

"*Might* not." Marley's knuckles whitened over the spatula, her eyes laser-focused on the bowl cradled in at her side. "That's only a maybe, and I'm not really crazy about those odds."

Oh. *Oh*. Something twisted, deep behind Cate's breastbone, but she shook her head despite the tightness expanding in her chest.

"I know it's scary, taking the risk of letting someone care about you again. Of caring for them back," she said, because, God, she really did. She might not have realized it at the time, but she could see now that she'd purposely kept people at arm's length after Brian and Lily had died. It hadn't just been everyone in town who had tiptoed around her and thought "poor Cate". She'd done her fair share of it to herself, too.

And if she could keep Marley from hurting, even a little bit, by letting her know that, then she owed it to her, and to Owen, to try.

Cate put down the bowl of jam filling she'd been mixing and took a step closer. "I also know that when you've lost someone close to you, it's hard to let other people in. You worry that something might happen if you allow yourself to hope or feel good, and you'll just end up hurt again."

"I don't..." Marley exhaled, her voice growing softer. "Does it ever go away?"

"The pain of losing someone that close to you?" Cate asked.

But Marley shook her head. "The fear of *getting* close again. It must go away, right? Because you did it with Owen."

Cate's pulse ratcheted, tapping harder at her throat. "What's going on with me and Owen is a little different than what's going on with your family."

"Is it really?" Marley asked, looking genuinely surprised. "I mean, obviously, you're his girlfriend and I'm his sister, so it's different in that way. But close is close. Weren't you scared to let him in?"

Since this wasn't about her as much as it was Marley, Cate dodged around the "girlfriend" thing in favor of answering the question without argument. "I think it was more like terrified," she said with a small laugh. "But once I took the chance and let Owen in a little, I actually felt better, and then the rest just sort of happened all on its own. I'm not saying I'm not still scared of being close to people sometimes, or that I don't feel sad about losing my daughter sometimes, too, but trusting the right people to care about you can make a difference in how scared and sad you feel."

"No. I can't trust Tobias," Marley said, her head shake adamant. "He knew about me all this time. From the beginning. I know my mom asked him not to come find us, but he was sending her money for me. He *knew*, and he could've come anyway, or at least called, or something, and I just... *can't.*"

"That's fair." Cate's reply clearly had shock value, and she used the ensuing hiccup of silence to continue with, "You can't force trust and expect it to work. But your brothers love you, Marley, maybe even more than you know.

It might be okay if you let them care for you a little, just to see how it goes."

Marley nodded. "Maybe."

Cate had a feeling the road to trust had a lot more potholes in it than that for Marley, and that her healing would take a lot of time, but for now, this was enough to start.

"Good," she said with a smile. "In the meantime, do you want to help me out here? This cake is kind of kicking my ass, and I could really use an assistant."

~

"IF I DIDN'T KNOW any better, I'd swear you're trying to kill me."

Owen pushed back from the plate-lined dinner table in his kitchen, grinning despite the claim. Between the storefront project that was humming along ahead of schedule and the temperate weather kicking their growing season into high gear, he'd had a long but successful week. Eli and Scarlett were set to arrive tomorrow from Dublin, just in time for family dinner, and despite the absolute fullness of his belly right now, Owen was happier than he'd ever been.

He had family and farm. And Cate was right there with him in the middle of both.

"Hmm," she murmured. "Death by cake? Really?" Her lips quirked into just enough of a sassy smile to make him pounce.

"I didn't say it wouldn't be a hell of a good way to go. But, seriously, as amazing as those test cakes were, I can't try another bite. At least, not for a while."

"You did just eat four slices," she mused, licking some buttercream off the edge of her fork thoughtfully. "Granted, they were kind of small, and we did have them instead of dinner, but I'll let you slide." She pointed the fork at him, her smile turning serious. "For now."

Owen pushed to his feet, moving across the floor to wrap an arm around her waist. God, he loved the way she seemed to fit against him like she was made for the space, her shoulders lining up with his chest, her mouth within perfect reach of his.

"The cake is going to be incredible," he said after sliding a kiss over her lips. "I know you're worried about it, and I totally get that, but really. You've got this."

Owen supposed most people would've probably gone with a good, old, reliable "don't worry" in this situation. But he also knew that telling Cate *not* to worry would be akin to telling him not to fret over bad weather or failed crops. Not worrying about something like this just wasn't in her DNA.

Her suddenly tense muscles were case in point. "The wedding is essentially seven days from now." She sent a glance to the window at the back of the kitchen, where twilight had already set Friday night into motion. "Hunter and Emerson have been really easy to work with, and I know I'm not a dolt when it comes to baking. It's just that making a cake for a function like this is so much bigger than anything I've ever even dreamed of doing. I'm scared it's not going to be perfect, you know?"

"Is anything ever really perfect?"

Whether it was the question or the laughter he'd pinned it with that made Cate's eyes go wide, he couldn't be sure. "Some things are," she said.

"Maybe to you, sure," he countered. "But I think perfect is more in the eye of the beholder than it is a golden rule, just like I know everyone is going to love Hunter and Emerson's wedding cake. Including the two of them."

Cate bit her bottom lip, and hell if that didn't make the way he was holding her that much more enticing. "I *am* really close to nailing down the final recipes for the flavor combination they chose," she admitted. "And now that Marley's helping me, things are going a lot more efficiently, too."

At the mention of his sister's sudden change of heart— or at least in attitude—Owen's chest tightened. "I know she seems to like baking, but she's been such a hard 'no' on anything having to do with our family, including this wedding. I still don't know how you talked her into helping you make Hunter and Emerson's cake."

"I pretty much just asked and she said yes," Cate said. "After the talk she and I had a couple of days ago, I think she was looking for a way to start connecting with you and Hunter that didn't feel awkward, and helping with the cake fit the bill. It doesn't hurt that she's actually got skills."

Owen thought back to the day he'd first caught Marley making brownies and smiled. "Hunter and I saw her mixing up some different flavors of jam filling today after we came in from working in the north fields, and she didn't run out of the kitchen when we stopped to ask her how things were going. In fact, she said she even changed her mind about coming to the wedding."

"She did?"

At Owen's nod, Cate continued, her eyes sparkling with genuine happiness. "I didn't want to push her the other day, but I was really hoping she'd change her mind. I'm so glad she decided to come."

He chuffed out a quick laugh. "I thought Hunter was going to pull a muscle, he was smiling so hard." In fact, his brother had been so happy about Marley's about-face that

Owen hadn't even been able to give him a proper ration of shit over it.

"Hmm," Cate said. "Somehow, I bet he wasn't the only one happy about her decision."

Ah, fuck. Busted. "We've got a long way to go to mend those fences," Owen said, choosing not to tarnish the moment by bringing up the fact that Marley had made it wildly clear that, while she'd attend the wedding and reception, what she *wouldn't* do was anything that involved their father, including family photos. "I'm just glad she's not pushing us all away, all the time anymore."

"I'm glad she's not pushing you guys away, too."

"Us," he corrected, the word slipping out before he could trap it between his teeth and bite it back.

Cate's brows knit together, and she pulled back to look at him in confusion. "What?"

For a hot second, Owen thought about hedging. But whether she realized it or not, Cate had played a huge part in getting Marley to start to come around, and she deserved his gratitude.

"I never would have gotten past square one with Marley if it weren't for you. I don't know that any of us would have. So, yeah, you're part of that. And I'm really thankful."

"For the record, I think you guys would have made headway on your own eventually," Cate said, her lips curving the slightest degree before she added, "after all, you do have your own brand of charm hidden beneath that serious exterior. But I'm glad my being here helped."

Owen pulled her closer. "Your being here does a lot more than help."

He leaned down, angling a kiss over her mouth. She opened for him in a seamless glide, their tongues touching with just enough suggestion to make his cock stir. The feeling was sexual, but kissing her made something deep inside of him feel good in a way that surpassed plain desire, too, and, impulsively, he pulled back to grab her hands.

"Come with me," Owen said, heading for the stairs.

"I thought you'd never ask," Cate replied with a laugh. But rather than giving in to the demand pumping down from the primal parts of his brain that wanted to strip her naked and fuck her until they were both sweaty and screaming and senseless, he bypassed his bed and headed directly for his dresser.

"Here." He pulled open the drawer he'd emptied a couple of days ago, his heart moving into his throat as he turned to look at Cate. But this was right—*they* were right. No matter how much she might have lost in the past, he wanted to be with her moving forward.

"What's this?" she asked, both her expression and her tone impossible to read.

"It's a drawer," Owen replied, and, Christ, was he really going to go the Captain Obvious route now, when it really mattered? "I mean, it's a drawer for you. To put your stuff in when you stay here. With me. If you want to."

"Oh."

Cate didn't say no, nor did she run screaming from his room, both of which, Owen supposed, were a win. She did remain quiet, though, with her wide eyes fixed on the drawer as if it might sprout teeth and snap at her, and fuck it. He might not know any fancy ways to say what he was feeling, but he knew this woman, knew how much he *wanted* her in his bed and his dresser drawers and his life, and that was enough.

"I know you might feel like this is a big deal," he said. "But it's not—not in the way you're thinking. I just...I like that you stay here. It's okay with me if you decide not to do it every night. I just thought this would make it easier for when you do. That's all."

"Oh," Cate whispered again, this one sounding worlds different than the one she'd uttered less than a minute before. "I guess it would be less of a pain than bringing an overnight bag every time."

Hope kicked through Owen's chest, bright and daring. "It's actually downright practical, when you think about it," he said, delivering just enough of a smile with the words to draw a soft laugh past Cate's lips.

"You really know how to sweet-talk a girl, don't you, Casanova?"

"I know how to sweet-talk you," he countered. Wrapping his arms around her, he pulled her close enough to breathe in the woodsy, herbal scent of her hair and the smell of her skin that belonged to her alone. "I have my own brand of charm, remember?"

Cate melted against him, the warmth of her body and the lush press of her curves and straightaways rekindling the darker part of the desire that had made him lead her up here in the first place. "That you do," she said.

"Does that mean you want the drawer?"

"Yes, I want the drawer." She kissed him just long enough to turn it into a promise. "But I want you first."

"I'm all yours," Owen promised in return.

And as he cradled her face and kissed her back, he knew that he meant it in more ways than one.

Just like he knew he was falling in love with her.

26

As she stood here in Owen's bedroom, with his strong, steady hands cupping her face and her belly fluttering with a sort of excitement and intensity she couldn't even name, let alone explain, Cate knew she should be scared. No, wait. That wasn't quite right. She should be downright fucking petrified. Not only was she getting close enough to Owen's entire family to befriend his prickly younger sister, bake his brother's wedding cake, *and* go to the fairy-tale wedding as his plus-one, but she'd spent every single day and night with him for the past few weeks, to the point that he'd offered her the roomiest drawer in his dresser, and she'd actually taken him up on the bedroom real estate. Little by little, Owen had moved past her defenses, over all the walls she'd strategically set up around her heart to keep him out. To keep the both of them safe.

And the scariest part was that it felt too right to be scary at all.

"Come here." Cate slid her arms around Owen's neck, pulling their bodies flush. He moved toward her so willingly that the flutter in her belly turned into a full-fledged back-flip, and, God, she couldn't get enough of this man.

"I'm here," he said. Keeping his gentle hold on her face, he kissed her again, slow, but not soft. He pressed his mouth to hers, and the two days' worth of stubble on his face created just enough friction to make her breath catch. "Just show me what you want, sweetheart."

Cate whispered, "All I want is you."

She eliminated the tiny fraction of space between them to reclaim the kiss. A sigh built in the back of her throat, swirling like a tiny storm before rising out of her. Owen coaxed her lips open to capture the sound, swiping his tongue first along her lower lip, then the smaller, more sensitive swoop of the one above it, tasting her thoroughly before tugging her lip between his own.

"*Ah.*" She made a noise that defied actual language, and Owen's smile grew dark over her mouth.

"You like that." He did it again before she could answer, and, again, she bowed into the provocative contact.

"Yes." Heat gathered between Cate's thighs, heady and insistent. Owen read her in less than a breath, his tongue skimming another path over the top edge of her lip before he pulled back to let his fingertips follow.

A wicked smile shaped his even more wicked mouth. "Good. Because if what you want is me, then I intend to deliver."

Cate paused, her heart tripping beneath her T-shirt. "You do?"

"Mmm hmm. Do you want to know how?"

Unable to get a verbal response past all the lust that had just made her sex squeeze with need, she nodded. Owen trailed one hand over her cheekbone, his calluses rasping against her skin as he hooked his index finger beneath her chin, tilting her face up to pin her with a glittering gray stare.

"I'm going to undress you." He flicked the button on her jeans open with his free hand as a preview, turning the juncture between her thighs slick even though he hadn't come close to touching her there. His fingers moved up, hovering over the midline of her body for a long, pulsing moment before he rested them on her breastbone.

"I'm going to touch you," he continued, both his stare and his smile turning downright sinful as he leaned in to place his lips an inch away from hers.

"Then I'm going to put my mouth in every single place you want it until you come apart under my tongue. And that's only what will happen *before* I get my cock inside you."

Oh. God. Cate fought the urge to just rip off both of their clothes and skip all the pleasantries in favor of having him inside her within the next five seconds. But she'd promised to let him have her, and what's more, it was what she *wanted*.

This man. Touching her. Kissing her. Pleasuring her and taking her any way he wanted to.

Starting right now.

Nodding, she lowered her hands to her sides and shifted back a half step. Owen raked a stare over her, so hot she swore she could feel it on her skin. The soft light filtering in from the hallway allowed her to see his gaze travel up over her jeans, then her T-shirt, lingering on the flare of her hips and the curve of her breasts before connecting with her eyes.

"So pretty," he murmured. Other than that first time in his kitchen, Cate hadn't felt particularly self-conscious about Owen seeing her pleasure. He certainly was skilled as hell at doling it out. But standing here, fully clothed and brimming with need for what only he could give her, she knew she should feel vulnerable.

Instead, she looked him right in the eye and trusted him.

He stepped closer, running his fingers over the top edge of her jeans. Anticipation pumped through her, turning into relief as he grasped the hem of her T-shirt and pulled it over her head. She'd gone for function over form when getting dressed this morning, choosing a plain, white satin bra that —ugh—bordered on boring.

Not that Owen seemed to mind. "Mmm," came a rumble of appreciation, deep in the back of his throat. "Now, turn."

Surprise stuttered through Cate's veins at the near-demand, but she did as he asked, pivoting on her heels to face his bed.

"Don't worry, I've got you," he said, proving it by wrapping an arm around her from behind. Even through his T-shirt, his chest was warm on her rib cage, and the unmistakable ridge of his cock pressing against her lower back sent a shot of arousal directly to her core.

"I know," Cate said. Owen's fingers slid over her belly, deftly lowering the zipper on her jeans and tugging the denim from her hips to reveal the white satin panties that matched her bra. She toed out of her sandals at the same time he pulled her jeans past her knees, until, finally, both were on the floor, forgotten.

Owen returned to standing in the spot behind her, his hands shaping her waist and his breath warm on her neck. True to his word, he let his fingers start to roam, first over her hips, then her sides, then her shoulders. He touched her as if he was memorizing every contour, and her heart pounded faster as she watched each glide of his hands. His exhale grew rougher when he got to her breasts, the sound making her nipples stand out tightly against the thin barrier of the fabric covering them.

"Owen, *please*." She arched into the contact, desperate for more, and he obliged in less than a heartbeat. One twist of his wrist freed her bra, his strong, capable hands feeling so wantonly hot on her bare skin that she cried out.

"I could spend forever listening to you make that sound," he said. Still at her back, he cupped both of her breasts, stroking circles over her achingly tight nipples. Each pass heightened her arousal even more, and oh, God —*oh, God, oh, God*—her clit throbbed so hard it nearly hurt with the sort of pleasure/pain that made her desperate to come.

As if he'd read her mind, Owen lowered one hand over the flat of her belly. Cate watched, entranced, as he dipped his fingers past the top edge of her panties, her gasp flying out when he slipped them over her pussy with ease.

"Ah!" She bucked into the touch, her body vibrating with need.

"There you are, so wet and ready," he whispered. "So goddamn beautiful."

She realized in that moment that Owen was watching over her shoulder, and even though she'd have thought it impossible, she grew even more turned on. Cate moaned in reply, watching, too as he teased her clit with his fingers. She widened her stance to give him better access, meeting each touch with a thrust of her hips. Owen tightened his arm around her belly, pulling her completely level against his chest. Using his new vantage point, he cupped her pussy and sank two fingers deep inside, the pressure so unexpected and darkly provocative that she saw stars.

Yet Owen's voice was steady behind her. "I have you, remember." He withdrew slightly, but only to press right back home. "Take what you need. I'm right here to give it to you."

Cate didn't wait to comply. Pumping her hips, she moved over his fingers, her inner muscles squeezing and releasing with every push and retreat. The heel of his hand rubbed against her clit, the slickness from between her legs providing friction that sent a tremble from the lowest part of her belly. An orgasm built from some hidden place inside her, twisting and growing stronger with each thrust of Owen's fingers. He lowered the hand that had been cupping her breast, sliding his fingers into the scant space between his opposite palm and her body. Between the pressure inside her pussy and the more direct contact of his fingers on her overly sensitive clit, she was lost. Her climax spiraled out from between her hips, wringing all of her tension free and knocking her breath from her lungs until finally, she was boneless in Owen's arms.

"Christ, that was hot," he said, his voice ragged and reverent. Cate registered the rapid rise and fall of his chest, the hum of need pulsing through him with the heartbeat she felt against her back, and she turned in his arms in one fluid spin.

"Now, it's your turn." She reached for the button on his jeans. "I want to make you feel good, too. Tell me what *you* want."

The chuckle filling the shadowy air around them shocked her, stilling her hands.

"Just you, sweetheart," Owen said, his gaze wide-open and steady on hers. "I only want you."

They made quick work of the few items of clothing left between them, her panties, his shirt and boots and jeans and boxers all finding the floorboards in quick succession. He guided her back over his bed, settling her in the center of the mattress before tucking in at her side. He followed through on his dark and dirty promise to kiss her anywhere she wanted him to, desire sparking back through her blood with speed and intensity that both surprised and excited the hell out of her as he worked her body with perfect strokes of his lips and tongue. But despite her rebounding arousal, Cate still felt empty, as if she was missing just one more piece that would make her whole.

"Owen," she whispered, pulling him toward her and rolling to her side so they were lined up, face-to-face. "Take what you really want. I want it, too. I want *you*."

Slowly, Owen nodded. Breaking from her only long enough to take a condom from his bedside table and roll it firmly into place, he returned to the spot beside her, brushing a kiss over her mouth that quickly deepened. Cate hooked one knee over his hip, using the leverage and some added momentum from her hands to roll him onto his back.

He arched up, the thick length of his cock jutting against his lower belly. His muscles, already bowstring tight beneath her, became even more rigid when she shifted forward to straddle his upper thighs, and she greedily gave in to the urge to slide her sex over his rock-hard shaft.

"Cate."

It was as much benediction as it was warning, and she heeded both. Tilting her hips, she angled even closer, until the head of his cock was notched at her entrance. Owen gripped her waist, bowing up into her at the same time she lowered down, and Cate was helpless against the moan working its way past her lips.

"Oh...*God*." She stilled, trying to adjust to the nearly too-tight fullness where she'd just felt so empty. Owen held her in place, keeping their bodies completely joined as he started to rock against her. The movement was just enough to let her inner muscles relax, and it quickly sent desire kicking through her blood.

Anchoring her shins to the mattress, Cate balanced her weight more steadily on her knees. She tested her pleasure, riding Owen's cock with thrusts that ranged from shallow to rapid to deep before sinking all the way over him until he filled her to the hilt. A high noise vibrated in the back of her throat at the combination of pressure and friction, and she leaned forward in search of both. The move brought his cock in direct contact with her already hyper-sensitive clit, tripping her right over the edge into another release. Owen let her ride out every tremor before rolling her to her back in a move so swift, they remained locked together, and Cate knotted her legs around the corded muscles at his hips, taking him as deeply as her body would allow. He was right there with her, though, thrusting harder and faster and filling her again and again, until his body tensed and he came with a shout.

Owen softened his movements, his body growing heavier over hers with each passing second. For a minute, they simply lay there, catching their breath.

And then he stole hers all over again by saying, "I mean it, Cate. All I want is you."

27

All I want is you.

The words had echoed in Cate's head for the past twenty-four hours. She'd been so stunned when Owen had said them that she hadn't been able to speak. She hadn't been able to say what was in her heart, which was that all she wanted was him, too. Once she'd gotten past the shock of what he'd said and what she felt in return, she'd wanted to say it back—hell, she'd wanted to shout it from the rooftops. But Owen had already kissed her forehead and turned to gather his clothes, giving her that crooked smile she loved so much and promising to go warm up some dinner.

They'd slid right back into their routine, talking and laughing and even wrapping up in blankets to have a couple of beers on his front porch as the stars rose in the sky. Today had been more of the same, with her happily testing out the last of the cake recipes and Owen working in the greenhouse while Hunter took farmers' market duty, and, as crazy as it was, Cate couldn't deny the truth.

Not only was she falling for Owen Cross, but with what

he'd said last night, they might just end up together instead of heartbroken.

"Hey! Are you ready?" Owen's voice delivered her back to the spot where she stood in his kitchen, and, God, how could her heart squeeze so hard at just one little smile from this man? "Eli and Scarlett's flight landed at BWI three hours ago, and he texted to let us know they breezed through customs and they're about forty minutes out."

"Oh, good," Cate said. She was dying to hear about Eli and Scarlett's stay in Dublin. And if they happened to have any inside scoop on the nuances of authentic Irish soda bread, all the better. "I was just finishing up. Marley and I made a bit of a mess in here with her buttercream lesson today. Trust me when I tell you that as delicious as it is, the stuff is like spackling paste once it dries."

Owen laughed. "Yeah, I saw her at the main house about an hour ago and she had frosting in her hair, so I figured y'all had had a busy day."

"Is she coming to dinner?" Cate asked. Marley hadn't mentioned it, and even though she had been tempted to ask during their kitchen session today, she'd also wanted to let the Crosses make their own inroads without pushing from her side. Not *too* much, anyway.

Owen's smile sobered, his gray eyes turning serious. "No. I asked her, of course, and with Eli and Scarlett coming home, I'd really been hoping she'd bite, but she said she had to work in Lockridge. I'm not sure she didn't volunteer for the shift just to get out of the house, but..."

Cate closed the space between them, smoothing the crease between his brows with her fingers as if she could erase it. "Baby steps. Today she showed me pictures of the dress she's wearing to the wedding, and she even seemed excited about how Emerson helped her pick it out, so that's something."

"She did?" he asked.

"Mmm hmm. She'll get there, Owen. With you guys and your father. Just give her time to figure out how."

He wrapped an arm around her to pull her against his chest. "Thank you for asking her to help with the wedding cake. Learning how to bake is really bringing her out of her shell."

"I'm glad it's making Marley feel more comfortable with your family to help with the cake, but I'm just as grateful to have her hands in the kitchen. She's an excellent assistant," Cate said, a warm feeling spreading out beneath her flowy, light blue tank top. "And while we're on the topic of gratitude, thank you for asking me to your family dinner tonight."

The smile Owen had ditched went on a comeback tour, making Cate's heart speed up just as much as it had the first time. "In case you haven't noticed, I kind of like you," he said. "And it's not as if you're a stranger to my family or our dinners. Why *wouldn't* I ask you to dinner tonight?"

Cate shook her head. "Don't get me wrong, I'm happy to join you."

Okay, so it was a teensy bit of an understatement, but she'd really come to look forward to spending time at the main house—and not just with Owen. She loved talking with Hunter and Emerson about their wedding plans, and she'd become downright addicted to crossword puzzles after Mr. Cross had turned her onto the ones in the *Camden Valley Chronicle* a couple of weeks ago. Still... "With Eli and Scarlett coming home for the first time since Christmas, it would've been okay to keep your first dinner together to just family."

"No, it wouldn't. I want you there. Plus"—Owen lifted a brow, turning to eyeball the pair of pies cooling on the ledge —"the only thing better than your peach pie is your strawberry rhubarb pie, and now I get to have both."

"You are terrible," Cate pointed out with a laugh, and he captured the sound with a kiss before pulling back and reaching across the counter for his keys.

"Terribly glad you're coming to dinner," he amended. "Now, come on. Eli, pain in the ass that he is, asked for Shepherd's pie for his first meal stateside, which means I've got a mountain of potatoes to peel, not to mention some prep to do for Scarlett's vegan version."

"Ah! Thank you for reminding me." Cate moved to grab the eight-by-eight baking pan she'd covered in foil and set aside earlier, lifting it with a flourish. "I can't believe I nearly forgot these."

"Okay," Owen said, waiting just a beat while she treated the peach pie to the same foil-wrapping treatment as the eight-by-eight pan. "What are they?"

She wrapped up the strawberry-rhubarb pie next, nestling everything in one of the baskets they used to transport her baked goods to the farmers' market. "Vegan cherry chocolate brownies."

They'd been a first for her, to be sure, but, actually, cooking with ingredients like flax seeds and coconut oil hadn't been too bad once she'd gotten the hang of things.

Owen's expression said he was definitely not sold on the idea of flax seeds, coconut oil, *or* vegan cherry chocolate brownies. "You made special brownies for Scarlett?"

"Well, yeah." Cate shrugged. "I mean, I murdered a few batches before I got them passably decent, but I remembered she's vegan from when she spent time here last fall."

Not too many folks came in to The Bar asking to read

the ingredients label on their beer bottle before they committed to throwing a few back. The fact had been pretty tough to forget.

"It didn't seem right to only bring desserts Scarlett couldn't eat," Cate continued, hefting the basket to her hip. "Plus, I had a lady ask me if I made vegan baked goods last week at the farmers' market."

Owen led the way to the front door, holding it open to usher her into the late afternoon sunshine. "As a specialty-produce lover, I'm all about the veggies. As a cattle farmer..."

"Totally a carnivore, I know," Cate replied with a laugh. "Most folks out here are, and I'm not sure that'll change anytime soon. Still, if we have enough demand, I don't mind coming up with a few vegan and gluten-free recipes to go with the rest of the baked goods we'll offer at the storefront."

"Huh. I never would have thought of that," Owen said, taking the basket from her to put it carefully in the back of his truck. "Guess convincing you to come on board was a pretty smart call."

She arched a brow even though she knew her ear-to-ear grin probably erased all the tartness she'd meant to dish up. "You and your sweet talk. My heart's all a-flutter."

"Only for you, sweetheart. Only for you."

The ride to the main house went by quickly despite the lingering kiss Owen had laid on her before putting the truck into gear. Emerson and Hunter were already in the kitchen, along with Mr. Cross, and after the chorus of hellos and the warm hugs that accompanied them, they all fell into orbit around each other to get dinner ready. As Cate helped Hunter arrange fresh-cut flowers and herbs in a pair of pretty mason jars and laughed at Owen and Emerson's potato-peeling contest, all of them calling out possibilities for Mr. Cross's crossword puzzle as they went, she couldn't help but feel good, all the way in her bones.

For the first time in a long time, maybe even ever, Cate felt like she was home. With Owen at her side and his family all around, she felt happy. Right.

Like nothing in the world could bring her down.

OWEN STOOD BACK and took in the kitchen with a huge fucking grin. Between setting the table, mixing up a triple-batch of sweet tea, and getting the salad and two Shepherd's pies from farm to fork (or, at least, in the case of the pies, to the oven), they'd put organized chaos to the test. But just as she had for weeks, Cate had fit right in with Emerson and Hunter and his old man, joking and pitching in and telling everyone all about her plans to try some new muffin recipes for the next farmers' market. Looking at her now, with her brown eyes sparkling and her cheeks lit up with excitement as she unpacked the desserts she'd made in between batches of buttercream frosting for Hunter and Emerson's wedding cake, Owen never would've guessed she'd been so resistant to start her own business, or to find her own happiness.

God knew he'd found his.

The familiar creak of the front door sounded off from down the hallway leading out of the kitchen, and Owen's pulse jumped like a big mouth bass at daybreak. "Eli?"

"I'm sorry," his brother said, his cocky grin leading the way over the threshold and into the room. His dark blond hair was a bit longer than he normally wore it, his T-shirt and dark gray hoodie definitely a little travel-worn, but, damn, he looked as at-ease and happy as Owen had ever seen him.

"Were you expecting someone else?" Eli asked with a wink no one else in the universe could pull off without looking like a dick. "The mayor, maybe? Or—I know!" He snapped his fingers. "Clint Eastwood."

"I see all that world traveling and a seven-hour flight hasn't made you less of a smartass," Owen said, but damn it, he was smiling too much for the words to be anything other than affectionate.

A fact which Eli had clearly picked up on. "Ah, come on. Admit it. You missed me and my smartass ways." He crossed the kitchen tiles to give Owen a warm handshake and shoulder-to-shoulder half-hug/clap on the back before looking at Cate and Emerson and adding, "'Scuse my language, ladies. I see my brother here still has an eloquent way with words."

Owen recovered just enough to arch a brow as Eli made the rounds with everyone in the kitchen. He had a pair of very *specific* words in mind for his brother right now, but Eli —the old swellhead—wasn't wrong. They *were* in the middle of their old man's kitchen, so he'd have to keep said directive to himself. At least until later.

"Where's Scarlett?" Hunter asked, spinning a gaze over the kitchen with a grin of his own. "She didn't get tired of you already, did she?"

Eli snorted, and, in this case, his confidence was extremely well-earned. He and Scarlett were so overboard for each other, they might as well be their own romance novel. "Not a chance, brother. We just got cell service as we pulled up outside, so she's on the phone with her dads."

A weird expression flickered across Eli's face, taking his smile down a notch. "So, before she comes in, there's something I should probably tell you."

"Everything alright, son?" their old man asked, his salt-and-pepper brows pulling low beneath the brim of his Stetson, and Owen had to admit, he'd never quite seen the look Eli was currently wearing on his face before.

His "yes" came out quick and honest, though. "Everything's great, actually. It's just—"

"Hey, everybody!" Scarlett said, appearing in the doorway to the kitchen. "Sorry I'm a little late coming in, but I wanted to let Bryan and Miguel know we got here okay."

She stepped into the room, her movements oddly a little hesitant. She was wearing a short, flowy sundress that swished around her knees and the sort of huge smile Owen had always associated with her unvarnished personality, her face almost glowing and her eyes wide and bright. But the kitchen had gone pin-drop silent, and in that moment, he noticed that both Emerson and Cate had skipped over Scarlett's smile to stare pointedly at the hand she'd splayed over the curve of her belly that had been hidden by her sundress when she'd first walked into the kitchen, and wait. Wait...

Holy shit. Scarlett was *pregnant*.

28

Owen blinked, watching as if from a trance as Eli wound his arm around Scarlett and gave up a sheepish grin.

"So, I guess the cat is out of the bag," he said, his expression turning genuinely apologetic as he focused on their old man. "I'm really sorry we didn't tell you sooner. We found out for sure just after Christmas, and we wanted to wait until after the first trimester to tell anybody. You know, to make sure we were out of the danger window."

Owen nodded dumbly, although he had not one fucking clue what a danger window was, let alone how long a trimester lasted.

Scarlett rubbed her belly, continuing where Eli had left off. "Then at the end of the first thirteen weeks, you two told us you were getting married," she said, looking at Hunter and Emerson. "We knew we'd be back here in the States for that, and Eli really wanted to give you all the news in person, so...surprise! We're having a baby."

So many thoughts flew through Owen's head that he had no prayer at capturing one and putting it to words. His brother—his *youngest* brother, who hadn't taken anything seriously in his entire life until six months ago—was going to be a father. At this time next year, Eli and Scarlett would have a baby. A family. The thought was totally surreal.

Hunter broke the silence first. "Holy crap, you two. That's great news. Congratulations."

"Thanks." Eli beamed. "Obviously, we were a little surprised, too. Us having a baby right now wasn't exactly part of our plan," he said, addressing the drop-jawed shock that had been evident on everyone's face—and probably still was on Owen's, because, *damn*—at the news. "We didn't want to take away from y'all's wedding, because it's really cool that you're getting hitched, but Scarlett and I do plan to get married in the next couple of months, before the baby comes."

"So, wait. When *is* the baby coming?" Owen blurted, and, clearly, no one was ever going to accuse him of being articulate.

Scarlett shared a quick, conspiratorial grin with Eli before she said, "He's due in August."

"Oh! You're having a boy," Emerson exclaimed, swooping in to hug Scarlett. "That's so exciting!"

Sweet Jesus, when was Owen's shock-meter going to top out? He squinted at Scarlett's stomach, which didn't look terribly big despite the definite baby bump beneath her sundress. "You can tell that stuff already?"

"We're twenty weeks tomorrow," Eli said, as if that cleared everything up. "We had an ultrasound last week when we were in London. See?"

He reached into the back pocket of his jeans, pulling out a grainy, black and white printout and passing it over to their old man, who Owen belatedly realized had been oddly silent since Eli had dropped his news on them.

"Here's your grandson, Pop. We'd like to name him Jordan Tobias, if that's alright with you."

Owen's heart seized at the mention of his mother's maiden name, then again at the definite sheen in his father's eyes as he took the photo from Eli and smiled.

"Well, I think Jordan Tobias is a right nice name. I'd be honored," he said softly. "I'm happy for you, son. For both of you," he amended. "Your momma would be so proud."

"Thanks, Pop." Eli cleared his throat and hugged their old man. "That means a lot to us."

"Well," Scarlett said, after she'd given out a hug of her own. "We're certainly excited to be home to tell you all in person and to celebrate the wedding. *And* to see a new face in the kitchen, too."

She sent a pointed look over Owen's shoulder, and damn it! He'd been so shell-shocked that he'd momentarily forgotten about Cate.

"Hi," she said. "I didn't want to interrupt your family moment—"

"Nonsense," Eli interjected with an affable smile and a shake of his head. "Word is, you've been putting up with this guy." He paused just long enough to shoot a cocky glance at Owen. "And that makes you pretty okay in my book."

Cate laughed. "It's good to see you, Eli. Congratulations."

Owen's pulse knocked at his throat as Eli's expression grew suddenly hesitant. "Thank you. I'm sorry, Cate, I didn't even think—"

"Don't," she said, and, aw, hell, Owen had been so stunned that he hadn't thought of it, either. Cate had done a lot of moving forward over the past month, but this had to be hard for her, having lost her daughter.

Still, her voice was quiet and sure. "Please don't apologize. You have great news, and you should celebrate it. Truly, I'm happy for you both."

"Thank you," Eli said, and Scarlett's nod punctuated the sentiment.

"It's really nice to see you here, Cate. I'm looking forward to getting to know you as well as everyone else does," she said.

Cate gave up the sort of smile that always hit Owen right in the solar plexus, and this one was no different. "Why don't I grab you something to drink and we can talk while these guys catch up? I'd love to hear all about London and Dublin."

"Ooooh, me, too," Emerson chimed in. "Let's go sit in the living room. It's nice and comfortable in there."

"I'll make up a pitcher of lemon water and join you two in a minute," Cate said. Emerson linked arms with Scarlett, the two of them heading down the hallway amidst some happy murmurs, and Hunter and Eli headed to the fridge with their old man to grab a couple of beers. Concern slipped between Owen's ribs, and he walked over to the far side of the kitchen, where Cate was cutting up a lemon with precise movements.

"Hey," he said, standing next to her in an effort to keep their conversation private. "Are you, ah, okay?"

"I'm fine," she replied. But she also wasn't dense, because she continued before Owen could voice the "really?" that had been brewing in his mind. "If you're asking whether Eli and Scarlett's news threw me for a second, the answer is yes. I'm human, and I miss my daughter. But their news isn't about me, and I really am very happy for them. They're clearly excited to be parents."

Owen paused. Everything she'd said made perfect sense, and what's more, he believed that she was genuinely okay.

She'd never been the type to bullshit anyone, least of all him.

So what was that weird feeling in the pit of his stomach, and why did it feel like it was settling in for a good, long stay?

Cate looked at him, her gaze narrowing in concern. "Are *you* okay?" she asked, lowering the knife in her hand and reaching out to squeeze his forearm. "You look so serious."

Owen opened his mouth, the word "no" hot on his tongue. But he couldn't even pinpoint the source of his unease, let alone come up with a way to articulate it, so he tacked on a smile instead.

"Are you kidding? I'm great," he said.

It was the first time he'd ever broken their honesty policy with an out and out lie.

THE ODD FEELING in Owen's gut faded a bit during dinner. Then again, it would've been downright impossible not to feel at-ease with everyone together, talking and laughing and dishing up seconds of the best strawberry-rhubarb pie in the county. He'd told Eli and Scarlett all about the progress they'd made with the storefront project and the success they'd had adding Cate's baked goods to their lineup of offerings at the farmers' market, then listened in turn as Eli and Scarlett had told everyone all about the stories they'd covered together in Europe and a few countries in Central America. Cate had fit right in with the boisterous group. Not that Owen was shocked by that at all—she'd seemed hand-made for his family ever since she'd stormed into the office like a cyclone, knocking some sense into him even as she'd knocked the breath right out of his chest.

Family and farm. Owen had one of those things well in-hand.

Now, he wanted the other.

"Ah, there's that serious look." Eli's teasing voice cut through the low light of the now-empty kitchen, and he ambled over to the spot where Owen had been tidying up the very last remnants of the mess from their family meal. "I've been wondering when it would make an appearance."

Owen worked up a smile, mostly to cover his thoughts, but—well, yeah—partly to counteract Eli's words, too. "I'm not that serious," he said, returning his attention to the last of the dishes in the sink.

"Sure you are," Hunter chimed in from the doorway. "But it's why we like you."

Ah, he couldn't help it. Owen let one corner of his mouth drift up into the barest hint of a smirk. "And here I thought you liked me for my charm and irresistible good looks."

Eli barked out a laugh, picking up a blue and white kitchen towel and drying the serving bowl Owen had just washed. "Jesus. You weren't kidding, Hunt. He really did grow a sense of humor."

Seriously? "You guys have been talking about me behind my back?" Owen asked, both of his brothers responding with the same well-duh expression.

"Uh, yeah, dude. We're your brothers. It's what we do," Hunter said. He sent a look in Eli's direction that said the two of them had traded more than just passing conversation about him, and Owen took a step back from the sink in surprise.

"I'm your brother, too, and I don't talk like that with either of you," he pointed out.

Eli took a turn with the half-smirk Owen had tried on a

minute earlier. "Well, Scarlett went to bed early to get ahead of her jetlag, and Emerson just went back to your place with Cate to talk about the last-minute details for the wedding cake she's making. What do you say we grab a couple of beers and change that, right now?"

"Okay. Sure," Owen said after he got over the pop of shock the offer had sent through his rib cage. Hanging the kitchen towel over the handle on the dishwasher, he took one of the beers Hunter had liberated from the fridge and followed his brothers out to the back porch. Unlike its counterpart on the front of the house, there wasn't anything fancy about the small stretch of boards just outside the back door. But also unlike the front porch, the rear deck was dark save the soft glow of the single bulb over the door leading to the mudroom and the muted flash of fireflies in the fields beyond the yard, and it housed three Adirondack chairs just perfect for kicking back a few beers on a Saturday night.

"Ahhh," Eli said, leaning back in the chair to Owen's left and kicking his jeans-clad legs out in front of him to look up at the stars. "I might've seen a lot of gorgeous places over the last six months, but I can't lie. I missed this."

"Really?" Owen asked. His brother had been so certain about leaving Cross Creek to pursue a career in journalism. Owen had assumed he wouldn't miss the place much.

Funny, Eli didn't hesitate. "Yeah, really. Don't get me wrong—I'm happier than hell traveling and freelancing magazine stories with Scarlett. It's definitely what I'm meant to be doing. But being here, with y'all around me...I might belong with Scarlett, but Cross Creek is still my home, you know?"

"I'll drink to that," Hunter said, lifting his bottle in the shadows. "So, does that mean you two are going to stick around for a while after the wedding?"

Eli nodded. "Scarlett's halfway done with her second trimester, and after six more weeks, she won't be able to travel by plane. We've got a couple short jobs planned on the east coast after that, but, otherwise, we're going to stay here in Millhaven until the baby is born."

"You're having the baby here?" Owen asked, taking a long swallow of beer in an effort to drown the unease filtering back through his gut.

"Of course. Scarlett and I want to be around family when this little guy comes into the world. Plus"—a grin hung in his voice—"we're gonna need all the help we can get."

Owen's pulse knocked at his throat, and even though he knew it might be bordering on ill-mannered, he'd never pulled any punches with Eli. Starting now seemed dumb as hell. "Jesus, man. You and Scarlett are having a baby. You're going to be a *father*. Doesn't that freak you out?"

To Owen's relief, Eli chuckled. "Dude. I still laugh at fart jokes and eat Lucky Charms for breakfast. Hell, yes, becoming a father freaks me out." He paused, surprising Owen when his tone turned serious. "I mean, obviously, Scarlett and I didn't plan to do this now. Getting pregnant was definitely a surprise. But I love her, and we've both always known we want kids. This might not be the most traditional way of doing things, but it fits us, and we're in it together. When things get tough, we'll figure 'em out."

"That's really cool, man," Hunter said. "Em and I have talked about having kids, too."

Owen nearly choked on his beer. "You have?" Was he the only fucking guy in Millhaven not to have considered procreation yet?

"Well, we're getting married in seven days, so yeah." Hunter laughed. "Of course, we've talked about it. We're not there quite yet. We'll obviously have to take her MS into consideration, but her doctors have all assured us there's no reason we shouldn't try when we're ready, and we both want a couple of kids. I don't think we'll be too far behind you and Scarlett in the grander scheme of things."

Owen blinked, unable to say anything past the shock jammed in his windpipe. Having kids had always been one of those things he thought he'd consider some day far in the future, a nebulous idea he couldn't even wrap his head around because he'd spent his entire adult life trying *not* to get whomever he'd been sleeping with pregnant. Even sitting here, now, the thought of having a baby was surreal.

And yet, both of his younger brothers had considered it; hell, Eli and Scarlett were *doing* it. Why did the thought seem so strange to him?

Didn't family and farm mean having kids?

"How about you?" Eli asked, bringing Owen back to the here-and-now of the back porch. "Think you'll get serious with Cate? You look awfully happy when you're with her."

"I am." Well, at least *that* was a no-brainer. "We're not, you know, talking about the kinds of stuff that you guys are, though."

He'd just given her a dresser drawer, for Chrissake. Although, come to think of it, she'd slept in his bed every night for the better part of a month straight. Would it really be so different if she moved in?

"But you really like her," Eli said, and Hunter answered before Owen could.

"Trust me, he does. He actually laughs on a regular basis now. And the other day, he even left work two whole hours early."

Eli lowered his beer bottle to the arm of his chair with a clunk. "Shut the fuck up. This guy? Who once slept in the greenhouse the night before the Watermelon Festival because he ended up working so late? He left the farm early? On *purpose*?"

"Are you done?" Owen asked, but damn it, a smile twitched at the edges of his mouth.

"Are you kidding?" Eli countered with a laugh. "I just got started."

The protest Owen was about to launch must have been obvious on his face, because Eli lifted his hands in concession.

"Okay, okay. So we're giving you a little shit. But, seriously, O. It's cool to see you with someone who makes you happy. Much as I love Cross Creek, and I get how much you love it, too, there's more to life than just the farm."

Owen's gut panged, his shoulders stiffening against the wooden slats of his chair at Eli's words. He'd always thought the family part of family and farm was something he'd figure out later, after all the work was done. He'd loved working the land and carrying out his legacy so much that he hadn't missed the rest.

But now he loved Cate, too, and as absolutely crazy as it might've seemed to him even two months ago, Owen knew Eli was right.

There *was* more to life than just the farm. And he wanted it.

All.

29

If a hundred years went by before Cate saw another piping bag full of frosting, it would still be too frickin' soon.

She stepped back on the floorboards in the dining room of Cross Creek's main house and examined her handiwork. Okay, fine. So she'd realistically only last about two days without hitting the kitchen. But she was damn glad that today and tomorrow would be those two days.

Even if Hunter and Emerson's wedding cake had turned out better than she'd dreamed.

Between her work in the office, baking and assembling the cake, and helping with the wedding preparations that had started bright and early five days ago, Cate had barely had time to breathe, let alone take a break that lasted longer than two minutes. But she spent all day at the main house. Overseeing things like deliveries and the tent set-up so Emerson could rest before the big day had made sense, and Cate had been happy to help, especially since Owen had been swamped with the storefront project and getting the farm ready for all three Cross men to take two days off.

She'd barely seen him over the past week, save a few sleepy moments when she' d crawled into his bed super late at night and a few more equally sleepy moments when he'd crawled out a few hours later. True to his straight-to-it nature, he'd left her a note on the bathroom mirror this morning, and, God, even now, hours later, the thought of it still sent a flush of warmth all the way through her.

Me. You. Right here after the reception. Let's make up for lost time.

"Oh, my God!" Emerson's best friend and maid of honor, Daisy Halstead, exclaimed from the doorway, delivering Cate back to the dining room with a snap. "Cate, the cake turned out *gorgeous*. Seriously, it'll be a crime to cut into it!"

She came all the way into the dining room for a closer look, a bottle of champagne in one hand, a pair of flutes in the other, and the hem of her pale blue silk dress swishing around her ankles.

Cate laughed, hoping her blush had taken a hike. "Thank you, but if Emerson and Hunter don't cut this cake and enjoy the hell out of it when it's time, I may be forced to cry." She and Marley hadn't killed themselves on all that fondant and buttercream and jam filling for a cake that was all aesthetics.

"Girl. I tasted the last round of test cakes you left in the kitchen the other day. Believe me, once Hunter and Emerson do the honors in a few hours, I'll be fighting folks for a giant hunk of that thing," Daisy said.

Cate looked at her watch, smoothing a hand over the slate gray dress she'd bought for the occasion because it had reminded her of Owen's eyes. "We're about an hour from the guests arriving. Can I do anything to help with the last-minute details?"

Daisy laughed. "You can help me and Emerson drink

some champagne. As for everything else, it's all been either delegated or done. Mrs. Montgomery runs an incredibly tight ship."

"I heard that," came a knowing voice from behind them. Emerson's mother walked into the dining room, auburn brows raised and clipboard in-hand.

"Meant purely as a compliment," Daisy said with a grin, and a very slight but very definite smile formed at the edges of the older woman's mouth.

"Then I suppose that's how I should accept it. I came to check on the cake," she said, her blue eyes widening as she took in the three-tiered confection that had consumed the last two weeks of Cate's life. "Oh, Cate, it's *lovely*."

Cate's cheeks prickled. "Thank you."

"I'm on several committees at Camden Valley Hospital. We can always use a good cake caterer for our charity events and galas. I'd love to speak with you further about some of our upcoming engagements. After the wedding, of course."

Cate channeled every ounce of her energy into not letting her jaw fall to the floorboards. "I, ah. That would be great." She'd put in for a small business license a few days ago, per Owen's suggestion, but, God, she never thought she'd use it. Not like this, anyway.

"Wonderful," Mrs. Montgomery said. "I'll be in touch. And, ladies"—her gaze drifted to the champagne in Daisy's hand—"please be prudent. A bit of bubbly is one thing, but a tipsy bride..."

"Not gonna happen, Mrs. M.," Daisy promised, crossing a finger over the sweetheart neckline of her dress. "Emerson wants to remember every second of today, I can assure you. No more than one glass before we send her down the aisle."

Emerson's mother smiled. "Well, then. Go on and have a little fun. I'll be back after I check on the attendants and make sure all is well with the gentlemen. If you'll excuse me."

Cate watched the woman depart in purposeful yet graceful strides. "Wow. I'm not sure if I should be impressed or terrified."

"Go for both," Daisy said, a grin covering her pixie face. "Come on, let's go pop this sucker and have a girls-only toast."

Nodding, Cate followed Daisy up the stairs of the main house and down the hall to what appeared to be a guest bedroom. Emerson sat at a small dressing table, her head thrown back in laughter at something Scarlett—who was perched on the four-poster bed in a dress that matched Daisy's—had said. She looked so beautiful that Cate's breath stuck momentarily in her throat. Her red hair was swept to one side in a low ponytail, her curls spilling over her bare shoulder. Her dress, with its lightly beaded bodice and fuller tulle skirt, was elegant without being overdone, and Cate couldn't help but smile at the sight of her.

"Oh, hey!" Emerson said, brightening. "You found champagne *and* friends. Talk about a win-win."

Cate looked around the room, suddenly feeling hesitant. "I don't want to—"

"If you say intrude, I'm going to throw something at you. You're part of the crew, so get your ass in here," Emerson warned, and Scarlett lifted a dark blond brow in agreement.

"She's been so laid-back until now. Don't give her a reason to turn into Bridezilla when we're so close to go-time."

Not in a million years could Cate picture Emerson turning into Bridezilla. She was too damned happy to be getting married to let anything hack her off. "Alrighty, then. Why don't I open that champagne so we can have a toast?"

A few minutes later, they'd uncorked the champagne and found Scarlett a bottle of sparkling water. Emerson lifted her glass with a mischievous grin, looking at all three women in the room. "Here's to us and the men who love us," she said, clinking her flute against Daisy's before taking a sip.

"Hear, hear!" Scarlett replied, tipping her bottle of water at Emerson.

Cate's heartbeat conspired against her, making her chest feel full to the brim with butterflies, and she took a nice, long sip of champagne.

"I can't believe all three Cross men are off the market," Daisy mused, sitting down next to Cate on the bench at the foot of the bed.

Scarlett shot her a sassy look. "I can't believe *you're* falling for the sheriff," she said, and Emerson gave up a laugh that came dangerously close to a snort.

"I can. She's had a crush on Lane forever. And the feeling is clearly mutual. That man is crazy about her."

A pink tinge climbed Daisy's cheeks, but Cate noticed she didn't deny the words. "Oh, like you're one to talk. You and Hunter have been cross-eyed for each other since high school."

"Sure have. Guess I should go on and marry the guy."

Emerson took another sip of her champagne, leading the way for the rest of them to drink up. They chatted and put some final touches on Emerson's makeup, with Scarlett snapping photos as they went. Things became a whirlwind from there, time seeming to fly as guests began to arrive and Emerson's mother returned from downstairs. Cate delivered a boutonniere to Emerson's father, then another to Mr. Cross, as well as a pretty bouquet of wildflowers to Marley, who was guarding the cake like a momma bear on full alert.

Last-minute tasks flowed from one to the next, until the wedding coordinator Mrs. Montgomery had hired to make sure things happened as planned gave the guests the signal to take their seats.

"May I, ma'am?" Lane asked, extending his well-muscled arm in Cate's direction.

She laughed. "Of course."

Looping her arm through Lane's much bigger, much brawnier one, she let him lead her down the aisle bisecting two groups of prettily decorated folding chairs. The tent, which had been set up yesterday and transformed this morning into a flower-filled space with generous glimpses of Cross Creek's rolling green fields from all sides, provided the perfect setting. Cate's heart tapped faster when Lane brought her right up to the front row and told her, "He made me promise to give you the best seat in the house," then faster still when Owen appeared at the front of the tent with Hunter, turning to smile at her over one shoulder.

And as excited as she was to be here, with the family who treated her like one of their own, Cate found herself counting the minutes until she and Owen were back at his house, and back in each other's arms.

OWEN WAS FAIRLY certain he'd never smiled so much or so hard in his life. But between his genuine happiness for Hunter and Emerson as they'd gone through their vows, the dozens of photographs for which he'd had to pose after the ceremony, and the obligatory meet-and-greet that had gone along with best man duties, he'd definitely filled his grin quota for the foreseeable future.

The only thing he wasn't grinning about was the fact

that he hadn't seen Cate for more than seven seconds in the last seven days. But finally—*finally*—the toast had been made and the cake had been cut (and devoured). Hunter and Emerson had just piled into a vintage Rolls Royce, ride courtesy of her parents, and headed off for a few days at a nearby mountain resort. The guests were beginning to disperse, the sun was on its way to setting, and Owen had a date to keep.

As well as a promise.

Leaving Mrs. Montgomery and his old man to oversee the cleanup with Eli, Daisy, and Lane to assist, he made his way through the dwindling crowd. Cate was standing at the back of the reception tent with Scarlett, and, damn, with the way the waning sunlight turned her skin a soft, glowing gold and that dark gray dress hugged every last one of her curves, she was the prettiest woman he'd ever seen, or would see again.

"Hey, there you are!" Cate said, her smile turning into uncut laughter as Owen wrapped his arms around her and pulled her close. "I was beginning to think you'd forgotten our date."

"Never." He fit a kiss over her mouth, proper enough for public, but only just.

Scarlett shook her head and laughed. "I believe that's my cue to go take a load off. Have fun, you two. I'm going to go eat the vegan cupcakes you brought and blame it on the baby."

"Goodnight," Owen said, Cate echoing the sentiment and giving Scarlett a hug before slipping in at Owen's side. Their feet shushed an easy rhythm through the grass as they made their way to his truck, and Cate pulled back to look at him through the growing shadows.

"Thanks for inviting me to your brother's wedding," she said softly, and guilt laddered a path up his spine.

"I wasn't a very good date."

"You were busy being Hunter's best man. And I wouldn't have missed the wedding for the world."

He cupped her face between his palms, kissing her just enough to remind him how little time they'd spent together this week. "Why don't we go do some celebrating of our own?"

"Are you kidding?" Her throaty laugh hit him in about ten places at once. "I've been waiting for that all day."

Somehow, Owen managed to get them from the main house to his cabin, then walk her over the threshold, although his colossal hard-on made the trip interesting, to say the least. A soft glow filtered down the hallway from his kitchen, and his pulse hitched as he shut the front door and reached for Cate's hand. He'd done most of the setup for their date after she'd left for the main house this morning, then slipped one of the catering guys an extra twenty to come down here and take care of the finishing touches about an hour ago. Now that it was nearly dark outside, the dozens of battery-powered candles he'd placed all over the kitchen looked even prettier than he'd hoped, draping the room in warm light and velvety shadows and making the pair of champagne flutes on the island glitter like diamonds. He'd cut the very best offerings from both the garden beside the main house and the small assortment of flowering plants they grew in the greenhouse, placing the blooms in a handful of large Mason jars around the room. The earthy, sweet smell of the peonies and lilies and various wildflowers and herbs scented the air just enough to make their presence known, but not enough to overpower, and Cate stumbled to a stop just past the entryway to the kitchen.

"Owen," she breathed, staring at him with wide eyes. "How did you...why..."

She trailed off in obvious surprise, but he answered her question anyway. "Because we're making up for lost time, remember?"

"It's only been a week," Cate said, and between the lift of her brows and her totally unvarnished, totally *Cate* reply, he had no choice but to laugh.

"That's not quite what I meant."

Slipping around her, he grabbed the small, padded envelope he'd left safely on the far side of the counter and returned to stand in front of her. His pulse echoed loudly in his ears, pounding to the rhythm of his shaky breath, yet, still, he didn't hesitate to press the envelope into Cate's hands.

Her mahogany brows tucked in confusion. "What's this?"

"It's a key," Owen told her. "I meant what I said, Cate. I want to make up for lost time with *you*. I know this might seem crazy, but I don't care. I love you. I love you and I want you to move in with me."

A soft sound resembling a gasp flew past her lips. "You want me to move in with you," she said slowly. "As in, live here in the cabin permanently?"

"I do." He knew he should take a second to let things sink in, or, at the very least, treat himself to a decently sized inhale. But, damn it, he'd kept these feelings under wraps for an entire week, waiting for the right time to let them out. He didn't want to hold back now. Hell, he didn't want to hold back *ever*.

He stepped toward her. "My legacy is family and farm. My mother dedicated her life to it, and it's what she wanted for me and for my brothers. Hunter found it. Eli found it.

And now I want it, too."

"With me," she whispered. Her eyes glistened with unshed tears, and—his heart twisted like a tornado—they looked like the happy kind. "Are you sure?"

"Are you kidding?' Owen laughed. "Of course, I'm sure. I want you. I want to wake up next to you every day. I know it sounds brash and impulsive as hell, but I want to marry you, and have babies with you, and—"

Her spine unfolded in one swift movement. "What?"

Oh, *hell*. He was completely graceless. She'd probably want some time to plan. "Well, obviously we could wait at least a little while to get married, but—"

"No, not that," Cate said, her voice strained. "The other part. About having babies."

"Oh. Well, we could wait for that, too. If you want." What was that odd look on her face?

His confusion doubled when she shook her head. "It's not that I want to wait. I don't want to do it. I'm not having any more babies, Owen."

A pause opened up between them, during which Owen tried to process both her words and his surprise. "I know you lost Lily, and I can't even imagine what that's like. But that doesn't mean you couldn't try again. It doesn't mean we couldn't try."

"Actually, it does." Cate took a half-step back, but Owen pressed forward to reclaim the space.

"I'm sorry. I don't understand."

A pained look crossed her face. She didn't scale back, though, looking him right in the eye as she said, "I never wanted children."

"What?" he asked, certain he'd misunderstood.

"I got pregnant with Lily by accident. I loved her once she was born, and I miss her every day, but...I never envisioned myself with children. Ever. And I don't now."

Shock knifed through Owen, making him blurt, "How come you never told me?"

This time, when Cate stepped back, he let her. "Because you never asked. Because I just started leaving my toothbrush here last week. Because you said you wanted just us. Me and you. And I believed you."

"Okay, yes. I said that," he allowed, his brain spinning to try and keep up with his runaway pulse. "But I meant it in the moment. Not literally."

Cate's laugh held no joy. "We had an honesty policy. You said *this* was what you wanted. You never said anything about wanting children with me once we started getting serious. If you had, I'd have told you."

"And what's so wrong with having children?" Owen bristled. His legacy was *family* and farm, for fuck's sake. He might not have ever thought about having kids because he hadn't found the right person for that, yet, but weren't they *supposed* to have kids to make a family? Wasn't that what his mother had meant?

"Nothing," Cate said, the honesty in her voice shocking him into silence. "Nothing is wrong with having children if you want them. But there's nothing wrong with not wanting them, either. And I'm sorry, Owen. I don't."

He scrambled to process what she was saying, coming up miserably short. "Okay, look, I know I'm springing this on you and maybe I got ahead of myself. Of us. But, I love you, Cate. Maybe in time—"

"No."

Frustration uncurled in his belly, low and hot. "You didn't even hear me out."

"I don't have to hear you out to know how I feel about

this," Cate said, but the softness of her words didn't lessen the blow.

"So, what?" Owen ran a rough hand through his hair, wondering how the hell this conversation had spun so quickly from something that was supposed to be perfect to this. "What I have to say doesn't matter?"

Cate shook her head. "Of course, it matters. But what you have to say won't change my mind. In fact, it can't."

"Why not?" he asked.

"Because I elected to have my tubes tied last year. There's no possible way I could get pregnant. Ever."

30

Cate knew the words would wreck any chance of happiness with Owen. They'd been painful to say, as if each one had been wrapped in razor wire, slicing her neatly to the bone. But the fact that they'd shred her hadn't stopped her from saying them.

As much as it shattered her heart to break his, they were true.

"You can't get pregnant," Owen repeated flatly, and the emotions in her chest rose another notch, squeezing her ribs.

"No. I can't."

Although she'd been certain she hadn't wanted more children well before the accident that had claimed Lily's life, she'd waited for two years after that to seek out sterilization surgery. Even then, she'd had to go all the way to Philadelphia before she could find a doctor who would even consider it, given the fact that she was young, single, and had lost a child. She'd gone through the counseling sessions recommended by the doctor, patiently endured the waiting period after signing the paperwork. And through all of it, she'd been sure.

She didn't want children. She hadn't even before Lily had been born. She'd loved her daughter with everything she'd had, but of this, she was sure.

Owen shook his head as if he was trying to get her revelation to stick. "But having your tubes tied...God, that's so permanent."

"That's the point," Cate said. Oh, *hell*. Yeah, it was true, but did her non-filter really have to choose now to make an appearance? "I'm not going to change my mind."

"Okay, but how can you be sure?" he asked, stepping back to pin her with a frustration-laced stare. "You never know what you might feel six months from now. Or a year."

Shock moved through her chest, followed quickly by a burst of anger. "Yes, I do. At least as far as this is concerned."

"And you never thought of bringing this up? You know how important family is to me. Christ, family and farm is my *legacy*, Cate."

Cate tried—and failed—to get a deep breath past the adrenaline and emotions surging through her veins. "I didn't bring it up in the beginning because I told you I didn't want any strings attached, and you swore we were just casual. It hardly seemed appropriate. Then, later, you said all you wanted was us, me and you. I thought..." Her treasonous voice caught, but she forced the rest past her lips. "You seemed really happy when we were together. I thought it would be enough for us to be a family of two. Not every family has children."

Owen exhaled, slowly and audibly. "Look. I know that losing Lily hurt you, and it makes sense that you'd be scared—"

Just like that, Cate's last thread of composure snapped. "No, you don't."

"I'm sorry?" he asked, clearly confused.

But all the emotions she'd been trying to manage burst free and spilled out of her. "You don't have any idea what losing my daughter was like for me, so don't say you know, because you don't. You don't know that the first thing I thought when I found out I was pregnant with her was 'please, God, anything but a baby'. You don't know how the guilt of that hurt me after she was born, and you sure as *hell* don't know how it wrecks me every single day now that she's gone."

Owen stared at her, his gray eyes round with shock, but now that she'd started, she knew she couldn't stop until she'd laid out every last one of her feelings. "I had a child, and I lost her, and that's something I'll have to carry with me for the rest of my life. But don't you *dare* imply that my loss is 'clouding' my judgment."

Cate slung air quotes around the word with a slash of her fingers, her anger rising along with the pitch of her voice. "I didn't make my decision because I was grieving. I made it because it's right for me. Being childless might not be what you want"—the finality of it sunk in, stabbing into her like a thousand vicious pinpricks, but, God, this had been sitting inside of her for far too long—"but my life isn't less important because I don't want kids. I have a legacy, too, Owen, and it's one I need to honor."

"Cate," he said, and even though it nearly tore a sob from the back of her throat, she shook her head and stepped back on the floorboards.

"I'm not the right person for you, Owen, and I should have known that all along."

"Can't we just talk about this for one minute?" he asked.

But as much as it shredded her to say no, she knew the truth.

A man like Owen Cross wasn't for her, after all.

"No. I can't give you what you need, and I wouldn't be able to live with myself if you lived a life with less than what you want and deserve. I'm going to walk out the door." Her heart seized at the thought, but oh, God, she knew it was the *right* thing, even if it was the very last thing she wanted to do. "Please, just let me go."

Cate made it all the way to her car, down the lane and onto the main road with Cross Creek behind her before she started to cry.

∾

"Wow. I don't mean to kick a guy when he's obviously down, but you look like crap."

Owen closed his eyes as if the move would change the fact that the words were very likely true. After replaying every part of his relationship-ending conversation with Cate in his head ad nauseam and—okay, fine—doing one too many shots of Jack Daniels to try and drown his sorrows before getting four hours of fitful sleep on the living room couch at the main house, he had to look as bad as he felt.

"Thanks," he said, clearing the rust from his voice as he looked at his sister. "Want some coffee?"

"Like that's even a question." Marley padded over to the coffeepot, which Owen had filled twenty minutes ago in an effort to kill his headache.

His heartache? Yeah, that was going to need something a hell of a lot stronger than coffee and Jack Daniels combined.

Please, just let me go.

Owen stuffed the memory aside. "You're up early," he

said to Marley, gesturing to her pajama pants and T-shirt, which read *Namastay In Bed* in big, bold print across the front.

"And you're here at seven o'clock on a Sunday morning looking like a walk of shame just waiting to happen," she quipped back, filling a mug to the brim before plopping down at the kitchen table next to him. "Shouldn't you be at home in your pajamas, having a life with Cate?"

Ah, hell. He should've known his presence here, especially in the same shirt and dress pants he'd worn to the wedding, would raise brows. But he hadn't been able to stay at the cabin last night, not when Cate's toothbrush still stood next to his in the bathroom and his pillows all smelled like her shampoo. "Yeah, that's a no," he said, hating the words but knowing he'd have to say them at some point. "Cate and I broke up."

Marley paused with her mug halfway to her lips. "What? What did you do to her?"

"Nothing. I don't know." Christ, he couldn't think. "It's a long story."

"Okay." But rather than leaving it at that and going on her merry way, Marley kicked her feet up on the chair across from her. "Start at the beginning."

She had to be kidding. "You want me to tell you my breakup story?"

"You slept in your dress clothes and you smell like a distillery, not to mention looking like the unhappiest human being I've ever clapped eyes on. So, yeah." She pinned him with a stare. "I want you to tell me your breakup story. It can't make you feel any worse, right?"

Well, shit. She had a point. "Fine," Owen said, certain she wouldn't let it go until he did. "Things had been going great between us lately. I mean, I guess they'd always been kind of great," he amended, and hell if *that* didn't make his heart sink even lower. "I asked Cate to move in with me last night."

"Wow." Marley's brows lifted. "Did she say no?"

"No. Not exactly."

He relayed the conversation as clearly yet generally as he could, wanting to get the point across without spilling Cate's personal business in too much detail. Marley took it all in, waiting for him to finish before tipping her head at him to say, "So, you never said you wanted kids, and she never said she didn't."

"Yep. I guess," Owen said, the ache in his chest spreading out a little bit farther at the words.

Then Marley surprised him with, "Okay, but *do* you want kids?"

"Family and farm are my legacy," he replied. "They're the two most important things in my life."

"I know. But that's not what I asked you."

He blinked once. Twice. Yeah, still no. "I'm not sure I understand the difference."

"I get that family and farm are your thing, or whatever," Marley said, shifting in her chair to look at him more fully. "But look at Eli and Hunter. They've both got ties to family and farm even though they're not doing the same stuff in the same way. Eli doesn't even live here anymore."

"No, but they both want to have kids one day, and it'll happen for both of them."

Marley lifted a slim shoulder in a shrug. "That may be. But isn't it possible that you're looking at this legacy thing just a little too rigidly?"

"It's not a legacy *thing*," Owen said, battling the frustration and irritation in his chest. "It's important, Marley. It's what my mother wanted."

Marley frowned, showing off some irritation of her own. "Don't get your panties in a twist. I hauled myself here from Chicago knowing full well our father didn't want me just so I could fulfill my mother's dying wish," she reminded him. "I know all about how important those are."

Damn it. *Damn* it. "You're right," he said. They'd have to tackle her issues with their father another day, but Owen knew she understood why this was important to him. "It's just...I don't know how to fix this. Cate doesn't want kids at all. Ever."

"Let me ask you a question. Did your mother actually tell you she wanted you to have a bunch of kids one day?"

"Well, no." Owen paused. "Not in those words, exactly. She just wanted us all to be happy, and she wanted family and farm to be a part of that."

Marley said, "Okay, but families aren't one size fits all, and they're not always what you think they'll be. God, I'm living proof. I'm sitting here, having coffee and giving love life advice to a grumpy, hung over older brother I didn't even know I had a year ago. But that doesn't really make you and I less of a family, does it?"

"No," Owen said, his chin lifting with the force of his realization. "It doesn't. But..." He trailed off, trying like hell to sort through the surge of thoughts suddenly crowding his brain. "I always thought my adult family would involve having kids."

"Is that because you *wanted* them? Or because you thought you should have them?"

Owen blinked. "I..." *Shit.* "I'm not really sure."

"Hmm. Close your eyes."

If Marley had asked him to put on a clown suit and teach her to juggle, he might have been less surprised. "What?"

She rolled her eyes and gave up an exaggerated sigh. "I don't have to do this, you know. I could be back in bed, catching up on my Netflix queue. So, are you going to humor me here, or what?"

Owen resisted the urge to tell her he knew damned well that if watching Netflix what she really wanted, she wouldn't hesitate to leave his sorry ass in the kitchen. "Fine," he grumbled. Settling in against the ladder back of his chair, he let his eyes drift shut.

"Good. Picture what you want in your head. No limits or anything. Just whatever you want in life."

For a second, he nearly protested. He was about as far from a touchy-feely, dive-into-your-inner-light kind of guy as you could get, and he really didn't know how thinking of things he wanted but couldn't have was supposed to make him feel better.

As if Marley sensed his hesitation, she added, "Trust me. Just do it."

With that, Owen gave in. He got the crazy, if-I-won-the-lottery stuff out of the way first, like a fishing boat and a new truck. A second later, he moved on to his father and brothers and Marley, picturing them all as a family, happily running the farm together. He saw Eli's and Hunter's kids. But he saw Cate most clearly of all, wearing that light blue sweater dress that had driven him crazy on her very first day at work and a smile so full of joy, he could look at it for hours, and oh, Christ, he *missed* her.

"Got it?" Marley asked softly. Owen didn't trust his voice with a reply, didn't want to let go of the image of Cate quite yet, so he nodded.

Marley continued, "Good. Now picture everything you can't live without."

The easy stuff fell from his mind's eye quickly, the boat

and the truck disappearing like smoke in a strong wind. Not surprisingly, his old man and siblings and their extended families stayed firmly in place, as did Cate, who was front and center.

But his own kids weren't there. Not anywhere.

Startled, Owen bolted upright, searching his mind's eye more carefully and forcing himself to be sure. He'd been so certain that family meant children, he'd never even considered the alternative.

He never realized he might not need children as much as he needed a family that fit his heart.

And that family was him and Cate.

Oh. Oh *shit*.

"I've gotta go," Owen blurted, scrambling up from the table and knocking his chair to the floor in the process. He reached down to right it, but Marley laughed and waved him off.

"I've got this. Go."

Gratitude slipped past all the urgency in his brain—how had he been so thick-headed?—and he turned to scoop Marley into a hug so fierce, she let out a soft "oof".

"Thank you," he said. "Really. I owe you one."

"I'll collect someday," she promised, although her trademark sass had been replaced by a strangely goofy grin. "Now, get out of here, would you? Your forever is waiting."

Right. Now all he had to do was figure out how to win it back.

31

Cate stirred the batter in the bowl in front of her without seeing it, smelling it, or even being certain what the final product was supposed to be. In her defense, after she'd come home last night and finished her cry in the shower, she'd done the only thing she could; namely, pulled up her big girl panties and taken out every baking dish, mixing bowl, and ingredient in her pantry.

For the first time ever, it hadn't been enough to take the edge off her heartache.

Lowering the bowl to the scuffed Formica in front of her, Cate blew out a shaky breath. She'd mentally replayed her conversation with Owen so many times, she practically had it memorized. Yet, somehow, the words stung equally hard every time she heard them in her mind.

Family and farm is my legacy, Cate...

Of course, she'd known that. For God's sake, it was why she'd resisted her attraction to him so hard in the beginning. She should've listened to her common sense from the beginning, but, instead, she'd trusted her stupid, needy heart. She'd believed she and Owen had a chance, just the two of them, and that it would be enough. But she should've known better—*had* known better from the start.

A man like Owen Cross wasn't for her. And now she had the broken heart to prove it.

Swiping her tears away with the back of one hand, she reached out to open the drawer holding her dish towels with the other, catching a glimpse of the blue and purple trivet peeking out from beneath the terry cloth.

"Oh," Cate whispered. Her guilt roared to life, just as it always did when she was inadvertently blindsided by a memory of Lily. Funny, this time, something even stronger rose up from her chest to meet it.

That something was forgiveness.

Cate took the trivet out of the drawer, cradling it with steady fingers. She'd spent a lot of time hiding from her guilt, and even more time punishing herself for it. She might not have planned to ever be a parent, but she'd loved her daughter from the minute she'd first held her, and she'd been a good mother.

She wouldn't ever forget Lily—God, she wouldn't ever want to. But it was time to begin forgiving herself. It was time to fulfill her own legacy and start the business she'd wanted for so many years.

Even if she had to do that without Owen in her life.

A sharp, rapid-fire knock sounded off from her front door, startling a soft curse out of her and prompting her to put the trivet on the counter with care. She wasn't expecting anyone, and it wasn't as if she'd get any sort of delivery at— she peered at the clock on her stove—eight o'clock on a Sunday morning. Who the hell could be banging on her door?

"Cate? It's me. Owen," he clarified, his voice trapping her

breath in her lungs all the way through the wood and steel. "Please, open the door."

Every instinct she had screamed at her to do exactly that. But she'd meant what she'd said to him last night. She couldn't give him what he really wanted, and she'd never ask him to compromise on having exactly what he deserved.

Cate rested her hand against the door, fighting the tears in her eyes as she stayed silent. A beat passed, then another, before Owen's voice came again.

"Come on, sweetheart. I know you're in there. I'd know the smell of your oatmeal raisin cookies anywhere."

Her heart twisted behind her T-shirt, pumping faster when he continued. "I came here to tell you something, and if I have to do it through the door or in the middle of town square or, hell, in the middle of *Times* Square, then so be it. I love you, Cate. No"—he paused—"it's more than that. I don't just love you. I want to wake up next to you every morning. I want to stand by you as you start the best cake catering business in the Shenandoah Valley, and I want to lean on you for support when things at Cross Creek get tough. I want you beside me at our family dinner table, and I want to fall asleep in your arms every night. I wasn't wrong about my legacy. I want a family. God, I need it more than I need to breathe. But I was wrong about what that family looks like. I don't need kids to be happy, Cate. I only need you."

Hope flickered in her chest, but oh, God, she had to be sure.

She opened the door a crack. "Owen, I meant what I said last night. I'm not ever going to want kids. You have to be certain—*really* certain—you're okay with that."

A half-smile tugged at the corners of his mouth, sending another curl of hope through her belly. "And I meant what I said last week. Perfect is in the eye of the beholder. For Eli and Hunter, that means having kids, but to me, perfect is having you."

Oh. "I'm sorry I didn't tell you sooner. I didn't mean to hurt you, or make you believe something that wasn't true," Cate whispered, but Owen shook his head.

"I didn't give you much chance to tell me before I went from a dresser drawer to proposing," he said. "But I mean it, Cate. All I need is this. Just me and you."

The tears that had formed in her eyes spilled over her cheeks, and she pulled the door open at the same time Owen rushed through it. "Well. I guess you have a way with words after all, Casanova."

"I love you, Cate McAllister," he said, wrapping his arms around her and pulling her close. "And I'm never going to stop. How's that for a way with words?"

"Seeing as how I love you, too, I'd say that's perfect."

And as she pressed up to kiss him, Cate knew they'd found the perfect family. Just the two of them.

Together.

EPILOGUE

Epilogue—four weeks later

Marley crossed her arms and glowered at the baked goods on the cooling rack in front of her. When she'd started this little endeavor three hours ago, she'd had no idea that chocolate chip cookies could be such a gigantic pain in her ass. Then again, she'd never had a clue about things like gluten ratios, consistency of oven temperatures, or the merits of ceramic baking dishes versus non-stick metal.

Judging by her last batch of cookies, a.k.a. chocolate-studded hockey pucks, she *still* didn't have a clue.

"Okay, so how come these came out like this?" Marley asked, lifting a cookie a few inches off the cooling rack to drop it to the empty baking sheet in front of her with an ominous *thunk*.

Cate, who pretty much never let anything rattle her, like, ever, made a "yikes" face, but didn't lose her smile. "Well, it could be a couple of things. Overmixing the dough will make it kind of tough, but it could also be that you're not used to the oven temperature yet. How long did you put them in for?"

Shit. Marley bit her lip. "The recipe said eleven to thirteen minutes, but when the timer went off, I still had to mix this batch for another two minutes." She pointed to the bowl full of cookie dough—her third try of the day, thanks —on the counter. "I was worried that if I stopped mixing, I'd wreck the dough, and it seemed like there was wiggle room in the baking time since it said eleven to thirteen minutes, so I stuck with mixing, but I guess I went over on time. It was more like fifteen minutes." She didn't add the "ish" that would probably make things more accurate.

"A-ha," Cate said, flipping a cookie over to reveal a bottom that Marley was ninety-nine percent sure wasn't supposed to look like *that*, and ugh, guess that explained the kind of burnt smell wafting through the kitchen, too. "Here's your culprit. They're just a bit overdone."

"A bit." Marley slid a hand to her denim-covered hip, and Cate lifted her hands, guilty as charged.

"Okay, girl. They're crispy critters. We can chuck this batch and just try again."

"Sorry," Marley muttered. "That was kind of dumb." Her cheeks burned with embarrassment, but Cate shook her head, refusing to let Marley avert her eyes. So annoying.

"You didn't burn them on purpose, and baking is harder than it looks. For now, let's focus on single batches rather than trying to get fancy and multi-task too many things."

Marley couldn't help it. She said, "Right. Because those homemade cinnamon rolls you made the other day were so basic."

Cate—quite possibly the only person in Millhaven who

spoke Marley's exact dialect of sarcasm—laughed. "Oh, my God, they were such a pain in the ass, right? They take forever to rise. And don't get me started on rolling that dough out. It sticks to *everything*."

"So, how come you made them, then? Did Owen leave the cap off the toothpaste? Or, wait, no. He didn't take the last cup of coffee, did he? That's unforgiveable."

Cate's penchant for baking crazy-complicated recipes when she was upset about something wasn't exactly a secret, nor was Marley's penchant for poking fun at her half-brothers (when she was upset or, you know, breathing. But it wasn't her fault they were easy targets). Cate had moved into Owen's cottage—well, guess it was both of their cottage now —a month ago, no looking back. A neighboring farm had bought the house Cate had once lived in with her husband and daughter in order to add the acreage for their dairy cows to graze. The house itself, which hadn't been in great shape to begin with, had been torn down, with plans for a barn to eventually go in its place. Marley had wondered if that had been hard for Cate—she knew she'd be *super* pissed if someone tore down the place where she'd lived with her mom in Chicago—like maybe the memories would all disappear or something once the place itself was gone. But when Marley had asked, Cate had just smiled and said no, she could keep the memories she needed inside her heart, and it was better if the land could be used for something good, like agriculture.

It had been pretty happy-sappy as far as Marley was concerned, but ever since Cate and Owen had decided to be a serious couple (barf), sometimes they got like that. Marley liked her enough to overlook it, and honestly, Owen *was* way less cranky now that he and Cate were living together.

"No," Cate said quietly, bringing Marley back to the sunny kitchen at the main house. Marley registered, too late, how much time had passed since she'd asked her nosy-ass question, and that a gentle smile had replaced Cate's wider, sassier grin from a few minutes before.

"Owen didn't make me mad. I was just missing Lily a little, and the cinnamon rolls were her favorite, so I thought I'd make them to cheer myself up."

Marley's heart pounded, her gut twisting into a tangled knot. God, she was such a jerk. "I'm sorry. I didn't mean to be all in your sh—stuff."

"You're not in my shit," Cate said, one corner of her mouth lifting in a wry twist. "I'd tell you if I didn't want to talk about it. But I'm learning that a lot of the time, it actually feels better to let those feelings out than to cram them in."

"You're starting to sound like a Hallmark card," Marley warned, taking the cooling rack full of crap cookies to the trash and dumping them in with a thump.

"Pretty sure Hallmark isn't big on words like 'cram' in their cards," Cate said with a laugh. "Anyway, it's the truth."

Dread settled low in Marley's belly. "Is that what your therapist told you? That you should embrace all your feelings in order to let them go, or whatever?"

Marley didn't fault Cate for deciding to start seeing a therapist to talk about her loss. It was cool; some people did, and it worked just fine for them. But she'd heard all the self-help, self-healing crap before, and she wasn't interested for herself, thanks. She only had so many memories of her mom. She wasn't letting *any* of them go.

Her mom had been her only parent. Her hero. Her best friend, the only person in the entire universe to really get her.

And now she was gone, and Marley couldn't afford to leave any of those memories behind.

"Sort of," Cate said. "I've only seen her twice, though, so we're still figuring out what works for me." The pause that stretched into the silence that followed filled Marley's chest with unease, especially when Cate added, "You know, it might not hurt if you—"

"Went to a therapist I don't want to see?" She kept the *with money I definitely don't have* part to herself. Her crummy retail job didn't exactly offer stellar benefits. Or, okay, any benefits.

Cate's spine straightened, just slightly, but it was enough, and shit. "You lost your mother, Marley, and grief is difficult. All I'm saying is that it might help for you to talk to someone who knows how to help you through it."

The back of Marley's throat pinched, a precursor to tears she would rather die than shed in front of Cate. She had to end this conversation, and she had to do it right now.

"Look, talking to strangers like that isn't my thing. But I'm good, okay?" Well, she would be. Just as soon as she scraped up enough cash to get out of this Godforsaken mapdot of a town.

Cate looked like she wanted to argue. But then Hunter and Owen came banging through the back door—*yesssss*—and Marley was able to exhale in relief.

"Smells like cookies," Owen said, leaning in to (ugh) kiss Cate before moving to the sink to wash his hands.

"Burned cookies," Marley corrected.

"We're going to give them another go," Cate countered, and God, this family was so upbeat sometimes, Marley could scream. Weren't they ever mad? Sad? Honestly, the closest she'd ever seen to ugly had been when Owen had screwed up with Cate just after Hunter and Emerson's wedding, and even that had only lasted for, like, twelve hours before he'd gotten his head out of his ass.

Although, Marley had to admit, she was glad he had, because Cate was okay. And Owen was a lot happier now that she'd moved in with him. And he cooked more here at the main house, which meant she didn't have to eat as many microwave burritos for dinner. Plus, now that Eli and Scarlett were back, too, there were enough people to keep the chatter going at the table. No one bugged her to contribute. Not much, anyway.

Which was good, because she wouldn't.

"Hey, did someone say 'cookies'?" Scarlett made her way into the kitchen with Eli right behind her and Emerson right behind *him*, and sweet, Marley could easily fade to the background now. Pregnant ladies always got a double-serving of the spotlight, and everyone was all too happy to talk about Eli and Scarlett's baby even though he wasn't even close to due yet.

"This batch is a teeny bit overdone, but we've got more dough, so, yes. There will be cookies," Cate said, leaning in to hug Scarlett, then Eli, then Emerson. "And I made a batch of vegan gingersnaps for the farmers' market yesterday. We can snag some of those, too."

Scarlett rubbed her belly, which was now a definite volleyball beneath her red-and-white striped shirt. "Thank you! I feel like I'm eating for triplets lately."

Marley barely bit back her snicker at the look on Eli's face. "Wait. We're *absolutely* sure there's only one kid in there, right?"

"You were right there for the ultrasound, cowboy." Scarlett waggled her blond brows and laughed. "This little guy is a single rider. Maybe a linebacker," she added. "But definitely just the one."

"Do you think he'll *be* a linebacker?" Hunter mused, grabbing a glass of water for Emerson before helping himself to one.

"Or maybe a scientist," she said, and Owen chimed in next.

"Or maybe he'll work the farm with his favorite uncle."

Hunter laughed. "So nice of you to realize he's going to like me best."

"No way." Owen shook his head. "I'm so much cooler than you. I'm gonna let him drive the tractor."

"I'm gonna show him how to jump off the rope swing down by the creek," Hunter countered, and Eli arched a brow.

"And I'm gonna kick both your butts. *I* wanna show him that stuff first."

Scarlett looked at all three men before letting out a sigh. "Maybe let's wait until he's born before we tackle tractors and rope swings, yeah?"

"Yes, ma'am," Eli said, kissing the top of her head as he ran a hand over her belly.

Everyone fell into a familiar pattern of chatty dinner prep, with Marley firmly on the (self-imposed) outskirts. Still, she didn't mind eavesdropping on her half-brothers' conversations. How else was she going to find out that Emerson had started a Move It group with some of her physical therapy patients, where they walked around Town Street every morning as preventive therapy, and that it was actually helping her with some of her joint stiffness, too. Or that Eli and Scarlett's Dublin article had gotten some serious international exposure after an Irish actress mentioned it on her Twitter feed. Or that Lane and Daisy were getting serious enough to talk about moving in together, *or* that Greyson Whittaker was still cranky about that five thousand dollar check that Eli had refused to cash last fall, and that the guy was still crowing on and on about how this year, Whittaker Hollow's peaches would yield the biggest and best harvest any of them had ever seen (if you asked her, Greyson sounded like a pretty big jackass. She'd never met him, personally, but on that, she and her brothers could totally agree).

As the group chopped and prepped and cooked, Marley just listened. It was better than sitting up in her room, she guessed, and they did all seem happy. Contrary to popular belief, she didn't *hate* happiness. It had just been so long since she'd felt anything other than this hole in her chest where all her happiness used to be that she was pretty sure she'd used her quota.

"Evenin', Marley. It's right nice to see you here for dinner."

She damn near jumped out of her skin, and God, how did Tobias always manage to sneak up on her like that?

"Oh," she said, her voice stiff and chilly in her ears. A fresh load of hurt expanded between her ribs, and you know what, this wasn't worth it. "Yeah, actually, I was just wrecking a batch of cookies. I'm not staying."

"Aw, come on," Eli said, apparently having overheard them. Damn it. "Who else is gonna help me poke fun at Owen if you don't stay?"

Marley shook her head. "You've got that covered without me. Plus, I forgot. I have a thing."

Okay, so she was going to go sit in her room with her earbuds jammed into place, waiting until they'd all eaten and gone their separate ways before creeping downstairs for cold leftovers, but whatever. It was still a thing in the literal sense, and she couldn't be here.

Being here reminded her of what she no longer had. She should've known better than to think she could belong with the Crosses. She wasn't one of them. She didn't want to be.

She was a Rallston. She couldn't forget it.

So, when Cate gave Marley her kindest smile and asked, "Are you sure you don't want to stay, just for a few minutes?" Marley had no choice but to shake her head.

"No, thanks," she said, walking out the door before anyone could protest, or—worse yet—she changed her mind.

∼

NOT READY TO LEAVE CROSS Creek just yet? Don't worry! I've got an exclusive letter from Owen Cross, including a recipe for spaghetti and meatballs, just for you! But before you get cozy with Owen, don't forget to grab the next story (yes! Marley's!) in the Cross Creek series, CROSSING HOPE, right here.

TO CLAIM your exclusive letter from Owen, just use this special link to become a VIP Reader. ** Even if you are already subscribed, click the link to get the letter ** It'll be delivered to your inbox! (you must use THE ABOVE LINK to get the bonus content)

READ on for an exciting excerpt from CROSSING HOPE, and stay tuned directly after for a complete list of all my sexy standalones!

. . .

MARLEY'S BOOTS clapped to a halt on the linoleum at the same time her heartbeat cranked way, way up in her chest. She blamed the former on the way the deputy—who had nervously picked her up from The Corner Market—had stopped short beside her, as well as the sight of her oldest brother Owen's best friend standing a few feet away, his face locked in disbelief. The latter was entirely the fault of the man planted next to Lane, though. Between his tanned skin, the tall, muscular frame that nearly gave Lane's a run for its money, and the inky black tattoo curling from beneath the sleeve of his T-shirt all the way to his left elbow, Marley really couldn't help the visceral reaction.

Even if the guy was leveling her with a dark and stormy gaze that said he didn't like what he was looking at in return.

"What the hell is going on here?" Lane's voice crash-landed in Marley's thoughts just in time to chase the flush from her face. What did she care what this scowling stranger thought of her, anyway? She had bigger problems at the moment, thanks.

Case in point. "I, uh," Deputy Collingsworth stammered, turning roughly the color of summer strawberries as he cleared his throat. "I made an arrest."

"I can see that," Lane replied tightly. "What I meant was, would you care to *elaborate* on exactly why it is that you've arrested my best friend's little sister?"

Marley's gut fluttered, but she refused to let the sensation get anywhere near her face. She'd known exactly what she was doing when she'd claimed those groceries as her own. Even if the steel bars and jail cell were a whole lot more real now that they were standing starkly in front of her.

Deputy Collingsworth straightened. "She was shoplifting at The Corner Market. Travis Paulson caught her red-handed, and she admitted it, to him and to me. What else was I supposed to do?"

Shock streaked over Lane's face, but it didn't last. "Radio me, for starters," he hissed, and the guy next to him released an audible, oh-please scoff that sent Marley's brows hooking up. She opened her mouth to tell Lane and the deputy and God and anyone else within earshot that she didn't want any special treatment.

But Lane was already shaking his head, the thought forgotten. "You know what, never mind. We've got a more immediate issue to deal with here."

"Okay," Woody said, enough of a question hanging in his voice that Lane huffed out a breath.

"I've also made an arrest, as you can see." He jerked his chin at Tall, Dark, and Scowling. "And we can't put two people of the opposite sex in the same jail cell."

The guy's face changed then, sending another curl of heat through Marley's blood. "By all means. Ladies first," he said, gesturing grandly at the single cell. His smirk was its own entity, taking over his unnervingly rugged and (ugh) undeniably good-looking face as if it had a life of its own. He could fill Wrigley Field with his arrogant attitude and ultra-cocky bravado. Even then, he was brimming with so much of both that he'd probably have to use a crowbar to cram it all in. Too bad for him and his sexy little smile, Marley was packing boatloads of backbone, herself.

And she was in just the mood to let it fly like a fifty-foot flag.

"Oh, no. Really. Age before beauty," she maintained, planting her hands on the hips of her cutoffs and smiling so sweetly at the wide-open door to the cell, she damn near needed a root canal. "After you."

The guy's black brows shot toward the tousled waves

falling over his forehead. "It wouldn't be gentlemanly of me to step on your cute little toes. Please. I insist."

Oh, my God, was this guy even for real?

WANT TO FIND OUT? Grab it here!

KIMBERLY'S OTHER BOOKS

The Cross Creek series (sexy small-town contemporary):

Crossing Hearts (Hunter and Emerson, second chance lovers)

Crossing the Line (Eli and Scarlett, opposites attract)

Crossing Promises (Owen and Cate, friends to lovers/workplace romance)

Crossing Hope (Greyson and Marley, forbidden lovers)

The Intelligence Unit Standalones (steamy police/detective romantic suspense):

The Rookie (Xander and Tara's story, opposites attract)

The Guardian (Garza and Delia's story, forbidden lovers, grumpy/sunshine)

The Grifter (Maxwell and Francesca's story, single-dad romance, second chance lovers)

The Rogue (coming in 2022)

The Agent (coming in 2022, tentatively)

The Saint (coming in late 2022)

The Station Seventeen Engine Standalones (super-sexy firefighter/cop romantic suspense):

Deep Trouble (Kylie and Devon's story, best friend's little sister/forbidden lovers) (prequel, with 1,001 Dark Nights)

Skin Deep (Kellan and Isabella's book, enemies to lovers)

Deep Check (January and Finn's book, second chance lovers)

Deep Burn (Shae and Capelli's book, opposites attract)

In Too Deep (Luke and Quinn's book, friends to lovers)

Forever Deep (companion novella to Skin Deep, Christmas wedding story)

Down Deep (Kennedy and Gamble's book, forced proximity)

The Remington Medical Contemporary Standalones (sexy medical romance)

Back to You (Charlie and Parker's book, second chance lovers)

Better Than Me (Jonah and Natalie's book, best friends to lovers/accidental roommates)

Between Me & You (Connor and Harlow's book, enemies to lovers)

Beyond Just Us (Tess and Declan's book, marriage of convenience/single parent romance)

Baby, it's Cold Outside (Emmett and Sofia's book, Christmas story/enemies to lovers)